D1363642

MUSIC
IN OUR TIME

MUSIC IN OUR TIME

TRENDS IN MUSIC SINCE THE ROMANTIC ERA

By

ADOLFO SALAZAR

Translated from the Spanish by

ISABEL POPE

GREENWOOD PRESS, PUBLISHERS
WESTPORT, CONNECTICUT

Copyright © 1946 by W. W. Norton & Co., Inc.

Reprinted by permission
of W. W. Norton & Co., Inc.

First Greenwood Reprinting 1970

Library of Congress Catalogue Card Number 75-97391

SBN 8371-3014-X

PRINTED IN UNITED STATES OF AMERICA

Contents

Part One

077166

Part Two

CHAPTER XVII

CHAPTER XVIII

CHAPTER XIX

CHAPTER XX

Introduction

ART is no more nor less than a means by which humanity expresses a certain category of ideas; these concepts are not purely logical, like those with which science deals, but intuitive. They operate not only within intellectual areas but upon the senses as well. It is obvious that by virtue of this double process art is an eminently social phenomenon; social because it is human, because it is a special means of communication between two poles that the work of art acts to unite: the author and the audience. It is social in all its consequences. The form society assumes at a given moment is reflected in the art of that moment. That art, so closely bound to the life it mirrors, is affected in an analogous way by the crisis through which the contemporary society may be passing.

The art of our time illustrates this parallelism in a most striking way. And it is the object of this book to exemplify this correspondence in the field of contemporary music. However, it is essential to point out from the beginning that the complexity of the material is such that it will be impossible to find precise formulas or to point out consequences with mathematical exactitude. It will suffice to trace a general scheme whence it will be possible to deduce the parallelism between the social and artistic phenomena of our time.

In the vast firmament of contemporary music shine an infinity of stars of all magnitudes; many are true stars shining with their own light, others are planets which do no more than reflect the light of the sun about which they revolve. The majority of writers on the music of today devote individual study to the musical stars of first magnitude. The others are grouped according to their nationality.

In my opinion this method does not lead to an understanding of the direction of present day music. It would seem better to investigate not the authors exclusively but their works. However, in speaking of the works themselves, it is necessary to guard against a myth. This myth maintains that the works of a certain author are the fruit of a given system of "intentions" which belong sometimes to the emotional field and sometimes to the technical. From this has been born a whole series of doctrines, now dated as the period of isms. They are in large measure conventional and artificial; we utilize them in a general way as the easiest method of referring to a given period, school, or group. The value of these isms is modified when we remember that even the most authentic of them, such as impressionism, symbolism, expressionism, are borrowed from other arts—painting or poetry—and that they are used in music in a general, almost metaphorical, way. It follows, then, that the isms that allude specifically to characteristics of the art of music, such as atonalism, polytonalism, and microtonalism, may be considered valid. Yet even here a certain caution is necessary. When we find the name of Stravinsky near that of Falla, that of Schönberg beside Debussy, Strauss associated with Wolf, we are not to infer necessarily that there exists between them a striking similarity or a spiritual relationship but rather that their respective orbits each revolve around the dynamic center represented by the particular musical problem under discussion. If we discuss here only the stars of the first magnitude we must remember that, as is the case with the heavenly bodies, their apparent size may not always reflect their true dimensions but may depend instead on their relative distance from us. Therefore, this book does not pretend to lay down indisputable judgments but rather to suggest points of view. Its pretension to relative objectivity rests on the fact that it does not discuss composers and their works from the point of view of the author's predilection but from that of the concrete facts as they present themselves. If I speak of tendencies, of leading ideas, I do not mean them simply in the sense of programs or theories declared more or less clearly by the composers themselves but I refer to the dominating concepts on which the creative work of each is based. These fundamentals have features in common which permit classification.

The surest way not to lose ourselves among the dubious theories and spurious personalities so often encountered in the field of contemporary music is, in my opinion, to keep sight of the thread of tradition. The study of musical history teaches us that all its facts are essentially linked together because they are manifestations of an art based on unchanging acoustical laws. From this point of view, each step in the history of music proceeds from the previous one by a gentle gradation. Only from a certain distance are we aware of the differences which divide the two. That which distinguishes two or more stages in musical art (provided that many centuries do not intervene) is the difference in the treatment of the musical material, in that handling of it we call style. This difference in musical style corresponds to a change in taste and to the changing function that the art of music performs in any given period of history.

The fact that music has acquired an increasing complexity and variety of sonorous substance as well as the fact that musical techniques have attained increasing virtuosity and manual agility has lately led to the belief that, if composers continue at an accelerated pace along this road of greater complication, they will reach solid achievements in an art of increasing brilliance, value, and merit. Thus has resulted a fallacy which is the cause of the most common flaws in the musical panorama of our day. There is no doubt but that the investigations of contemporary composers within the field of harmonic possibilities or in the mathematics of sound have opened up a multitude of new perspectives. But usually these investigations overlook the fact that music is the effect produced by sounds on human sensibility or, in other words, that music is simply a vehicle for ideas which, although specifically musical, nevertheless continue to be ideas. We frequently encounter, therefore, vehicles of sonority lacking in feeling; they are merely technical procedures which do not satisfy any need for expression. Indeed, it may be said that contemporary music possesses a greater number of means of expression than ideas to be expressed; techniques such as microtonalism, for example, are designed to serve ideas as yet unborn while atonality or polytonality are employed to interpret traditional ideologies. Throughout the history of music we observe that the number of aesthetic ideas that humanity expresses musically is restricted. The value of musical art does not reside in these ideas but rather in the purely musical way in which these ideas are made to act on the emotions. The musical faculty is not awakened by aperitifs or stimulants such as quarter tones, unusual dissonances, or ingenious effects of tone color. These devices are effective because, through his use of them, the artist brings to fruition a previous desire of the musical faculty. The interplay of these two elements constitutes the dramatic adventure of the creative artist who strives to discover means to satisfy the vague need of the society in which he moves. In opposition to this normal and historically proven process, our own musical panorama is a rich storehouse of things often useless for the inner life of the artist and of society.

The present abundance of aesthetic systems or, rather, the breaking up of traditional aesthetics corresponds to a universal disintegration apparent in all aspects of the present epoch; in art as in politics, in religion, and in philosophy.

Despite slight differences, the man of the twentieth century is physiologically, intellectually, and aesthetically the same as the man of the nineteenth century. He will probably maintain this similarity in the twenty-first century. We may therefore undertake a description of the contemporary musical panorama by using those lines that come from the past as our principal guides and by seeing if they have maintained their vitality in the present or whether they are becoming exhausted.

In music perhaps more than in any other art the organization of the structural elements into a coherent, meaningful whole is of prime importance. The principle of organization, of course, is subject to infinite variation. By and large, however, music may be classified according to two basic concepts: that of the music of oriental peoples, not subject to the regulating principle of tonality in the occidental sense, and that of Western music which, although deriving historically from the other, has established itself as an entirely different sonorous and artistic phenomenon.

In Western or occidental music, in general, musical structure is based on the principle of tonality. The rhetorical paradigms known as forms which appear in treatises on composition are various historically accepted ways of manipulating this principle. More or less disguised, these forms continue to maintain the coherence of present day music while introducing external differences which bring variety, originality, and charm.

Now, as has been said, other music exists which does not have tonal coherence. Its coherence, then, derives from other principles the analysis of which would lead to a study of oriental monody that does not lie within the purpose of this book. However, these principles may be described succinctly as: rhythmical structure and arrangement, combinations of vocal and instrumental tone colors, combinations of agogic processes or the unity and contrast of movement, and dynamics or unity and contrast in sonorous quantity. All oriental music follows, in addition, the principle of consonance as the determinant in the leaps taken by the voice. In accordance with these elements, oriental music seeks formal principles in the arrangement of sounds in motive groups while variety is achieved by means of melismatic ornamentation or rhythmic complexity.

Now these elements also exist in occidental music. Some penetrate deeply within it; others remain superficial, rhetorical devices. In effect, the greater part of the investigations made by modern composers under such terms as atonality, polytonality, microtonalism, and polyrhythm spring from attempts to introduce into the occidental musical system these unifying principles of oriental music. But with all this, and even in the instances where these attempts have been most successfully realized, what is the musical thought expressed? It does not suffice simply to reproduce this or that effect of oriental music but to create an occidental work in which such means have been utilized. That which man expresses through music is a psychological complexity ordinarily called his "soul." The soul of the occidental has a structure and a capacity for achievement entirely different from the soul of the oriental. For this reason his music has entirely different bases. When the occidental composer adopts oriental procedures (often without knowing that they have this origin), he still continues to express his occidental soul. Thus we are confronted with the paradox that such a composer may wish to express, atonally, emotions of accredited romantic derivation or, polytonally, rhythmical constructions of the baroque period or, microtonally, harmonic relationships with a basic tonality! It is obvious, then, that methods of procedure serve only as a provisional classification and that composers of our day are united more or less closely to the aesthetic tendencies traditional in European music to which they add, as external attributes, these exotic techniques. Most important for us to determine is to what extent they have made new contributions to the makeup of our music, up to what point and in what evident ways they have transformed form and tonality.

Part ONE

Chapter ONE

EVERY artistic age takes shape under the impulse of an illusion. In the beginning this illusion has an almost religious significance. A program emerges with the pretensions of a credo and artists, moved by proselytism, swear by a new faith. If the movement possesses a sound basis for existence and if these artists have succeeded in creating works of intrinsic merit, the public accepts their creed and doctrines. The artists, having already accepted as incontrovertible the fundamental truths of their faith, now take account of the inner weaknesses in their first productions and dedicate themselves in the second stage of the movement to the creation of more robust works, firmer in structure and firmer in their specific, technical ingredients. When this movement reaches its climax and the aesthetic principles upon which it is founded are obvious to all, then the truly creative artist turns his gaze toward new horizons.

Without this initial illusion, art could not exist or at least it could not exist as an entity profoundly rooted in the spirit, and the technique on which it is based would never rise above that of the manual arts. Yet, at last, the illusion fades while the works themselves remain. These persist as living things at least as long as the illusion which inspired them persists in the consciousness of the public; that is to say, they remain so long as they fulfill a social function. In time, that basic idea, that ideal, and the works which it engendered are supplanted by other ideals which, in their turn, engender works of a new texture. The earlier works then either disappear or remain in that lethargic state characteristic of "culture." Thus historians who examine works of art are accustomed to associate them with what is known of the motivating forces which gave them birth. These forces have almost always been explained by the artists themselves or by their accepted spokesmen; but in retrospect it is sometimes difficult to perceive clearly the inner relationship between the theory and the resultant works of art. Often the two appear somewhat incongruous, at times, even antithetical.

Nevertheless, whatever may be the forms in which the style of each age takes concrete shape or becomes intelligible, they are permeated with a meaning and a desire for expression which a detailed knowledge of the period recognizes as congruent with the general aspects of its life. The external forms of style are symbols which the artist uses to express, within the realm of each art, the way of life in his epoch and, while each stylistic motif lacks meaning when isolated, the sum total possesses a convincing eloquence. We are more clearly aware of this when the period with which we are dealing is not too remote as, for example, the romantic or the baroque periods. Thus we may readily perceive that the profuse ornamentation of Couperin's fragile music for the clavecin reflects the dress and manners of the aristocratic court of a monarch such as Louis XIV while the theatricalism of the baroque, visible alike in churches, palaces, gardens, and settings for opera and ballet, inspired monarchs to become imperial actors in their private theaters. Again, if we penetrate deeply into the motivating forces which determine the transformations of styles we comprehend how the rococo, with its curves inspired in the shapes of seaweed with its clinging, sea shells, corresponds in its expressive sense to the age of Louis XV. Proceeding further in time, we are able by dint of study to recognize that the stylistic forms of Renaissance music or the polyphony of the Gothic or the plain song of the Romanesque periods were, indeed, authentic means of expression in their day. We may even go so far as to declare any other stylistic forms as inconceivable in these epochs.

Every style has at its command an adequate technique. The artist's problem is to discover at each moment in the life of society and in its art the means by which to give external reality to the intuitions he absorbs from the social environment about him. When he realizes these intuitions fully in his artistic medium, he becomes the artist of his age and his work a characteristic product of the period. It is scarcely necessary to point out that the weaker his intuitions the easier it will be for him to handle his technique, the less problematic the work and, in consequence, the more commonplace the result. There are moments of plenitude in every age when the artistic credo becomes a facile interplay within the reach of all; fortunately, these moments are brief and new problems always arise to maintain the dramatic tension of artistic creation. Then begins a period of experimentation during which the artist is finding himself while to the observer he seems to have lost himself. If a period is so complex as to be slow in declaring itself, as has been the case in the first four decades of the twentieth century, the general perplexity may reach chaotic proportions. Thus it is obvious that, if we wish to study the state of art in our times and speculate on its future tendencies, we cannot take as our point of departure the panorama that now presents itself but rather we shall have to turn back to that clearly recognizable moment when the art of music took an unmistakably new departure.

There must be some way of determining the uncertain dividing line between the present and the past. When, in fact, does the present period begin?

If we examine, to begin with, those aspects of our art that have a firm sense of historical continuity, we may say that the present begins when the line relating it to the past undergoes a deviation either because it becomes more and more inoperative or decadent or because it shows unmistakable symptoms of reaction. The observer, by analysis, usually succeeds in finding the moment of crisis, a moment which often passes unobserved at the time, and is to be seen only later after the current of events has produced a difference clearly perceptible in its external form, that is to say, when a change in style has become obvious. In reality these transformations in the style of an art do not possess a "zero hour," a line of demarcation. Nevertheless there always exists some point in the chain of events sufficiently well characterized to permit the historian to select a point of departure in his description of a new period without losing contact with the earlier one. This continuity in history is the unique guarantee of authenticity against the often extravagant imagination of some historians; history as a succession of human facts has, like humanity itself, a limitless link with the past.

With the necessity we feel, then, of finding a symbolic zero hour, which shall we choose? It seems clear that since we descend from the century of romanticism (whether as continuation or as reaction, our music derives ideologically and technically from that of romanticism—a fact we are going to verify presently), the zero hour will appear to be that moment when the romantic current shifted—either because it was engendering special types which deserved to be considered postromantic or because a reaction against it was in process which showed a desire to relate itself to an outmoded classical discipline called neoclassicism. The critical moment, then, seems to take shape when the musicians of the nineteenth century who most conscientiously practiced the symphonic forms protested the tendency of other contemporary musicians toward a dissolution of form. We observe at that moment the double process we have already pointed out, namely, a deviation from the original direction and, on the other hand, a reaction. The expression of the second tendency is to be found in the famous manifesto of 1860 signed by Johannes Brahms, Joseph Joachim, Julius Otto Grimm, and Bernard Scholz. Appearing in the spring of that year in the Berlin periodical *Echo,* it was directed against those musicians whom the review *Zeitschrift für Musik* termed a "neo-German school."

Among the signers of this manifesto and those musicians who later adhered to it, only the names of Joachim and Brahms signified anything to their contemporaries, who saw in this act a violent protest against the Wagnerian group and against the tendencies enthusiastically proclaimed by Wagner in his extensive polemics. They attributed to Joachim a personal dislike for Wagner because of the latter's pamphlet on Jews in music. Brahms at this time was a young composer and a distinguished pianist greatly admired in both respects by his adherents but he had as yet written nothing profoundly characteristic,[1] nothing capable of competing with the creations of Wagner who was then approaching his peak.[2] Nevertheless the manifesto was significant and announced a new point of view in that it took issue with the other group for its extreme attitude in favor of a music of the future.[3] The issue was joined, then, like many another in later times and it at least served as a point of departure with consequences which resulted in a profound break between the followers of Wagnerian principles and those who, with Brahms, advocated the return to the closed forms. Wagner considered these forms as unfruitful as all romantic music not destined for the stage, even including the symphonic poem of his friend Liszt and the poematic symphony of Berlioz.

In order to understand the true importance Brahms's manifesto had in the year it was published and the importance of the year itself in the transformation romantic music underwent during the second half of the nineteenth century, it is necessary to get a glimpse of the general situation as regards European music at the moment. In the first place, Wagner, the man whose music of the future was so much debated by his own compatriots, reached his zenith in 1860. *Tristan und Isolde,* the work in which application of romantic musical ideas reached the limits of their possibilities and of development "within the concepts so far recognized in music" was receiving its final touches in 1859. In 1861 *Tannhäuser* had its famous performance and was hissed in Paris. Wagner was beginning work on *Die Meistersinger von Nürnberg*. Between these two years, in the momentous year 1860, were born two German composers who were to continue the lyricism of Wagner although in different forms: Hugo Wolf and Gustav Mahler. Liszt had given up his career as virtuoso and was living chiefly in Rome where he retired for a time after donning the garb of *abbé*. A new star of the piano was dazzling all Europe by his brilliant tours which began in 1860: the Russian, Anton Rubinstein.

This year was likewise decisive in the development of a new movement beginning to spread through Europe; a movement at once liberal and tra-

[1] Brahms was born in Hamburg in 1833. In 1860 he was in the service of the prince of Lippe-Detmold. At this time he had written the Serenade in D, Op. 11, for orchestra, the First Concerto, Op. 15, for piano, the Trio, Op. 8, in B, the first version of the German Requiem, the sonatas for piano, Op. 1 and 2, and some other pieces for piano, organ, and chorus. At this time also, Brahms had already published his Third Piano Sonata in F Minor, Op. 5, on which Robert Schumann very justly could found his hopes of a new direction in German music. But although the influence of Schumann may be seen in this work, the influence of Liszt predominates. The sonata belongs to the year 1853, the same as that of Liszt's great sonata dedicated to Schumann. Brahms visited Liszt shortly after in Leipzig. Liszt tried to draw him into the group of young Germans but Brahms refused chiefly, so it appears, because of his disgust for the atmosphere of adulation that surrounded the "great virtuoso."

[2] *Die Walküre* was finished in 1856, *Tristan und Isolde* in 1859.

[3] The "Art Work of the Future" by Richard Wagner dates from 1850, "A Message to My Friends," the letter to Villot, from 1851. "The Music of the Future" belongs to 1860.

ditional; its music, born under both influences, is called nationalist. In Russia it was the outcome of the liberal government of Alexander II which culminated, about 1860, in the liberation of the serfs. The movement produced a lively interest in the art of the Russian people, especially in popular arts and crafts and above all in music. Musicians like Mily Balakirev, writers like Vladimir Stassov, the painter and architect Victor Hartmann were outstanding in their defense of national art. It is worth remembering that the famous series of pieces for piano by Modest Mussorgsky, Pictures at an Exhibition, were inspired by drawings of Hartmann. Michail Glinka, who in the period of the expansion of romanticism in Europe had created Russian national opera (*A Life for the Czar* first performed in 1836), had died a few years before, in 1857. In the previous year the death of Schumann—the first to recognize Johannes Brahms as the new messiah who would redeem German musical art from its disintegrating tendencies—had occurred.

Another event of great importance for the development of nationalism in music occurred in 1860 when Bohemia acquired political freedom after many years of slavery under the Austrian yoke. From 1860 date the symphonic poems, still inspired by romantic themes, of the man destined to be the founder of the Bohemian national school: Bedřich Smetana. He was then living in Sweden where a strong national feeling was rapidly spreading. This movement reached a moment of brilliance with the work of Gade, Sinding, and Grieg and still continues in full vigor with Jean Sibelius.

Turning westward, a certain tendency toward musical nationalism is discernible in France toward 1861 with the teaching of Saint-Saëns in the École Niedermeyer; profoundly French, it was on the surface romantic in the style of Liszt's "poems," while possessing a classical purity of form. France was then passing through a Mendelssohnian phase in concert music after the greatest achievements of French romanticism in the finest works of Berlioz: *Les Troyens* and *Béatrice et Bénédict* (about the same period; *Les Troyens* first performed in 1863). In the following year Jakob Meyerbeer, the German Jew who was the founder of French grand opera, died leaving as his heir Charles Gounod, whose *Faust* had its première in 1859. Georges Bizet, one day to be proclaimed by the most acute of German philosophers as the antidote for the infectious miasma of *Tristan,* was at this time engaged in the composition of little symphonic sketches, unimportant and picturesque, yet completely representative of the French spirit. The great Italian opera composer Giuseppe Verdi, the contemporary of Wagner, was at this time acquiring a reputation for his postromantic operas like *Un Ballo in maschera* (1859) and *La Forza del destino* (1862). Both were written to librettos of the most extravagantly romantic character, one based on a work of Victor Hugo, the other on a drama of the Spaniard, Angel de Saavedra, duque de Rivas.

Thus it is theater, all theater, from Wagner to Verdi—whether in the music of Bohemia, Russia, Italy, or France. There scarcely appeared an important symphonic work. Only the piano maintained its prestige, thanks to the remarkable virtuosity of its performers. Chamber music—which with the symphony had reached its moment of greatest development in Beethoven's last period—had fallen into disuse like all the manifestations of the sonata form. Richard Wagner was pleased to predict its disappearance as an exhausted form. Johannes Brahms, whose works of apprenticeship maintained an equilibrium between the exaggerated classicism of Eduard Marxsen and the tepid romanticism of Willibald Cossel, began a resurrection, a revivification of this form with a solid base in the Beethoven tradition. The sonata form, impoverished after Beethoven's death, tended toward a disintegration of its essential character with the great symphonists of the second generation of romanticism, Berlioz and Liszt, while with the pianistic composers, Chopin and Schumann, it dissolved into scintillating fragments or took on a new appearance.

This year of 1860 shows the beginning of the chief tendencies of the second half of the nineteenth century which were to lead to the music of the present day. We have: (*a*) an extension of form and an amplification of tonality after *Tristan;* (*b*) poematic symphonism which, from Berlioz to Liszt, became assimilated to Wagnerian harmonic and orchestral expression with a simultaneous relaxation of the inner relationship of form; (*c*) the invention of small forms, principally experimental in structure, harmony, and aesthetic character; (*d*) a reaction to form in the sonata for piano, in chamber music, and in the symphony. These tendencies do not pursue a parallel course but, as is natural in periods as complex as the nineteenth century and our own, they frequently display an interchange of the characteristics appropriate to each at the same time tending to enrich the personalities of the artists and the inner meaning of their works.

Chapter TWO

THE CREATIVE artist, always audacious in his investigation of new means which may nourish and extend his art, has frequently been hampered in his advance by more timorous spirits. These have been found less among the laity than among professional musicians, those conformers for whom scholastic legality is inviolable. Among the audiences for new works, the receptive and the intolerant maintained an unstable equilibrium during the romantic period. Although the laggards opposed any obviously perceptible novelty, many unorthodox innovations passed unnoticed. At the end of the last century, however, when it became generally accepted that it was the composer's obligation to *invent,* intolerance developed on the part of the supporters of extreme or systematic innovation. Composers hastened to throw themselves headlong into search for the new, whether legitimate or chimerical. Discoveries and novel inventions in the realm of all the arts took on such a rapid tempo at the end of the nineteenth and in the early years of the twentieth century that none of them had the opportunity to exploit their inner possibilities nor to unfold their aesthetic content. Hence arose the confused situation apparent in the art of our own days.

Present day historians of music, preoccupied with noting what techniques have served the cause of new aesthetics, have written descriptions of harmonic procedures rather than histories of music. The already extensive bibliography for contemporary music consists mainly of studies in modern harmony: sometimes as an evolution of classical harmony, again as an analysis of more or less arbitrary procedures. Until very recently, moreover, these investigations included the study of mechanical means of inventing harmonies and even complete systems of music based on mathematical relationships arbitrarily invented from beginning to end. Naturally, since in all these systems the musical "function" is completely lacking, they have failed or rather will fail through their inadequacy as aesthetic phenomena.

Some of these authors are motivated by a desire to demonstrate that the formulas usually accepted as modern already occur in romantic music and even in that of earlier periods. They are thus led to suggest that the artists of those periods foresaw the music of our day. Such suggestions imply an error in perspective. The harshnesses and shocks encountered in the polylinear writing of some polyphonists, including certain cases in Bach, do not derive from a tolerance toward harmonic effects and dissonances but, quite the contrary, stem from the fact that these effects were heard not harmonically but contrapuntally. In the same way, the bitonality of some of their *fugato* passages is not an indication of the amplitude of their tonal feeling but, on the contrary, shows that their feeling for tonality was not so predominant as in the period immediately following (i.e., the Viennese or classical period). When Schubert or Berlioz, Mendelssohn or Weber employ certain harmonic combinations, it is not for the purpose of serving an aesthetics which they have not as yet perceived. Sometimes these modernisms occur quite unconsciously, brought about by exigencies of writing or of style; at other times they are flying sparks which hint at a new future. Both cases are legitimate and should be studied as symptoms of a later transformation. Yet, when they are encountered in conscious and systematic use by present day composers it would be frivolous to consider them romantic procedures. Similarly, to think that Guillaume de Machault was modern (although this great musician of the *ars nova* was so in his own time) because he employed consecutive sevenths is as ridiculous as to say that a modern composer is medieval because he employs a certain procedure known to the fourteenth century. Similarly a composer of today is not modern solely because he employs formulas taken from the scores of Schönberg and Stravinsky. A composer like Fauré can display a musical sensibility delicately touched with new shadings without employing unusual devices.

An artist is not old or young, antiquated or modern because he uses certain technical methods. Newness, in order to be authentic, must be combined with other factors, some of which are not clearly perceptible at the moment when the artist uses them. What is essential is that the artist truly expresses the needs and aspirations of the time in which he lives and for which he works. It is false, therefore, to say that there are artists who write for posterity. This idea results from a complete misunderstanding of the artist's environment or from mistaking the vulgar and superficial appearance of a certain type of society for the true expression of the time; the aesthetic attitude of a period is always in strict agreement with the other contemporary features of style, although sometimes these are not definable until much later.

The idea of modernism proceeds from Richard Wagner. This man, so extraordinary as an artist, was equally so as theorist and producer. As often happens, the theorist and the critic were at the service of the producer who struggled against odds in getting his music heard and sought arguments for it which he hoped would impress the artistic world. As a creative artist he was deeply intuitive; his aesthetic need proceeded from the profound depths of a strong personality and expressed itself in large part by traditional means as well as by new ones which were their logical development.

On the other hand, as a theorist, as the interested defender of his works of art, Wagner was moved by a legitimate but, in a sense, commercial desire. In depreciating or belittling the music around him, in evaluating history according to his own taste, in posing as the necessary continuer of traditional German thought, Wagner deceived himself (if he was sincere) without succeeding in deceiving his readers; they gradually accepted his music without necessarily accepting his theories. Wagner thought he was constructing the art of the future when in reality he was constructing that of his own day along with other artists whom he surpassed but who, like him, appear to us to be the last composers of romanticism. What Wagner would have considered monstrous, however, was that the means which he designed as a vehicle for his own deepest musical thought were to be utilized not long after him to express quite different needs, although of the same emotional family. The chromaticism of *Tristan* was destined to lead so far afield that one of the most profound consequences of this aspect of Wagnerian art, namely the art of Claude Debussy, appears on the surface as a reaction to it. This reaction Debussy sought at one time to demonstrate in his projected musical setting of the Bédier restoration of the *Tristan* legend. In more than one respect the prelude to *L'Après-midi d'un faune* is the French consequence of the formal and tonal dissolution implicit in *Tristan*, while the *Martyre de Saint Sébastien* might be called Debussy's *Parsifal*. Between the extremes of the exuberant chromaticism of *Tristan* and the tonal fluidity of *Pelléas et Mélisande* lies the whole period of transition from the twilight of romanticism to the dawn of a new epoch.

Wagner at the end of the romantic period and Debussy at the beginning of our own are the "inventors" of genius, between whom took place the aesthetic and technical transformation that shaped the course of music from the nineteenth to the twentieth century. Other men sought in the inventions of geniuses of the past the means to prolong an art in which they and their audiences felt at home. Whatever their importance, it is evident that they will not create a new aesthetic world; yet they act as a counterbalance, maintaining an aesthetic equilibrium.

If we go back into the past to seek the sources of those inventions by which our art lives, we find that the romantic age which ended in Wagner was already well defined in all its essential characteristics in Beethoven. Further back still, the baroque which ended in Bach had earlier found dramatic expression in the madrigals, for one or more voices, particularly in those of Monteverdi. Before Monteverdi, musical ideas of tonality and harmonic concepts belong to a world of sonorities associated with intuitions very different from those which integrate our own. The dramaticism of Monteverdi's great vocal compositions, however, fully satisfies our emotions, although generally speaking his harmonic sense seems to us lacking in density. Nevertheless one finds in Monteverdi chords that have only recently been exploited to their fullest extent. There is constant invention in Monteverdi, in his melody and harmony as well as in his orchestration. Although his inventions disappeared quickly (for they never became crystallized as formulas), the entire harmonic repertory of seventeenth century music is to be found in Monteverdi. It remained for the eighteenth century to give order to that harmonic material; it added little of importance in this respect although it added much as regards form and the treatment of expressive elements. The great musicians of the eighteenth century, contrapuntists like Bach, as well as composers of musical dramas from Rameau to Gluck, and the composers of symphonies of the second half of the century, all found ample scope within this harmonic repertory. Beethoven himself was nourished by it. But his feeling for tonal dissonances—such as the chords of the dominant seventh and ninth and the diminished seventh—strengthen the tonal value of this harmonic material; to the same degree, his originality manifests itself in the expressive quality of his modulations which follow the unfolding of his ideas with a dramatic power and with an intensity which take precedence over formal considerations.

This feeling for modulation becomes ampler in power of expression and in variety of tonal color as used by Schubert, while his treatment of the chord of the ninth and even of the seventh produces entirely new effects. Modulation with Schubert has already become fluid material and is no longer a procedure to be used for considerations of form or dramatic effect but is felt as an essential property of the sonorous fabric. This incorporation of the inventions and discoveries of earlier pioneers into the normal vocabulary of the later composers is the natural process of evolution of the art and continues to affirm itself throughout the course of romantic music. At first, however, romantic composers were unable to define these earlier ideas objectively and, for the sake of a better comprehension of them from their own point of view as well as from that of the public, they clothed them with poetic verbiage. Berlioz speaks of a feeling for the infinite, of the immensity of the starry night. Schumann and Chopin find in such evocations admirable excuse to justify their harmonic feeling. In a clearer and more rational manner, Mendelssohn explains in a famous letter to his sister Fanny that what he wishes to express in his Barcaroles or Songs without Words is just what his notes say, not any kind of poetic thought or feeling but purely and simply a musical idea. Nevertheless, like his companions, Mendelssohn had recourse to descriptive titles. This device, however, was imposed by the general poetic tone of the period and was the only way, for the moment, in which to make himself intelligible to a public whose musical understanding had not reached the composer's degree of perception. There was urgent need and obligation to discover technical means for the translation of the feeling implicit in the age: vague and restless in the social mass, ever clearer to the composers who were creating a new technique for new intuitions.

The process is analytically observable in the extension of a feeling for chromaticism which reached a critical point in Chopin. Fifty years ago, Sir Henry Hadow pointed out that the modulatory passage of the Nocturne in E Flat (No. 2, Op. 9, beginning with the twelfth measure) should be interpreted not as a rapid series of modulations but as a kind of sonorous iridescence enveloping the principal modulation. This transformation of the musical material or—as a certain German critic expresses it—this transformation of the "sonorous ideal" (such as consonance, timbre and quality of the material) is not inherited by Chopin from the great figures of the romantic music of the first period. Chopin drew on other, more modest, sources such as those suggested by Hummel, Field, Moscheles, Kalkbrenner, Bellini, and Spohr. It is important to point this out because it shows that the transformation of aesthetic feeling in romantic music was taking place among all the artistic groups of the time—the most modest as well as the most brilliant.

As far as Chopin was concerned, this was the more natural because it came by way of the technique of the piano which interested him more deeply than the symphonies of Beethoven or the melodies of Schubert. Music came to him through his fingers and new harmonies and chromatic richness unfolded for him by means of pianistic figurations. Passages in the sonatas or concertos of Hummel (such as those pointed out by Gerald Abraham, who finds in Hummel the connecting link between Mozart and Chopin) [1] are already strikingly Chopinesque and even approach the sparkling brilliance of that composer.

An especially typical ingredient of romanticism is its predilection for music of popular inspiration. Peasant songs or the popular music of village and town had been used for a long time past in music but like the striking harmonic effects already noted, it was used only by exception and was assimilated, as in Haydn, to conventional musical rhetoric in a kind of game that hid the popular tune within the formalism of the symphonic melody in order to please an elegant audience. Beethoven, who harmonized (on commission) a considerable number of popular songs of different countries, did not find any special attraction in them for they were incongruent with his dramatic genius. Schubert, on the other hand, found his finest inspiration in Viennese popular songs, as did Chopin in Polish music. In the case of Chopin, as later with the national composers and with those who based their music on the tonal feeling in peasant songs, the songs of Poland proved suggestive in

[1] Gerald Abraham, *Chopin's Musical Style* (Oxford: 1939), Ch. 1.

various ways: sometimes for the modal feeling of this music (exploited also by Mussorgsky in the polonaise in *Boris Godunov*), again for its typical rhythms which opened up original means of harmonic treatment, again, too, as suggestive of form as in some of the rondeaux and finales of Chopin's concertos where juxtapositions of short passages of a popular character call to mind the mazurka.

The pianistic formulas of Chopin are propitious for the development and repetition of chromatic patterns in formations such as diminished-seventh chords and linked successions of chords by semitones, of which his études and preludes offer such eloquent examples. The effect of headlong modulations, leading directly to atonality in contemporary composers, has a precedent in the succession of diminished sevenths in Chopin. Nevertheless, his repetition of the same kind of harmony leaves in the ear an effect of unity which is not as yet atonal but which raises an interrogation resolved in the chord of resolution at the end of the passage: an effect frequently found in music of the eighteenth century. Yet with what new pianistic effects and color in Chopin! Chopin's use of chromaticism, indeed, is not simply a harmonic effect but is a kind of dissolving of the tone into an infinity of chromatic radiations which he produces by surrounding his melodies, normally diatonic, with a sonorous cloud in the Italian coloratura style. The series of chromatic chords occur as passing chords between two different positions of the original chord.

Much has been said about the Italian quality, especially that of Bellini, in Chopin's melodic ornamentation—a quality which proceeds in great part from the *bel canto* style. This florid writing, however, always takes on a truly admirable pianistic stylization in which Chopin utilizes all the formulas included in the repertory of the keyboard and to which his inventive genius adds many subtleties. Ornamentation is so congenial to Chopin's spirit that some critic has asked if in certain cases it can really be called ornamentation or whether it is not rather the stylistic manner required by his thought, like the arabesques of the oriental or Gothic styles. Thus an extremely baroque line becomes, in Chopin, true thematic substance. Many of his richest melismas would lose meaning were they deprived of all their paraphernalia of gruppetti, trills, mordents, and portamenti. In the same way he uses retards, passing notes, anticipations, appoggiaturas, borrowed chords, elisions, and other techniques of writing to wrap his harmonies in a sonorous veil which is the very substance of his ideas and which constitutes one of the most evocative ingredients of the romantic vocabulary.

What in Beethoven was melodic improvisation, the source of such rich results in his sonatas, in Chopin becomes ornamental improvisation, a sudden blossoming of embroideries for agile fingers. Chopin's repertory of chords is that usual in his day but among them abound those formed by added dissonances and those resulting from the alteration of the notes constituting the chord. He rarely employs the high chords that result from the natural resonances, including the chord of the ninth and the secondary forms of the seventh; in this respect, Chopin remains distant from such later composers as Wagner and Liszt and from the early composers of our century. Certain devices that have led to present day harmony come from Chopinesque sources such as (*a*) the reiteration of a passing note in a repeated pattern, which reiteration gives to the note a real harmonic value or (*b*) the constant replacement of a note by another to which the ear naturally attributes the rights of the first.

This procedure brought about other important consequences in an extended conception of the grand form in the music of the romantic period. The grand form—sonata, quartet, or symphony—is based, as is well known, on the solid interrelation of the three tonal functions: tonic, dominant, subdominant. If Chopin was able in his use of ornamental passages and chromatic progressions to maintain, in the majority of cases, the original harmonic feeling, he achieved a great deal. Yet the repetition of these procedures was to lead the way to a weakening of the tonal structure so that, in the case of the sonata, it could only follow the form at a distance. The tonal structure tends to relax, especially in the central or development section which is normally modulatory, and this dissolution contrasts artificially with the obligatory tonal strictness of the first section where the thematic material of the work is presented. The latent form is felt as a promise which, in Chopin and other romantic composers after Beethoven, is not fulfilled. Once the exposition section is presented, with a schematization which denotes the effort these composers made to follow the precepts of an aesthetics no longer theirs, it is evident how they flee to more attractive fields, either in search of new harmonic relationships or for the opportunity to improvise on the keyboard. Because it provided the latter opportunity, the concerto acquired an attractiveness not offered by the sonata. The fantasia tended to take the place of the latter in music for solo piano. In one instance Schumann was even tempted to name one of his fantasias "Concerto without orchestra"; this contradiction in terms eloquently suggests the transformation of form in the romantic period. The development of the symphony from Berlioz to Liszt shows the same attempt to pour new wine into old bottles. This tendency is also evident in those later composers who find in the music of Wagner an expression that they wish to confine within the form of the classical symphony, a form that had become rhetorical, as we shall see in the next chapter.

Chapter THREE

JOHANN SEBASTIAN BACH was, as we know, the last great contrapuntist: the last great musician for whom counterpoint was the normal medium of expression. Mozart was also a great contrapuntist; his art, however, in this respect derives not so much from the German as from the Italian tradition, learned after the conservative manner of Padre Martini. Nevertheless, no one would think of Mozart's musical idiom as contrapuntal. On the contrary, the idiom in which Mozart found such admirable freedom, the idiom that fills the new art of his period, the art of the symphony for orchestra, was the triumphant consequence of a struggle begun in Bach's lifetime between the contrapuntal tradition and the novelty of harmonized melodism which brought to instrumental music accents borrowed from opera. Telemann, champion of melodism against the contrapuntism of his close friend Johann Sebastian, was victor in the struggle and his epoch, sharing his taste, did not forget that fact. Telemann, born four years before Bach, was to be "the young"; Bach "the old." The latter's sons, especially Philipp Emanuel, who was Telemann's godson, carried along by the current of the times, rapidly left behind the rich contrapuntal art cultivated by their father.

Counterpoint, to be sure, exists in the symphony, in the sonata of the new epoch, but it is disguised: it has become a technical means, essential for treating smoothly the voices of the orchestra, for giving lightness and grace to the accompaniment of a melody; it is no longer the principal means of expression. Beethoven's mastery of counterpoint is unmistakable in certain of his works such as the fugue with which he intended to end the Quartet, Op. 130 (numbered separately as Quartet No. 16, Op. 133) but these works are the exception with him. Schubert and Weber are mediocre contrapuntists. It has been emphatically said of Chopin that he was ignorant of the rudiments of the art. The winds of romanticism were blowing over the land of harmony; the expression developing in music was to be *dramatic,* proceeding from lyrical sources. For the second generation of romanticists, for Chopin and Schumann especially, the *expression* of their music, above all their music for piano, possesses clearly defined characteristics; it is specifically musical, concerned with sound and its combinations, with harmony, with tonal color. But romanticism, a spiritual movement derived directly from poetry and the theater, did not yet have, in the time of Schumann and Chopin, terms sufficiently clearly defined to show wherein consisted the expressive quality of its music. To make itself understood, music had recourse to the terminology of poetry: immensity, the night, the feeling for nature, picturesque terms such as barcarole and ballade or, again, a term associated with another typically romantic sentiment, irony. Thus are born carnavals, humoresques, scherzos or, again, inconsequential brief pages, *Bunte Blätter,* novelettes, which fluttered a moment in the musical atmosphere like butterflies and quickly disappeared.

But some composers realized that they were experimenting practically with musical material. So Chopin and later Liszt entitled as études pages which are not simply studies for the exercise of the fingers but studies in sonorities, experiments in instrumental color which arise from the predominance of a formula, a harmonic pattern or a specific interval. The études of Claude Debussy later confirm this tendency under new conditions.

The decline of the old contrapuntal style in France and Italy had other, less favorable, results than in Germany. An entire art of transcendent importance reached its peak in Germany in the symphony and in chamber music without ever entirely neglecting counterpoint. In the more easy-going society of the Latin countries the change took a different course: *opera buffa* and comic opera came to the fore. Symphony and chamber music are aristocratic forms. Comic opera is essentially popular and the Encyclopedists like J. J. Rousseau declared in favor of it because it reflected a social movement. This movement was to lead to romanticism; but first it led to revolution—the French Revolution.

One of the principles of the Revolution was art for the people. Great festivals were organized; they were secular festivals with a religious character centering around the cult of reason, of the supreme being, of the heroes and, above all, the cult of the dead. The composers of the music for these grand ceremonial processions and choruses were men trained in the light style of comic opera. Regardless of what might be the solemnity of tone demanded by the occasion, two things remained intact in principle: a melodic facility in the style of the popular tune and harmonic simplicity. The most "learned" musicians, like François-Adrien Boieldieu for example, excused themselves by insisting that they were *not* harmonists and declared that they did not understand the strange and mysterious diminished seventh chords of the young Berlioz.

Nevertheless, it was Berlioz who, at the dawn of romanticism, led the violent struggle in favor of harmony and symphonic music (with little or mediocre counterpoint) amid the sterility of French music. He had been preceded, however, by musicians with a fine ear: Le Sueur, who sought exaggerated expression in orchestral color and in the color of harmony or Reicha, who proclaimed the need of composing in well-constructed forms. Berlioz, possessed of a passionate temperament cut to the measure of the times, understood music as a kind of hyperaesthetic poetry. The poetic commonplaces of the day found their counterpart in his music; there the heroism and triumph of the glorious dead are combined with the mysterious enchantments of nature and witchcraft. He found in Gluck nobility in the dramatic expression and in the tone of the flute "a solo"; in Beethoven he appreciated the heroic and the pastoral. The Ninth Symphony, however, troubled him; nearer to him was *Der Freischütz* with its huntsmen, its sentimental airs, its solo instruments, the power and color of the orchestration in the evil spirit episodes.

It is scarcely possible to conceive what French music in the romantic period would have been without Berlioz. His symphonic overtures dating from 1828, the *Symphonie fantastique* belonging to the famous year 1830, his great dramatic symphonies like *Harold en Italie* (1834) and *Roméo et Juliette* (1839), his operas which began then and culminated in *Béatrice et Bénédict* in 1862 and in *Les Troyens à Carthage* in 1863—all are gigantic works for their time and, in many pages, worthy of immortality. It is not strange that Wagner and Liszt should see in Berlioz the prophetic figure who appeared at the threshold of the music of the future. The question indeed arose, when *Les Troyens* was recently performed at the opera in Paris whether Berlioz might not occupy today the place now reserved for the composer of *Tristan*—if the latter had not existed.

To his own discomfiture, on hearing the Prelude to *Tristan,* Berlioz was forced to declare that he did not understand a single note.[1] Such is the march of time and of art! Berlioz had not understood much more of Beethoven's Ninth Symphony, which Wagner set himself to "discover" and which became one of his favorite war horses. Yet, to what degree did Wagner comprehend the complete meaning of Beethoven? The chamber music of Beethoven was almost unknown at the mid-point of the century. When Liszt inherited the artistic dictatorship of Goethe at Weimar and undertook to organize its musical life, his programs included composers as recent as Peter Cornelius and Saint-Saëns; yet it never entered his head to perform the quartets of Beethoven. This, however, belongs to the history of chamber music and we will come back to it when we speak of the composers who initiated a return to pure forms.

The harmonies of Berlioz, which seemed so incomprehensible to the composer of *La Dame Blanche,* could not have been more modest and were those employed then by contemporary German composers. But in Berlioz they appear united with an expression so intense and an orchestral color so unique

[1] See his collection of most suggestive and interesting articles entitled *À travers chants,* "Concerts de Richard Wagner," "La musique à l'avenir," ed. Calman-Lévy (Paris), p. 311.

that they produced a startling effect on his contemporaries: an effect which disappears completely in a simple piano transcription. With him, as with his predecessors and followers, the significance of his harmonies lies in the way in which he uses them and in the originality of the ideas behind them; thus it is that he gives unsurpassed expression to romantic emotions. A performance of the *Symphonie fantastique* always produces an amazement which increases when we consider the contemporary musical picture and it makes us regret the absence of works like *Roméo et Juliette* in the concert repertory of today. Edward Dannreuther, who is not overenthusiastic in his criticism of some of Berlioz's works, justly says that the chromaticism of certain passages of *Roméo et Juliette* (*"Roméo seul—Tristesse"*) compares favorably with the introduction to *Tristan und Isolde,* which it seems to have influenced as other pages influenced certain of those in *Tannhäuser*. And he adds, in a burst of generosity, that the love scene contains some two hundred measures of the richest, most delicate and most passionate music that exists; nothing in all the repertory of French music can approach it and nothing, except *"O sink Hernieder, Nacht der Liebe"* of the second act of *Tristan,* can surpass it.[2]

More than his harmony, Liszt appreciated in Berlioz his orchestral color, really unique in the art of his time for its richness and evocative quality (only Weber's *Freischütz* offers comparable passages). The remarkable orchestral inventiveness of Liszt (today it is said that Joachim Raff, who assisted him in his instrumental arrangements, collaborated effectively in the numerous novel effects in Liszt's orchestrations) derives from Berlioz and ends in Wagner. From the point of view of form also, Liszt stands between the two. More graceful, more independent, more ingenious in his devices for preserving the unity of form than Berlioz, Liszt reaches admirable heights in his great oratorios and in the Sonata in B Minor. He is not so fluid nor so untrammeled as Wagner in his symphonic dramas, for Wagner never proceeds except under the stimulus of feeling which, when it achieves genuine realization, discovers by its own virtue its proper form.

In Liszt's music, chromatic and diatonic procedures alternate, carrying their respective qualities to extremes as compared with the general practice of the time. His religious feeling led him to seek expression in reminiscences of modal music, especially notable in his oratorio, *Christus*. Modal color, so frequently sought by contemporary French composers, had already suggested itself to the romanticists; and one remembers especially the famous passage, *"in modo lidico,"* in the Quartet No. 15, of Beethoven. The Lydian mode appears in Chopin inspired by popular song; here, however, it is the natural result of the national Polish scale. In certain pages Berlioz uses modal color

[2] Edward Dannreuther, "The Romantic Period," *The Oxford History of Music,* VI, Ch. 7.

with ineffable simplicity and tenderness, as in his *Enfance du Christ,* so rarely performed today.

The harmonic character of Liszt's chromaticism is no longer an external phenomenon, a shower of tonal sparks. It penetrates deeply to the very roots of Liszt's music to infuse it with a different feeling, something profoundly new, both for the meaning of the melody and for that of the harmonic relationships. The musical idea itself is chromatic in essence, very different from the ornamental chromaticism of Chopin. Even the form was soon to display its consequences, not as yet in the symphonic poems, which are regular in structure, but in the works of Liszt's final period such as the Sonata in B Minor, a gigantic attempt to achieve a grand form for piano outside the classical pattern.

In this attempt Chopin had preceded Liszt and, in the *Fantaisie Polonaise,* initiated a type of large-scale construction which death prevented him from developing. Looking back, one can see Chopin's incessant preoccupation with the problem of form; his is a logical, methodical process which rejects any idea of improvised construction even when improvisation dominates the development section both melodically and in the carrying out of modulations. In the Scherzo in E Major, Op. 54 (1843), the form is still traditional with its two motives in the tonic and dominant, a development section, and a recapitulation whose solitary first motive leads to the trio, in C-sharp minor. This tonal relationship at the third (normal in this case because it is the relative minor) appears in other works of Chopin but without the relationship of mode. The trio returns to major and the two initial themes reappear in their respective keys, after which follows a development section and coda.

Not only do the key relationships become more complicated in Chopin's larger works but the themes increase in number: from the orthodox two to three in the A Flat Ballade (1841) to four in the *Fantaisie Polonaise* (1846), which has an additional central theme in a section that leads to a transition passage and thence to a recapitulation of the first section with its first two themes or motives. Both of these appear in the same key (the fundamental, A flat) after a modulatory introduction which touches on the minor. A working-out of conjunct tonalities follows between the repetition of the first theme (A flat) and a passage in B flat. The latter, after modulating, leads to a new theme in B major. The central section, *più lento,* is in G-sharp minor (the enharmonic of the principal key, in minor) which leads to B major, returning via minor and major to the initial tonality in A flat. The construction, firm and completely satisfying, is of great originality and interest. It is based fundamentally on the principal motive and key: the first theme and the key of A-flat major. The importance of the first theme is confirmed when it is heard for the second time in the first section after the episodic motive no. 2. Later on, the interest maintained during the unfolding of the other thematic passages is kept alive as if by an extensive digression until the original key and motive reappear, the latter followed within the key by motive no. 4, which brings the work to an end with a peroration. Presented schematically, the work unfolds thus: that is, a whole structure moving back and forth.

A♭ major and minor		A♭ major and minor
B major	or	C♭ major
G♯ minor	otherwise	A♭ minor
B major	expressed	C♭ major
A♭ minor and major		A♭ minor and major

All this variety of material is presented in a work of moderate length but Chopin tends to shorten the recapitulation section in other works of greater extension. This tendency is of capital importance in his conception of the sonata and, in fact, is an entirely modern conception. Chopin shows, thus, that he has discovered the principle of foreshortening. The classical Viennese composers such as Mozart were not content with less than an integral and literal repetition, in the first sections of their sonatas and in the recapitulation, a system derived directly from the *volta* and the *da capo* of aria and dance forms. But the modern audience does not need to hear again a complete repetition of a section. Just as in painting, the layman by virtue of perspective has learned to see a considerable extent of space between two points that are actually very close together, so Chopin taught him to hear "in perspective" by foreshortening these secondary sections which he presents merely for the sake of the symmetry and equilibrium of the form. This effect is to be observed, for example, in the Sonata in B Minor, where the first theme is greatly abbreviated while Chopin gives more importance to the second, the cantabile. The procedure is still more notable in the Sonata in B-flat Minor, where the second theme attracts the attention to such a degree that the first disappears entirely in the recapitulation. The fact that this treatment results from a well-calculated criterion, a new manner, less formal and more lyric, of conceiving the sonata is clearly evident in the construction of the A Flat Ballade. It has three themes: the second lies at a third below the tonic (A flat —F), the third is in the principal key (in which the theme in F is also repeated) leading by modulations to the first theme in the original key, while the third theme, considerably shortened, serves for the final peroration. The idea of shortening the first motive reappears in the Ballade in F Minor (1842); here, too, the chromatic sequence which we have observed as the basis for melismatic ornamentation, so characteristic in Chopin, is converted into a real structural and tonal idea.

Chopin's two sonatas still preserve the classical division into movements.

The romantic criterion tended to assimilate the sonata with other larger forms such as those just discussed. This idea preoccupied Schumann, who if not so rich in harmonic invention as his colleagues nor so original in his feeling for dissonance, is fully their equal in the profoundly creative character of his motives. The form of the larger sections of a composition engrossed him and, after the experiments in his first sonatas where he tried to convert the tonal dualism of the themes into a difference of character, he produced the splendid *Fantaisie,* Op. 17 (1836), in which the romantic form, ten years before the *Fantaisie Polonaise* of Chopin, finds its unequivocal affirmation. The *Fantaisie* of Schumann had an ideal precedent in those of Schubert and his own sonatas, Op. 11 (F-sharp minor) and Op. 14 (F minor), show the way. But the goal of the romantic grand form achieved by Liszt in his Sonata in B Minor, dedicated to Schumann, did not appear until 1853. This is the year when Liszt and Wagner understood for the first time the meaning of melos and for the first time reflected on the form of the great quartets of Beethoven's final period.[3]

From a fundamentally chromatic feeling as regards melodic structure, Liszt's sonata has recourse to clearly diatonic passages when he wishes to express an ample, serene tone; the short, agitated motives find a greater plasticity in chromatic processes. The models of Schumann and Chopin were before Liszt whose work, neither so rich in quality as those of Schumann nor so suggestive for the originality of writing and for tonal relationships as those of Chopin, has the advantage of maturity of form. As with Chopin, the introductory section to this sonata has a tonal and thematic value and the melodic extension of the second motive dominates the first which by its character is less capable of development. In reality, they are not two motives but two contrasting members of a single motive; and the second member, by reason of its melodic extension, is capable of creating an entire section. The extraordinarily advanced construction of this sonata runs no risk of shocking the listener because in its fundamental lines it preserves the classical tonal relationship: B minor, F-sharp major, B major.

The two outstanding qualities in the music of Richard Wagner are the character of the thematic material and the powerfully expressive harmony. Since both are at the service of a dramatic idea made clear and concrete by stage performance their character and their dramatic quality are legitimate. Wagner had much more liberty as regards tonality than his contemporaries and predecessors because in writing for the stage he was not restricted to the closed forms in which tonal unity is essential. Yet Wagner made of his strong feeling for the dominant seventh and ninth a solid core around which he could weave as many chromatic modulations as he liked. Series of ninths

[3] Berlioz, *Les Soirées de l'Orchestre* (On the Beethoven Quartet Society of London). R. Rolland, *Musiciens d'Aujourd'hui,* p. 255. H. C. Colles: *The Oxford History of Music,* VII, Ch. 2.

were soon to become one of the commonplaces of impressionistic harmony; but the fact that in Wagner they preserve their character as chords of the dominant is of prime importance because they thus maintain a unity of tonality which the impressionistic series, as in Chopin's passing chords, do not have. Yet, since the effect of the chord of the ninth is very strong, it loses its character as a passing chord with the result that it dissolves the general tonal feeling, the tonality of the piece.

The repertory of Wagner's chords differs little from that of the romantic school and his way of using them can scarcely be called revolutionary in view of what his contemporaries were doing. His originality consists in the originality of his ideas and of his intuitions, which found expression in the current musical vocabulary. We shall not be long in confirming that the most important step forward made by music between the nineteenth and the twentieth centuries, that of impressionist harmony and even of expressionist atonal harmony, are only further steps along the same road. The genius of the individual may vary greatly; his means change relatively little. This fact is important because it at once assures historical continuity and maintains the legitimacy of inventions. Let us remember that even with the poets of the extreme vanguard, as they were called before the present cataclysm, the fundamentals of language were preserved. Whatever the extravagances of the Dadaist or the surrealist, the syntactical relationships of subject, verb, and complement continued and the agreement of gender, number, and case remained intact. The same is true of music. Recently some arbitrary minds have sought to transplant the art of music to realms of their own invention not based on the reality of the aesthetic-acoustic feeling. A great part of the up-to-the-minute new harmonic resources and the complicated ultramathematical proportions for writing music, drawn from goodness knows where, utterly disregard these fundamentals. It is not our purpose to treat them in this book.

Chapter FOUR

WHATEVER may be the aesthetic value of the doctrines of Richard Wagner, they failed from the practical point of view; linked so intimately to his unique personality in his double capacity of composer and poet, they remained for the most part beyond the reach of his contemporaries in whom this double gift, rare in the history of music of more recent times, did not exist. Those who, comprehending the scope which Wagner wished to give his doctrines, tried to write dramatic poems which they afterward set to music only succeeded in exhibiting their mediocrity in both respects. August Bungert (1846-1915) awakened initial interest with the first part of his tetralogy, *Homerische Welt,* which began with a Circe (1898) and concluded with the Death of Odysseus (1903). Bungert, who lives in the memory of Germans for his comic opera *Die Studenten von Salamanka,* presented in 1908 an opera which he conceived as an interpretation of the mystery: "Where are we going?" and "Whence have we come?" Philosophy translated too directly into musical terms has produced discouraging results and the *Warum? Woher? Wohin?* of Bungert seems to have been too vague both for the author and his audience.

Wagner himself must have recognized that the horizons indicated by his "dematerialization" of the musical substance in his chromaticism were Faustian horizons in which the vagueness of the image did not lend itself to scenic realization. Spohr, in whom chromatic richness was already acquiring significance, wrote a *Faust* as early as 1816, although it did not avoid theatrical conventionalities any more than did the much later, bourgeois *Faust* of Charles Gounod. The Faustian theme, which created a whole postromantic philosophy, suggested to Wagner *Eine Faustouvertüre* (1839-40) in which he contradicted his own arguments on the futility of purely instrumental music after Beethoven. The new version of this overture, which he made in 1855, possesses an importance within this realm of ideas which contrasts with his lyric pieces for Goethe's drama written in 1832.

Arrigo Boito, one of Wagner's most legitimate followers, carried out the Wagnerian point of view expressed in "Opera and Drama" in 1851 by writing a little known operatic *Faust* in 1868 (supplanted by a shorter, more realistic version in 1875). However, his Italian temperament bound him too closely to purely scenic considerations from which he freed himself with difficulty to enter the lyric spaces where Fausts move at their ease. The Faustian idea attains something like its fullest meaning with the *Doktor Faust* which Ferrucio Busoni left unfinished at his death in 1924 and which is the direct descendant, among post-Wagnerians, of a romanticism then in its vanishing phase. Busoni intended that this work should reach the stage; however, those who obtained possession of it held it within the more propitious realm of symphonic music.

Attempts like those of Vincent d'Indy or those of Ernest Reyer to bring the Wagnerian drama to France—the former with *Fervaal* (1889-95), the other with *Sigurd* (1883)—proved in their literalness that, even though they comprehended the full intention of Wagner, it was not in the theater that they were to realize it. D'Indy, in fact, is more successful in his symphonic than in his dramatic production while Reyer is today no more than a name. Their intention was superfluous because a theater deeply imbued with the romantic spirit had existed in France since Berlioz and there was no reason to confuse Wagnerian orchestration and a declamation specifically appropriate to Wagner and to the German language with things belonging to a foreign culture.

In his correspondence with Liszt, Wagner complains bitterly of the lack of understanding displayed by those of his admirers who were entranced by his music but who failed to understand his drama. Apparently, they did not see as he did that both elements were united equally in his art which wished to be not musical but dramatic or, rather, musico-dramatic. If novelties of transcendent importance exist in his harmony, in the contour of his motives, in his orchestration, it is because these are dictated by a poetic energy to which they give form. Those composers who seem to have comprehended his purpose as made explicit in his writings were only able to follow him at a level far below his genius; on the other hand, those who penetrated his musical thought did not follow his aesthetics in the theater but either made compromises with the artificialities of the operatic stage (as did Cornelius, Humperdinck, and later Strauss, Siegfried Wagner, Hans Pfitzner, and Franz Schreker) or else cultivated the field of the symphony and the symphonic poem. This field flourished luxuriantly after Wagner, both from the point of view of his symphony of expression, as in Bruckner and especially Mahler, and in the formal symphony of Brahms and his successors. Both symphonic and dramatic composers were guided in their music by intuitions much more pertinent than any philosophical or literary ideas. This fact explains their essential soundness whatever may be the merits which our aesthetic sensibility or our tastes, already very distant from theirs, may attribute to them.

The great romantic orchestra after Berlioz, Liszt, and Wagner disclosed a new symphonic concept, in which the instrumental material itself is made to have an expressive value of its own; this value developed simultaneously, at the end of the romantic era, with that assumed by the chord as an acoustico-aesthetic element. Thus, we find the use of harmonic color (that is, harmony as an expressive value) combined with appropriate instrumental timbres to be the primary objective of musical thought. The clearest example of this is to be found in the Prelude to *Tristan*. In this work, all the harmonic means—dissonance, chromaticism, modulation, the juxtaposition of chords—which formerly served to enrich the harmony or extend the tonality have now been converted into what may be called *pure expression,* in the expressive value of the chord itself.

In the piano, beginning with Chopin and Schumann as well as in the orchestra of Berlioz, Liszt, and Wagner (to mention the most essential names) this aesthetic transformation of the instrument continues to take place; from now on, the quality of sound of the instrument itself, as well as the harmony and the motives for which it is the vehicle, will be counted as possessing an expressive value. It is most important to stress the fact that we are concerned here with an expressive value, not merely a sonorous one, because that which lies at the basis of this transformation—namely, the expressive, dramatic, human will—is the essence of romanticism. This human quality, which saturates the instrument with the dramatic feeling the composer wishes to transmit, impelled Beethoven to utilize the voice in the last movement of the Ninth Symphony. Wagner saw the importance of this fact but he interpreted it to mean that instrumental music was worn out, its possibilities exhausted by Beethoven, and that it had become necessary to fuse the tones of the orchestra with the human voice: a fusion which, in his point of view, led logically to the theater. But in describing the relative values of melody and harmony in "Opera and Drama" he shows that his artistic intuition had gone further than his critical reasoning. The voice is a sonorous element, a physiological instrument, which just as in the case of the orchestra acquires a pure value per se. The fact that it is produced by a human being gives the voice an emotional power, a warmth of feeling other instruments lack. Yet, except for the articulation necessary for the interplay of vowels and consonants, the voice in this sense does not actually need to sing *words.* Language, when sung, tends to become pure sound, pure vocal color while the semantic value of the words becomes redundant: everything is now expressed in musical values. Almost all of *Tristan und Isolde* testifies to this fusion of voice and orchestra. The duet in the second act, the death of Isolde are thrilling proofs that the stage, so important to Wagner, is actually an unnecessary duplication of effort. This fact, so well understood by the lovers of Wagner's art, gives to Wagner's scenes the same auxiliary, suggestive, subordinate role as that implied by titles such as Nocturne and Forest Scenes in the piano music of Schumann or by the poetic allusions which impressionist music affects.

Harmony, according to Wagner, provides an emotional frame for the vagueness of the melodic line. To fulfill this function, the harmonic value of the chord requires a plurality of instrumental elements, either in vocal or orchestral combination. The coexistence of both, after the Ninth Symphony, satisfies all the desires of the romantic or even the postromantic symphonist, who can perfectly well do without the help of the stage or an explicit dramatic plot. These become redundant since the orchestral harmony is now capable by itself of expressing synthetically all that develops so slowly on the stage (especially slowly in the Wagnerian theater). To Wagner's great annoyance, the composers of the final phase of romanticism thought of the theater as an enormous dead weight from which pure symphony freed them. The symphony, fed by such ideals, was to become an art totally distinct from the classical symphony or that of Beethoven. It was a different art which Berlioz foretold in *Harold en Italie* and in *Béatrice et Bénédict,* above all in *Roméo et Juliette* and even in the *Damnation de Faust*. These works lie half-way between the theater and the older symphony—the symphony which was obsolete for Wagner but which nevertheless was to be propitious soil for the post-Wagnerian symphonists, with Bruckner as the first and outstanding example.

The powerful affirmation of tonality in the symphonies of Beethoven, so vigorously accented in the finales of each movement, arises from the fact that Beethoven perceived that tonality is a human or, as I have called it, an acoustico-aesthetic phenomenon. For Wagner, the pure chord is the stream which flows to our world of sonorities from the mysterious springs of the universe; it is the channel by which the human soul relates itself to elemental forces. These blind forces lie at the heart of the meaning which the chord possesses for the human being and the chord itself reaches its most complete statement in the timbres of the orchestra. With the marvelous intuition of the artist, Wagner translates his feeling for the primitive world, for the life which sleeps even in the depths of the waters, in the Prelude to *Das Rheingold* where one hundred and thirty-six measures in gentle succession intone the single chord of E flat. This is, one may say, the expression of the chord solely for the sake of its pure sonorous value. And it is precisely this mystic value of the chord that is to be the nucleus whence will germinate and blossom, like enormous but unfragrant sunflowers, the nine symphonies of Anton Bruckner.

Anton Bruckner, the humble musician of a country town, was filled with harmonic mysticism; a mysticism founded, as I have suggested, in the cosmic value of the chord. The dramatic quality of his true predecessors, Liszt or Wagner, even Berlioz, was limited in Bruckner to this feeling for sonorous infinity with scarcely any other shadings except the reminiscences of the music of his native land, the Austrian Tyrol, that appear in the scherzos of his symphonies and his quintet. The vast fluidity of his first movements and of his adagios in no way suggests the fervent Catholicism of this organist of the small provincial town of Linz.

This provincialism never left Bruckner even in his mature years, when he was professor of the Conservatory of Vienna. Through his ingenuous feeling for nature, and by virtue of his simplicity of mind and soul, Bruckner expressed himself without false intellectualism or sophistry.

This seraphic quality has been attributed likewise to César Franck, but in a very different sense. What in Franck is a feeling for form and for contrapuntal writing is, in Bruckner, a simple yet extended exposition of thematic material, solidly based on the arpeggio of the chord which sings (frequently in the violoncellos or the horns) amid the atmospheric murmurings of the tremolos. Both men were organists and their instrument influenced them strongly; however, the effect of organistic improvisation that appears in Franck is most carefully reworked while in Bruckner this effect is transferred directly to the orchestral score. The tremolos of the high strings translate the "right hand" part while the lower strings and brasses (in combination with the Wagnerian tubas) announce the peaceful and ecstatic melody the "left hand" improvises. Showing little variety and displaying little need of it, the nine symphonies of Bruckner seem like so many different essays in the expression of a single thought: a thought whose essence is a kind of hypnotism produced by the chord spun out in foamlike melodies.

So vast is the structure and so meager the writing in these symphonies that some of the admirers who surrounded Bruckner in his old age suggested cutting them here and enriching them there with contrapuntal graftings. The composer, who only succeeded in gaining recognition at about fifty and whose works were not performed frequently thereafter, consented to these collaborations, which conductors like Löwe and Schalk proposed. Yet the possibility of editing a new Bruckner without revisions (as in the case of *Boris*) seems unlikely, since, at least outside of Austria and Germany, Bruckner's music appears to have exhausted the interest of present day audiences.

For Bruckner, as later for his disciple Gustav Mahler, the orchestra is, in accord with Wagner's concept, "the materialization of the harmonic idea in operation"; an idea that has a human meaning because it is born in the emotion of the creator. Without this animating content, the mere union of certain sounds lacks aesthetic value. For Wagner then this primary emotion, source of creation and artistic communication, is a vital necessity in art. This point of view is, in its turn, the basis of romantic aesthetics as distinguished from the formalist aesthetics. The latter proclaims that artistic pleasure is derived from the satisfaction that form provides in the interplay of the elements comprising the work.

The creation of the sonata-symphony form is the result, after much travail, of the latter point of view. Romanticism subordinated the question of form to the strong expressive need of an age for which form (excepting naturally that unity without which no work of art of any kind can exist) was no more than a kind of inherited convention or foundation upon which the work must be built. Form is regarded as a first principle which can be modified as the expressive necessity of the creator requires. A romantic criterion, this, whose best exponents are Bruckner and Mahler while the opposite criterion, which proclaims the supremacy of form as the construction of sonorous elements having value in themselves and not for their expressive meaning, had as its most ardent advocates at the moment Johannes Brahms and his supporters.

Anton Bruckner was ten years older than Brahms but his works are approximately contemporary with the symphonies of Brahms. The latter, in fact, did not approach the symphony until he felt himself secure in the formal construction of works to which he gave a specifically symphonic treatment, in the sense of the organic development of the form. For him the symphony is simply the result of the amplification, in the orchestral medium, of the chamber sonata. In both mediums Brahms needs no other sonorous elements than those utilized by Beethoven in bringing the sonata form to its ultimate fulfillment. In contrast rises the expressivistic criterion of Bruckner; this is not dramatic in the theatrical manner of Wagner but is saturated with Bruckner's religious feeling. That is not to say that the religious character of Bruckner's music takes on a definitely liturgical aspect (except in his sacred works) for it is a pantheism of vague outline awakened in him by the harmonic phenomenon.

This type of intuition, impregnated with what German aesthetic psychology calls a process of *Einfühlung*—or the injection of human emotion into the artistic material—was, generally speaking, something unknown to Brahms in the construction of his sonatas and symphonies. Brahms, like all the composers of his day, produced his works of art under the universal imperative of romanticism: the imperative of emotional expression. Brahms accepted this mandate in his lieder and small piano pieces, but his criterion of form prevailed in works of grand construction.

The first essays of Brahms in the symphonic form were his serenades, Op. 11 and 16, which date from 1860; that was the year of the famous manifesto, which he signed with Joachim, against the music of the future and the symphonic poetry of Liszt and Wagner. Brahms, who in 1854 had received an offer to enter the Conservatory of Cologne, preferred the post of court musician offered him by the prince of Lippe-Detmold. In accepting this post (1857), which committed him to regular, systematic production, like Haydn in his day, and to the tradition of the quiet, methodical life of a small German court, Brahms demonstrated his inclination toward a traditionally Germanic type of life and society; this life reflected itself promptly in the form of his compositions. When he gave up his post four years later, about 1861, it was in order to retire to his native city to complete the works he had planned at Detmold but which he had not been able to compose there, due to the distractions of his official duties. The serenades for orchestra were completed at that time, but we must wait for his first symphony until he has written the strongly symphonic chamber works such as the Piano Quintet in F Minor (1861-65), the two sextets of 1862-1866, and the first two quartets for strings (1865-73). Brahms's First Symphony was first performed in 1877, in the old-fashioned society of the small German court at Karlsruhe. The following year, his Second Symphony appeared.

In the time that elapsed between Brahms's serenades and symphonies, Anton Bruckner first became known. His First Symphony (aside from earlier, unedited essays) dating from 1865, was first performed in Linz in 1868 when Bruckner was forty-four. It was not heard in Vienna until 1891. Bruckner was thirty-seven when, without giving up his post as provincial organist, he went regularly from Linz to Vienna to study counterpoint under old Simon Sechter—the same Sechter of whom Schubert had requested similar lessons not long before the immortal author of the C Major Symphony left this earth. In Bruckner's First Symphony, the principles which inspired him are already manifest, if not under the aspect of the hypnotic influence of the chord, then certainly under the other-worldly influence of melody. Bruckner's Second Symphony, very similar to the first and in the same key of C minor, was first performed in 1873. Both these works antedate Brahms's First Symphony by several years.

The partisans of the one and of the other composer began to express their admiration violently. Bruckner was exalted for his expressive qualities and for his Catholicism, while the formal perfection of Brahms was declared by *his* admirers to make him worthy of being considered the legitimate successor of Beethoven. To this end, Hans von Bülow and other ardent panegyrists regarded the First Symphony of Brahms as the "tenth symphony." On their side, the Brucknerites thought that the poetic and expressive feeling of Beethoven's Ninth Symphony could only be understood by Bruckner; indeed, his followers—Mahler among them—attached great importance to this last symphony, even to the extent of using the human voice in their own symphonic work. This, Bruckner did not do, for he only employed voices with orchestra in compositions destined for the church. In the field of chamber music, Bruckner produced his Quintet in F Major, dating from 1879 (first performed in 1881). This was the unique essay of Bruckner in this type of music; here the characteristics of his inspiration show themselves subject to a formal imperative—derived not so much from rhetorical precepts as from the relative restrictions of the sonorous resources of a quintet compared to the cosmic possibilities of the orchestra. Brahms, on the other hand, continued his production of chamber music. His Clarinet Quintet was performed in 1891 at the little court of Meiningen. Brahms's last symphony had appeared six years before. He died in 1897. Bruckner had preceded him by one year, leaving unfinished his Ninth Symphony (begun in 1891).

Bruckner and Brahms, unlike their ardent supporters, were men of great breadth in their appreciations. It will be remembered that Brahms showed great esteem for Wagner even though the latter accused him of lacking a German spirit, something that astonishes those who are not German. On a certain occasion, when both symphonists met, Brahms said to Bruckner that he regarded him as the greatest symphonist after Beethoven.[1] Eduard Hanslick and Hans von Bülow claimed this historical honor for Brahms; Hugo Wolf, Ferdinand Löwe, and Franz Schalk claimed it for Bruckner: it is obvious that the truth lies between the two extremes. For, if Brahms thought to continue Beethoven's inspiration, it was by way of his own criterion of tonality. Bruckner, for his part, had understood the expressive meaning of the Ninth Symphony and the dissolution of form to which it leads, in the light of Wagnerian romanticism and had fixed his efforts to that end. Hugo Wolf and Gustav Mahler felt, under such stimulus, the authenticity of Bruckner's genius and believed it fitting to pursue the same road by way of their own inspiration. And each did so, most fruitfully, after his own fashion. Wolf provides the link to the programmatic symphonies of Richard Strauss. Mahler leads to the formal and tonal dissolution of the modern Viennese school in Schönberg and Berg.

We shall meet both these composers of the last years of the nineteenth century in the next chapter.

[1] Probably this was a sarcastic compliment. R. H. Schauffler tells us of Brahms's jokes at Bruckner's expense as well as the vacillation of his judgment regarding Wagner.

Chapter
FIVE

THE MUSICAL production of Hugo Wolf, like his life, was brief; both were intense. Wolf had completed his work at a time when Bruckner, one of whose earliest supporters he was, first began to be known. Possessed of an intellectual brilliance that betrayed a mental abnormality, Wolf lived a solitary existence completely wrapped up in artistic meditations which were interrupted only by long periods of insanity. Having premonitions of these spells, Wolf worked feverishly at the composition of brief poetic pages—deeply intense in vocal as in harmonic expression—when his mental state permitted. Even in his periods of health his state was far from normal. The exuberance of his genius alternately overwhelmed him or again exhausted itself, leaving a sterility which made him desperate.

Wolf composed scarcely any work of great length. Only his symphonic poem Penthesilea can aspire to the category of a grand form. If Wolf prefers the work of small compass, it is for a reason comparable to that of Schumann—his mental infirmity. The creative idea, inspiration, came to Wolf intermittently but so urgently that he must needs seize it and confine its volatile spirit in forms where it might be condensed before it evaporated. This inspiration was in essence intensely dramatic. It required a formulation with strongly marked features, as in Schumann's writings for piano or in the Wagnerian leitmotivs. Just as Nietzsche's works present a series of isolated thoughts, each one of which receives epigrammatic form while the complete idea evolves from their juxtaposition or interlinking, so Wolf's series of lieder unfold a general thought of which each song presents a single facet.

While the art of Mahler is the logical continuation of the expressivistic sense of Bruckner's symphonies, that of Wolf comes to be its antithesis. Both start from the Wagnerian concept of harmony as expression but, while the one dilutes it in vast orchestral digressions, the other condenses it in a few brief pages for solo voice. These songs of Wolf derive from the Wagnerian dramatic idea and from the Wagnerian use of the voice as a means of humanizing and crystallizing the expression of instrumental harmony. In this sense Wolf's lied is as different from the traditional song as Wagnerian drama is from opera.[1] Or rather, Wolf's lieder are like the lieder of Wagner in relationship to certain works of which they are the seed. Recall, for example, *"Träume"* or, in general, the series of five poems by Mathilde Wesendonk set to music by Wagner. The creative process in Wolf seems to parallel this model without assuming its consequences. With Wolf a preliminary meditation on the poem was followed by its musical realization which took place rapidly, one might almost say unconsciously, as was the case with Wagner in the composition of *Tristan.* Wolf looked upon some of his completed works with perplexity, almost terror. Writing his friend Werner that he had finished (in 1888), amid a Hoffmanlike exaltation, the composition of forty-three poems by Moericke in a space of three months, he says that some of them "sound so frightfully strange" that they frighten him and he sympathizes with the poor wretches who one day will have to listen to them. Cruel indeed for the ear and for the spirit, as has been said, are the ten songs of religious hallucination based on texts of Spanish origin; and his Penthesilea is one of the most acrid and virulent works in the postromantic repertory before Richard Strauss.

Form predominates in Schubert's songs, even in those as deeply expressive as the "Erlking" and "Margaret at the Spinning Wheel." Schumann's lied, freer of form, is nevertheless solidly constructed, and to this end Schumann took the liberty of modifying verses and changing words in the poems whose meaning inspired him. Wolf, and this holds true also for Wagnerian drama, follows in his musical settings the slightest inflections of the poetic text, translating them plastically, that is to say, as if they were intended for the stage: a dramatic process rather than a strictly lyric one. In this way the form of his songs is modeled on that of the poem but not in the sense of Schubert's form or of that of popular song, which parallel the regular structure of the versification. Rather, as in the case of Wagner and later in a whole group of musical settings for poetry which developed with impressionism, Wolf's form is composed of an intimate combination of the details of the verse-melody; the harmony no longer has a tonal connection with the form but is freely molded for the sake of expression. One of the most painfully conceived, although rapidly realized series of Wolf's lieder is the collection of Spanish songs in the German arrangement by Heise and Geibel, composed between 1889 and 1890; these poems had tempted other composers before Wolf, among them Schumann and Brahms. Romain Rolland reminds us that it has been said of this group of songs, the *"Spanisches Liederbuch,"* that it was for Wolf's art what *Tristan* was for Wagner. An *"Italienisches Liederbuch,"* finished in 1896, followed the Spanish, and in it Wolf attempted to simplify his writing

[1] Not always, however. The feeling of tradition is so strong in all the great German composers that something of Schubert's lied may be perceived in songs of Wolf such as *"Frühling uber's Jahr"* ("Goethe Lieder," No. 28) and *"In der Frühe"* ("Moericke Lieder," No. 24).

and his form. Thereupon he set himself to translate musically the profound emotion of Michelangelo's poems. The music for some of these dates from 1897. At this moment, however, when the lonely musician believed himself definitely cured, he was seized by another attack of insanity from which he never recovered. The final illness was long drawn out: Wolf did not die until 1903.

If one considers the dynamic value of chromaticism and of the dissonant chord which in Wagner's concept—and this concept sums up that of romanticism at its height—does not have simply a tonal and sonorous value but is intimately bound to human expression, one will see clearly why Wolf found in it his primary element. The partisans of sonorous objectivity (such as his enemies, the followers of Brahms) could reproach him, from their limited point of view, for his lack of rhythm, his melodic diffuseness, and his disordered harmony. But Wolf's real purpose has been described as an empirical letting-go, which was later to have extreme consequences in the world of Viennese music and which was undoubtedly adequate to his need for expression. The theory set forth above as to how an invention or discovery appropriate for a specific moment becomes transformed at a subsequent stage into a rhetorical formula can be observed already with Wolf himself, in whom (in the "Moericke Lieder" for example) dissonance as accented appoggiatura, passing harmonies, and chromatic procedures common to Wagner and Bruckner, tend to become the norm.

His highly developed harmonic idiom, like his writing for piano and voice (not to be thought of as harmonized song nor even as song enveloped in harmonies but as song which forms part of a sonorous complex constituted of voice and piano, in the same way that the voice and orchestra are one in Wagner), matured in about three years. His forty-three *"Gedichte von Moericke"* belong to the year 1888. The twenty songs set to the poems of Eichendorf, begun in 1886, are of the same year. The fifty-one *"Gedichte von Goethe"* are of 1888-89 and the forty-four *"Spanisches Liederbuch"* are of 1889-90. His first compositions, like the Quartet in D Minor (1879-80), only disclose Wolf's painful efforts during his youth to acquire a technique which he learned by reading the scores of Berlioz and Wagner. A period of choral compositions occurs between 1881 and 1891 and between these two dates belongs the bitter adventure of the queen of the Amazons, wild Penthesilea suggested by a poem of Kleist.

Neither in his collection of Spanish songs nor in the Italian ones did Wolf intend for a moment to suggest a local color. Neither he nor Beethoven in songs of the same type nor Schumann nor Cornelius nor Brahms are nationalists, even though they may very truly be composers of their nation. But their nation was Germany, not Spain nor Italy; one would seek in vain for a meridional accent in the *Italienische Serenade* which Wolf wrote in 1893, shortly after the first collection of his *"Italienisches Liederbuch."* Nor is there a more picturesque liveliness *à la espagnole* in his comic opera *Der Corregidor* (1896) than is to be found in *Fidelio.* The Spanish quality of both, like that of the other composers mentioned (as well as the Arabic flavor of the *Barber of Bagdad,* by Cornelius), never passed beyond the romantic commonplaces. Wolf left only partly sketched (four scenes of the first act) another piece for the stage *Manuel Venegas* [2] which, like *Der Corregidor,* is based on a work by Pedro Antonio de Alarcón.

It is important, however, to point out to overenthusiastic admirers of the Wagnerian music drama that, except for isolated cases, composers like Wolf reacted violently against Wagner's theater. Let it be understood clearly that this was a reaction against that heavy, antitheatrical theater devoid of action, against that transplanting to the stage of poematic symphonism. In this respect Wolf reacted against the Wagnerian theater in exactly the same terms as Nietzsche did when he hailed, in *Carmen,* the excellence of Latin genius. When one of his friends, knowing Wolf's desire to compose music for the stage, offered him nothing less than a libretto based on the life of Buddha, Wolf returned it, much irritated, saying that it was necessary to become emancipated from Wagnerian musical drama and that the musical world should be spared new headaches. What he desired, explicitly, was to write a comic opera with all that that implied. The letter he wrote in 1890 to his friend Grohe is categoric. Romain Rolland reproduces it in his sympathetic article on Hugo Wolf and it merits translation:

"In his art and for his art Wagner realized a work of liberation of such magnitude that we may rejoice that we need not attempt an assault on heaven since he has already conquered it for us. It is far wiser to seek in that beautiful paradise a pleasant little corner. I would like to find it not in the desert as a refuge with water, locusts, and wild honey but in the company of gay, original spirits amid the strumming of a guitar, amorous sighs, moonlight, etc., etc., in short: in a comic opera, a quite ordinary comic opera, without the lugubrious specter of a Schopenhauerian philosopher in the wings. . . ."

Yet Rosa Mayreder's libretto for *Der Corregidor* did not translate the sparkling style and delicate humor of Alarcón nor did Wolf's muse possess dancing feet.

Of the three great continuers of the Wagnerian spirit in instrumental terms, apart from the stage, Gustav Mahler is at once the least literal and the most genuine. There is no special paradox in this yet the genius of Mahler and the works which reflect it are full of conflicts. Born in a small town in

[2] Based on Alarcón's novel, *El niño de la bola.* Wolf also left incidental music for Ibsen's drama, the *Feast in Solhaug* (first performed in Vienna in 1891).

Bohemia, he soon went off to what was then the capital of the empire as well as of the musical world. Vienna had acquired this honor from her great classical and romantic symphonists and, at the end of the century, she wished to maintain her prestige in a final display of brilliance.

Mahler's professors in the Conservatory of Vienna are scarcely remembered: Julius Epstein for piano, Robert Fuchs in harmony, Theodore Krenn in what is commonly called composition: the study of the classical forms. As regards counterpoint, Mahler's natural gifts seemed so remarkable to Joseph Hellmesberger Sr. (then director of the conservatory), that he considered it advisable to excuse him from studying it. The date of this dispensation, 1875, is worth remembering as proof that Mendelssohn's "resurrection" of Bach in Leipzig had not even yet come to be considered as an essential feature of romantic aesthetics; counterpoint's principal advocate, Max Reger, had only just been born. Weakness in contrapuntal studies hampered Mahler throughout his career.

Mahler entered the Vienna Conservatory at the same time as Hugo Wolf. The undisciplined Wolf left it shortly, less at his own wish than at that of his teachers. Mahler remained scarcely a year longer. In 1878 he made an acquaintance which was to be of the utmost importance in his life. Anton Bruckner had been professor of theory and organ in the conservatory since 1871 (when he began his Second Symphony), and 1875, when Wolf and Mahler entered that institution, Bruckner began a series of lectures on the theory of music at the university. Mahler began to follow these courses in 1877, abandoning them in 1879. At this time he had already formulated "his idea." Bruckner, from the time that he had been chosen to conduct an audition of the *Meistersinger* before the first performance in Munich, had become the Viennese apostle of Wagnerianism and of an art which was acquiring importance at that time owing to the influence of Wagner—namely, the art of the orchestral conductor, of the conductor of the romantic orchestra. In 1880, Mahler began his career as conductor and also that of composer. *"Das klagende Lied"* is his first important work and is already symptomatic of his future art.

The classical and romantic composers had ordinarily been pianists. Next to Berlioz, Wagner was the first composer to be not pianist but conductor: from sonorous microcosm to macrocosm. This was a fundamental ambition with Mahler whose production oscillated between the popular song—the vocal microcosm—and the supersymphony, which he found in Bruckner and which he carried to a height of feverish sensibility.

His was a vast illusion; a vision of the symphony in which the romantic illusion was dissipated in a whirlwind of sonorous metaphysics. The credo of the nineteenth century unites in Mahler its most characteristic phases: the impulse toward nature embodied in the symphony by Beethoven, Berlioz.

and Liszt, the cosmic urge, harmony conceived as the precise expression of dramatic emotion, the mysticism of Bruckner which Mahler raised to the category of Nietzschean pantheism in his canticles to night and his verses of Zarathustra which are declaimed in his Third Symphony. "Oh, man! Take care! What says the deep midnight?"

Mahler's rise as composer was rapid. Fame, in contrast to Bruckner's case, was not long in coming to him. The former's belated admirers understood what they were to find in the pupil's works. Mahler's admirers, like himself, expected more than his symphonies were capable of giving; offspring of an enormous temperamental vitality and of a tortured, restless, and unsure process of realization, they were creations in which the illusory exceeded reality and where the contradictory was the nucleus of the expression, the source of their dramatic quality. The drama exists in the artist while it is only reflected indirectly in the work or is reflected negatively by what it lacks, by what it fails to realize, by what is not achieved: a tantalizing figure of which each symphony shows a different side.

So it happens that Mahler's best commentators—Adolph Weissmann among them—show more sympathy, more comprehension of the man than admiration for his works which remain difficult of analysis and escape rationalization; this leads to the worst of critical corollaries: to saying that the man is superior to his work and that it is therefore legitimate to admire the work in proportion to our admiration for its author. This is a dangerous evasion which, in trying to save them both, exposes the man and his work to the same risk. The role which Mahler thus plays in the music of romanticism is not a fortuitous one; he suffers the misfortune which befalls the artist in the final phase of a period when, like the temple of the Philistines, the whole structure is demolished by the Samson who is its first victim. Mahler thought himself the legitimate successor of Beethoven; so did Brahms and Bruckner but for different reasons. This difference is based on the individual aesthetics of these men. Lieder and symphonies represent a musical microcosm and macrocosm: not on account of their respective dimensions but for their capacity to reach expressive depths; for this reason, Mahler moved from song to symphony, just as the acorn engenders the oak. In a simple melody, in a children's popular song, Mahler heard the musical murmurings of the cosmos. He tried to capture it in his symphonies: the end excuses the means.

Mahler's First Symphony appeared in 1888 after many series of songs. Four more symphonies follow at irregular intervals: sometimes five or six years pass between one and the next; again they follow in successive years. Between the Fifth and the Sixth (in 1902) intervenes one of Mahler's most profound productions, perhaps the most intimate, the most truly felt and the most vividly expressed: the *"Kindertotenlieder."* Finally three of his biggest works appear: the Eighth Symphony—in two parts in which he introduced the old Latin hymn *"Veni, Creator Spiritus"* and the Faustian invocation to the *"Höchste Herrscherin der Welt"*—is followed in 1907 by another of the works which will do more for Mahler's glory than his vast digressions: the symphonized poems on "The Song of the Earth" (*"Das Lied von der Erde"*), said to be reworked by Hans Bethge from a hypothetical Chinese original.[3] One year later, in 1908, the Ninth Symphony appears. This time for orchestra alone; a trace of humor, perhaps, to confuse overingenious critics. Shortly after, on a day in May, 1911, Mahler died in Vienna.

His complex personality, the unevenness of his achievements, the confusion which one finds in his works, his essential originality and his frequent borrowings, his ambitions and their obstacles, his inconsistencies combined with his abilities, his superficiality, hand in hand with his very real depth, make of Mahler the most paradoxical figure in the whole field of music (not without a certain similarity to Berlioz' genius) and provide a basis for conflicting criticism. In either, one thing is inevitable: a passion, a vehemence equal to his own creative spirit and to his life itself. One cannot imagine a moderate admirer nor a disdainful detractor of Mahler. "Wild," "ultraromantic," "disordered" are epithets appropriate to an art such as his based on strength of character and on the power of suggestion. Mahler passes a little into our century but what passes is only his shadow. The artist and his art are backward-looking phantoms of an age already vanishing; they are the last echoes of an art in process of dissolution, the final decline of a once magnificent art which bids farewell in a burst of sunset glory. Is the expressionism which immediately follows Mahler a belated, dying splendor or the nimbus of a new day which no sooner dawns than it begins to disappear? Beside it Mahler's art appears vigorous and powerful, at least in its expressive strength.

It is a curious fact, worth mentioning, that the dividing point in the current of the romantic symphony involves the burning question of Semitism. Wagner's Jewish ancestry is open to question; Wagner, if we are to believe the testimony of Friedrich Nietzsche, struck out—on Nietzsche's advice—one of the first lines in his autobiography: "My father was a Jewish writer

[3] *"Das Lied von der Erde,"* says Adolf Weissmann, "is his leave-taking of the world, Mahler's farewell to life, even though it was followed by the composition of the Ninth Symphony and even though Mahler was to sketch a tenth." Weissmann thinks that it is Mahler's most perfect work, that it is a poematic symphony in which the voice expresses the dramatic meaning which inspires it: it is, therefore, a program work for voice yet one may perfectly well consider it as a series of lieder with symphonic interludes, a series inspired by a general emotion, like the more famous ones of Schubert. It exhales a feeling of solitude, of depression, of the world's sorrows—also, it is true, the joys of spring and the beauty of youth—but melancholy is the keynote of the work. A male and a female voice alternate in the different sections. The orchestration is clear and succinct without complications of texture.

by the name of Louis Geyer."[4] Let us leave to iconography the solution of a mystery which certain politicians, as vile as they are barbarous, can interpret as "a crime against the state." As regards Mahler, who never denied his ancestry, he is what authoritative writers call a modern Jew and is by nationality a German. He was one of the many who had descended from Palestine through fifty or sixty generations but who, rooted for centuries in middle European lands, feel that soil to be inalienably theirs. Above all other considerations, he felt and proclaimed himself to be fundamentally German. It is as easy to attribute his excellences to racial characteristics as to impute his defects to the same cause: the one like the other is so much hocus-pocus.

Mahler is unmistakably a German dreamer and an artist—like dozens in other countries—whose imagination traveled faster than his hand could build. Mahler found himself compelled to return again and again to his initial ideas in order better to see their outline, to come nearer to their possibilities, moving around them a thousand times like the sculptor who cannot decide to put his chisel to the block of marble. His delays are translated into diffuseness of form, his uncertainties into a lack of sureness in technique, the vagueness of his thought into an inability to control his idiom, his volubility, his restlessness, the capriciousness of his fantasy into incoherence. At the same time, his ambition to express himself through many formulas degenerates into rhetoric and his indifference toward a choice of means appropriate to the matter treated results in poverty of style. His works are like a flood where float the wrecks of many a proud hope and where great gifts are lost in a vast disorder.

To Mahler's carelessness may be attributed two of his most characteristic qualities. On the one hand, a lack of discrimination as to the originality of the elements he utilizes brings him within the danger zone of the laws of property. The borrowings are dissolved, to be sure, in the current of his eloquence, more verbal than sincere (although sincerity is not lacking; still less, enthusiasm). The other, indirect consequence is his preference for the diatonic since a post-Wagnerian or post-Brucknerian chromaticism would have obliged him to repress his penchant for converting to his own use the fruits of his neighbors' harvesting. The repertory of formulas of every kind invented by romanticism had been exhausted by Wagner; and Mahler, like Brahms, although from a different point of view, thought that it was necessary to cleave to Beethoven. Brahms felt this from the point of view of form, Mahler from that of content, and each according to his own conception of Beethoven's form and content.

If Brahms had not abandoned his early career as concert pianist, he would

[4] See the third volume of *The Life of Richard Wagner* by Ernest Newman (1937-39) and "Wagner's Autobiography," II, *Essays by James Huneker* (New York: 1932).

doubtless have bequeathed to us the tradition of Beethoven's piano music. Mahler, in fact, is one of the best accredited creators of what we understand today, in the greater part of the musical world, as the Beethoven tradition. Nevertheless, caution is necessary. In one of the famous festivals celebrated in Strasbourg in 1905, Romain Rolland heard Mahler's interpretation of the Choral Symphony. A French "Beethoven tradition" goes back to the heroic days of the Société des Concerts founded by Habeneck (1828) whose fame, it is said, had even reached Beethoven in his last days. However, it is not to be thought that Romain Rolland would compare Mahler's version of the Ninth with French performances. It is not hard to believe that, as Rolland affirms,[5] it was an "unspeakable performance. I could never have believed that a German orchestra, conducted by the chief Kapellmeister of Austria, could have committed such misdeeds. The time was incredible; the scherzo had no life in it; the adagio was taken in hot haste without leaving a moment for dreams; and there were pauses in the finale which destroyed the development of the theme and broke the thread of its thought. The different parts of the orchestra fell over one another and the whole was uncertain and lacking in balance—a neurasthenic rendering of Beethoven. . . . No, this was not Beethoven; it was Gustav Mahler." And, in fact, in these phrases Rolland grasps Mahler's personality as a composer and the stability and instability of his talents, the sureness and unsureness of his realizations, the poise alongside the unbalanced character of his genius.

Richard Strauss once said that the musician's loftiest compositions within the limits of his art are worked out amid a profound silence by a coldly calculating, self-confident mind. We find entirely the opposite in Mahler: a nervous temperament which was exasperated by the slightest incident of his existence, an impetuous nature which alternated between exaggerated action and remorse. The composer in Strauss's sense brings into play his technical skill to achieve the effects he purposes. Mahler's excitability and his feverish workmanship expose his noblest inspirations to failure. Spurred by an ardent faith, he writes poems imbued with an intense mysticism, such as his Second Symphony, with its eager accents which yearn to lose themselves in the creator. Soon, however, his spirit reacts from its momentary exaltation; skepticism follows fanaticism and his voice expresses the desolation of those crying in the wilderness. Perhaps Mahler was the first to recognize the defects of his works, conceived and carried out in the enthusiasm of an impassioned mind yet with a tremulous hand. From hot to cold: this in part accounts for the contradictions that are to be found in his exceptionally anomalous character. With his easy faculty for being enkindled by any phase of the beautiful, he frequently degenerates to triviality. He was not simple, like Bruckner, but

[5] In *Musiciens d'Aujourd'hui*. Translation, *Musicians of Today*, ed. Claude Landi (New York: 1914), pp. 218-219.

ingenuous, sometimes falsely so. His failures are as pretentious as his ambitions. To retrieve himself he turns to irony, an accredited romantic device, but in our eyes no more than an easy expedient. Again he seeks what he believes to be innocent superficialities, like his spring cuckoos in the country, his children who imitate the sound of Easter bells, his use of the schoolboys' round, *"Frère Jacques, dormez-vous?"* His artificial ingenuousness only sets the audience's teeth on edge. And a mystic fire promptly follows, the sudden splendor of artificial fireworks with which we have been familiar since Loge and the enchanted fire of the Valkyrie. Like his race, Mahler has an inclination toward metaphysics yet without serious consequences; and we must be grateful that he does not insist on Messianic prophecy, so unfortunate both for art and humanity: his hopes of redemption are kept to himself. In this he, as well as ourselves, are gainers.

Mahler is not so reserved, however, that his discretion prevents him from being the hero of his symphonies nor does it prevent him from making clear that he is the principal actor of his tragedy. His symphonies, then, are grand autobiographical structures, but not program symphonies in the sense of those of Berlioz, from whom he derives so directly and to whom he bears so close a resemblance. If these structures are not very solid, the defect lies in the fact that, like Berlioz, Mahler believed that expression and form in Beethoven were two distinct things and that it was only sufficient to follow this form more or less rigorously in order to shelter within it a whole emotional process of such intensity—so they thought—as to permit them to compare themselves with their illustrious model. Yet Beethoven's was a disciplined mind! Did either Berlioz or Mahler ever trouble to analyze the strictly objective, firmly dispassionate means by which Beethoven achieved such heights as in the Fifth and Seventh symphonies? It seems that neither Mahler nor the great Frenchman had ever thought of the advisability of counting the measures in the "constructive" sections of their works just as the architect calculates the resistance of the columns which will have to bear the weight of his sculptured pediment. Mahler and Berlioz set themselves problems without solving them. In the Beethoven of the Ninth (perhaps also in the Beethoven of the last sonatas and quartets), Mahler saw the ideal image of the great architect with whom, at the height of his glory, the material begins to become diluted in vague forms. He started from this lofty eminence and it is no wonder that he lost his head in the clouds.

Chapter
SIX

THE EXPRESSIONISTIC symphonism of the postromantic era ends, practically speaking, with Mahler. For some years into the twentieth century, instrumental music continued to cultivate in the large orchestral forms a poematicism, which is derived from the program symphony of Berlioz and the symphonic poem of Liszt, and which finds in Alexander Scriabin and Richard Strauss its most representative and most valuable figures. Another stream which flows from romantic sources is the picturesque instrumental music chiefly inspired by the local color and by the popular music of various countries: this is national music. Although its beginnings are a century old, its consequences are fresh and vigorous in our own day. Nevertheless, although the nationalist movement thus appears to be relatively modern, it must be recalled that its foremost promulgator, Michail Glinka, was born before Schumann and Chopin, before Mendelssohn, Liszt, Verdi, or Wagner.

In history, political nationalism is a modern concept. A feeling for the national was one of the sentimental aspects of romanticism. At first it appeared negatively, as nostalgia, homesickness; later it took the form of a delight in old customs, in country dances, in the family home with its typical furnishings, its hunting trophies on the walls, its cuckoo clocks; all this decorative paraphernalia constituted one of the charms of the old operas where peaceful village life and its honest sentiments were translated into appropriate music. But the campaigns of Napoleon aroused a new feeling of nationalism, a fervent love of country hitherto unknown, by bringing war to the people themselves, by invading the fireside, by inflaming hearts not only with hatred but also with a spirit of romance and adventure. With Napoleon, Europe felt new winds blowing and the breath of liberty stirred the peaceful dust on the things of the past. Some countries, invaded by "the little corporal," turned on the invader; others who had long mourned their lost liberties rose against their rulers. Liberalism shook the society of capitals and penetrated to villages where a medieval servitude still reigned. All that was national became a motive of poetic inspiration in romanticism; as musical inspiration it gave color to a lyric theater in the native tongue, discarding the Italian which had become as indispensable to opera as Latin to the Mass. Later, with the coming of revolutions, patriots rushed into the streets, often to the tune of a march or a song heard in the theater.

There have always been local differences in art, even in those times when the language of art was thought to be universal. Universality even in the church, its chief promulgator, was never more than an illusion. Today that illusion lies in believing that the national can possess an equally great expressive scope. The desire to dominate seems to be innate in humanity. Emperors dominated in the name of universality. Unbridled nationalism led again to imperialism. Thus a political as well as an artistic cycle is completed and we are witnessing its final effects. In architecture, in painting, in music, and above all in literature (since belles-lettres only possess their full meaning where their language is spoken), the art of Europe has consistently demonstrated characteristics typical of climate, race, society, and individual idiosyncrasies, all tempered by the circumstance of an existence in common. North and South, East and West, each has impressed its special mark on the whole history of art. The history of music has seen oriental influences succeeded by others typical of the extreme West; Italian influences follow Flemish; polyphony at first is Nordic, later meridional; opera begins by being Italian and aspires to be classical, universal, but by extending itself it takes on different aspects. These differences were once considered as the natural results of the diversity of the world; thus one spoke of the differences between schools. The words "culture" and "nation" had not come into general use. The ancient word "enlightenment," however, struck root in the native soil and, along with the feeling of inalienable liberty which makes each people different from the next, was born the consciousness that to each belong norms of feeling and understanding, of culture which are peculiarly its own and which it soon demonstrates in its works of art. Belated echoes of worn-out arts reverberated within national consciousness: vestiges of music preserved here and there in remote villages; reminiscences of manual arts in the building of houses, in the decoration of furniture and fabrics, in regional costume and household utensils; all these fragile survivals persisted with a tenacious resistance. They formed a barrier against the fashions from the capital, dangerous fashions which incessantly continued to undermine tradition for the sake of politics. When nationalisms (as distinct from nationalism) awoke in Europe in the first decades of the nineteenth century, they carried in their fiery wake political vengeance joined with the resentment which lay dormant in subjugated peoples. These nationalisms made use of local color, with its historical prestige, of all that appealed to a feeling for the picturesque, the popular, the traditional, the religious, the emotional. Aside from political aspects we observe another in which all these facets of nationalism find their full expression. It is the theater: national opera.

Russia, situated on the extreme confines of Europe, was a country whose frontiers extended deeper into Asia than into Europe itself. Her peoples, descended from ancient races, scarcely felt or understood the recent importations from the West; to them the idea of culture was as new as it was superficial. Yet, on the other hand, they possessed arts of ancient lineage, traditions, local dialects that were incomprehensible in the capital of this "empire," even a special form of religious ritual distinct from the Roman. Russia, disturbed by novelties of a social and artistic order which reached it from afar, agitated by new political ideas, likewise coming from the West—though by very different routes—seems to have been the first country to feel the strong repercussions of the various aspects of nationalism, especially in art.

Thus it is that a Russian, Michail Glinka, gave the initial impetus to nationalist music and, specifically, to its most characteristic form: national opera. When Glinka was born, the old musical world was taking its leave and a new one was coming into being. According to the Old Russian calendar, Glinka was born May 20, 1803; according to the New Style the date was June 2.[1] At the other end of Europe, in a little village near Grenoble, there was born on December 11, 1803, one of the musicians whose influence on all his contemporaries, Glinka included, was to be considerable: Hector Berlioz. The death of Boccherini in Madrid in 1805 brought to a close that world we are accustomed to consider classical. At that time the new genius, Beethoven, was at the height of his powers: 1804 is the date of the Eroica, dedicated momentarily to Napoleon. To the year 1805 belongs the first version of *Fidelio* or *Leonora* which is already an opera with a picturesque Spanish flavor, at least in its plot.

Delicate in health, Glinka traveled widely: Germany, France, Venice, during the most ardent years of the romantic fervor; later, at the mid-point of the century, he went to Spain where he spent several years. In Paris, Glinka met Berlioz whom he considered the greatest musician of the day; and Berlioz, in gratitude, dedicated to him some flattering remarks in his *feuilletons* of the *Journal des Débats*. Glinka had presented, in 1836, his opera *A Life for the Czar;* it had a tremendous success with the public and aroused, as a reaction, the animosity of the aristocrats with their foreign tastes who dubbed it "music for coachmen." What they did not suspect was the future importance of coachmen in Russian music as in the "picturesque scenes" of *Petrouchka*. More appreciative than Glinka's contemporaries, musical history recognizes *A Life for the Czar* as the first truly successful national opera, in which are to be found all the principles that characterize the movement.

[1] 1803 according to Grove and Cobbett; 1804 according to others.

This historical opera was followed in 1842 by another with a romantic plot somewhat in the manner of Weber's operas of this type. But, here again, Glinka utilized chiefly music of popular inspiration. The kind of music appropriate for *A Life for the Czar* was of a rustic type. That of *Russlan and Ludmilla* required melodies with a picturesque strangeness, with an oriental flavor which the Russians do not have far to seek; for these melodies are to be found in the frontier districts of Asia, from the Transcaucasus to the Urals. Despite the exotic interest of the music of *Russlan and Ludmilla,* the work did not have the spectacular success accorded *A Life for the Czar*. It is said that, in his discouragement, Glinka set out on new travels and found in Spain the country which appealed to him most: Granada, above all.[2] His travels through Spain took place during the years 1844-47; thus he had sufficient time to learn the meaning of popular Spanish music and the kind of orchestration appropriate to it. Three compositions in a manner half-way between that of the fantasy and the rhapsody appeared in 1848. Two of them were inspired by Spanish, though not Andalusian, music: A Summer Night in Madrid and the Jota aragonesa. The other work was a reply to the accusation, "music for coachmen," with which the elegant world had scorned Glinka's music of Russian inspiration. This work was Kamarinskaya with a completely plebeian theme which scandalized aristocratic ears, as Dostoevski tells us in one of his novels. Later on, as a result of new travels and new compositions of a poematic character (such as Tarass Bulba inspired by Gogol), Glinka, who was constantly preoccupied with the study of popular music, reached the conclusion that this music preserved within itself the still living essence of the ecclesiastical modes. He worked on this idea during his last years. In 1856 he went to Berlin to study ancient music with the celebrated theorist, S. W. Dehn, and there he died in the following year.

In his early years Glinka had been a disciple of John Field and had thus inherited romantic doctrines directly from one of their most outstanding originators. The musicians destined to create the body of Russian music proceed from Glinka, if not directly, at least from the same doctrines. The group of nationalist composers known as the "Five" of St. Petersburg carried these doctrines to their ultimate fulfillment, both in the field of music for the theater and in instrumental music; in the small forms as well as in those which aspired to greater length. The charm and picturesqueness of their theatrical compositions and their success throughout Europe considerably surpassed the modesty of their instrumental works; nevertheless, the vivid coloring, the brilliant orchestration of the latter exercised an indubitable influence

[2] In these years Spanish musicians like Hernando, Oudrid, Barbieri, and Gaztambide were reviving the zarzuela in a very popular atmosphere. Popular Spanish music, particularly dance music, spread throughout Europe in the first decades of the nineteenth century. The Symphony on Spanish Airs by Mercadante dates from 1843.

on European music, especially in the Latin countries, even though these compositions were slow to become known outside of Russia. The visit of Czar Nicholas II to Paris in 1896 contributed to the closer relationships between France and Russia and portions of the great nationalist operas, along with symphonic compositions by this group, began to be heard in the Occident. The lecture-recitals of Pierre d'Alheim with Marie Olenine and other artists, in the early part of 1896, made known in Paris the lesser works of Mussorgsky. Some years had still to elapse before *Boris Godunov* appeared on the French stage (in 1908, in a series of concerts of Russian music organized by Sergei Diaghilev, whose famous Ballet Russe dates from the following year) but its score was discussed as an amazing mystery in Parisian artistic circles and it is said that the copy that Claude Debussy read in his studio was that lent him by Camille Saint-Saëns.

Between Glinka and the "Five" appears the notable figure of Alexander S. Dargomyzhsky (1813-69), whose musical career began in 1851 with a romantic opera based on Victor Hugo's novel *Esmeralda.* It had small success. Shortly after appeared another opera *Russalka* (on a poem by Pushkin), in which the romantic fairy tale in Weber's style was accompanied by music of popular origin. Although the work again had little success with Dargomyzhsky's own public, it attracted attention in certain foreign countries such as Belgium and England where its author at last achieved recognition in 1864, almost ten years after the opera's first performance. Along with songs in which the color and expression of Russian music are handled with great delicacy and melodic charm, Dargomyzhsky introduced poematic instrumental music of an originality which matched the power of his instrumental color. Dargomyzhsky strictly followed the point of view of Glinka concerning the organization of the vocal part of opera. This system, much used thereafter, consisted of a recitative on simple lines, lightly supported by the harmonies in the orchestra; between these scenes of exposition were interpolated passages of song when they were required by the intensity of lyric feeling. A famous critic, W. von Lenz, said of *Russalka* that it was a "recitative in three acts." What would he have said of *Boris Godunov* or *Pelléas et Mélisande?* It is important to note the milestones which mark the development of the contemporary lyric theater.

The feeling and the form in Dargomyzhsky's large instrumental compositions are those of the fantasy but are combined with a classical tonal construction giving them a unity and coherence which the picturesque fantasy was beginning to lose. Dargomyzhsky, in fact, was well acquainted with the classical technique in composition and wrote some chamber music (two quartets and three trios as well as vocal music for duets, trios, and chorus) which is worth mentioning in view of what is generally supposed regarding chamber music in his country at that time. The influence of Liszt's piano style, which was to be constant in the group of the "Five," appears in a Slavic Tarantella. It is interesting to compare this work with Islamey, the most ambitious work in the field of keyboard music by Mily Balakirev, the spiritual leader of the "Five." Balakirev was approximately twenty-five years younger than Dargomyzhsky and thus his junior by almost a generation, while between Glinka and Dargomyzhsky there was only ten years' difference. Balakirev was not, however, the oldest of the "Five," since Borodin (1834) and Mussorgsky (1835) were born before him.

The posthumous opera of Dargomyzhsky, the *Stone Guest,* on the poem in which Pushkin reverts to the story of Don Juan and his tragic adventure with the Comendador, has been considered the bible of the theater. On his deathbed, Dargomyzhsky confided (in 1869) to Rimsky-Korsakov the completion of the work. The latter composer, who was destined to finish or arrange the operas of others of his comrades, such as *Prince Igor* of Borodin and *Boris Godunov* of Mussorgsky, thus began that series of noble efforts which have since been severely criticized. The system of composition of the *Stone Guest* is that already presented in *Russalka.* Composers like Cui, Tchaikovsky, Glazounov, Liadov, and Rimsky himself, who placed more confidence in the effectiveness of a lyricism based on vocal forms and on well-defined orchestral passages, departed from the extremes of Dargomyzhsky's recitative. The latter, it is said, in his fidelity to prosody and the literal text, did not alter a single verse of Pushkin's work. Dargomyzhsky's criterion in this respect can be traced by way of Borodin and Mussorgsky to *Pelléas;* while composers of nationalist operas based on popular themes, as in the Spanish zarzuela, find a simpler expedient in spoken recitation.

The ardent, proselytizing spirit of Mily Balakirev was enkindled by the flint of Glinka's nationalism and the liberalizing winds of the rule of Alexander II fanned its fires. In his early youth, Balakirev came into contact with a curious spirit who might have deflected him from his future work of propaganda. This was the musician and critic Alexander Dimitrievitch Oulibishev who, after publishing his famous biography of Mozart in 1844, in 1867 launched an attack on Beethoven, his critics, and his commentators such as Lenz. However, the spirit of the day was more decisive than all that Oulibishev could have expounded concerning Mozartian forms.

The library and the little orchestra which Oulibishev maintained in his country retreat at Nizhnii Novgorod (now Gorki), the native city of Balakirev, were far more profitable to Balakirev than the theories of the dour musical historian. The classical musical studies of the young musician were restricted in the beginning to the composition of scherzos, mazurkas, nocturnes, and waltzes. Oulibishev must have realized that a new spirit was stirring in European music, a spirit whose breezes reached him in printed form under the signatures of Berlioz and Liszt scarcely, as yet, under that of

Wagner. In a burst of generosity, he sent Balakirev to St. Petersburg. The first pianistic attempts along with a letter from Oulibishev to Glinka were the only equipment Balakirev had for the task he had set himself. The pioneer enthusiasm of his eighteen years was more telling and Glinka, who had not forgotten the bitter disillusionment of *Russlan,* became so fond of the young propagandist of a new school (its cornerstone was Glinka himself) that he conferred upon him the official title of his successor and disciple. In witness thereof, he offered him some of the Spanish themes he had brought back to the imperial capital on his return from Spain; Balakirev used them in a serenata that is not listed among his works. The items which figure in his brief catalogue are headed by an overture on the theme of a Spanish march. Then follow two symphonic poems, Russia and Tamara, and another overture on three Russian themes. Balakirev, who studied the classic form with his friends and disciples, analyzing everything from Handel and Bach to the romanticists, showed his learning in a symphony (which appears as Op. 5). An overture to *King Lear* is his contribution to the romantic atmosphere and another overture for Lvov's opera *Undine* completes his works of extended inspiration. The entr'actes for the above-mentioned play of Shakespeare are his only known attempts in music for the theater.

Mussorgsky was the first budding musician to associate himself with Balakirev, under whose influence he came in 1857. Rimsky-Korsakov and Borodin followed later. These were the three who with Cesar Cui formed in 1863, under the leadership of Balakirev, that invincible group which claimed to be a "new school of Russian music." Tchaikovsky joined their leader in the year 1868 on the occasion of a visit to the capital but he was not long in separating himself from them, probably because he found them too autocratic in their opinions and too weak in technical methods. At this time, Tchaikovsky had in his notebook two nationalist operas—the *Voyevoda* which reached the stage in 1869 and *Undine* which, like the former, was destroyed, except for a few passages. The nationalism of Tchaikovsky springs from more purely European streams than that of the others and, although these too ran deep in the soil of Russia, Tchaikovsky gave them shape in works of symphonic form to which he felt himself more attracted. As a composer of operas, he followed the example of Anton Rubinstein (whose operas date from 1852-89; the most famous of which is the *Demon,* 1875) more than the recitative style of Glinka and Dargomyzhsky. In his operatic works Tchaikovsky, who was as Russian as can be imagined, aspired to an occidental brilliance which Balakirev's group scorned but which, for his own part, Cui also cultivated with the smallest possible amount of nationalist color. Various passages from these early operas passed into a symphony that is heard today because Igor Stravinsky has felt it worth reviving. This is Tchaikovsky's Second Symphony on themes of Little Russia, which dates from 1872 (although an earlier version, it appears, was discussed with Balakirev). Tchaikovsky also brought to St. Petersburg in that year his First Symphony, just completed, and an overture on Danish themes, like those of Balakirev on Spanish melodies.

Tchaikovsky's career, both in its theatrical and symphonic aspects, was much more fecund than that of the nationalists—except for Rimsky—and with resulting unevennesses. His operas, some of which like *Eugen Onegin* (1879) and *Pique-Dame* (1890) form the foundations of the modern Russian lyric theater, deserve to be better known outside of his own country. Some of Rimsky's operas are so weak in plot that the orchestral brilliance of certain passages cannot conceal a rather flimsy inner structure. On the contrary, Tchaikovsky tended to accent the dramaticism of his operas in a manner which may be called veristic and which left its mark on this Italian idiom. In his symphonic works, moreover, Tchaikovsky occupies the highest place among postromantic symphonists.

Although, in his symphonic poems and poematic overtures, Tchaikovsky leaned toward strong dramatic contrasts which derived quite directly from Berlioz, in his symphonies he sought a solidity of form within a notable originality of concept. If national color scarcely appeared in Tchaikovsky's symphonies except in the Second, their romantic quality, on the other hand, has a profound expressiveness which is not indebted to the current of Wagnerian symphonism and which, after Beethoven, was unknown to the romantic symphony in combination with such solidity of form. After all reservations have been made concerning his talent and his tendency for turgid rhetoric and oratorical exaggeration, Tchaikovsky may be considered as the true continuer of Beethoven's symphony: if not in form, then certainly in emotional content. This aspiration is summed up and concentrated in the Sixth Symphony, known as the Pathétique, like Beethoven's famous sonata. This symphony, with the Fourth and Fifth, form the symphonic triptych that produced the most powerful effect on the emotions of the general public in Europe during the last third of the century.

Tchaikovsky's enormous popularity at the end of the last century and during the first decades of the present one declined considerably after the more richly picturesque music of the "Mighty Five," with its attractively exotic melodies, reached western Europe. The first performance of *Boris* took place in 1874; *Prince Igor* remained unfinished at the death of Borodin in 1887; Rimsky's first opera goes back to 1873; yet it must be remembered that these works did not reach Paris until the first years of the new century. Their novelty is thus associated with that period in which were written Debussy's *Prélude à l'Après-midi d'un faune* (1892), the three nocturnes—*Nuages, Fêtes et Sirènes* (1897-99), *La Mer* (1903-05)— and also *Images* (heard for the first time in 1909) as well as *Pelléas et Mélisande,* the completion of which extends from 1892-1902.

The instrumental works of Rimsky were first known in their versions for ballet. They rapidly became indispensable on symphony concert programs in France, Italy, and Spain. They became known much later in Germany. All the great symphonic works of Rimsky, including their revisions, are prior to the new century. His First Symphony of 1862 he rewrote in 1884; the Second, *Antar,* is of 1867; the Third, in C minor, of 1872, was revised in 1886; the *Sinfonietta* on Russian themes is of 1880; the *Capriccio Espagnol* dates from 1887; Shéhérazade from 1888, as also the overture on Russian liturgical themes entitled the Great Russian Easter. His last operas, however, belong to the new century: *Czar Saltan* of 1900; *Kastchei the Immortal* of 1902; *Pan Voevoda* of 1904; and Rimsky's last work, which has been considered by some commentators as a kind of Russian *Parsifal,* the *Tale of the Invisible City of Kitezh,* was first performed in 1907. Rimsky died in 1908, leaving unpublished a work which brought him to the threshold of modernity: *Coq d'Or.* After slight retouchings, this opus first reached the stage in a private theater in Moscow in 1909.

Rimsky-Korsakov wrote, in addition, chamber works in which the nationalist color is lacking. This is also the case with the quartets of Borodin and the famous one in D major by Tchaikovsky (of which the overpopularized andante is constructed, it is said, on a monotonous phrase chanted by a poor beggar under his window). In addition to this quartet, Tchaikovsky wrote two later ones, and also a trio and a sextet. In the first of his two quartets, Borodin develops in his own way a theme from the Quartet Op. 130 of Beethoven. His two symphonies (between 1862 and 1877) are earlier than his finest and most successfully realized work: the sketch entitled In the Steppes of Central Asia which belongs to 1880. Cesar Cui did not write symphonic or chamber works of a serious character but some suites in popular vein are equivalent to the little, picturesque sketches of Bizet (1868-72) and of Massenet (1865-81) in which a facile orchestration of attractive color fully satisfied, between the sixth and eighth decades of the last century, the moderate musical demands of a superficial public. It was the period of the brilliant successes of Moritz Moszkowski and of inferior Italianism and Hispanicism. For his part, Mussorgsky never attempted to compose music of an abstract character such as the symphony, even in the poematic vein, still less quartets and quintets. His great instrumental compositions, such as The Rout of Sennacherib or A Night on Bald Mountain, approach more nearly the symphonic poematicism characteristic of Berlioz (1867-75). From this point of view, such music of Mussorgsky's lacks significance; on the other hand, his pages for voice and piano and for piano alone are at the threshold of a new feeling in music. His Songs and Dances of Death, of 1875, and the Pictures at an Exhibition, of the previous year, inspired by the baroque orientalism of sketches by the architect Victor Hartmann, belong to the very years when Brahms was meditating his "return to the past."

In France, meanwhile, Georges Bizet (1838-1875), a contemporary of Balakirev, affirmed the nationalist criterion. Essays like the Provençal music of *l'Arlésienne* and the oriental passages of *Leila* and *Djamileh,* were followed by songs of such distinction as *"Les Adieux de l'Hôtesse Arabe,"* and, at the end of Bizet's career, by the notably successful exotic national color of his opera *Carmen* (1875).

It is well to recall that musical orientalism, a sequel of the picturesque so much in favor in French painting after the campaigns of Napoleon in Egypt, always had cultivators in France. The mention of the Desert by Felicien David, which goes back to 1844, suffices as reminder. (David, who traveled in the Orient between 1833 and 1835, furthermore, wrote some pleasing *mélodies orientales.*) Another successful orientalist came between David and Bizet: Léo Delibes, who in *Lakmé* (1883) left pages worthy of more consideration than is generally accorded them by writers on music; one of his songs, *"Les Filles de Cadix,"* which may well be termed admirable, is like a seed which, sown in 1872 on fertile ground, produced in *Carmen* its most luxuriant blossoming.

The picturesque charm of the water color, with its light, dextrous, fresh tone, was cultivated by two French composers whose respective works obtained an immediate success although, like the works themselves, that success was superficial and passing. Édouard Lalo's *Rhapsodie norvégienne* and the *Fantaisie* (both inspired by motives from a source which Lalo thought popular but which was really the private domain of an individual author of Norway), his Russian Concerto and his Spanish Symphony, dedicated to Pablo Sarasate, belong to about 1880. The *Suite Algérienne* of Camille Saint-Saëns, his barcarole, *"Une nuit à Lisbonne,"* his Jota Aragonese, and his *Rhapsodie d'Auvergne* belong between 1880 and 1884. His concerto for piano and orchestra, *Afrique,* appeared in 1891 and his *Caprice Andalouse,* for violin and orchestra, in 1904.

This facile, picturesque genre had its repercussions in Spain also. Almost all the Spanish composers of the last decades of the century fall into it. It suffices to mention a couple of works, the most important in the style: *En la Alhambra* ("In the Alhambra") of Tomás Bretón (1850-1923) dates from 1880-81; the *Fantasía Morisca* ("Moorish Fantasy") of Ruperto Chapí (1851-1909) belongs to 1879. More ambitious, Felipe Pedrell moves only in the sphere of the theater. His *El Comte Arnau,* in which popular Catalan songs appear in the romantic atmosphere of the ballad in the style of Lenau or Wieland, and the *Sinfonía jubilar* or *Glosa* for solo, chorus, and orchestra, are the most important works belonging to Spanish nationalist symphonism prior to the present time. As a composer, Pedrell was a postromanticist who felt and understood music first after the Italian style, next after the German. The direct influence of his music on the young composers was nil because all these works, conceived in an atmosphere completely foreign to them in the aesthetic as in the technical sense, were stillborn; recent attempts to revive them have proved futile. On the other hand, although Pedrell's nationalism and his interest in folklore were entirely theoretical, nevertheless it is that aspect of his work which gives him an important and original place in the history of Spanish music. Of this aspect we shall speak in its appropriate place.

The nationalism of his great predecessor Francisco Asenjo Barbieri, this time authentic but derived from the popular districts of the capital, poured itself into the same stream of the popular theater whence it sprang and, if it inspired some instrumental music, this was of the most ordinary kind, even though it might be seasoned with the salty wit of the Madrilenian. In order to encounter in Spain a nationalist music of real artistic value, we must wait until her musicians have been nourished by European currents, above all in Paris; and so, both the picturesque pianism of Albéniz and the various aspects of the art of Manuel de Falla will be considered in their fitting time and place.[3]

[3] See Chapter XXVIII.

Chapter SEVEN

WHILE German musicians of the last third of the nineteenth century labored to give a new meaning to symphonic art, either by reverting to the pure forms or by bringing to their elaborate symphonism a Wagnerian harmonic expression, nationalist composers sought their expression and the charm of their music in other directions. Like the romanticists, they were anxious to endow their motives or melodies with a strongly distinctive character but, instead of seeking this quality in personal expression, they sought it in a common inspiration, in the material of collective creation. This implies, first, a creation based on the stylistic commonplaces of a given period and, second, a task of adaptation and polishing of an easily manageable kind. While an art that is based on the material of collective invention may lack characteristic individual qualities, it possesses in exchange the reflections of moods and the varied shadings which the collaboration of many individuals instills in such artistic production.

From the beginning of the century of romanticism, then, the nationalist composers and the composers of abstract music follow different paths. Only at the end of the century, when the increasing acuteness of their expression and the refinement of their harmonic and orchestral material carried both groups to frontiers of musical intuitions beyond which nothingness lies, only then did they meet. Thus it happens that the conception of the value of harmony in and for itself and that of instrumental values as means of expression come together in both schools. It is easy to distinguish the expressivistic or the "popular" ancestry of the majority of present day composers; nevertheless, both types appear to understand sonorous values in the same way. Thus it comes about that the composers of expressivistic origin abandon the human drama as a source of inspiration while the composers of "popular" ancestry relinquish their picturesque and decorative aims. That which is specifically sonorous acquires first place with both and the form which they strive to shape has for its plastic material values of an exclusively musical nature, no longer reflecting a dramatic basis.

Let us see by what successive stages nationalism in music found itself in contact with that other, primarily symphonic, course taken by postromantic art. This latter art was above all German: the art of the Teutonic genius, one may say, the voice of its "deep midnight." The nationalism suggested in its earliest romantic poetry, the national picturesqueness of its earliest operas, exotic in *Fidelio,* native in *Der Freischütz*, was cast aside because national feeling found its most profound and intimate expression in the abstractness of its romantic music for piano or orchestra. The symphony and chamber music are, in this sense, as congenial to the German temperament as operatic *bel canto* is to the Italians (we refer here particularly to the later nineteenth century). From Beethoven on, instrumental music is the typical expression of that German society into whose farthest corners filtered the romantic spirit, from the great symphonic orchestras down to the needlework which decorated the armchairs; from opera to the bookplates, from Bayreuth to the Christmas-tree candles.

The picturesque nationalism we have seen develop in Russia, like that in Scandinavia and Bohemia, has no true reason to exist in Germany or in Italy whose most solid art is, in its essence, national. The same occurs in France and in Spain, too, where nationalisms in the style of *Manon* or in the more rustic style of *La Dolores* come late. Instrumental music, symphonism, had declined notoriously in France after Berlioz and the very fact that Saint-Saëns strove to raise its level reveals the point to which it had fallen. The picturesque and popular quality of Lalo's symphonies had a laudable aim but they were too slight in texture. The appearance of César Franck brought about a great elevation of the spiritual level, but, this time, in terms not traditionally French.

In Spain, instrumental music, expressivist and picturesque symphonism alike, lacked tradition in the early nineteenth century. There was an effort to cultivate agreeable pastiches which ranged from a pallid Mozartism and Beethovenism to trifling imitations of Mendelssohn, Weber, Liszt, or Raff. Genuinely Spanish nationalism belonged to the theater and, in Spain as in Russia, instrumental music was the exception during the last part of the century.

Musicians who composed primarily for the theater such as Bretón and Chapí took their first steps in writing symphonies and chamber music. The quartets of Chapí are a plausible attempt to infuse national color into a loose and disconnected form. Good musicians of an originality which felt itself stifled by the requirements of a fashion dependent on German music found their way when they breathed the popular atmosphere; it suffices to recall Vicente Arreguí (1871-1925) and Bartolomé Pérez Casas (1873-) among those who composed pages of noble vigor and lively coloring. This road of poematic symphonism and national color culminated in the work of two composers of real fiber and stature: Conrado del Campo (1879)—and Oscar Esplá (1886) whose works are chiefly symphonic.

Del Campo, a fecund composer, starts from a romanticism which, even if Germanic in musical substance, is purely Spanish in sentiment. Del Campo's *Caprichos Románticos* for string quartet belong to his first period. Other quartets, to the number of seven, emphasize the German aspect of his romanticism but they are preferable in their vividness and warmth to the cold indifference of those by Bretón or Arreguí, and to the empty, yet gracefully inventive, nationalism of those by Chapí. Enrique Fernández Arbós, the famous director of the Symphony Orchestra of Madrid, wrote in his youth pieces for trio with a discreet picturesque color in which the first violin plays the important role. They are pleasant pages with an old-fashioned Spanish quality in the spirit of Lalo and Sarasate, a spirit which springs directly from the *cancioneros* or from the popular pieces of Manual García, Ocón, and other Andalusian writers.

The vast orchestral canvases of del Campo, expansively written, vary from a romanticism in Berlioz's vein (*La Divina Comedia*) to a picturesqueness with a Madrilenesque or Andalusian flavor. His rhapsodic structure, in which the suggestion of eager improvisation is sustained by a warmth of feeling and a spontaneity in the working-out, sometimes lacks nicety of balance. More solid in workmanship, more deliberate in thought, profuse, complex, inclined toward an elaboration of his material, is Oscar Esplá who by preference finds inspiration in the mountains and the sea of his native province of Alicante. Esplá knows how to see and feel on the grand scale of vast horizons. His works are ambitious and for the most part are known better by their titles than in performance. His work of first importance, Don Quixote's Vigil at Arms, is a powerful composition of considerable extension with a richness of color and wealth of material through which run fleeting echoes of popular song; the whole is conceived in a vein of poematic symphonism which, deriving from the soil of German postromanticism, reflects the most recent and extreme developments of European music from all sources. Yet in Esplá as in del Campo pulsates the profound individuality of the Spanish musician which rises above the closely woven web of his environment and the complex sources of his technique and his aesthetic criteria.

Nationalism in the countries of Central Europe dates, as in Spain, from the second half of the century. In Spain, the only object had been the desire of its composers to take part in the musical currents which then had prestige. Bohemian nationalism, the first to follow the Russian both in time and in importance was, above all, colored by political resentments; these grievances, while perfectly justified, were after all extramusical. Polish nationalism in the first half of the century, like the Spanish of the same period, consisted simply in the adoption, on the composer's part, of folk models—chiefly of their dances or of some usable element in their folk songs. Out of all this, Chopin was able to create music of the highest order in the depths of which lay a popular national art. Like a grain of musk it may perfume the whole casket but it is prone to lose its precious qualities unless used with discretion. The system began with the Hungarian rhapsodies and the potpourris of folk songs. It is one thing to go in search of folk music like the Russians, the Bohemians, and the Scandinavians; it is quite another to derive from it, as did Chopin. The first process resulted in a variety of consequences but it engendered a whole artistic movement. The latter, in the first half of the century, produced only the art of Chopin. More recently, it has resulted in another quite different kind of art in which are to be included the soundest composers of the music of today from Bartók and Stravinsky to Manuel de Falla. Theirs is an art which, proceeding from the national and the popular, is neither the one nor the other but a universal art.

First, however, let us examine that type of national art in which the Bohemians and the Scandinavians, the most significant contributors in this movement, carried popular feeling into the symphonic and chamber-music forms which keep their memory alive (not to mention their theatrical works, little performed in other countries than their own).

From the last decades of the eighteenth century until the romantic nationalism of the post-Beethoven era, the composers of both Czechoslovakia and Bohemia were satellites of German art. Gluck, Stamitz, and Czerny, among others, were natives of this Central European region but it is difficult to see in what way their popular roots influenced their art.

Situated at the crossroads where an infinity of races have passed during Europe's lifetime, Bohemia and Moravia, or Czechoslovakia, as all this territory was called when joined as a political unit, has known from remote times the constant alternation of domination and freedom. It is, likewise, a region traditionally rich in musical talent. During the middle years of the last century, its fight for freedom was a powerful stimulus for those of its musicians who formed the national Czech school with Bedřich Smetana and, later during its years of political independence after the war of 1914-18, with such a turbulent musician as Aloys Hába.

Bedřich Smetana was born in the same year as Bruckner, in 1824, the year of the Ninth Symphony. Nevertheless, the Bohemian, in contrast to the Austrian, derived nothing from it and, again in contrast to the latter, did not feel any attraction for a music lacking concrete emotions. Even though both drew their symphonic music from their innermost being, what in Bruckner were the expressions of vague sentiments, in Smetana were autobiographical pages: to him they were a way of bringing to the symphonic poem or to the string quartet episodes with a dramatic quality not sufficiently plastic for the stage, his preferred medium. One of the greatest symphonists of western Europe, César Franck, was born two years before Smetana. In the years immediately preceding, Robert Schumann and Franz Liszt had made their bows before the public as pianists. Smetana, who was a child prodigy, was fascinated from childhood with the impression of two prodigious virtuosos: Mozart and Liszt. After a little time had passed and the young Smetana was capable of reflection and of a surer taste, he realized that the figure of Mozart was enshrouded in legend while, on the other hand, that of Liszt was of the tangible present.

An example near at hand indicated his path as a Bohemian composer: this was the Chopin of the mazurkas and polonaises. Smetana's first compositions are popular dances, those typically Bohemian polkas which Smetana gathered in various collections from his earliest years, in 1832, down to an advanced age in 1878—yet which, despite their charm and freshness, are scarcely known outside his own country. Smetana's youth was disturbed by political excitements. Karel Čapek has left us a picture of the youth of the patriots of 1848. Their national revolution was smothered and the regime of the secret police which followed was intolerable. Some artists, like Smetana, succeeded in leaving the country. Smetana accepted a post in an academy of music in Göteborg, Sweden.

Overcoming his nostalgia and his loneliness, Smetana turned a deaf ear to his sorrows and began to compose romantic pictures in the vein of the symphonic poem. The themes were derived sometimes from Shakespeare (*Richard III* in 1858), sometimes from Schiller (*Wallenstein* in the same year). This period was decisive in the political life of Bohemia. The war between Franz Josef and Napoleon III in Italy, which restored to that nation the territories held by the Austrian empire and which forced Italy to cede Nice and Savoy to France, ended with the defeat of Solferino and the peace of Zurich at the end of 1859. The imperial talons relaxed their hold on Bohemia, the national idiom began to be heard everywhere and, in fact, a lyric theater arose in 1862 to present operas in the Czech language.

The Czech lyric theater had an immense influence on the musical education of the people of that country from this time on—almost equal, one might say, to that which the new zarzuela had in Spain at its revival in the middle of the century. Bohemian musicians declared that the imitation of the classical masters or of the most outstanding of contemporary foreign composers could not speak to the Bohemian soul and Smetana, furthermore, asserted that even less adequate was the method of introducing the popular song into art music in mere imitation of an artless model. What was requisite was the composition of music "felt" in that way, that is to say, felt by the native composer with no other model but the work of those masters who, in his own village, first taught him the rudiments of their art as they played the melodies of country dances on their rustic violins. The nationalism of Smetana, which from 1864 until 1883 without interruption took the form of compositions for the theater, possesses the immense advantage of "truth without authenticity" (as Manuel de Falla was to put it). That is to say, the national is reborn in specifically artistic terms and not as an adaptation of the popular "document." It is this that Mussorgsky (and even Tchaikovsky) achieved in Russia in contrast to their companion composers in whom literalness, truth to say, was never systematic but who nonetheless possessed to a lesser degree the ability to re-create truly popular melodies.

The first of Smetana's national operas was his masterpiece. He never again "hit the mark" as in the *Bartered Bride.* The similarity of this opera, so charming and so popular in every sense, to some of the best Spanish zarzuelas is remarkable. This similarity continues to our own day when we compare works like *La Dolores* of Bretón, which is one of the masterpieces of the Spanish national lyric theater (and which was so recognized in the musical Europe of the time—1895) with Czech operas of such merit as *Jenufa* of Leoš Janáček (1904), the most notable Bohemian national opera in the modern repertory. True it is that Bretón did not exercise the same care in technical niceties and harmonic refinements as did Janáček but, on the other hand, there is in the first a spontaneity, a simple earthy naturalness in the unfolding of the drama that make the episodes of *Jenufa* seem artificial and exaggerated.

As was also the case with Spanish composers of national operas, Smetana fell into the error of using historical themes. *Dalibor* (1868) and *Libussa* (1872) are works of this type which have survived four or five others. In them the action develops slowly and insipidly, and the lyric passages which are interspersed do little to arouse the interest or the emotion. The same thing was repeated in the Russian theater, even including that of Rimsky-Korsakov, as also in that of Smetana's successor, Antonin Dvořák.

The symphonic production of Smetana developed in a series of vast orchestral canvases which are included under the common title, *Má Vlast* (My Country); they are: *Vyšehrad,* Vltava (the river Moldau), Šárka, From Bohemia's Meadows and Groves, *Tábor,* and *Blanik*—all are symphonic pages which Smetana composed between 1874 and 1879 and came to be known (though infrequently) in Europe and to have certain consequences. One of these consequences is the Spanish series of landscapes which Bartolomé Pérez Casas entitled To My Native Land (1893), later reduced for practical considerations to the limits of the Suite Murciana; this work came at a period when the new music of the advanced Russian school had not yet reached Spain. Pérez Casas anticipated it with an unusual mastery, as compared with his contemporaries, in instrumentation and in harmony as well as in his use of popular motives.

While in his compositions for piano, Smetana followed with facility the models of Chopin and Liszt, in his orchestration he does not deviate from the pattern of Central European symphonic works. Since the formation of the classical orchestra, the orchestra of the Viennese symphony to be precise, the three musical countries of Europe developed their instrumental genius differently, each one demonstrating a development and a perfection of the instruments of its preference. Italy, the country in which bowed instruments had reached their greatest brilliance in the epoch of the *concerti grossi* and the virtuosos, continued its predilection for strings in the orchestra of its opera; the Italian operatic orchestra did not progress in the romantic era except for occasional details in Verdi and Boito. Germany, on the other hand, beginning in the seventeenth century, displayed a great affection for municipal orchestras of wind instruments and continued perfecting them until they became the heart of the Wagnerian orchestra. Naturally, Wagner utilized whatever improvements were made in the wood winds—improvements due chiefly to French workmanship—which contributed thereby a special purity and mellowness to the instrumental whole. Yet whatever may be the genius of Wagner in this respect, it is the expressive quality of his brasses which is outstanding; and the orchestra of Bruckner, like that of Mahler or of Richard Strauss, can no more be imagined without its nucleus of brasses than the orchestra of Claude Debussy can be conceived without the technical refinement of the wood wind instruments.

The nationalist composers, except for certain of the Russians, made no great discoveries in the field of orchestration; instead, they confined themselves to introducing into the general scheme of the romantic orchestra such popular instruments as occasion demanded. In their orchestration as in their harmonies, they followed their individual tastes with very little modification of the technique they had already learned. This technique had been drawn (*a*) first from the treatises of Berlioz and Gevaert, (*b*) later from the appendix Richard Strauss added to the German translation of Berlioz's treatise (which meant that they took as the basis of their orchestra that of the French musician, so outstanding a discoverer of orchestral shadings), (*c*) finally, from the treatise on orchestration by Rimsky-Korsakov, not so much a method as it is a collection of typical Rimskyan formulas which cannot be followed too closely without serious prejudice to a composer's originality. However, as is well known, this is always the danger of learning orchestration in the treatises or scores of the masters if the inexperienced composer does not feel within himself the source of a new sonorous palette.

Antonin Dvořák, who inherited Smetana's position as leader of the Bohemian national school, felt less than he the attraction for orchestral color. Although he was a composer of national operas, which have been little performed outside his own country and which, like the one entitled *Undine,* repeat in all its aspects a plot often treated by early romantic and nationalist composers, Dvořák reacts more strongly to the suggestion of classical forms. Violinist in the orchestra of the National Theater, under the direction of Smetana, Dvořák followed the style of that national opera and of that master. His first theatrical productions were comic operas (1874). His first grand opera of tragic character followed shortly (*Vanda* with a Polish plot, in 1875). But Dvořák also wrote quartets, trios, and serenatas for string orchestra, almost without interruption throughout his life. These works of a general character alternate with songs and pieces in popular style; but there is no stylistic intermingling of the one with the other. The symphonies came later, beginning in 1880, when Dvořák reached his fortieth year and his talent and technique were mature. The operas are few but those that have been published maintain his character of national composer.

Preoccupation with abstract form during most of his career prevented Dvořák from feeling any inclination toward poematic symphonism. Curiously enough, however, toward the end of his life he wrote five symphonic poems at a stretch in 1896. These poems are little known. On the other hand, Dvořák acquired an extraordinary renown through a casual circumstance: namely, for treating symphonically, with great correctness and sureness of form, some themes of the North American Negro garnered as the result of a visit to New York in 1892. Dvořák treats dance themes and melancholy songs of the Negroes, such as their spirituals, both in his famous New World Symphony and in certain chamber-music compositions, all of which promptly became well-known and popularized with the nicknames, "Negro Symphony," "Negro Quartet," or "Negro Quintet."[1]

Thus, Dvořák appears as a pioneer in his interest in the Negro folklore which has enjoyed such vogue in recent years but this interest is scarcely more than incidental in his career as writer of Bohemian national operas or as composer in classical forms. Brahms, who esteemed him and advised him in his youth (even arranging the grant of a pension by the Society of the Friends of Music of Vienna), contributed to Dvořák's reputation in Germany. Those works with such novel themes made him promptly popular in Latin countries. However, when these lands heard the quartets in which he made use, always in the same formal manner, of native motives such as *dumkys* and furiants, the knowledge among western European countries of nationalist

[1] Today it is said that these Negro motives are not really so authentic. "Many of the tunes which he used were really Irish tunes colored with a Negro brush." Charles V. Stanford, "Some Thoughts concerning Folk Song and Nationality," the *Musical Quarterly* (New York: 1915).

In a letter to the Czech conductor Oscar Nedbal, in 1900, Dvořák affirmed that he had not used *textually* a single Negro song but that he "tried" musically to write in the spirit of these national American melodies.

William Ritter (author of a biography of Smetana) explained that the "Negro symphony" is so markedly Czech in feeling that it is considered as typically national throughout Bohemia.

music had already advanced considerably and their preference was for the rich colorings of the Russian orchestrators.

A little more than ten years younger than Dvořák, Leoš Janáček, a Moravian by birth, brought to the new generation of his countrymen the postromantic Bohemian nationalism of Smetana and of Dvořák. Janáček's most significant production is in the theater. As happened with the masters who preceded him and who were of immense importance in his country, Janáček scarcely has become known beyond it. Yet visitors to the Czechoslovakian capital invariably found the works of the two older men in the National Theater and at least the *Jenufa* of Janáček in Prague's delightful Viennese rococo German Theater. The poems of Smetana reached the height of their vogue with European orchestras some years ago and are no longer played. The "Negro Symphony" continues in the repertory of these orchestras while the chamber music of Dvořák is never absent in that of quartets of every rank. But who knows Janáček beyond the confines of Czechoslovakia—his symphonic poems (one of which sings the epic of Taras Bulba, after Gogol) or his trios, his sonatas and quartets, still less his many songs and choral works? In the field of vocal music nationalist composers found, as can be well imagined, an especially propitious field. Janáček, furthermore, cultivated folklore in its documentary aspect and the collection of Moravian popular songs he published with Josef Bartoš, about 1901, contains pages of delightful freshness. His study on "The Musical Structure of National Songs" (1901) is considered as important as those of Béla Bartók on the same subject but I do not believe it has been translated into the languages in use beyond his own country. Josef Bartoš is the biographer of Antonin Dvořák and of Zdenko Fibich, the Bohemian musical contemporary of Janáček (Fibich, 1850; Janáček, 1854) whose symphonic pages are nationalist to the same degree that his operas are postromantic. Also of the same generation is Joseph Bohuslav Foster, whose symphonic music is of more importance than his music for the theater.

Joseph Jiránek (1855), who was a pupil of Smetana, belongs to that generation; his work is primarily didactic and with him the nationalist Czech music comes to possess a technical method which assures it a unity and coherence which the other national schools did not achieve in the same degree. Rimsky-Korsakov's treatise on harmony is not one of his best works although, on the other hand, his treatise on orchestration is. However, counterpoint in Russia has a master of the first rank in Taneiev.

The succeeding Czech generation starts out with Vitězslav Novák (1870), a Bohemian, who was pupil of Dvořák and whose national feeling tends to encompass more universal values, especially in his chamber music. Novák marks the transition to the younger generation. His pupil was Boleslav Jirák, a Czech born in Prague (1891) and one of the authentic masters of what may well be called the Central European school. What is national lies deep within him, submerged in the subconscious of the musician while he aspires to a new type of universality. Jirák can write an opera on Apollo or "Songs of Home," a psalm, or a suite on the Colors of the Rainbow. He is as much Czech in the one case as in the other. This is generally true of the other Czech composers of the same age: Otakar Jeremiáš (1892), for example, a Czech and also a pupil of Novák, who has written an opera on the *Brothers Karamazov;* and even with the young composers of the neighboring countries, like Božidar Širola, the Croat (1889) (countryman of Dragan Plamenac, a musicologist of high rank). Hungary counts among its most recent composers talents of such powerful temperament as Tibor Harsanyi (1898) and Alexander Jemnitz (1890). The latter is further removed from the nationalist influence; the former is perhaps nearer it in feeling. Marcel Mihalovici, the Rumanian (born in Bucharest, 1898), in his Rumanian Caprice (1939), relegates the nationalism of Enesco to a remote past. Yet Enesco, like his younger compatriot and even like Harsanyi, has felt more than one breath, more than one perfume wafted by Parisian breezes.

Chapter
EIGHT

CENTRAL EUROPE was not the only region traversed by the road of musical nationalism. In the Scandinavias, the road led, after mediocre works like those of Svendsen and Sinding, to the only nationalism that is still vigorous today without, in general, rising to the degree of refinement reached by two composers who discovered that loftier type which may be called intrinsic nationalism: Carl Nielsen in Denmark, little known outside his own country, and Jean Sibelius, who has found an amazing success with the North American and English public (which are inclined to accept with docility the opinion of their music critics).

At one time, the musical history of the Scandinavias was little more than a satellite addition to that of Germany. The modern age begins for these countries in Denmark, nearest to the German cultural center; Johan Peder Hartmann (1805-1900) composed music for the stage to some of the tales of Hoffmann. During these years the institution for musical education in highest repute in Central Europe was the school founded by Mendelssohn in Leipzig. After his death, it lost the freshness and flexibility that characterized his talent and became a conservatory of formalistic, traditional, and pedantic teaching.

For this reason the famous School of Leipzig was more prejudicial than useful to the Scandinavian musicians who continued to go there to study the composition of symphonies, quartets, and other formulas which were much too ample for the gentle, delicate inspiration of their country's music. In spite of this misguided training, Scandinavian composers began to attract the attention of the rest of Europe. The first was Niels W. Gade (1817), friend of Mendelssohn and Schumann, who died in 1890 in Copenhagen. Gade was a highly estimable composer. If his pleasant and agreeable talent is not especially apparent in his symphonies (eight) or in his poems of a clearly romantic derivation like the "Daughter of the Erlking" (*Elverskud*) or in his concert overtures like Hamlet and Michelangelo, or in his cantatas Kalanus, Psyché, *Der Strom, Frühlingsphantasie,* and *Frühlingsbotschaft,* it is certainly demonstrated in his songs *im Volkston,* in his *Nordische Tonbilder,* in his *Volkstänze,* in his suite Holbergiana and in the sonatas (like the Fourth, in B flat,

Op. 62) for piano and violin with the subtitle, *Volkstänze im nordischen Charakter*. True, these are pages of a predecessor of Grieg but they merit a more faithful memory than they have known.

Gade's compositions for piano, among which are numerous *Frühlingsblumen, Arabesken,* and *Novelletten,* show an ingenious and facile writing which appears to have been a direct model for Grieg (1843-1907). Grieg received a solid education at the School of Leipzig but a desire for inspiration led him to Copenhagen, to Hartmann and Gade, at the early age of twenty. There he met a youth of his own age who had made himself the champion of Norwegian nationalism and who was living in exile in Denmark apparently on account of his political enthusiasms. Rikard Nordraak (1842-66) is a perfect example of the young nationalist author of about 1860, in whom the fading flower of romanticism is touched with the gay colors of the dawn, in literary works opulent with grand phrases and noble gestures. Nordraak was furthermore a musician of unusual talent who had studied with Kullak and had composed—besides the Norwegian national anthem—incidental music for the *Mary Stuart* of Björson as well as for his *Sigurd Slembe*. Nordraak's genius showed itself at its best in his improvisations. In them he united the legendary themes of Scandinavian poetry with popular melodies; he described to Grieg his projects for heroic operas, for vast symphonic sagas, for works of combined poetry and music that he might very well have realized himself, had he not died at the age of twenty-four.

The fondness for vast sonorous structures, typical of composers of the north, is ever present in the Scandinavians. Grieg, a disillusioned disciple of the School of Leipzig, did not share these enthusiasms but utilized his good technical apprenticeship for the creation, in his own style, of compositions of brief dimensions possessing powerful inner solidity—music that, although inspired by popular airs, is not what is commonly understood as popular music; it is subtle piano and chamber music in which art conceals art and in which, despite an apparent fragility, the trained musician can recognize the composer's distinguished craftsmanship. The three sonatas for piano and violin and the Quartet in G Major contain, within the flexibility of form necessary to this type of inspiration, tonal relationships of an attractive effect and harmonic touches already close to impressionism. In writing for orchestra, Grieg appears full of anxiety lest he crumple the fragile petals of these wild flowers which require the tenderest handling. In his use of the wood winds, in the grace with which he makes the violin sing about the orchestral palette, Grieg already approaches French music at the beginning of the century. The French, indeed, knew how to appreciate this musician's reserved, discreet, and delicate naturalness, the "bite" of his orchestral timbres, and his modern feeling for harmonies.

Grieg's reputation, even in his own country which until then had shown no great enthusiasm for his music, dates from the first performance of his setting of Ibsen's *Peer Gynt* in 1876. From then on, Norwegian musical youth had almost no other ideal. On the other hand, Christian Sinding (1856-) was the musician preferred by students who sought amplitude in form without losing contact with popular music.

In the neighboring country, the romantic ardor appeared late. The Royal Academy, founded by Gustave III at the end of the eighteenth century, only served to give Sweden musicians of weak personality, who faithfully followed German trends. Only toward 1880 did the influence of Wagnerian drama provide some stimulus among composers like August Södermann (1832-1876) and Ivar Hallström (1826-1901), who had already written nationalist operas well furnished with popular songs. Wagner's influence was inevitably strongly felt in the country which gave birth to the mythical poems he dramatized. Anders Hallén (1846-1925) composed music for *Harald Viking* which was performed in Leipzig in 1881 on Liszt's recommendation. The latter's influence, like that of Berlioz, is evident in Hallén as well as in Emil Sjögren (1853-1918), who is fairly well known for his agreeable romances while Tor Aulin (1866-1914) has received recognition beyond his native land for his chamber works.

Among the younger writers of symphonies of extended treatment, for which these northern composers experience an undoubted fondness, Kurt Atterberg (1887-) has made himself known, partly on account of the prize he received in Vienna in 1928 in an international competition to celebrate the centenary of Schubert's death. He attempted, in that competition, to encourage a return to the form of vast dimensions sustained by the melodic interest, as in the great Schubertian compositions. The symphonies of Atterberg (five) are of solid construction but free in form; they are logically sound with a melodism supported by the rhythmical and tonal structure. Strictly speaking, Atterberg might better be considered in the section dealing with the cultivators of the formal symphony yet the character of his melody is clearly national without being literally so. In the sense described above, Atterberg's music is derived from a popular feeling which he treats freely and without specific poematic meaning.

From this point of view, Atterberg carries further the criterion of the two greatest symphonists of Scandinavia: Carl Nielsen and Jean Sibelius. Construction is a constant preoccupation with both and their form is obviously the product of meditation. Nevertheless, the stimulus of their inspiration is poematic: Nielsen's romanticism is of the south while Sibelius prefers the clear broad outlines of his native landscape. Denmark and Finland are austere countries; but, in all climes, youth has a warm heart and spring comes to those lands with an overwhelming force and exuberant joyousness. The long days have a smiling brightness; the trees, in perfumed flower, overflow the countryside and inundate the city streets; one catches fleeting glimpses of a milky sea. Carl Nielsen (1865-1931) possessed a restless imagination which he knew how to direct with a judicious technique. Among his six symphonies, one entitled Expanse well represents the character of his talent. He has been called the Sibelius of Denmark and his works, among which are two operas and a number of chamber-music compositions, merit at least as much appreciation as those of the Finnish master. Nielsen's music is often visited by meridional lyric breezes which he treats with nobleness and originality though not without a certain austerity belonging to his temperament. His operas, *Saul and David* and *Maskerade,* are very distant in their atmosphere from his native island of Fyn. Among his symphonies, those entitled *Die fire Temperamenter* and *Das Unauslöschliche* give an idea of the poematicism or, better, the expressivism which places them in the line of Viennese symphonism after Mahler; yet the character of Nielsen's phrases and the carefully planned order of his form belong to a composer of the north.

With the death of Nielsen, Sibelius is the composer of most serious import among those of his generation (1865) in the Scandinavian countries. He, like Robert Kajanus (1856-1933) and other young musicians, received his early instruction in the National Conservatory under Martin Wegelius. After studying in Berlin with Bargiel and A. Becker, he went to Vienna in 1890 to seek Goldmark, whose overture Sakuntala already old (1865) at that time as well as his suites and (symphonic) poems still maintained a prestige strengthened by his opera the *Queen of Sheba* (1875).

From his first poem *En Saga* (Op. 2), to Tapiola, written as a gesture of gratitude to the audiences of the United States for the recognition which they accorded his Seventh Symphony, Sibelius' inspiration is that of a spirit wandering in gentle or gloomy mood through the woods and fields of his native land. He himself says that nature is the book that inspires him; his vast compositions, some of which have a slight historical basis, are really extensive friezes in which the theme is the Finnish landscape. Karelia, legends like the Swan of Tuonela, Lemminkaïnen, Ukko, the Daughter of Pohjola, Luonnatar, Kullervo, Finlandia, and finally Tapiola are the high points in an extensive production which includes more than a hundred works. Among these are no less than eight symphonies, in addition to the poems and fantasias mentioned. There is also a quantity of minor works such as sonatas and sonatinas, piano pieces in more or less conventional forms. In these may be followed, in appropriate proportion, Sibelius' typical manner: clear and short ideas which follow each other with a vivacity of dynamic contrasts and which are linked together in short periods, whose juxtaposition leads to climaxes or points of greater lyric intensity. Yet, generally speaking, his language is that of postromantic poematicism and his system of symbols is that created throughout the whole period of romanticism through Wagner. This language of symbols of an epoch which survives in the symphonists after Wagner with a content already exhausted. To it Sibelius can add very little with his folk melodies or picturesque suggestions of a distant country stimulating to the imagination though they may be. So it happens that all the composers without exception who at the present time continue to move within the limits of poematic or expressivistic symphonism suffer from comparison with figures of the past. Their personality may be strong, as in the case of Sibelius, or weak, like that of meridional composers of symphonic poems; they may use a clear and sober orchestration or a lively and polychromatic one with harmonies seasoned to excite the palate but, in short, they are composers still living in the nineteenth century.

In France, in Italy, in Spain, and in America, there are many such composers. Really, except for those eminent cases of musicians who began their careers in this way but later were wise enough to "change their skin," the majority do nothing more than go around in the circles of the nationalist merry-go-round. I have mentioned some names belonging to Spain. In France the figures of Florent Schmitt (1870) and Albert Roussel (1869-1937) stand out among an abundance of works and authors. Both, like so many other French composers of today, have notably enriched the procedures known as modern in the realm of harmony and, in fact, their harmonic writing, like their orchestration, is full of clever details. The effect of works like *En Été, Musiques de plein-air, Le Palais hanté, Rêves,* or *Mirages,* among the orchestral compositions of Schmitt, is in general terms that of postromantic poematicism but these symphonic studies are worked out in terms less vague in outline than are similar German compositions. In this respect, as in the contour of their phrases and their unmistakable "air," they are typically French. The exoticism of Schmitt's *Antoine et Cléopatre,* that of Albert Roussel in Padmâvatî, Evocations, *Poème de la forêt,* or *Pour une fête de printemps* also belong to the subject under discussion. The same may be said of Vincent d'Indy in pages like *Symphonie Cévenole* or *Jour d'été à la montagne;* as well as of many others of his compositions which are directly derived from Wagnerian symphonism. But in d'Indy there is an obsession for achieving logical and robust constructions, which carries him beyond the limits of poematicism, and in this connection we shall return to d'Indy as well as to other composers who, after him, derive from that great architect César Franck.

The desire for expression overflowing formal limits predominates in musicians like Schmitt and Roussel. The latter wrote a symphony, a suite, a concerto, and a great deal of chamber music. Schmitt's chamber music or piano pieces cannot contain themselves within their frame and eagerly confess it in their titles as in the amusing *Sonate libre en deux parties enchainées* and

Ad modum Clementis acquae. One must be grateful for this because when writers of pure symphonies like those fresh from the classrooms of the Schola Cantorum adopt the severe demeanor appropriate to such a lofty task, what they produce is not very alluring.

A lyric Italianism, quite distinct from folklore but with sufficient power thanks to its lyricism to move beyond the literary, ultraintellectualized means which first produced it, was that of Gabriele d'Annunzio. The once famous author of *Il Fuoco* and *La Nave* wished to forge an Italy that would correspond politically to his poet's dreams and there were many who, without realizing that to bring the dreams of poetry down to the vulgar level of everyday life may result in irreparable damage, used his fiery harangues to inflate reckless political programs which have had their terrible consequences. D'Annunzio desired to create a musician in his image and he found his material in a youth honored by the Conservatory of Parma. This honest provincial town found itself raised to the lofty regions of Parnassus—in exchange for its famous cheeses and its Stendhalian reminiscences—thanks to the talent of one whom d'Annunzio was pleased to call Ildebrando of Parma (or Ildebrando Pizzetti according to the civil register which recorded his birth on September 20, 1880). Whether of Parma or of any other place, Pizzetti is a wholly Italian composer especially in that lyric air which he gave his operas, an air of less amplitude than that of his literary models but with a resonance eminently scenic and theatrical. His first fully realized work is the *Fedra* of d'Annunzio (1915) after which followed other operas of diverse derivations—some of them owing their text to the composer himself like *Debora e Jaele* (1922)—down to the recent *L'Orseolo* (1933) which seems to show a flagging of the ready inspiration which had filled his music for *La Nave* (1917), for *La Pisanella* (1913), and for the *Sinfonia del fuoco* (1915).

This symphony, really an arrangement of one of the first attempts to provide the cinema with music of high quality (for d'Annunzio's film, *Cabiria*), demonstrates better than any other the content and formal consequences of the poematic symphony. Primarily a composer of operas, the rest of Pizzetti's production for orchestra or chamber instruments is but the sonorous shape he gives to inspirations felt by and for the stage; they have an unmistakably theatrical accent. His Summer Concerto, his poem "The Last Hunt of St. Humbert," his *Canti della stagione alta* foreshadow the work of another composer who, though not indebted to him directly, carries to its ultimate consequences in our own time this symphonized poematicism, a man whose Italianism derives not from the opera but from the orchestra of the Russians.

In fact, after seeking his technique, curiously enough, in the colorless Germanicism of Max Bruch and, later, in the superficial polychromy of Rimsky-

Korsakov, Ottorino Respighi (1879-1936) discovered the rustling of the pines and the gentle murmur of the fountains of Rome. A facile, agreeable composer whose characteristics are within the reach of sensibilities which still respond to the commonplaces of the romanza and the aria, Respighi has left, in Pines of Rome, Fountains of Rome, in Church Windows, Botticelli Triptych, the Birds, and in Roman Festivals, pages of uneven merit among which are agreeable landscapes saturated with bucolic poetry and expressed with a palette of delicate tints. At the same time his heroic notes betray a conventionality tending toward bad taste; the triviality of his inspiration is revealed in the two compositions which sum up his life's work: the Pines and the Fountains of the eternal city.

Of a loftier inspiration, sounder in his realizations, with a lyricism of noble spirit in which may be heard an echo of the enthusiastic d'Annunzian lyric, is Gian Francesco Malipiero, younger than Respighi by a few years (1882) and, perhaps, the most notable contemporary musician of the unsettled peninsula. The *Sinfonia del Mare,* the *Impressioni del Vero* in three series, among which are to be found a coloring which does justice to the rich palette of the Venetians (such as *I Cipressi e il Vento, Baldoria Campestre,* and *I Galli*), or the graver inspirations of his *Pause del silenzio* and the *Ditirambo tragico,* where the palette is more somber, carry the career of Malipiero to his most recent symphonic productions in which appear a poematicism somewhat mild in tone. Malipiero's great virtue is his imagination. From it flows a thoughtful workmanship with an originality of sentiment which discovers forms that are neither commonplace nor arbitrary; simple, yet at the same time substantial, facile yet clean cut, as his songs and chamber music abundantly testify.

The Victorian age brought to English music of the second half of the nineteenth century an air which it had lacked since the distant days of its ancient glories. Like the royal house, which descends from German princes, Victorian music felt continental influences, that of Brahms above all. Sometime before, W. Sterndale Bennett (1816-75), accomplished musician and friend of Mendelssohn and Schumann, had brought home something of the perfume of continental music in his poematic overtures, such as the Naiads or Sylvan Nymphs, and in more than a few of his works for piano and chamber instruments. These were of the type stipulated by the romanticism of the School of Leipzig where, indeed, these works had their first performance. As is natural in an English musician, the production of Bennett abounds in anthems, cantatas, and oratorios.

Mendelssohn was the passion of the England of the romantic period; his reign was succeeded by that of Brahms, whose influence—by way of Hubert

H. Parry (1848-1918) and Charles Villiers Stanford (1852-1924)—has a kind of blossoming in the chivalrous, noble music of Edward Elgar (1857-1934). Elgar was, however, a nationalist composer. This genre was cultivated in England somewhat later than on the Continent, rather inconsistently indeed, since the science known as folklore is in name at least an English invention. It goes back, in fact, as early as the year 1846, to the time when Glinka was making discoveries in Spanish folklore. If popular song was already alive in England, in Russia and in Spain, in Bohemia or in Scandinavia at that time, its methodical study is a modern discipline. The first Folklore Society was founded in London only in 1878, and shortly after in Spain in 1881, and the first methodical collections (or re-collections) of English folk music, those of Cecil James Sharp in his medieval Morris Dances (Moorish Dances, the very ancient morescas, still alive in Somerset) date from the first years of our century.

A last echo of poematic symphonism in England, flowing directly from the romantic sources of Berlioz, Liszt, and Wagner, is to be found in the operas, poems, and overtures of Alexander Campbell Mackenzie (1847-1935). He had studied in Germany but, a true Scotchman, he possessed a strong national feeling which pervades his Scottish Concerto, his Pibroch, and the Burns Rhapsody, while the rest of his work displays a romanticism tinged with a special quality which is unmistakably insular. The same is true of all these British musicians, even though this delicate flavor eludes the perceptions of those on the other side of the Channel.

Of the post-Victorian composers or, in other words, those of the same generation as Rachmaninoff in Russia, Ravel in France, and Falla in Spain, Vaughan Williams (1872) must be mentioned first and following him Holst (1874-1934) and Holbrooke (1878). Here again we observe how insufficient chronology alone can be, for a composer like Frederick Delius (1862-1934) and another like Granville Bantock (1868) outstrip their contemporaries in their modernity of thought and method and associate themselves with the younger generation. In the figure of Delius one can well observe the transition from the past century of romanticism to the new era of impressionism. As for Granville Bantock, his compatriots consider him one of the outstanding leaders in the development of national music. A restless talent, he has left his mark in this aspect of English music as well as in symphonic poematicism, where he displays an imagination strongly plastic in quality. Remarkably fertile in ideas, he projected no less than twenty-four symphonic poems for Southey's *Curse of Kehama,* while the life of Christ inspired him with the idea for an oratorio in ten parts.

His choral writing marks an important date in this traditionally English musical art. Every Englishman, no matter how sedentary, how addicted to the comforts of life (a phrase especially invented for that country), dreams of distant horizons. Bantock let his fancy wander to the Persia of Omar Khayyám; to the Palestine of the Song of Songs; to classical pagan lands in Pagan Chants and to other climes more accessible today (especially in illustrated books, in histories of art, and in the folders of tourist companies) such as Egypt, India, China, and Japan; these countries possess the inestimable advantage for the occidental composer of permitting him the pleasure of experimenting with supposedly exotic scales and harmonies suggestive of far-off lands.

Yet his countrymen are more grateful to Bantock for his experiments, better realized, in the field of Scottish folklore with the inevitable Pibroch; this long, warlike melody is improvised by the Scots on their bagpipes with endless variations on an old and well-known theme, the *urlar,* which is slightly related to the Alpine *ranz des vaches.*

Among the English composers of this generation and connected with this tendency, Ralph Vaughan Williams is, I think, the most outstanding. Arthur Eaglefield Hull said of him that the most important thing for Vaughan Williams is to be English and next to be a musician: when both elements are not properly combined, his music suffers. I leave to Hull the responsibility for this opinion. In the series of songs with string quartet which Vaughan Williams composed on the admirable stanzas by A. E. Housman, "On Wenlock Edge":

> On Wenlock Edge the wood's in trouble;
> His forest fleece the Wrekin heaves. . . .

(*A Shropshire Lad,* XXXI) are to be found, I believe, the most delicate tints of an inspiration very near to being impressionist as well as the most dramatic accents in present day British music. Of a similar character are his songs "Toward the Unknown Region" by Walt Whitman (1907) but it is in his Pastoral Symphony (1922) and in his London Symphony (1914) that his inspiration finds the ample horizons that it needs. His ideas derive from the field of poetry and are translated into a sober and powerful melodism; the development is not dictated by the poematic content but by a vigorous feeling for the form, which has an eminently contrapuntal texture while the harmonic combinations which this brings about are never utilized in and for themselves.

The ancient airs and legends of Wales, enveloped in a romantic atmosphere derived from Wagner (an influence from which he later freed himself), inspired in Rutland Boughton (1878) a scenic lyricism in which the principal part is given to the chorus. Boughton wanted to produce his operas in the environment evocative of times gone by and of their setting. Thus he wished to convert the little town of Glastonbury into a kind of Bayreuth for his Arthurian dramas (staged by Reginald Buckley). In the *Immortal Hour,* a legend of princesses and magic dreams by Fiona Macleod, Boughton found his greatest success; its generously melodic music and diatonalism stand in contrast to the experiments then being made along very different lines by Central European composers.

Gustav Holst is to be connected with Vaughan Williams for, although the poematic character of Holst's works belongs to an earlier style which Elgar, Bantock, William Wallace (1860), and Frederick Corder (1852-1932) had cultivated, his technique, through Vaughan Williams, approaches impressionism. A suite in oriental style, Beni Mora, no more than salutes from the distant West the orientalisms of Ippolitov-Ivanov. Holst's chief work to be known beyond his native island is the symphonic suite, the Planets: a symphony in its formal concept and texture, a suite because it consists of a series of pictures in which Mars, Venus, Mercury, etc., are described symbolically in episodes which are far from cosmological but which rather reflect the atmosphere of the Strand, the banks of the city or Hyde Park and which are not altogether exempt from a certain British stodginess. English critics see in this series of symphonic pages one of the masterpieces of their contemporary music. The foreign observer cannot go so far; the orchestration seems somewhat thick and ponderous, and the general ideology does not inspire light thoughts. Josef Holbrooke (1878), on the other hand, is not known across the Channel. His imagination leans toward a neurotic romanticism somewhat in the vein of Poe and, indeed, his symphonic poem, the Raven, was his first success and gave him a reputation rapidly confirmed by his music on another of Poe's poems, Ulalume. It is easy to say of Holbrooke that he is an English Berlioz and the comparison appears justified. In the cantata, Byron, his romantic temperament lets itself go at will. His opera, the *Children of Don,* crowns these enthusiasms in the form of an operatic trilogy in the purest romantic, one might almost say Weberian, tradition. The demoniac delights him; one of his chamber works is entitled *Quintette Diabolique,* in a tone which reminds us of Scriabin. His eloquence gushes unchecked from a lively imagination with the almost inevitable consequence that the result is uneven, lacking in self-criticism, and contains sterile passages which make the work fall apart. Arnold Bax (1883) appears in sharp contrast to Holbrooke but Bax belongs to a generation with different ideals as is shown in his concept of form and in his predilection for the most fluid material. At the same time that the turn of a phrase is often typically national, Bax's music approaches that which, in the Île de France, enchants the sensitive ear. This is the best commentary on works which are rather melancholy, contemplative, of a slow yet noble measure incapable of affectation. The same may be said of another composer whose true distinction is also somewhat faded today, Cyril Scott (1879).

All due reserves made, especially in regard to harmonic and orchestral technique, I believe that Eugène Goossens (1893) has a closer relationship to Holbrooke than to Charles Wood (1866-1926) or to Charles Stanford, his teachers. Goossens, belonging to a Belgian family established in England, is distinguished by an original imagination which is manifest concretely in his program pieces and abstractly, although unmistakably, in his chamber works; here, his originality of thought has its vividly exact counterpart in the technique. His Miniature Fantasy and his Two Sketches for string quartet profoundly interested those of us who were young during the years of the first world war. Youthful vivacity took on another note later and the Eternal Rhythm, Op. 27, falls into a metaphysical sonority between Scriabin and Holst which did not attract us so much. His first symphonic poems are entitled Perseus and Ossian; the more recent symphonies, of 1938 and 1940, fluctuate between the poematicism of Two Nature Poems and the formal abstraction of the symphony written for the Cincinnati Orchestra which Goossens conducts. Spanish themes have attracted him since his youth: his Op. 23 is a prelude to Verhaeren's *Philip II;* an opera, *Don Juan de Mañara,* was first presented at Covent Garden in 1937 but is of somewhat earlier date. These are baroque themes and are strongly flavored with the whole repertory of dissonances yet, in them, the desire for a dense, closely knit technique combined with a vivid line and a brilliancy of expression seems to be the object of much thought with this important musician.

The last lines might also apply to the Dutch-born Bernhard van Dieren (1884-1936) with the necessity of accentuating in them the mystical quality—that is to say, that mysticism of the sound itself, in dissonance and in "writing," which harassed Scriabin and fascinated Bruckner. Van Dieren was a philosopher-musician—a serious symptom. A notable writer, a great part of his activity was in the field of literature until in the last years of his life, unfortunately short, he dedicated himself with more ardor to the composition of music. His pieces have an obscure, willful character, a little like that of Jacob Epstein in sculpture (whom van Dieren interpreted in a book on the sculptor, 1920). A year before his death, van Dieren published a book of powerfully suggestive essays, *Down Among the Dead Men:* this idea of diving into the Homeric Hades, the abode of departed souls, seems to have preoccupied him in his musical activity. However profound it may be, it is never attractive; the aggregate of his *Klang-Ideal,* still less so. Nevertheless, van Dieren did not lack his enthusiasts like Cecil Gray, who wrote a little book (delicious in its acidity) on the composers of our day; among its disillusioned pages only one name survives unscorched, that of van Dieren.

Among the most recent young composers, William Turner Walton (1902) may be singled out as a post-Brahmsian if one views him through his Concerto for Violin (1939), or as an expressivist if one considers his overture-suite-ballet Façade (1922-36-38), which is an interesting, well-worked-out series of pages of half-spoken, half-sung declamation with accompaniment. This type of intoned recitation, somewhat different from that cultivated in Germany by composers all the way from men as mediocre as Arnold Winternitz (*Die Nachtigall* on the same Andersen tale as that of Stravinsky) or Gustav Levin ("*Das klagende Lied*") to the *Pierrot Lunaire* of Schönberg, finds in Walton extremely unusual accents.

Chapter NINE

THE GROWING plasticity of the character of the motive from Schumann on and the integration of the sonorous symbol with dramatic feeling, ever more concrete in Wagner, led inevitably to the stage. If the musical motive—that is, a guiding leitmotiv, a symphonic counterpart to dramatic action—parallels episodes of a dramatic nature, it follows obviously that the forms and variations of the music will come only in part from purely musical considerations; the rest will come from the dramatic intentions born within the composer's creative faculty. The part that springs from the musical drive of the motive is the bond which unites this music to the cosmos, to the elemental forces of the universe. The other part, that related to the expressive force of the composer, is the bond which links this music to human emotion. The proportion between these two extremes determines whether the dramatic symphony will be more symphony or more drama.

Beethoven's motives are no longer simple formulas of sound from whose objective evolution the symphony is born, as in Haydn and Mozart. The extramusical meaning of his motives was recognized by Beethoven himself. From his time on, the deep and ever-widening gulf which separates the music of the nineteenth century from that of the preceding centuries is apparent. Keeping this in mind, one understands what Wagner really meant when he said that the pure forms, the closed forms of the sonata, were outmoded by Beethoven. Wagner could not imagine that, after Beethoven, there could be musicians for whom the motive might exist without emotional content. Yet such there were, as we know, although the musical current of greatest force in Wagner's time was that which carried symphonism toward an expressive intensity which, above all in Wagner's *Tristan,* was at once both musical and dramatic.

If it is indeed so, if it is true that a certain group of notes and harmonies really *are* Tristan's yearning, then the intoxication of the lovers, the despair of absence, the drama itself must become meaningful to us not only through the ear but through the eye as well. At the same time that the orchestra plays upon our deepest consciousness, we see the action represented palpably and tangibly upon the stage. The dramatic symphony, then, finds completion in the musical drama and constantly tends in this direction.

Thus argues Wagner. But it is no less true that, if we shut our eyes and follow with our inner being the episodes of the unhappy love of Tristan and Isolde, the music which this bitter tragedy awoke in Wagner's creative imagination will seem, to some at least, still more expressive than when we contemplate the live figures—figures only too often less than ideal. We have reached, then, a point when we must assert that the concrete reality of the stage is unnecessary and that we may faithfully follow the dramatic action in the music alone. In other words, we can conceive of a symphonism that is dramatic but not theatrical.

However, if we eliminate the theater, the dramatic quality of the symphony easily loses its clarity of outline, its motives are no longer as explicit as in Wagner; it no longer deals specifically with Sigmund or with Isolde but only with the emotion which fills them and of which they are simply the bodily expression. We shall, thus, enlarge the compass of this meaning, even though the outlines of the motive which translates it become somewhat blurred and lose something of that shape which appeared so concrete to Wagner. From dramatic symphonism we proceed to a symphonism that is expressive of human emotions.

Two ways are open in this direction. Mahler's symphonism deals with undefined emotions in intangible terms, displaying a Faustian vagueness which combines very well with the general character of music but which in compensation requires a more circumscribed, formal treatment; here the symphony must provide its own support without the material aid of dramatic action. On the other hand, other composers with ideas less vague, less general, would rather preserve the clarity of Wagnerian outline in their motives, even though they may believe the stage to be superfluous; they do not wish to present to the audience a drama constructed in successive episodes but rather the dramatic meaning of those episodes. This road, which we saw opening in the lieder of Hugo Wolf, leads us directly to the symphonism of Richard Strauss. And the symphonism of Richard Strauss leads us, in turn, directly to his dramas. In him the process is simply an intensification of that constant interplay between emotional content and form which we saw being established in all romantic music from Beethoven on.

Precise calculation was the indispensable element in the classical symphony. Now it is the imagination which is in play. Classical motives were as explicit as two plus two. Those of romantic symphonism are dramatic. This is Florestan. This is Eusebius. This is Harlequin. Here you see Isolde beside the dead Tristan:

There comes Don Juan, in love with love:

Yonder you see how Tyll Eulenspiegel dances, his feet in the air, sticking out his tongue at the silly world:

The interpretation of the motive on the part of the listener is entirely voluntary. He is presented with a proposition by the composer and he accepts it or not, just as he does in the case of the windmills of Don Quixote or the flute of The Faun. This process is a cumulative one; simple imitation gives way to allusion. The simple figure, transplanted to a superior plane, becomes an ornamental arabesque, just as the acanthus leaf and the thorns of the blackberry become decorative motives by the purifying power of style. Harlequin makes his entrance in Carnaval with a stumble. Petrouchka twists and turns like the puppet he is. We see Tyll Eulenspiegel's derisive gesture as he thumbs his nose to mock us. But the phrase which the violoncello sings to describe Don Quixote presents an idea in which literal imitation has now disappeared, leaving only the feeling of the ideal aspiration of the knight. The two monks converse via their respective bassoons in simple thematic fragments. The gesture has now passed far beyond the theme of Don Juan; but the anguish of the high B flat in the basses in the scene describing the beheading of John the Baptist in *Salome* no longer reflects a plastic allusion nor any gesture translated into sound; it is the fruit of the intuition of the artist.

We are dealing, I repeat, with a proposition. We can take it or leave it. If we accept it, we accept the composer's art. If we leave it, we have rejected it. That is our privilege. And so, if the artist cheats a little, as is frequently the case with Richard Strauss, indignation on our part will only be ridiculous just as it would be to try to discover the tricks of the sleight-of-hand artist or the illusionist. It is better to let ourselves be willingly convinced. Otherwise we had best not see the show.

The character of the motive springs, then, from the primary translation of the gesture (or the grimace) and moves to the highest degree of symbolism which can exist in a particular harmony or in a special timbre. It is always a process of filling the symbol with a significance which ordinarily we do not accept in its entirety as the artist presents it but which we interpret according to our taste along the general lines which he suggests; this procedure holds good from the four notes of the Fifth Symphony to the program works of Berlioz and Liszt or the Wagnerian drama. In the classical symphony the listener need only follow the composer's manipulations. In the romantic symphony it is a question of collaboration. For this reason romantic art is called emotive. The artist communicates to us his emotional reaction, stimulates us by his translation of it into sonorous form. Classical art reserved this category of sensations for its lyric theater. It is, however, the indispensable condition of all romantic art.

It is desirable to emphasize at this point that it is not a question, between the early and late romantic composers, of phenomena different in kind but, rather, different in degree. With the classical composers, the rhythmical regularity of the harmonic pulsation and its extension in balanced periods tend to approximate the closed sections of forms modeled on the dance. With the romantic composers, the plastic irregularity of their motives, subjected to a process not eurythmic but dramatic, approaches pantomime. Wagner could say that Beethoven's Seventh Symphony was an "apotheosis of the dance," or, what amounts to the same thing, that it was conceived as a grand dance full of a Dionysiac content. The Carnaval of Schumann is already pantomimic. The symphonic poems of Richard Strauss are absolutely so. The classical forms, with their regular periods, are comparable to the structure of verse. The others compare with free verse or simply with prose of a more or less elevated style; it lies with the composer to make us fully aware of his whole scheme within the compass of a symphonic episode in the same way that we perceive the symphonic development of the Seventh Symphony as a closed dance form. Poematic symphonism leads to ballet if it is built in regular periods, to pantomime or the drama if it develops freely.

In his fecund and original career as composer, Richard Strauss (1864) follows a line of action entirely normal for a composer of the final period of romanticism, that is to say, of the post-Wagnerian era. This process may be outlined thus: works of classical form, symphonic poems, poematic symphonies, dramas. The four periods are clearly defined in the catalogue of his works: quartets and sonatas (with some pieces for voice) succeed each other up to Op. 13 in 1884 when he reached his twentieth year. A short Serenade, Op. 7, for a group of instruments without strings already reveals, in the treatment of the four horns and in turns of phrase for the wood winds, characteristics which will later on receive their complete development just as his early pages for piano present brief motives which foreshadow the merry pranks of Tyll Eulenspiegel.

Strauss's first big work dates from 1886 and is a symphony or rather a symphonic fantasy, since Richard Strauss never applies to his works, even those which belong most clearly to the type of symphonic poem, any other name than that of symphony. This work, Op. 16, bears the title *Aus Italien* and initiates a series of grand poems—Don Juan (Op. 20, 1889), Macbeth (Op. 23, 1889-91), Death and Transfiguration (Op. 24, 1890), Tyll Eulenspiegel (Op. 28, 1895), Thus Spake Zarathustra (Op. 30, 1896), Don Quixote (Op. 35, 1898), the Life of a Hero (Op. 40, 1899), and the Domestic Symphony (Op. 53, 1904).

After this last symphonic composition, Strauss begins his series of operas. Two first attempts (in 1894 with *Guntram* and in 1901 with *Feuersnot*) are nothing more than preparatory essays. His first opera comparable to his last great symphonies is *Salome* which dates from 1906; this is followed by *Elektra* (1909), *Der Rosenkavalier* (1911), *Ariadne of Naxos* (1912-17), the ballet, the *Legend of Joseph* (1914), the *Woman without a Shadow* (1919), *Schlagobers* (the humorous ballet which might be translated as *Whipped Cream,* 1924), *Intermezzo* (1925), *Helena in Egypt* (1928), *Arabella* (1933), *Die Schweigsame Frau* (1935), *Friedenstag* (1938), and *Daphne* (1938). Between the version of *Ariadne of Naxos* and the *Woman without a Shadow* appears still another symphonic work of grand dimensions, the Alpine Symphony.

Strauss's youthful period with its sonatas, pieces for piano, and chamber music follows, with a docility not exempt from flashes of originality, the romantic models from Mendelssohn and Schumann to Brahms. It is a period of solid apprenticeship, of an admirably sure mastery of technique. But soon the young composer must have felt that he had completed the traditional cycle, and in his student notebooks appear musical sketches in which a youthful romanticism, with all its consequences, is ready to burst out. It is said that Alexander Ritter, who was one of the first Wagnerites (1833-96), and author of chamber music and symphonic poems, as well as of a couple of operas, had a decisive influence on Strauss whom he introduced to the poematic symphonism of Berlioz and Liszt and to the significance of this symphonism up to and including the Wagnerian lyric drama.

In any case, Strauss would have found his own way very soon for, in addition to his impulsiveness, a violently egocentric temperament led him toward a dramaticism in which he was himself the protagonist. While this was not so easy to effect in opera, it was very easy to accomplish in the field of expressive symphonism—whether in Strauss's Don Juan, enjoying every beauty and breathing every fragrance or in the Life of a Hero where, in order to eliminate all doubt as to the hero of the biography, appear motives from his earlier works, first disfigured by the struggle against his detractors, then sweetened and softened with pleasure at the thought of his enthusiastic and highly intelligent audience. The disillusioned Domestic Symphony is, symphonically speaking, the last page of this biography in which domestic accents in all their triviality ("just like his papa! just like his mamma!" are heard in one episode) supplant the accents of the heroic. Strauss still paints himself under the name of Professor Stork in a humorous light in his opera about family quarrels entitled *Intermezzo.* After that the Straussian vein seems spent in *Helena in Egypt* where the ultraromantic phantasmagoria of Hoffmansthal has the same hotchpotch effect already visible in the *Woman without a Shadow* with its symbolist argument and its metaphysics of an opium dream. Strauss lives on, to his misfortune, at a time when politics has made him the visible head of an official art. It appears that the compromises which that exalted position required have given a dubious value to that *Friedenstag* (Day of Peace) mentioned above.

Romanticism, since it proceeded from the artist's inner emotions and from the necessity of expressing his keenest reactions, had been systematically egocentric but usually so only in those vague, discreet terms where the personal was veiled beneath an anonymity of good taste. The "objectization" of the motive, by way of the Wagnerian leitmotiv, the clarity with which facts came to be expressed by orchestral figurations with increasingly realistic force make this autobiographical element ever more concrete; in the music of Strauss it is revealed with a transparency beside which the episodes of Berlioz or of Mahler seem vague and imprecise, like their emotions and their harmonies.

But Strauss's desire for strong definition in the motive, for precision in every branch of technique—melodic, harmonic, and orchestral—forces him to descend from the poetic longings of Don Juan, from the metaphysics of Nietzsche which he realized in dance terms, to the minute details of Don Quixote's adventures. Thus the personality of the ideal knight is described by a series of variations of the principal theme, entrusted to the solo violoncello (the violin being the protagonist in *Heldenleben*); between them occur various episodes depicting with a crude realism—masterly in technique but so puerile in its meaning that it is redeemed only by its strongly ironic vein—the bleating of lambs, the whir of the windmills (using a wind machine to make the illustration perfectly clear), and the petty description of the ordinary incidents of everyday life.

Strauss's realism finds an acoustical idiom so adequate for his will of expression that it scorns pedagogical interpretation. Take, for example, the simultaneous production of the sounds C♯, A♯, E, F♯♯, G♯ in the low wood winds against a tremolo of high A-B♭, as Salome kisses the trunkless head of the Baptist, or the ending of Zarathustra in a simultaneous C major and B major. Yet the first group of notes has a sonorous value of its own with an effect of mystery in timbres admirably suited to the scene; they do not need to be analyzed as the chord of the dominant of the key of D (C♯, E, G, B♭ with an appoggiatura A♭ for an A♮ heard in the high tremolos). The second case is to be understood as an extension of the fifteenth harmonic of C, namely B, which the ear tends to confuse with the sixteenth, the fourth octave above the fundamental, a dissonance which acquires interest from the combination of the penetrating timbre of the piccolo with that of the fundamental C sounding solemnly in the lower strings.

An eloquent example of the inadvisability of interpreting academically some of the most realistic harmonies of Richard Strauss occurs in the famous opening of his Alpine Symphony where all the instruments of the orchestra slide simultaneously through all the notes of the descending B-flat minor scale. At a given moment, then, all the notes of the scale are sounding together. Is this to be interpreted as a chord of the thirteenth, built not in thirds but in successive seconds? Not at all. It simply corresponds to the very ordinary effect on the piano when the foot holds down the pedal. The value of Strauss's harmonies on occasions like those cited does not consist in the tonal relationships of the various chords with each other; it is not really a question of chords with a functional value determined by the dissonances which they contain. Such dissonances have a value in and for themselves; they are percussive dissonances with an expression which has its function in realizing the composer's intention in the same way that noise, cacophony, the wind machine are used for the painting of effects which have nothing to do with harmony proper.

Something analogous occurs in Strauss's writing. The complexity is often great but it is necessary to decide whether it is a question of real contrapuntal effects or simply of a complication of lines designed to achieve a special idea of confusion. Every sonorous moment, seen as it were in the microscope or in slow motion, may assume the form of a chord, a group of lines in sharp dissonance. But that is not what we are dealing with: the effect is exclusively mechanical as in the case of the passing chromaticisms or pianistic chromaticisms in Chopin; in Strauss it assumes the technique of rapid modulations, alterations, and appoggiaturas of every kind. Nevertheless, his feeling for the basic tonality is so sure that it admits of the superposition of as many tumultuous agglomerations as suits his purpose as musical painter or dramatist. Oswald Spengler is correct when he says that this type of music which, strictly speaking, began to develop with the first romantic composers but which appears most fully defined in Strauss and continues with the impressionists, actually has more to do with painting than with music. This truth becomes especially evident in comparing the poems, symphonies, or operas of Strauss with *Tristan*. What is expression in *Tristan* is painting in Strauss or, if you wish, what in Wagner is the expression of dramatic emotion is in Strauss the expression of the external situation. Even when it is not a question of wholly descriptive passages such as the flocks of sheep, the windmills, the candle with its dying radiance in Death and Transfiguration but of a human situation, Strauss still prefers to transcribe its external character, not with a musical passage expressive of the emotion (as for example, the first measures of *Tristan*) but rather by an instrumental imitation of the gesture, a gesture of anger, of sarcasm, of mockery. In this respect, Strauss is closer to the worthy Kuhnau and his Biblical Sonatas than to immediate predecessors such as Wagner. Strauss, like Rameau, can imitate the bleating of sheep or the cackle of hens but Rameau immediately uses this imitative jest as a motive for an abstract development whereas Strauss is satisfied when he has finished his pretty picture.

What distinguishes the motives in Wagner's art is their mobility, their capacity for symphonic development. The motive in Schumann varies little. The *idée fixe* of Berlioz undergoes scarcely any change in passing to the symphonism of Liszt, who stands midway between Berlioz and Wagner. The motive becomes transformed to the point of extinction in Mahler. In Strauss it is almost congealed as is sometimes the case in those motives of Wagner which represent specific objects (like Siegfried's sword, the casket containing the magic potions in *Tristan*). Strauss takes occasion to modify the orchestral and harmonic background against which the motive appears by changing the orchestral color and by dynamic variations, somewhat as the stage director manipulates the lighting with a shift from a sinister blue to an exultant red, from a mysterious half-light to the brilliance of midday. It is the brasses, above all, which carry out these tricks of orchestral phantasmagoria in Strauss, in contrast with the tremolos in the strings, in *fff* or *ppp*, and the subtle sonorities of the wood winds.

When Strauss makes use of this method of composition in his works for the stage, he need only let himself be led by the plot. Nevertheless he prefers to prolong the moments of climax in extended instrumental sections, rounding out the formal construction of the work with a sure hand. When the stage is lacking, the structural basis of the music must of necessity be strengthened; for this Strauss need not rack his brains to invent new forms, like Schumann or Liszt; he need only adapt the sonata form, the rondo, or the variation form. If the basic foundation of the form and the tonality is classical, his rhythmic organization will match it. The vivacity and eloquence of his treatment of rhythm is, indeed, very remarkable and, whenever he finds the slightest opportunity to treat the rhythm in dance fashion, he does so in a masterly way.

His inventive processes, however, do not show so much subtlety. Once he has found the gesture motive, his ingenuity lies mostly in his technique. Thanks to his powerful technique, Strauss is able to present us with a picture which is extraordinarily original in its line and color and which has, at the same time, a foundation solidly based on classical principles. This procedure is one of cold calculation (a method which Strauss strongly upholds) with nothing impulsive about it as in Berlioz. In all this, Strauss displays a shrewd choice of method for the audience perceives the effect desired by the composer and, at the same time, feels the constructive robustness of the work. In a sense, this is the technique of the designer of stage settings; a broad musical brush sketches a transitory background against which Strauss projects the dominating motives by means of appropriate instrumentation. The impressionist painters, such as Claude Monet, proceed in this fashion: spaces of a vague coloring against which stand out vivid touches of geranium, of chrome yellow, of violet.

If he finds a ready-made motive, Strauss does not hesitate to make use of it. He uses *"Funiculi Funicula"* just as Albéniz inserts *"La Filadora"* in his rhapsody Catalonia. On a certain occasion, the Spanish conductor Joseph Lasalle, returning in the same train with Richard Strauss after a performance of *Salome,* started to whistle repeatedly near a window where Strauss was sunning himself in a wayside station:

Strauss, who got the point, replied jokingly with the phrase:

Strauss understood what Lasalle meant and answered him. "Of course everybody knows that it's a motive from the *Barber!* [1] But with what a different expressive purpose! As great a difference, certainly, as that which exists between the initial motive of the Eroica Symphony and that of the overture of Mozart's youthful little opera *Bastien et Bastienne.*

The peril does not lie in the borrowing. The peril consists in the ease with which the method leads to a mixture of styles. Strauss's vigorous personality can avoid this pitfall. When the tendency develops, however, as in some of his present day successors, we find a stylistic potpourri, perhaps the most disagreeable thing of which a composer can be guilty.

[1] In Strauss, it is actually:

Chapter TEN

RICHARD STRAUSS was a man of his time. In the last decades of the century, the lofty ideals of the romantic artists had declined perceptibly. The halo which surrounded them as representatives of the spiritual qualities of the society in which they lived was fading and the prestige accorded to the artist shifted to those who had until then been less highly regarded: the scientist, the engineer, the doctor, and the professor inherited the almost prophetic aura with which romanticism had surrounded the artist. The sign and seal of the new age was the word "technique." Mechanical inventions satisfied the desires of a middle class which formerly had sought its highest spiritual satisfactions in literature and music.

This change in customs at the end of the nineteenth century was due to a new sense of convenience. Everything—from a culture made easy by handbooks and by popularized knowledge to distant journeys facilitated by tourist agencies—everything came within the reach of the middle-class pocketbook. Ease and comfort are words with a pleasing sound; their ingratiating tones effected the most profound and at the same time most superficial revolution attempted in the nineteenth century. Everything was simplified: lithographs and improved reproductions placed the masterpieces of painting within the reach of the middle class; amateur photography came to replace drawing and painting; the player piano, the phonograph, and later the radio eliminated the tedious study of that indispensable and cumbersome piece of musical furniture in the corner of every respectable parlor—the piano. The arts, the great ennoblers of the spirit on the lofty plane of the romantic ideal, became, after the middle of the century, the polite accomplishments of young ladies and gentlemen of good society. It was not long before even the small effort these attainments required was obviated by the marvels of technique. Mechanical facility at low cost!

Two phenomena brought about by this state of affairs developed side by side: on the one hand an easy-going art arose, ready to adapt itself to new demands; on the other, as a reaction, societies of a more or less private nature appeared, organized by people of means and good will who were anxious to preserve the former prestige of art and for whom certain artists continued to produce without making unworthy compromises. Thus, art became not a function of society but a counterfunction to it. This art was no longer impelled by the advancing movement of society but, on the contrary, became an art which, indifferent or hostile to contemporary tendencies, turned its eyes to the past. All reaction is born in this way. Thus, Brahms in Germany and César Franck in France, despite their fundamental differences, fostered an art that declared itself against the ethics of Wagnerian symphonism and that proclaimed the necessity of abiding by pure form.

At the end of the century, music had lost the symbolic character in which had been concentrated the loftiest impulses of society. Neither the heroic qualities of Beethoven, the lyricism of Schubert, the melancholy intensity of Schumann, the growing dramaticism in instrumental terms from Berlioz to Wagner, nor the richly musical virtuosity from Chopin to Liszt found place in this new age of cheapness, comfort, and ease. French grand opera, the last art to sum up the spiritual atmosphere in which it was born, had a vulgar successor in the operetta, that descendant of the French *opéra comique* and of the German *Singspiel.*

The last great artistic-social creation of the nineteenth century, the symphonic concert, continued to maintain its prestige because its dynamic social character enriched it, as it matured, with all the perfections of the orchestral art; the art of composition for a large orchestra (still of so recent achievement) and that of conducting developed hand in hand. In addition, the public concert offered a variety of fare on the same program and became increasingly popular while, through innumerable reproductive devices, it reached every kind of audience, from the provinces to the boulevards. Governments, through their ministries of fine arts, subsidized symphony orchestras. Thus, the idea of organized culture arose simultaneously with that of organized economy.

Musicians for whom the symphony orchestra and the symphony concert became the normal medium of expression reacted in various ways against the increasing vulgarity of life. Two of these ways constituted the most elevated aspects of the art of the time and were likewise those embraced by the artists of greatest stature in the first decade of our century. One form of this reaction consisted in enriching the expressive material without, however, departing from the level of comprehension of the average public. The other consisted precisely in leaving that level and in appealing exclusively to a more "refined" audience. Both stood on common ground in that they spoke eloquently to the conscience of their respective circles.

In the aesthetic medium of poematic symphonism, we observe the realism of Richard Strauss. In that rarer atmosphere which prefers the refinement of the material elements of sonority and the type of sensations thereby expressed, we have Claude Debussy. Last, in the field of the theater we find an accentuation of the effects and the emotional situations derived from the Russian theater of Tchaikovsky and Mussorgsky. This, becoming united with the intensification of effect in Strauss's operas, leads to the lyric sensuality of Giacomo Puccini, and culminates in the tendency known as verism. Such fondness for reality, a convention peculiar to the later years of the nineteenth century, corresponds directly to realism in literature from Flaubert to Zola and the Goncourts. Simultaneously, the rich idealism expressed in exquisite subtleties of accent and of sensation corresponds to similar moments in the poetry of Baudelaire, Verlaine, Mallarmé, and their most distinguished followers, particularly in France: for it happens that this newly engendered aspect of musical art is, above all, French.

Before we examine the new aspect which the art of music acquires at the moment the twentieth century makes its appearance, we must first consider a musical period in France, a knowledge of which is indispensable to the full comprehension of this new art. The period prior to the art of Claude Debussy is that of the formalist symphony of César Franck and corresponds, chronologically, in French music to that of Johannes Brahms in Germany. Why, then, did we not consider it at the same time that we alluded to the symphony of Brahms and its return (or desire to return) to Beethovenian forms?

The reason is simple. César Franck did not wish to return to a state of things where form, tonality, and instrumentation would closely resemble Beethoven's symphonism. Franck desired to continue further the lines of this symphonism but not in an expressivistic sense like Bruckner nor in the poematic sense of Mahler after him nor yet in a direction that would lead to dissolution and vagueness of form. Nevertheless, he wanted to retain the human expressiveness won for music after Beethoven. Franck, then, wished to include both features in his symphonism: that which would carry him beyond Beethoven along the path indicated by romanticism and that which would preserve him from the excesses of German postromanticism which had announced themselves with *Tristan*. Franck therefore sought a middle way. Yet two other considerations moved him: he could not remain insensible to Wagnerian art and, indeed, appropriated those of its elements he could assimilate without risk to his individuality; on the other hand, he was profoundly national, if not for his interest in picturesque color, then certainly in the intimate essentials of his art. His successive productions show how his criterion proceeded to define itself after experiments of one kind and another until there begin to appear works of a typically Franckian nature: the *Rédemption,* a poematic symphony; *Les Éolides,* a symphonic poem; the Quintet in A Minor; Symphonic Variations; Sonata for Piano and Violin; Symphony in D Minor; Prelude, Chorale and Fugue; Prelude, Aria and Finale (between 1884 and 1888); Quartet; and Three Chorales for Organ (1889-90).

César Franck, by birth a Belgian and thus a native of a country which, like Franck's art, lay between Germany and France, was ten years older than Brahms and died seven years before him. *Les Éolides* dates from the same year as the first performance of Brahms's First Symphony (1876). The Quintet (1878-79) is approximately contemporary with the three quartets of Brahms, the last of which was written in 1875. Franck's Symphony in D Minor dates from 1886, the year of Brahms's Fourth and last symphony. Bruckner, who began his career as composer late, like Franck, gave the first performance of his First Symphony in 1868 at a time when the Belgian musician had only composed his first pages. Bruckner still continued to produce after the death of both masters and Mahler, whose First Symphony dates from 1891 (the year after Franck's death), followed immediately.

Amid the bland harmonies and the disdain for counterpoint in which French musical romanticism was born, heir to the amiable muses of the *opéra comique* who had not yet lost either their chastity or their decorum, there existed in France a high regard for the classical concept of form and this spirit was Franck's only master. Anton Reicha had been made professor of counterpoint and fugue in the Paris Conservatory in 1818; Franck entered this class in 1834 at the age of twelve. Reicha had just published his treatise on *L'art du compositeur dramatique* (1833); some years before had appeared his *Traité de haute composition musicale* (1824-26), which still merits a glance from composers of our own day. In addition, Reicha had a tremendous prestige on account of his friendships with Haydn, with Beethoven, and with other famous composers in Vienna during the first decade of the century. The contact with Reicha, then, must have seemed to Franck like coming into contact with Beethoven himself. Connoisseurs of Franck have seized this early period in Franck's life as an excellent opportunity to proclaim him (although obviously not for this reason only) the true successor of Beethoven. This inheritance is still in litigation since it is claimed with equal insistence by the partisans of Brahms as well as those of Bruckner and even of Mahler: some from the point of view of form, others from that of meaning. Enthusiasts aside, it must be admitted that the art of the symphony, which had declined both in form and meaning after Schubert, did not revive until the works of these four masters. Each in his own way gave the post-Beethoven art of the symphony a period of real eminence. The four symphonies of Brahms and the single one of Franck, though contemporary in date, are not so in meaning for Franck's looks forward to the following age while those of Brahms stand inflexible, as monuments commemorating a past art.

It is not with the symphonies of Brahms that César Franck's Symphony or his chamber works are to be compared but with the music of the post-Wagnerian Viennese symphonists. Such a comparison will show that, while in the latter there is an unrestrained amplification of the form, there is in Franck's work a notably successful attempt to adhere to a traditional conciseness while using entirely new material, neither poematic nor expressivistic but truly symphonic. The symphonism of Franck's ideas appears in the D Minor Symphony and in the Sonata for Piano and Violin, in the Quartet and in the Quintet, and it results from the use of motives that are capable of being developed organically.

Symphonism, it should be repeated, means "the organic growth of a motive" organized in a satisfactory form. This process, realized in classical times in the sonata form, is based essentially on the interplay among the three consonant tonalities whose fundamentals stand in the relationship of tonic-subdominant-dominant, that is, a relationship between keys situated at the distance of a fourth and a fifth. We have seen how, beginning with Chopin, this consonant relationship came to be extended in a similar sense between two keys at the distance of a third, although this was formerly considered as a change of mode between a major key and its relative minor, of which the tonic of the first is the mediant. It is also known that the Sonata in B Minor by Franz Liszt is constructed in relations of keys at a distance of the third, even to establishing a "chord of tonalities" of five tones which thus form a tonal complex similar to that which the chord of the ninth has within it (G, B, D, F♯, A♯). The tonal combinations in the structure of Franck's Quartet, his most carefully worked-out composition from this point of view, answer a similar desire for tonal amplification now not as simple harmony but as a tonal complex upon the ninth, a process that seems to reveal the significance of acoustico-aesthetic evolution.

As regards arrangement of the motives, this Quartet of Franck is likewise very interesting and recalls in part the sonata by Liszt already mentioned, where an initial theme (G minor) intervenes between the development of the principal motives (B minor) producing, then, an ample middle section in D major. Calling the opening of Franck's Quartet (D major) "theme *x*," as does d'Indy, we find it again in the middle section (F minor), after the exposition of the principal motives (D minor and F major). This theme *x*, in a *fugato* development in B-flat minor (as in the *allegro energico* of Liszt's sonata), leads to the development of the principal motives (G minor—B-flat major) and the restatement begins to lead to B major and D major, in which the theme *x* serves for the final peroration just as in the case of the introductory motive used by Liszt.

D'Indy considers the structure of the quartet a sonata form inlaid in a lied form. Liszt's sonata could be understood as a lied form inserted into the sonata form. Nevertheless, Liszt seems further than Franck from the classical model of the sonata which, with essential differences, is the basis for the Sonata for Violin and Piano and the Symphony in D Minor, as we shall presently see. Both musicians understood the thematic extension and the tonal dynamism of the classical sonata in the same way but the variation (the grand Beethovenian variation) like the fugue has in Franck an abstract feeling while in Liszt it is poetic; it would be dangerous, nevertheless, to draw too fine a line of distinction between the one case and the other.

In this way, it has become a commonplace to call the initial motive of the Symphony in D Minor (it consists of three notes, minor second followed by a diminished fourth, a favorite procedure of Franck's) the theme of faith or the *motif de la croyance* as his disciple Guy Ropartz christened it. A religious interpretation of music noble in line and movement is too easy and, at most, the Symphony of Franck simply reflects his "seraphic soul" as Alexis de Castillon put it (a more generous judgment than that suffered by Bruckner whose detractors attribute his mysticism to mental weakness and imbecility elevated to the category of "motive power"). The *motif de la croyance* pulsates everywhere in the Symphony but sometimes it is mysterious in the lower registers with a doubtful note like the interrogatory *"Muss es sein?"* of Beethoven's Quartet in F, Op. 135. But the doubt is resolved in triumphant affirmation as soon as the diminished fourth becomes a perfect fourth. Wagnerian symbolism of harmonic expression appears here in all its glory.

Franck's Symphony, falling as it does between two works so typical of his genius as the Violin Sonata and the Quartet, shares their structural characteristics, both in its thematic formation—Franck submits little motives to the detailed working-out process of the laboratory—and in its tonal leading, which is much simpler than in the Quartet but which seems to anticipate the latter. It is important to examine both these details of procedure, so Franckian in nature, since, in contrast to the Brahmsian reaction, they represent the most advanced phase after Beethoven and Liszt of the transformation of musical form.

The symphonies of Beethoven are planned according to two systems: one, the harmonic-rhythmic, derives the entire structure of the opening movement from a short initial motive; this is the case in the E flat symphony, is especially true of the C minor, and is found in general in all the symphonies with odd numbers. The even-numbered symphonies reflect Beethoven's other system of planning a symphony, a concept that bases its free melodic commentary on a cantabile phrase presented at the beginning of the movement. This double point of view existed in the classical Viennese school; for example, the first type is found in Mozart's G Minor Quintet (K. 516) while the second type is found in his E flat symphony (K. 543), where the melodic exposition of various asymmetrical passages is continued but not specifically developed, with the result that the initial melody is actually heard again only in the recapitulation. H. C. Colles says very neatly that Mozart in one case "sets out" in search of "beauty" and, in the other, "starts from beauty" in search of new adventures. In Franck, we find both points of view combined so that the first motive, *de la croyance* with its three questioning notes, is followed by different melodic passages which, in combination, constitute the exposition section of the symphony. So varied and abundant are these passages that, as Colles points out, it is merely arbitrary and conventional to look for a "second idea" in the Franck Symphony.

In short, the fundamental idea remains undeveloped, forever concealing its innermost nature. This feeling of unfulfillment produced in the first movement finds compensation by the transplanting of the thematic nucleuses of the opening movement to the motives of the succeeding sections; the concluding movements are thus united in a kind of thematic ring which exponents of this school have labeled the *cyclical method*. The system may be as complicated as desired. Franck's Sonata for Piano and Violin, like his Symphony, is based on three motives which constitute, to use d'Indy's words, "its melodic framework." The Quintet and the Quartet are based on four cyclical themes. If the expressive units are as clear and well defined as in the Symphony, the listener can easily follow their sequels, tracing them throughout a lengthy fugue and variation. On the other hand, if the listener cannot identify them on their first appearance, he can still feel the thematic unity of the music and the consequent solidity of the form. The unsystematized cyclical principle is as old as the sonata form and is present in Beethoven;[1] furthermore, the *idée fixe* and the leitmotiv are simply aspects of poematic symphonism where this same struggle for unity seeks its goal through dramatic as well as thematic unity, while in Franck it is purely musical and abstract. The method has great attraction for those composers who like to write more or less complicated combinations of their themes and variations. It leads to music that is as pre-eminently objective as that of Bach himself; but it has its risks, equal to those in the old contrapuntal music, of becoming simply a trial of skill, a game of musical solitaire, and this charge may be brought, if not against Franck, certainly against some of his disciples.

The cyclical method is not limited to this kind of marquetry work in the interplay of motives; it also has a tonal aspect. Both features are combined in the fugue where the motive and the countermotive pursue each other in a game of hide-and-seek through the tonalities of the tonic and the dominant. Now we know that the interplay of tonalities can be much more extensive, so that we can imagine one of the motives modulating throughout the entire field included in the sharpened keys (in other words, by ascending from fifth to fifth) while the other modulates in the flattened keys (descending in fifths). Franck called these modulatory notes "tonal poles" which, by a simple mechanical device, seem to lead to bright tonalities when the harmonic

[1] For example, in groups of compositions like the quartets Op. 130, 131, 132, and 133.

progression ascends by fifths (by the dominants) or to dark tonalities when it descends by fifths (by the subdominants). The two poles of the Quintet carry out a very simple design: the bright pole is F major with its tendency toward the sharpened keys of the dominants; the dark pole is F minor and descends by the flattened keys of the subdominants. In the Quartet, the poles are D major-minor and F major-minor with similar manipulations. In the Symphony, however, these maneuvers are carried out with greater clarity than in any other work. As is well known, the exposition in the classical sonata is repeated more or less integrally because the composer thought that the listener would not otherwise be able to fix the elements of the exposition firmly enough in his mind to understand their treatment in the succeeding development section.

At the beginning of the nineteenth century, the habit of listening to classical works brought about the omission (on the part of the performers) of the repetition of the exposition, in the same way that the *da capo* was omitted in the minuet. Franck, however, felt that his play of combinations was so extended as to require that the exposition section be heard twice, but each time with different tonal effects. In the Quartet, the re-exposition draws the two motives to the tonic, as in the recapitulation of the ordinary sonata-allegro movement. In the Symphony, the situation is different. The first exposition is in D minor; the second is in F, the mediant of the tonic key. As Franck explained to his pupils, the Symphony is really in two keys, D and F, and the double exposition is necessary in order to permit the emphasis of each tonal pole separately; this interchange continues throughout the entire work with the final triumph of D major–F major over D minor–F minor. The pole D leads to tonalities greatly altered by sharps, such as B major; the pole F moves to tonalities greatly altered by flats, like B-flat minor. If there really is such a thing as tonal color and if certain tonalities exercise a definite effect on the composer's inspiration (Paul Bekker has admirably shown the different effect of keys like C minor and E flat in Beethoven), the tonalities—D, F, B♭, F♯, and B—were undoubtedly favorites with Franck.

The instrumentation of Franck's symphony presents certain peculiarities such as his use of the English horn and the bass clarinet—this last as a bass to the two usual clarinets and the former as a singing instrument in combination with the harp. Franck's use of the cornet-à-pistons as one of his brass choir has been criticized; the instrument undoubtedly produces a rather coarse effect but Franck's reason for using it has been attributed to his admiration for such writers of comic opera as Monsigny, Dalayrac, Grétry, and Méhul. The cornet-à-pistons was common in theatrical orchestrations and Franck kept it, apparently for this reason.

Among the French symphonies contemporary with that of Franck belongs the Third Symphony of Saint-Saëns. His first two follow closely the classical pattern (a procedure regarded by symphonists of the time either as an advanced exercise in composition or, on the other hand, as a risky undertaking which could easily lead to disaster if one strayed too far from the precepts of the contemporary schools). Saint-Saëns' Symphony in C Minor displays tonal adventures which moved the composer to dedicate his work to Franz Liszt, as if to designate that worthy as his model. The tonal plan, which some writers such as d'Indy consider shocking, is wholly logical and marks the use, later very frequent, of the Neapolitan sixth as the representative of a cognate tonality. The four movements form in their succession a kind of grand cadence: tonic minor–subdominant major to tonic minor–tonic major, in which the chord of the Neapolitan sixth assumes the function of the subdominant. The instrumental novelty in this symphony of Saint-Saëns is his use of the organ. As regards the union of its movements in two and two, the explanation may be found in the tonal plan pointed out above.

Among later French symphonists Vincent d'Indy, Ernest Chausson, and Guy Ropartz belong to the school of Franck; others, like Albéric Magnard, do not. Paul Dukas must be included in the first group. He like d'Indy wrote works tinged with picturesque coloring, sometimes with popular motives or again with an explicit program. Nevertheless, the constructive element predominates throughout over that poematicism which may lend a certain color to the music but does not affect the solid formalist concept of the work.

D'Indy, like Saint-Saëns, wrote three symphonies, the first and last of popular inspiration. The First, in G, Op. 25 (1886), for orchestra with piano, is based on a French mountain song which, coming as it does from the region of the Cévennes mountains, gives the work its title, *Symphonie Cévenole.* To the Third is given the title *Sinfonia Brevis de Bello Gallico,* Op. 70, and from its dates (1916-18), may be deduced to what struggle it alludes. The Second Symphony, in B flat, Op. 57 (1903), follows the traditional form, constructed on two cyclical themes of a decidedly chromatic character which could be called Wagnerian.

The Wagnerian influence, in fact, had already appeared in Franck's first poems, and notably in the chromaticism of *Les Éolides,* while that of Liszt came from direct contact with the great virtuoso in Brussels. Franck, then in his twenties, composed his first trios and submitted them for criticism. The Fourth, Op. 2, is dedicated to Liszt who played it occasionally in Weimar around the year 1853, the year of the Sonata in B Minor. As early as 1842, Franck was not yet what was later on called a Wagnerite; but d'Indy tells us how enthusiastically Franck admired the great German and how he had the habit of "warming" his imagination by reading from his scores. This influence of Wagner constantly increased in France, in symphony and chamber music as well as in that of the theater. With sincerity, if somewhat over-enthusiastically, d'Indy describes the influence of Wagner on French musicians which reached its culmination with the war of 1870 and coincided with the founding, in 1871, of the Société Nationale de Musique, devoted primarily to the cultivation of chamber music. Furthermore, d'Indy points out that French opera of the second half of the century—Thomas, Gounod, Massé and Bizet—is contemporary with the Wagnerian influence: "a beneficial influence" felt by practically all the composers whose chief works belong to the years after the midpoint of the century. In his brief study, *Richard Wagner et son influence sur l'art musical français* (Paris, 1930), d'Indy published a long list of works in which this "happy influence" appears to him indubitable: a list which begins with *Psyché, Les Éolides,* and the Symphony of Franck and ends with *Pelléas et Mélisande* of Claude Debussy. D'Indy obviously exaggerates. Yet he does not hesitate to include in the sphere of this influence Lalo, Saint-Saëns, Duparc, Benoit, d'Indy himself in most of his symphonic compositions, Chausson, Guy Ropartz, G. M. Witkowski, Albéric Magnard, and Paul Dukas; among works for the theater included in the last "thirty years in the development of the Wagnerian impulse in France," d'Indy mentions the operas of Reyer, Chabrier, Alfred Bruneau, Magnard, d'Indy, Charpentier, Chausson, Dukas, Pierre de Bréville, Ropartz, and also Debussy.

In point of fact, the symphonies and chamber music of Chausson and Ropartz follow very closely, sometimes even too insistently, the procedures of their master, Franck. Even more than his one classical symphony, Chausson's Concerto for piano, violin, and string quartet has interest for the seriousness of its aim and the minute care of its treatment. The single symphony of Guy Ropartz is based on a Breton chorale, elaborately treated. As for the four symphonies of Magnard, they are of a more classical style but are ponderously written and heavily chromatic. The shadow of "father Franck" falls on the two brothers, Joseph and Léon Jongen, natives of his own birthplace (Liège, 1873 and 1884). The older one achieved an important place among Belgian composers. Although both wrote, like everybody else at that time, poematic music, Joseph Jongen owes his reputation chiefly to his chamber music which, despite his serene and well-considered ideas, does not escape a heaviness of material which seems to be habitual with the pupils of the famous school.

While the treatment is again very precise and the construction carefully thought out, although lacking in ideas of commensurate originality, the material is very different in the only Symphony (in C major, 1896) of Paul Dukas, as well as in that composer's single Sonata for Piano (1900). Both works, although not cyclical, have a unity of tone and of ideas which connects them in their external aspect to that method. The tonal plan is also related to that of Franck in its progress by subdominants, which seems appropriate to

Dukas' music of this type with its somber thoughtfulness, its measured movement, and a sober quality which is not relieved by upward flights at the dominants. Whatever may be the merit of these works (and they are, undoubtedly, among the most robust and most successfully realized French compositions in abstract form), their author will be best remembered as the composer of *L'Apprenti-Sorcier* (1897) and *La Péri* (1907). No matter how brilliant the orchestration nor how vivid the imagination in its flashes of intense color, it is his preoccupation with structure, with the inner solidity demanded by the complex harmonic treatment which absorbs Dukas above every other consideration, not only in these last-named compositions but also in his opera *Ariane et Barbe-Bleue* (1907). The necessity of conforming to a strict design is a great advantage when the harmonic material tends to slip through the fingers of the artist who tries to mold it. It is a danger clearly visible in *Ariane* and one over which the symphonic works of Dukas show better control. It is especially true where the imagination has such free play as in the *Apprenti-Sorcier* yet here the cleanness of the motives and a realism comparable to that of Strauss, gives clarity to the musical texture which maintains the interest and hides the somewhat diffuse and rhetorical treatment of this symphonic scherzo. Dukas has left us in this work an eloquent example of French art immediately prior to the period of Debussy.

The Wagnerianism which d'Indy attributes to Dukas is, in point of fact, but a pallid Germanic romanticism. His first works are concert overtures in pre-Liszt style and find inspiration all the way from Shakespeare (*Le Roi Lear,* 1883) to Schiller's *Götz;* but these works are no more Teutonic than the overture to *Polyeucte* (1891) is French. It is a period of transition in French art. If we want to find a definite boundary line, d'Indy has indicated it in *Pelléas.* Yet Claude Debussy, *musicien français,* had already unmistakably affirmed his national spirit in the final decades of the century of romanticism. Prior to the above-mentioned composers, romanticism had been propagated under the Wagnerian aegis. But a renewal of style, taste, and feeling occurred. It was the age of *le renouveau* and these social considerations of style, taste, and feeling required specific and adequate musical means of expression. It was Claude Debussy who provided them.

The gentle spirit of Gabriel Fauré, at once so musical and so poetic, provides a transition from the dying splendors of Wagnerianism to the delicate tints of the dawning French impressionism. Fauré is essentially (except for his songs and piano compositions and for his less important music for the theater) a composer of music in the closed forms. Yet in him, as in so many musicians of his country in the following generations, his music transcends the limits of the pure forms with inflections, which are imbued with a unique quality—a spirit which, from the beginnings of romantic music, may be described unhesitatingly as the spirit of poetry. In Fauré, the poetic and the musical are so fused into one substance that it is difficult to decide whether he is more musical in his songs (to texts of Verlaine, for example, or Samain, as most characteristic of his inspiration) or more poetic in his quartets. But if in his chamber music Fauré relates himself to a type of inspiration close to German romanticism; in his songs, an art of noble lineage in the country beyond the Rhine, Fauré creates an art entirely French destined to endow the music of his country with pages of the most beautiful and characteristic French inspiration, comparable to the lied in German music. The chanson in France has a distinguished tradition for it formed a whole section of French music in the days when medieval polyphony felt the first vivifying breath of the Renaissance; Frenchmen never left off composing songs, of which there exist many fine, although little-known, examples from Berlioz to Delibes. But the chanson of Fauré, as prelude to those which Debussy was to compose on texts of the same favorite poets, created a new art for French music and, indeed, for world music.

In this chapter our interest is primarily with Fauré as a composer of music in the closed forms. But, from this time on, French music of the purest form is music perfumed with poetry and in the case of Fauré as with his contemporaries and successors, it is almost impossible to speak of form as such; the general and constant keynote in all of them is that emotion which penetrates to the root of their harmonies, which seeks in their modal inflections an evocative accent of something evanescent, of a *parfum impérissable* which continues to breathe from the sensitive pages belonging to this new age of French music.

Verlaine is the poet of Fauré. He is also the poet of Debussy, with his poetry's delicate orchestration in which

> . . . nuance alone joins
> dream to dream and flute to horn.

It would be sufficient to compare the music to which Fauré has set the immortal pages of Verlaine with that which Debussy wrote to pages of the same poet in order to trace the direction of French music in this period of transition: the music of Fauré shows gray tints that often border on inexpressiveness. Something of the same sort occurs in certain chromatic turns of phrase and that which was a mere hint in César Franck becomes something quite obvious in Fauré: senility, the babbling of the dotard. The chamber music of Fauré is also not exempt from these moments of emptiness; yet the quartet (1925), the two piano quartets (1879, 1886), the two quintets (1906, 1921), the trio, Op. 120, and the sonatas for violin are the best chamber music in this period of transition; works of serene equilibrium but of thoroughly robust construction which mark the final decline of the postromantic art of chamber music just as the numerous barcaroles and nocturnes are faint echoes of the piano music of another day. They seemed to await the final extinguishing of the last gleams of the romantic genius in order to be reborn in another form: a new form yet one closely bound to that of Fauré. And, from what we know of his symphony (in D minor, 1884, unpublished, and perhaps destroyed), it seems to have been a kind of meeting point of the inspiration of Mendelssohn with that of Saint-Saëns.

In the warm and perfumed atmosphere of Fauré's genius matured talents as diverse as those of Ravel, Aubert, Koechlin, Schmitt, and Roger-Ducasse, all of them stronger and more vigorous as regards form than their master yet no less suggestive nor exquisite; clear examples of that indefinable union between the specifically musical and the unmistakably poetic. This typical union, if the typical exists in the music of today, reaches to the younger generation: Jacques Ibert (1890) was a direct disciple of Fauré but he was also a pupil of the sober Gédalge, and his feeling for form assures a well-knit coherence not only in his chamber works but in his poematic compositions like *Escales* (1922) and the symphonic scherzo *Féerique* (1925). A strong feeling for construction is the dominant characteristic in a musician like Arthur Honegger (1892); he finds inspiration not only in poetic or dramatic episodes but also in others of a more modern and perhaps more questionable type, such as a game of Rugby, skating, or the noisy rhythm of the locomotive—all of which may be reduced to mechanical formulas conspicuous more for their rigid construction than for their poetry. Ibert and Honegger have composed numerous operas and ballets. Later on, we shall return to Honegger in connection with his experiments in atonal texture.

Like Honegger, Darius Milhaud (1892) was a member of the one time famous group of *Les Six* (*Les Six* of Paris like the "Mighty Five" of St. Petersburg). If, on the one hand, he may be mentioned here for his predilection for the closed forms (albeit strongly imbued with a sense of the picturesque and the dramatic), he must still be considered elsewhere as the champion of polytonality. Georges Auric (1899), another eminent member of the group, is above all a musician with a lively and subtle plastic imagination, a composer of ballets. The delicate orchestral pages of Germaine Tailleferre (1892), like those of Francis Poulenc (1899), derive their strength, happily enough, more from the innate power of a deeply musical temperament than from an academic purpose. The unfortunate Pierre-Octave Ferroud (1900-36) perhaps showed most strikingly the power to achieve well-knit forms; to this same ambition aspired Georges Migot (1891) and Roland Manuel (1891) without possessing the same power to achieve it; yet, beyond that, they undoubtedly possess the plastic and poetic quality which so closely united young French musicians with their colleagues in the arts of painting and literature. Migot is a painter while Roland Manuel is an excellent critic and distinguished man of letters; like Milhaud and the rest, they represent the spirit of France, of that France between two wars.

Chapter
ELEVEN

HOW CAN we account for a reform, a reaction like that of Brahms which offered, after countless experiences in every kind of beauty, a symphonism possessing the externals of Beethoven's art yet lacking its essence?

Romanticism, from its birthplace in the north, had always looked toward distant sunny lands with their palm trees silhouetted against intense blue skies. This was, to be sure, only one aspect of romanticism; but this irrepressible yearning for the south, for Romanic lands, was simply the final phase in the nineteenth century (a phase which political aspects of the twentieth confirm), of that legendary "march to the Mediterranean" which, from remote times, swept the blond barbarians of the north toward the lands of dark-eyed Venuses. Musical history, since the time when music began to acquire characteristics which may be termed specifically European, shows a continuous flow of inventions from the north which either were attenuated in the warm meridional sunshine or else flowed back again, enriched with more glowing accents. The Renaissance madrigal is the final Latin form of the Nordic art of polyphony. Instrumental forms acquire their definitive shape in the Italian baroque. The austere contrapuntal style of the German masters of the north eyed, with a curiosity mingled with fear, the conquests of Italian melodism; and it finally succumbed to those charms with the death of Bach, who had himself been under the influence of the south. Handel, Telemann, Johann Christian Bach surrendered without a struggle to the Guelph Circe. Hasse and Mozart became essentially Italian composers.

This was the unquenchable, expansive attitude of those German artists who longed to soar beyond their native heath. Others, however, remained at home. Chorale, organ preludes and variations, counterpoint, canon, and fugue were their daily bread. Their thought tended toward the abstract, toward the introspection of their austere Protestantism in contrast to the baroque pomp of meridional Catholicism. The Reformation was a national bourgeois reaction. Brahms implied a new reaction, a new Reformation. Brahms's symphony is the unconscious revolt of traditional German music, of the north German, austere, abstract, intractable, against the invasion of sensuality in German music during the middle decades of the nineteenth century. This explains the nature of Brahms's success: clamorous in the north, indifferent in the south. His influence was practically nil in Spain and in Italy (although Martucci's return to the polyphonic style which had been lost in Italy is cited in connection with Brahms) while his music lacked relevance in France which had Franck as progressive champion of the great symphonic tradition. In England, Brahms's influence left fairly deep traces while in his own country it produced Max Reger, a musician who, although not sharing Brahmsian ideals, was to base his art on the specific values of texture.

The earliest influence of Brahms in England is due to Joachim who, especially after the founding of his famous quartet group (in 1869), contributed much throughout Europe to the development of the taste for chamber music. Two English musicians felt themselves profoundly affected from the first by the advance of Brahmsism: Hubert Parry (1848-1918) and C. V. Stanford (1852-1924). Together they constituted an entire stage in Victorian music and Joachim acknowledged their relationship to Brahms by including Stanford's viola quintet in the established repertoire of his group.

To understand adequately the character of English music in the last part of the century one must bear in mind two factors: (*a*) the peculiar tone which English music derived from the Handelian tradition along with its firm belief in the oratorio; (*b*) a belated appreciation of the very rich treasure of English popular song. Almost without exception, English composers have confided their finest inspiration to music for chorus, organ, and orchestra; this gives their repertory a unique character reflecting the influence of the established church on a musical society.

The aura of the neo-Germanic School reached England in the persons of Clara Schumann and Joseph Joachim. Parry was first to feel this influence united with that of Brahms. Stanford, for his part, showed in addition to this the attraction which the art of Verdi exercised on his vocal music. The latter influence like that of Brahms, however, was very new in England at that time; contemporary British tradition favored the placid, sexless freshness of Mendelssohn's music, adored by the English in the nineteenth century as they had adored that of Haydn and Handel in earlier times. The music of Elgar offers a delicate combination, a little cold, courtly, and wholly well bred, Mendelssohnian in essence and Brahmsian in the discretion and sobriety of its form. Thus, even when the music alludes to Mediterranean lands (In the South) or to their charming inhabitants (Dorabella) it is always formal and never permits great depth of emotion in the theme. Elgar's symphonies, likewise, have a faint perfume of the drawing room, an aristocratic air which made appropriate Elgar's appointment as Master of the King's Musick.

National flavor of a kind appears in Elgar and directly after him nationalism becomes naturalized in England. As compared with the music which this movement inspired in the rest of Europe, English musical nationalism is somewhat pallid and colorless yet it has a delicacy a little like the incomparable perfume of the English sweet pea. We have alluded in another place to the most significant English composers in this vein. A late echo of formal symphonism in England is to be found in the young composer, W. T. Walton (1902) who, through the teachings of Hugh Allen and E. J. Dent, is related to the Parry-Stanford period. Symphonic formalism takes on diverse aspects in the composers of northern Europe, in Scandinavia, as in those of Central Europe but among them, the Concerto for viola and orchestra by Walton shows the Brahmsian tradition most vivid and intact.

Among German composers with whom abstractness of ideas and a primary consideration of technical values of the sonorous texture assume the function of inspiration, Max Reger (1873-1916) must be mentioned before any other. *Satzkunst,* the art of "writing"—as the motive power which replaces former sources of inspiration whether the plastic and emotional ones of romanticism or the formal and abstract ones of the Brahmsian reaction—is today a commonplace; but it was not so to the same extent before Max Reger. Present day composers who choose "writing" for their muse may swear by Bach. Yet Bach would surely have rejected this homage for he knew better than anyone what a difference lies between the pedantic joiner of forced contrapuntal lines and the musician of profound emotions who, like himself, employs counterpoint as his idiom. The superiority of Reger over the scriveners of our day consists in the fact that the closely joined, carefully worked contrapuntal texture of his compositions is his true medium of expression, his characteristic idiom.

However, does Reger really express anything over and above his craftsmanship in his weaving of subtle tonal strands? We find in him a new phase which the music of our time assumes, whatever its derivation, if its creed or profession of faith consists in the assertion that specific values (harmony, texture, color) take precedence over every other consideration. This phase has come to be known as that of art for art's sake. Such a concept explains the decline in vitality and the slow anemia which has overtaken certain elements in the music of our day to end, after running its course, in a blind alley and in the conventions of a musical set or clique. While certain composers—for example, Igor Stravinsky, Bartók, or Manuel de Falla—are like the manipulators of engines which generate powerful energies, others, like Reger and his followers, develop a fruitless career over their writing desks. Theirs is not the field of artistic intuitions but of technical conventions.

In Reger we find the first of those numerous "returns to Bach" which occurred in the first decades of the twentieth century. While Reger confined his interest exclusively to the linear texture, disregarding Bach's powerful nervous rhythm, others tended to cultivate this rhythmic element and proceeded to emphasize as a principle what in Bach was merely accidental: his shocks and frictions or, again, his method of modulation which, while discreet within the limits of tonal security, can be continued along the path of indiscretion. It is scarcely worth while to mention here the truly guileless pretension regarding the bitonality that some present day composers claim to perceive in the real fugues or real canons of Bach's time and from which they think to proceed to what they call polytonality. Yet this pretension is curious for, if polytonality is the result of the pulsation between the motive in the tonic and the countermotive in the dominant, this result would have logically presented itself some two centuries earlier. What actually happened was exactly the contrary—namely, the real fugue fell into disuse before the ever stronger feeling for tonal harmony and instead the so-called "fugues within the key" (tonal answer) appeared in practice. The feeling of uncertainty conveyed by the real fugue through the too swift alternation of two tonalities at the distance of a fifth was a weakness derived from earlier times when the modal feeling was still strong (as in Bach himself); never for a moment did it predict the polytonality of twentieth century stamp.[1]

Reger was a composer who may be termed industrious rather than fecund. The reader will understand what I mean if he recalls the enormous production of Bach or of Mozart, always fresh, vital, apt (without denying passages in which the composer nodded) as compared to the prolific output, criticized even by his contemporaries, of a Telemann, for example. Reger's assiduousness was his inspiration. Objective music and the problems his writing continued to pose were his great joys as a composer and their solution, sometimes achieved, sometimes left incomplete, awoke certain specific emotions, substitutes for the usual forces which moved other composers. A poetic stimulus would have been incongruous in the robust simplicity of this Bavarian peasant, still less the contemplation of form. The form took shape by itself as Reger went on writing like one who weaves an interminable strand. Nevertheless, Reger was a musician by temperament and did not allow the form to run away with him, in contrast to those frequent cases of objective or neocontrapuntal works in which the composer ends by being thrown by his steed; or again, in which the work stops abruptly, without warning, as if the driver, his brakes gone, had crashed into a wall.

Consequently, Reger's musical production was copious. What is its meaning today? His works lie chiefly within the limits of chamber music: nu-

[1] See Chapter XXV.

merous trios, quartets, quintets, and duets for piano and violin which bear the title of sonatas. His first compositions were lieder and organ and piano pieces but in 1896, at the age of twenty-five, Reger produced his first *Klavier-Quintett,* now Op. 64. His last chamber work is a group of suites for solo violoncello, Op. 131, dating from 1915, shortly before his death. Midway appeared his works for orchestra, all of them composed within the space of five years, from the *Sinfonietta,* Op. 90, of 1905 to the Concerto for piano and orchestra, Op. 114, of 1910. Reger did not fail to pay his respects to the spirit of the age in a *Romantische Suite* but already the word *romantische* suggested an allusion to things past.

In his four symphonic poems inspired by the paintings of Boecklin, we find Reger in the odd position of one who wishes to "go along with the current," contributing his suite so as to be left in peace.[2] Boecklin is an artist capable of inspiring the most obscure symphonic digressions (as witness Jean Sibelius). Reger's temperament, furthermore, tended toward digression but not here nor in his *Vaterländische-Ouverture,* for in these works he is not in his polyphonic vein. His is an equivocal concept of polyphony, for, at a time when harmonic feeling presides over every formation, it has the meaning simply of "writing in various parts" upon harmonic procedures more or less solidly established. Paul Bekker aptly calls it "plurivocal homophony" and to justify this label, it is only necessary to compare the preludes, fugues, and chaconnes of Reger with the models of Bach.

Meanwhile, certain composers who had begun their careers at the height of nationalist music observed how this star was beginning to decline. They recognized this decline in the surrounding scene as well as in themselves so that they were led directly to a means of reaction and, thus, to an attempt to put to use their experiences as nationalist composers in forms by which tradition might accommodate itself to contemporary ideas. Among these composers, Alexander Konstantinovitch Glazounov furnishes the most eloquent example. He was an early pupil of Rimsky-Korsakov yet it was the later influence of Tchaikovsky which matured a talent of a facile, clear, attractive type, of indubitable individuality with features derived both from the nationalist group and from the more formal ones. Glazounov, who began his career as a prodigy at the age of seventeen (his First Symphony appeared in 1882; he was born in 1865), seemed to that famous Russian group to be the genius better fitted than any other of its members to carry their ideals to the highest fulfillment.

[2] Reger also payed homage to the most advanced romanticism of his day in transcribing for piano Penthesilea of Hugo Wolf and a number of his songs as well as some of Brahms and R. Strauss.

Born into a prosperous middle-class family, without economic cares and praised from adolescence, Glazounov's youthful period was like that of Felix Mendelssohn, to whose talent his own bears a certain resemblance. His early efforts were chamber works and the guidance of Balakirev was, for the moment, more notable than that of Rimsky. Balakirev's pride was evident in the fact that it was he who directed the first performance of the symphony, Op. 5, when Glazounov, in his student's uniform, took the applause. The tendencies of the "Mighty Five" triumphed brilliantly in the symphonic poem, Op. 13 (1885), based on the adventures of the legendary river pirate, Stenka Razin. This work, which had been preceded by some pages of oriental color, is indeed a good example of the triumph of nationalist ideas. However, in this very year, 1885, Glazounov began to see a great deal of Tchaikovsky in his country retreat, Kamenka. It would seem that the young Glazounov was deeply impressed by this environment which possessed the lofty atmosphere of criticism and discussion characteristic of European musical circles. Even though Glazounov's works after this date do not disclose a direct influence in their melodic or harmonic idiom nor in the form of his symphonies, this contact with Tchaikovsky nevertheless accentuated the eclecticism toward which Glazounov had been inclined from his earliest production.

The symphonic texture in Glazounov is lighter than that of Brahms and even than that of Tchaikovsky. Of its own choice, it moves within the lines of the classical symphony. On the other hand, Tchaikovsky's symphony took on a dramatic somberness which the clear, somewhat cool, spirit of Glazounov always eschewed. Glazounov's melodic material, while not deriving from the popular repertory, as in the most typical compositions of the "Five," nevertheless had an agreeable nationalist flavor a little like the first symphonies of Tchaikovsky. Indeed, Glazounov's symphonies seem to realize what Borodin tried to achieve in his Second Symphony (1887) and in his quartets too, which are structurally weaker than those of Glazounov although animated by the same spirit and turn of sentiment.

Glazounov wrote eight symphonies—the last two, Op. 77 and 83, in the first years of the present century. His command of the form is perfect as is his control of the orchestration, always clean and lucid, but perhaps his inspiration in these last works is not so fresh as in those of the middle period between 1890 and 1896. In all of them, as in his more colorful pieces, Glazounov is a conservative composer, like Mendelssohn in his day; his technique, however, never suffers any retrogression on that account. In 1899 he was appointed professor of orchestration in the Conservatory of St. Petersburg, of which he was director from 1909 to 1912. The soviet government conferred on him the highest honor it had invented for an artist: the title "Artist of the People," which Glazounov shared with Gorki and with very few others. In 1922 the new government reinstated him as director of the conservatory but not for long.

In the spring of 1928 an international congress was celebrated in Vienna in memory of Schubert, and Glazounov was sent there as delegate for the soviets. He never returned to Russia. The south had completely won him. He was not unknown there; in his youth he had traveled across Spain from Barcelona to Gibraltar in the radiant springtime of 1884, the year preceding his friendship with Tchaikovsky. Glazounov had then carried back to Russia a number of Spanish melodies, as Glinka had done forty years before. The Spanish or oriental music in Andalusian style of Glazounov appears in his ballet *Raymonda,* without important consequences. After living some years in Paris, Glazounov died in 1936 in an old hotel where Glinka once had lived.

Without denying that during the first decades of the second half of the last century there existed a marked conflict between the group with nationalist leanings and the Central European orientation of Tchaikovsky, it is certain that this divergence of ideals was less abrupt and striking than is ordinarily thought. We have seen that some of the composers of the "Five" essayed the writing of music in formal style while at the same time Tchaikovsky's national feeling is well defined and profound. In each case it is a question of proportion, which influences the treatment of the material and hence of the form. The symphony of Glazounov seemed to reach a point of equilibrium. With his works, the former cleavage disappeared and there is no longer need to talk of formal or nationalist composers.

Once the equilibrium is established, as occurred in Spain with Falla, the later composers—Taneiev, Scriabin, Rebikov, Rachmaninoff, Miaskovsky, Stravinsky, Prokofiev, and the most recent to appear, Alexandrov and Shostakovitch—never lose it. They may tend somewhat more toward the picturesque in writing works destined primarily for the stage, especially for the ballet (the art most in vogue in Europe after the appearance of Diaghilev's Ballet Russe), or they may turn toward a Germanic symphonism, abstract and abstruse somewhat in the manner of Bruckner, like a few of the Shostakovitch symphonies. Yet in all of them the formal principle has a predominant place, and color, however powerful and attractive it may be, is secondary. This can be seen in Stravinsky's works which, although composed for the theater, are pre-eminent in their form and therefore continue to keep their place in the concert hall.

Of Taneiev and Miaskovsky, as of other Russian musicians of their generation, it is almost impossible to speak at first hand for few of their works are known outside of Russia and it is not easy to consult those that have been published—often by order of and at the expense of the soviet government.

Of Rebikov, who at the age of fifty in 1916, was hailed as "the father of Russian modernism" we shall speak in another chapter, where his art can be more appropriately considered than here.

Sergei Taneiev (1856-1915) was ten years older than Rebikov and almost ten years older than Glazounov. He was Tchaikovsky's favorite pupil and his role in the history of his country's music is quite similar to that of Glazounov; yet his work lacks the fineness of quality which characterizes that of the latter and which gave Glazounov renown throughout western Europe. Despite his age, Taneiev is a relatively recent composer for he began to be known as such only in 1892 with a cantata, St. John of Damascus. A man of extreme scrupulousness, he permitted only one of his three symphonies, the Third, to be printed (in 1898). An opera, *Orestes,* as well as others of his compositions have become properly appreciated only since his death.

The greater part of his life was devoted to teaching. His technical meticulousness led him to work twenty years over his famous (in his own country) "Manual of Counterpoint" and inclined him to underestimate in his youth the group of "Five" whom he considered purely amateurs, Mussorgsky being the greatest of them although the least skilled technically. Later, when Rimsky acquired the requisite technique, Taneiev was one of his friends but Rimsky said that in his presence he felt as timid as a beginner. In a sense, Taneiev represented the Russian counterpart of d'Indy, who was somewhat older, in his opinion regarding the necessity of understanding and practicing old musical forms while he anticipated Reger, many years his junior, in his resurrection of contrapuntal writing—not simply as a method but imbued with life and movement. Taneiev was a conservative but as a teacher he set his pupils on the advanced way, leaving them free once they had command of their technique; to this Scriabin and Rachmaninoff bear testimony.

A pupil of Nikolai Rubinstein, Taneiev was an excellent pianist. Introduced by Tchaikovsky in his first public concert in 1875, he rapidly acquired a reputation and toured for some years as a virtuoso; this resulted in his slow development as a composer. Extremely exacting in this phase of his art, he left only thirty-six numbered works. The Third Symphony, dedicated to Glazounov, shows a scrupulous choice of melodic material but, like his chamber works, it is diffuse and the development section is lost in a motley contrapuntal texture. He seems a little like the Brahms of some decades past, especially to the Latin mind. Yet Brahms was profoundly antipathetic to the Russian composer who longed constantly, albeit in vain, for the joyous pen and the swiftness of thought of Haydn or Mozart. Taneiev was a man of vast musical, literary, and philosophical culture; he was first of all an intellectual composer. He knew what he wanted and he applied himself diligently to its accomplishment but the butterfly of inspiration eluded him and, when he caught it, it was only to dissect it and preserve it in a glass case.

Although Scriabin and Rachmaninoff received from Taneiev their *conscience du métier,* so meticulous in that master, they did not inherit his enthusiasm as contrapuntist. Had it been otherwise and, given Scriabin's instinct for hazardous experiments, who knows to what lengths of neopolyphony he might have gone. More discreet than Scriabin, Sergei Rachmaninoff showed from the first an eclecticism somewhat comparable to that of Glazounov, especially in the sense of casting ideas imbued with a well-defined romantic sentiment into unexaggerated forms. This is, as we have seen, quite common among the artists of the last decades of the century except for those who, through theoretical principles, desired to affect a strict formalism. The balance between form and content is established a priori by all the post-romantic artists from a romantic point of view; that is to say, ideas of romantic color and sentiment are treated in such a way that this sentiment either predominates or else consents to confine itself within the concrete limits of the form. The latter is the case with Rachmaninoff and, in general, with those Russian composers who followed the teachers of Moscow, such as Tchaikovsky and Taneiev, instead of leaning toward the license and technical laxity of the musicians of St. Petersburg. As is well known, Rimsky-Korsakov, the last of the latter group, reacted violently against this amateurish technique. After Glazounov, however, it is no longer possible to differentiate between the two schools, which finally became firmly united in Rachmaninoff.

Rachmaninoff, who made a reputation as a pianist before he became known as a composer, wrote a copious series of piano pieces of the type of *Morceaux de fantaisie*. His real career as composer began shortly before he became professor in the Conservatory of Moscow, when he wrote his most important operas, *Aleko* (1892) and *Francesca da Rimini* (1906). His piano concertos are followed by symphonies, the second of which shows the influence of Tchaikovsky, without further developments. Rachmaninoff was an artist who took his art as he found it without showing any desire for reforms or transformations; the art of the symphony in his time was so broad that he was able to avoid any difficult problems and his ideas were not so original as to impel him to find other means of expression. He was prolific; the easily achieved effect seemed to him the normal process for the artist of the twentieth century. Rachmaninoff's chief merit consists in having achieved an unforced and well-balanced combination of the romantic and the classical.

The dramatic character of Rachmaninoff's opera *Francesca da Rimini* proves this. According to some of his commentators, Rachmaninoff did not wish to compose music too intensely dramatic, wherefore he allowed the drama to unfold of itself while the music gradually proceeded to disregard it, following the situation and the characters at ever increasing distance although never ceasing to be agreeable and pleasing to the ear. This is, in a sense, the procedure which composers for the films were to cultivate later, providing music as an anodyne to keep the ear entertained while the sight is absorbed in what it sees on the screen; thus Rachmaninoff sensed a wholly new field of present day art. Yet, neither the prediction nor the thing predicted do honor to either artist or spectator.

Concerning the other composers worthy of mention in Rachmaninoff's generation, a few lines will suffice partly because their works are rarely performed outside their own country and partly because they reproduce, more or less, the characteristics already described in connection with that composer. Among these men are to be mentioned Glière, born in 1875; Vassilenko, in 1872; Akimenko, in 1876; Catoire (1861-1926); the brothers Krein—Gregory, born in 1879, and Alexander, in 1883—who bring this generation of Russian composers down to the last years of the century. Of all the group, Nicholas Miaskovsky (1881) is the one who has produced the most numerous and most interesting symphonic works. A pupil of Annette Essipov and of Liadov, he wrote some poematic compositions (Alastor inspired by Shelley's poem and Silence after Poe) but his great contribution to contemporary symphonism consists in his symphonies and chamber sonatas. His career as engineer and his intellectualism connect him with the composers of the 1860's,[3] but, aside from any pictorial or picturesque qualities, his music is strikingly subjective and finds its best expression in the large forms. He treats these with a complex technique in a manner somewhat similar to the expressivist German symphonists of which we have spoken in the preceding chapters, except that this subjectivity is dominated always by a vigorous conception of texture which relates him to the ideas of Reger and his polylinear construction. Miaskovsky amplifies the sonata form considerably, although its characteristic form presides over the general composition of the work. Within these outlines, Miaskovsky moves with such ease that up to the present time he has composed more than twenty symphonies; the twenty-first was magnificently rewarded by the soviet government with the sum of a hundred thousand rubles. The quality of his ideas is somewhat poetic and his formalism is, therefore, not reactionary. Nevertheless, he is not a romanticist because the form dominates the psychological and poetic nature of his ideas; his work is really a contemporary consequence of postromantic symphonism.

A young Russian composer who emulates the fecundity of Miaskovsky has turned, with a degree of sincerity not for us to analyze, to the lofty regions of that romantic symphonism which reached from Berlioz to Tchaikovsky.

[3] Phrases such as the theme of the Andante in his Fifth Symphony in D major, Op. 18 (1918), constructed on the four notes D, E, F, A belong to ancient popular Russian music.

He is Dmitri Shostakovitch (born in St. Petersburg in 1906), whose Seventh Symphony has been the object of widespread acclaim. This fact is of little interest to us here except as it indicates that quality of an art of the masses which his work possesses—a quality that has advantages from the point of view of success as well as disadvantages from the point of view of quality.

Shostakovitch, whose First Symphony (performed in 1926) had been well received, thought it appropriate to celebrate in his Second the tenth anniversary of the October Revolution. Apparently the practical revolutionaries resented this kind of artistic intrusion and when, in 1930, he presented a humorous version of Gogol's comedietta, the *Nose,* the official critics of the official newspaper *Pravda* accused the young musician of leftist tendencies and of middle-class decadence (not without its amusing side!). Two new symphonies followed but were ruined by the scandal of the first performance of an opera entitled *Lady Macbeth of Mzensk* (1934) whose plot dealt with erotic and criminal complexes so much in vogue in the contemporary German theater. Shostakovitch was severely censured; it is well known to what possibilities one exposes himself who disregards the opinion of the state in a totalitarian country.

However that may be, Shostakovitch decided to stay on the safe side, indicating that he understood popular and bureaucratic psychology. With his Fifth Symphony (1937) he obtained a tremendous success. In the face of a triumph with the masses all opposition was routed, Shostakovitch was vindicated, and official favor arrived with such leaps and bounds that the young musician received the Stalin Prize (together with Miaskovsky) of a hundred thousand rubles, awarded by the soviet government for his Quintet, Op. 57. It is a pleasing work, easy to listen to, well worked out, and in its final movements betrays a Franckian tendency combined with a salonlike music. In 1939 was performed his Sixth Symphony: in my opinion, his best-developed work. In 1941 comes his apotheosis in the Seventh Symphony which America received enthusiastically in 1942. Let us see, rapidly, what are his outstanding characteristics.

Even though Shostakovitch's First Symphony reached Europe (via North America instead of direct from Russia) accompanied by a publicity unusual for a young composer—he was called a Russian Mozart—the work did not arouse great enthusiasm in those who recognized Straussian echoes in its First Movement with its motives in the vein of Tyll Eulenspiegel and the banal climaxes (still perceptible in his later symphonies). Its Mendelssohnian scherzo reveals, like the model, superficiality and a sure musician's hand while the slow movement salutes the glories of a Germanic Valhalla in the same degree that the final movement revives the picturesque national music of Shostakovitch's own country. From every point of view it is the work of a young author with all the attendant excellences and drawbacks. The facility of Shostakovitch in inventing motives which do not have a great deal to say is abundantly exhibited in his preludes for piano, scarcely more than undeveloped sketches. Who would reasonably suppose that behind them was hidden a prolific composer of symphonies—and of very extensive ones?

Yet the incompatibility is not so great when it is seen that the symphonies do not develop as a genuine growth from initial motives but as long ecstatic perorations, lengthy digressions which, to a certain extent, display an inspiration similar to that of Bruckner. This is clearly apparent in the Fifth Symphony, Op. 47, where the young Russian's propensity toward diffuse form manifests itself unrestrainedly. The ecstasy aroused by "the mystic value of the chord" seems to dominate this symphony while in the following one a more concrete, a more plastic, dramatic episode connects him with the other great postromantic symphonist, Gustav Mahler, with whom he shares triviality of expression and unevenness of dynamics. A venerable model bent his frowning brow on Mahler as on Shostakovitch in this symphony: Hector Berlioz. If imagination in Berlioz's vein can be confused with eloquence, Shostakovitch is an eloquent composer—eloquent perhaps in the manner of the political orator, of the haranguer of the masses which, indeed, for him seems to be a desirable aim. His Seventh Symphony, Op. 60, confirms this point of view in its exaggerated dimensions, in all the apparatus of its orchestration, in its noise without grandeur, and in the weakness of its content. In this symphony Shostakovitch makes a profession of faith of his patriotic feeling, writing as he did during the siege of Leningrad, his native city. From the point of view of the composer's emotions as a citizen, his attitude is most praiseworthy but that does not come within the purview of the musical critic. Shostakovitch himself has written some vibrant pages for the press in this connection, affirming that he fights, with his compatriots, for the sake of culture against barbarism. However worthy of gratitude such an intention may be, it is difficult to hear it without sarcasm. To such extremes can political excesses drag European culture and its history!

If culture consisted solely in the conquests of mechanics, the Soviet Union would have two young composers to sing the epic of iron in Alexander Mossolov (1900) and Julius Meytuss. In his time, Prokofiev had celebrated it in his music for a cubist ballet, *Le pas d'acier*. Mossolov achieved momentary fame for his Iron Foundry, first performed at one of the festivals of the International Society for Contemporary Music at Liège in 1930. As in its model, Pacific 231 of Honegger, the formal outline is clear because it reduces itself to a continuous movement which goes back to the old structure of the spinner. Mendelssohn would have been able to do as much, accentuating the dissonances ad libitum and providing an insistent orchestration.

Chapter
TWELVE

THE CONCERTO (1926) of Manuel de Falla clearly illustrates the transformation of musical nationalism, after its purely romantic stage, which composers born in the final decades of the last century were to effect. The new direction given to musical nationalism led to a realm aesthetically opposed to that in which it originated—to the realm of pure forms. On the surface this may seem paradoxical, yet it is simply the consequence of that expansive tendency innate in all types of nationalism, whether in art or in politics. In effect, nationalism, having been born as a reaction against regimes which restricted the liberty of the artist, now advances irresistibly impelled by the very force of the energy which gave it birth. Thus, it scarcely achieves its first triumphs when, no longer content with them, it aspires to impose its originality and to insist on its own merits as compared with other styles, be they classical or of recent importation. In its desire for expansion it wants to be known beyond its local frontiers. If composers like Glinka and Smetana returned to their native land from exile and had no desire for further travels, their immediate successors, on the other hand, feel the urge to travel, to make themselves known throughout Europe and even in America. Tchaikovsky, Dvořák, and Grieg traveled quite extensively; with what they received as well as in what they gave, a fruitful interchange became established.

The qualities of a nationalist art which are observed in foreign countries are not those most lovingly attributed to it by its creators. Foreigners see in it new features which they desire to assimilate to their own art. These features are the elements which possess a certain capacity for becoming universal. Very rapidly, in proportion as a nationalist art possesses these elements, it becomes international. And thus it obtains the expansion and prestige to which it aspires. As a consequence, and in order to achieve increasingly better title to this universality, nationalist musicians gradually give up local characteristics in order to intensify universal elements: that is to say, they will abandon the picturesque, the conventionally patriotic, the interest in local manners and customs for the sake of accentuating the specific values in their art.

The immediate result is obvious: the equation, "Race — expression," becomes "Form — expression." Ethnic values, which manifested themselves musically through certain modal characteristics in the melody, in harmonies implicit in it, in the use of characteristic instruments, in rhythmical peculiarities, in elements of local color, tend to assume, by virtue of this process, the quality of ethical, ageless values.

This transformation from the ethnic to the ethos in music is not something which has just come about in our day. It is to be observed in an unmistakable manner in all the romantic composers; especially in those with aspirations toward form of the loftiest kind.[1] It is obvious that Wagner is as German as Delibes or Bizet are French or as Mussorgsky is Russian, but it is in Liszt and in Mahler where such transubstantiation appears undeniably among works in the grand form. Why? one may ask. What is Hungarian in the B Minor Sonata? What denotes Mahler's Jewish origin in *"Das Lied von der Erde"* or in the *"Kindertotenlieder"?* Specialists in oriental music know that there is something mysterious, yet unmistakable, which gives such music its special quality. This volatile substance saturates certain formulas which, because of their spiritual essence, receive a specific designation within their generic character as *maqamâts, rāgas,* etc., or in other words as the ethos of their modes as the ancient Greeks would say.

There is an ethos in this sonata by Liszt, in the symphonic works of Mahler, in the piano compositions or operas of Mussorgsky, in the pages of Grieg, of Debussy or Ravel, as in those of Albéniz and Falla. There is an ethos beyond the purely material elements of rhythm, harmony, modal color or timbre. This ethos, which exists in all the music of history, comes down from former times to our own through style (even though the idiosyncrasies of the individual composer may also play a decisive part). This ethos in present day music proceeds from aesthetic peculiarities contributed by the nationalist composers in the romantic period and even more pronouncedly in the postromantic: from nationalism first, next from that which constituted the essence of the aesthetics of the last years of the old century and the beginning of the new: impressionism or expressionism, atonalism or microtonalism. When this ethos is not sufficiently defined, it is because the art with which it is linked is itself not clearly defined. Nationalism, with Manuel de Falla, has passed into the realm of universal values like the impressionism of Debussy. Let us leave to the partisans of Viennese atonalism and of Czech microtonalism the responsibility of a like affirmation in their regard.

[1] Some motives from Scotch, Irish, and Welsh songs which Beethoven arranged for piano and strings in 1809 passed to his larger works, like the Irish one on which he based the initial motive of the final movement of the Seventh Symphony. See Charles V. Stanford, "Some Thoughts concerning Folk Song and Nationality," *Musical Quarterly* (New York: 1915).

I intentionally referred to Mahler a moment ago from the point of view of his Hebrew origin. In contemporary art there is an important section in which one may observe how concrete nationalist inspiration combines with a vague ethnic sentiment and one may see how this ethnic feeling, lacking minutely local characteristics, aspires to take shape in works of an eminently formal nature; it is this branch of contemporary music which shelters Hebrew musicians who, in our day, make public acknowledgment of their sources of inspiration in the abundant and magnificent stock of traditional Hebrew melodies. The musician in whom these characteristics are best exemplified, it seems to me, is Ernest Bloch.

Ernest Bloch is by race a Jew and by birth a Swiss. One can well comprehend that from his infancy Bloch heard more clearly the voice of his blood than that of political geography for, from the safety zone of Swiss neutrality, a musician would be able to approach composition in terms of the most abstract form more readily than anywhere else, since he could consider himself exempt from any nationalist pressure or proclivity. Ernest Bloch, educated principally in Paris, sought his inspiration in the robust pages of the Scriptures. The Scriptures possess a music which is its own, the music of the recitation in the synagogue. Yet Bloch did not intend that this music be used to paint symphonic poems with Biblical arguments in which Hebrew melody would be an indispensable ingredient. What Bloch actually produces is a Hebrew nationalism. And it will be understood that, since there does not exist a Hebrew nation but only a race with strong musical traditions, this music will play a part analogous to that played by regional melodies in the music of the nationalist composers. For Bloch this implies an added advantage, as compared to the nationalists in general, because his melodies have deep roots both in time and in space and thus lack limitations in both respects. Nevertheless, they are national motives at bottom and this suggests a limitation in comparison with such composers as Stravinsky, Bartók, or Falla, who started from nationalism but later freed themselves from it.

In contrast to many Jewish composers who figure in history not in their character as Jews but simply in their character as composers, Bloch brings to music his Jewish inheritance before every other consideration, that is to say, he acts as a native of a Jewish fatherland although the branches of his genealogical tree are stirred by every breeze and its roots are buried in every continent. His melodies are purely Hebraic, sometimes even literally so. The universality of the Hebrew lends these melodies an amplitude which national melodies, restricted by their very nature to a narrow ambitus, do not possess. Bloch, as Falla once said of himself, seeks the essential authenticity without subjecting himself to textual exactness. This is the case of all advanced nationalists who, with one foot firmly planted in the reality of the given melody, soar freely in the realms of imaginary discant.

Impelled by their national ardor, all nationalist composers tend toward the epic. Smetana is the best example. So also Sibelius. Of Bloch it has been justly said, by a writer as keen as Guido Pannain, that his is an epic spirit. Smetana could write a series of symphonic pages which he entitled *Má Vlast* (My native land). Others could write historical operas in which, happily, history took second place, such as *A Life for the Czar, Psokovitaine, Prince Igor,* or *Boris Godunov.* The epic of Bloch is to be found in the books of Kings, Chronicles, Psalms, or Proverbs, in the unpolished memoirs of Ezekiel, of Amos, or of Zacharias. Obviously, Bloch does not follow literally any of these writings. When he wrote Schelomo (1916), however, the spirit of Solomon inspired his muse and in his Symphony of Israel, of the same period, beats an ardent pulse with an accent no one could mistake.

This spirit refuses to conform to the restrictions of a brief sketch. It is an inspiration which needs wide spaces, open seas, vast skies, overwhelming deserts. Bloch naturally leans toward large constructions. But in them the motive is too vague of outline and the ambition to expression too eloquent for them to find a structure of objective preciseness. The subtitle of Schelomo, Hebrew Rhapsody, is that which is more or less appropriate to all the others, be they concerto, symphony, or better, simply psalms, poems, or episodes.

Bloch has written a considerable number of works of small scale: they do not represent the true Bloch but are rather the tribute demanded of each composer by his country and his age. Except for some pages of Hebraic picturesqueness (Baal-Shem, From Jewish Life, *Trois Poèmes Juifs*), his Landscapes, Nocturnes, and Poems of Autumn conform to the music about him as do his suite and sonata (1920), the quartet (1916), and the quintet (1923). In like manner he pays his debt to his native Switzerland in his overture Helvetia (1930) and in a symphony and a quartet which sum up his impressions as an Alpinist; moreover, he pays a debt of gratitude to the new continent in his symphony, America (1927).

One may find in his chamber works the same Hebraic inspiration as in other of his compositions. Nevertheless what predominates in them, in my opinion, is Bloch's fiery, dramatic temperament. And in them as in his works of larger dimensions, this dramatic quality of pure romantic origin struggles to find an equilibrium and balance in the form to which the musician very clearly aspires but which is outstripped by characteristics of temperament. In this lies the drama of such strongly original artists as Bloch—a drama which overtakes all those artists, past and present, who seek varieties of form appropriate for ideas not listed among those that have been the object of a previous formal treatment. Bloch is confronted with problems of style typical of this group of composers, as a result of their very struggles with the form. For this reason, the rhapsody, the form which does not completely mold itself but which pulsates uncertainly and indecisively although the author may have fitted it as neatly to his thought as a glove to the hand, is that which is appropriate to Bloch's entire work.

It is immediately evident, with the case of Bloch in mind, that Italian composers such as Alfredo Casella, Mario Castelnuovo-Tedesco, and Vittorio Rieti have risen, in varying degree, above an initial rhapsodic style (in the sense described above) to concentrate on forms of a much more solid and concrete type. Casella's Italianism is unmistakable in its lyric sense, in the quality and turn of the melody, and in everything which has been or is understood as Italian in music. I do not think that his early rhapsody Italia (1909), however, composed at a time when Casella was under the spell of Mahler, possesses much more significance in his work than does the Helvetia in that of Bloch.

The facility with which Casella has allowed himself to be impressed by the aesthetic and technical influences of strong personalities, from Mahler and Debussy to Ravel, Stravinsky and Schönberg, has been much discussed. Even Alban Berg seemed to him, in a moment of enthusiasm at his first hearing of *Wozzeck* (1930, in Aachen), to be the best composer in the world. Yet his *Serenata* (1927) indicated the direction of Casella's true ability and personality which, if not profoundly original, is at least firmly outlined after an assimilation of his many first influences. His excellent technique and the clarity with which he applies it is an invaluable asset. His irony, his spirit of burlesque, a certain touch of caricature—all provide a twist that eludes the censure of pedantic criticism. These qualities were present already, it seems to me, in his *Due Contrasti* (*Grazioso, Antigrazioso,* 1910), perhaps the first youthful work in which are defined certain aspects of Casella's personality which from then on were to continue their development. Thus, for each idea presented, Casella seems to pose an opposite; that this device has a great advantage as regards form would seem to be demonstrated by his most recent works.

The aspiration toward a form which is precise in its objectivity (that is, neither expressive nor descriptive) appears frequently among the younger composers of today. It is the dominant quality in Vittorio Rieti who combines it with great precision of line and texture. A ballet of burlesque type, *Barabau,* performed in 1925 by the Diaghilev company, first brought him recognition. Thereafter the rest of his works were to be of an eminently formal character: a sonata for four instruments (flute, oboe, bassoon, and piano), a symphony, concertos (for piano, for violin, for harpsichord). A madrigal for twelve instruments and an *Orfeo,* along with the earlier works, show that the Italianism of Rieti seeks to express itself with the conciseness and sureness of style of the classic age yet his language is of our own day.

The rhapsodic element, on the other hand, predominates in the work of Mario Castelnuovo-Tedesco. His youth was dominated by the influence of the neoromanticism of his master, Pizzetti. Lately his works have been of the formal type: sonatas, a trio, and concertos. (The concerto is much favored by the most recent composers for several reasons: the objectivity of its ideas may be expressed in passages of an instrumental virtuosity combined with modern harmonic successions; at the same time, the form, not prescribed by rule, is precise, yet free.) His *Concerto italiano* for violin on popular themes is of a more conventional nationalism. His Dance of King David (1925) leads to an evocation of the Israelite landscape; his opera, *La Mandragola* (1926), to an historical evocation which fortunately serves as no more than a neutral background against which polytonal combinations unfold without prejudice to the form.

Swiss by birth, French by adoption, Arthur Honegger offers problems similar to those discussed in connection with the Italian composers from the point of view of aspiration toward form. The French musician of our day has a freedom from restraint as compared with his colleagues in other countries for they are still held by the nationalist idea, no matter how much they try to free themselves from it. For musicians who have assimilated the Parisian atmosphere, everything which leaves their hands will reflect this environment, everything will have the stamp of the latest vogue. In them the national and the Parisian are identical. So long as they content themselves with the small forms, as do Poulenc and the infinity of small composers of the boulevards or the suburbs, the case does not present difficulties; in the closed forms the situation is different. Honegger, like other contemporary Parisian musicians, feels the desire to find clear forms for his music yet the spirit of Paris palpitated within these forms at their birth.

It is evident, then, that the realization of a robust form appropriate to the character of the composer's inspiration, whether it proceeds intuitively or is the fruit of a long technical process, reveals itself only after a penetrating, critical search. The process of finding form for form's sake, that is to say, an academic concept, is rare among contemporary composers even with those who momentarily turned to the employment of an idiom in imitation of Bach or Mozart. As occurs in the modeling of the human form, the exterior appearance is the result of the interior form and arrangement of the organs; in other words, what is perceptible in the outside form is the consequence of a pressure from within. So it is in music: a copy of the classic form without the other elements will have no more verisimilitude, no more natural color, than a garment hanging on a clothes tree has to the human form.

In contemporary art, the composer's aesthetic sense is appealed to by considerations of so many different kinds—harmony, rhythm, instrumental color, not to mention style and expression—that it is difficult for him to seek to give sonorous life to his thoughts in the neutral field provided by the piano when this instrument is not used from the point of view of its color possibilities.

Thus it happens that we find, almost without exception, every modern composer turning to the small forms. Form for form's sake which would result from the cultivation of the sonata for piano is, in our day, the exception.

After Liszt's Sonata in B Minor, the grand form for keyboard instrument scarcely exists except in César Franck's music for piano and for organ. These works all belong to his period of maturity and they are, as is well known, the *Prélude, Chorale et Fugue* (1884) and the *Prélude, Aria et Finale* (1886-87) for piano, and the Three Chorales for organ dating from 1890, the year of his death. Franck, who meditated much on the problem of form, had written more than twenty years before the first of the works mentioned a *Prélude, Fugue, et Variations* for organ, directly inspired by the music of the great classical organists. It is not, then, in the organic development of the sonata but in the compositions in three great sections that Franck can apply his favorite procedure of the grand variation and his cyclical treatment of the motives. In this way, Franck succeeds in giving independent value to the variation in and for itself; when it takes shape in various motives combined with each other as well as in the variation proper, this method produces one of Franck's finest works, the Symphonic Variations for piano and orchestra (1885). In this work the theme proceeds to define itself as the variations succeed one another in a manner similar to that of the Chorale in E Major, where, as Franck said, the actual chorale is not really the one alluded to in the title but the one that finally arises as an apotheosis after the long series of variations on the seven motives or melodic fragments which are enunciated at the beginning of this vast musical frame.

The musical discourse, so characteristic of the sonata, occurs in Franck in instrumental terms. It is not two themes which converse and contrast with each other but sonorous media—piano and orchestra—which carry out the dialogue in the Symphonic Variations. This is probably the reason which has led almost every modern composer to prefer the duet of piano with violin or violoncello (or rarely the viola) to the sonata for piano alone unless the work is conceived not according to classical models including those of Brahms but with the object of realizing in this very sober sonorous medium a new type of original composition.

The most successful sonatas of our day, in this sense, are sonatas for piano and violin from that of Franck and those—so fresh and personal—of Grieg [2] to those of Franckian inspiration like the one by Alexis de Castillon and that of Guillaume Lekeu (1892). The sonatas of Saint-Saëns and those of Fauré

[2] Grieg wrote an early Sonata for Piano in E minor, Op. 7, constructed on short themes and not without its charm while in his Symphonic Pieces, Op. 14, for four hands, he comes to grief in attempting an element not his. Nevertheless, if his clear but limited gifts are lost in the symphonic variation, he knows how to give an attractive turn to this procedure when it is animated by the rhythm.

serve as a transition in French art to those which, conceived under a different aesthetic criterion, nevertheless betray their native origin as in Honegger or in Milhaud. In Germany, Hindemith has written a number of sonatas for violin, violoncello, or viola with piano yet he has not undertaken the sonata for piano alone. Bartók wrote two for piano and violin and one for piano, dating from 1926, in which appears a pallid yet not impersonal reflection of similar works by Brahms. The constructivist tendency which we have remarked in speaking of the modern composers mentioned above is to be observed in the fact that they are substantially the only ones who have written sonatas for piano: for example, Prokofiev, with five works in this form, Roy Harris with two, and Roger Sessions with one. Milhaud has one to his credit, dated 1916.

Spain, which possesses in the Sonata for Piano and Violin by Oscar Esplá one of its most valuable compositions, also produced the brief and crystalline Sonata for Piano (1931) by Ernesto Halffter. From it there escapes a certain aroma of Granados, although neither the latter nor Albéniz ever wrote a sonata, preoccupied as they both were with genre pieces or with concerto movements where the weakness of structure is only partially concealed by picturesque virtuosity. Malipiero in Italy likewise confined himself to character pieces. Neither he nor Respighi nor Casella have written sonatas for solo piano while, on the other hand, they have composed sonatas for duet or trio. Rieti has written some sonatinas (that of Ravel is to be recalled as perhaps pointing the way), as if he felt a certain hesitancy before so imposing and severe a pianistic form as the sonata.

Bloch and Villa-Lobos are prodigal with sonatas for two or three instruments with the piano among them. When others undertake an extended form for the piano they either follow the baroque model of prelude and fugue like Busoni, who wrote only one sonata for piano (1880), or that of the toccata and variations like Honegger (1916) or that of the fantasy, like Falla in the *Fantasía Bética* (1919), in which it is made evident, as in the Islamey of Balakirev, that melodism of a pronounced nationalism and harmonic or keyboard color are materials of too weak consistency to carry of themselves a work of great dimension. The sonatas for piano of Stravinsky (1903 and 1924) are separated by more than twenty years; yet, as is typical of this composer, his powerful personality and unmistakable individuality have placed their stamp on works conceived during very different spiritual states.

The aspiration toward the grand form in the solo keyboard instrument appears in France with Franck, either in his baroque types of music for the organ or in the big variations in the style of Beethoven. The latter type characterizes the stern and austere Sonata, Op. 63, in E minor of Vincent d'Indy for piano solo (of 1907, three years after the Sonata, Op. 59, in C for piano and violin). D'Indy, twenty years after the sonata of Franck, makes use in his turn of vague initial themes which take on plastic shape as the work unfolds to end in a kind of apotheosis, triumphing both through the now radiant quality of the themes and by the enunciation of the principal tonality, after which the work seems to subside again into the gray atmosphere in which it was born, quietly dissolving in mists. Less directly derived from Franck's aesthetics, yet at bottom recognizing this debt, is the Sonata in E-flat Minor of Paul Dukas (1900), a vast construction in four scenes in which somber tones strike contrasts with a cold brilliance more in the vein of a Boecklin than of a Delacroix. We have already alluded to this work which, with its Variations, Interlude, and Finale (on a theme of Rameau), provides the most substantial part of the production of Dukas for piano (as limited in numbers as it is scrupulous in workmanship, like all of his work, orchestral or operatic). This sonata, with those of d'Indy, represents the most serious achievement in this form in France and in the music of Latin countries after the Sonata in B Minor of Liszt.

The most genuine impulse toward the composition of the sonata as a form especially appropriate to the keyboard is to be found in a unique and distinct manner in Alexander Scriabin. It is easy to fall into error in discussing this great Russian composer because the most important part of his work, that of his last years, is linked to the expression of mystic ideas which seek translation through the unusual effect of certain harmonies. But this mysticism and the harmonism inseparable from it are more apparent than real and proceed more from a certain theosophism then in vogue than from the tendency to acoustical ecstasy or chordal hypnotism typical of a Bruckner. What concerns us in this chapter is the way in which Scriabin finds in the sonata form—exactly as it is defined in the textbooks—a medium completely adequate, yet obviously in no sense academic, for the expression of his thought, in the same way that the melodic and harmonic vocabulary of Chopin served as Scriabin's model in his early work. In this he resembles other more recent composers who have expressed ideas undeniably their own in an idiom taken from a Scarlatti or a Johann Sebastian Bach or a Pergolesi, following a movement initiated by Reger, Strauss, Busoni, and Stravinsky and represented at the moment by the Symphony in C Major by the author of the *Sacre* himself.

It is important to emphasize that the early Chopinism of Scriabin is a kind of language and not the mere reproduction of a past style. In the same way, Scriabin finds the traditional sonata form perfectly adequate for his first sonatas and his first symphonies, down to the one entitled Divine Poem. The structure of his motives, their articulation in phrases, and the development of his periods are derived by Scriabin from the architecture of classical music; similarly, his orchestra is based on the classical equilibrium which requires no change even for the expression of his theosophical ideas. Scriabin's orchestra is the prolongation in a new sonorous element of the characteristic qualities of the piano, that is to say, he follows the old concept which understood the orchestra as a piano powerfully amplified. Thus Scriabin felt no great necessity for changes either as regards form or color. The important thing for him consisted in the translation of a vehement dynamic impulse, an eroticism (very far from Chopin), as his commentators have termed it, which by virtue of its mysticism ceases to be a sensual passion and converts itself into yearnings of a cosmic order.

And it is a curious fact that such a profound vehemence could find its adequate harmonic idiom in the natural series of harmonic overtones. His so-called "mystic chord" in five intervals at the fourth (C, F♯, B♭, E♮, A, D) only confirms the tonal potentiality of the fundamental and implicit resonances, not included by Scriabin in his chord (C, C, G, C). In the tone poem, Thus Spake Zarathustra, Strauss insinuates something of the sort: first he affirms in an overwhelming manner this series of consonances. Afterward, and finally, he can allow himself to superimpose on them violent dissonances, drawn from the natural overtone series. Scriabin goes one step further in taking for granted the fundamental consonances; yet, as is readily comprehensible, the step is not excessively great. Neither the classic structure of the phrase nor of the form suffers seriously thereby.

Scriabin's power lies in the vitality of his rhythm and in a lyric impulse which such enthusiasts as A. E. Hull term a "soaring" which mounts to the highest lyric regions. This is true. The fragment of a sonata entitled *Vers la flamme* could be presented as his most faithful portrait or, for the quality of its lyricism, the page for piano entitled *Flammes sombres* (Op. 73), Prometheus, the *Poème du Feu,* and his *Poème Divin,* his ardent *Désir* and *Caresse* (Op. 57)—all are like sparks flying from a passionate temperament. Scriabin's normal expression is that suggested by the title—"tragic, satanic"—given some of his poems in which ecstasies, dreams, and mystery abound. The strength of his personality makes the work of Scriabin individual, even in pages still permeated with Chopin's idiom. On the other hand, his conformity in the matter of form gives him an advantage that the poematic symphonists and mystics, Bruckner and Mahler, lacked. Scriabin, unlike them, did not need to dissolve the form; the principal reason for this, perhaps, lies in his rhythmical regularity. He animates it with his vivid inner dynamic energy but he does not need to dislocate it. If from the point of view of tonality he seems revolutionary in his use of that hypothetical chord in dissonant fourths, what has been said suffices, I believe, to make clear that, although the tonality with Scriabin is expanded to include its near neighbors, it never reaches the breaking point.

The last six sonatas for piano by Scriabin probably represent the most important music of this type written in Europe between 1908 and 1913 and we may even add that, after this date, in the years between the first world war and the second, there have been no sonatas written for solo piano worthy to be placed beside them.

Only the sonatas of Sergei Prokofiev (written between 1909, Op. 1 and 1924, Op. 38) deserve mention as springing from the spiritual source of Scriabin's music; a source from which Prokofiev departs only when he falls into a pallid neoclassicism, as in his *Symphonie Classique,* Op. 25. His humor (*Scherzo humoristique,* Op. 12), which reached a certain crudeness in *Sarcasmes,* Op. 17, reflected a passing vogue in Europe which found rather ingenious and spontaneous expression in Erik Satie and in Lord Berners. *Visions fugitives* for piano (Op. 22) still recall the model; while the so-called *Choses en soi,* Op. 32, rather approaches the pieces by Arthur Lourié entitled *Synthèse, Formes en l'air.* Lourié is mentioned by some musicographers as another of Scriabin's disciples along with Léonidas Sabaneiev, his biographer, and the brothers Alexander and Gregory Krein. Of Alexander Shenshin, who is said to have extended Scriabin's treatment of the pianistic arpeggio, and of Alexander Vaulin, who seems to have carried still further his polyphonic texture, very little has been heard recently.

The Englishmen, John Ireland, Albert Coates, and William Baines (who died very young) are among the occidental composers who show the influence of Scriabin. A nearer neighbor, Karol Szymanowski, the short-lived Polish musician possessed of unusual originality and a striking technique, and the Lithuanian, Michael Churlionis, reflect more or less directly the emotional restlessness of Scriabin and a personal, intellectual vitality. Despite his premature death, Szymanowski brought to realization works of such powerful fiber as his three symphonies (the Third, with solo voices and chorus, is a Nietzschean song of night), his three piano sonatas, and various pages for piano in which the national Polish flavor alternates with a modernism (Metopas, 1915; Masques, 1916) more in sympathy with the tendencies in Central Europe of the period.

We have alluded incidentally to the chamber music of the composers whom we have been considering. Except for Scriabin who, like Chopin, wrote nothing in this form (a trio and a sonata for violoncello, episodic works, are exceptions which prove the rule) which was incongruous with his specific talent for keyboard composition, the vast majority of contemporary composers have paid homage to that quintessence of pure form, the string quartet. But with the exception of Brahms's three quartets, it seems to be the case as with Schumann, that the large majority of modern quartets, while important, take secondary place in comparison to their composers' pianistic achievements. Only that of Franck suggests a genuine effort, in large measure realized, to find a form at once solid and original; a genuine accomplishment even when tempered by whatever reserves one may make regarding the composer's talent and methods.

It was not until the quartet of Debussy (1893) and that of Ravel (1903), together with Debussy's last sonatas, that we find string-quartet music worthy to be mentioned in high terms. In the case of most composers, the quartet figured as an academic work or else as one of compromise or experiment. Nevertheless, there are attempts in the formal domain worthy of mention, such as those of Arnold Bax in England, those of Joseph Jongen in Belgium, and of Gustave Samazeuilh in France. It is only as we approach the most recent period that we encounter works of indubitable importance. The series of brief pages by Gian Francesco Malipiero entitled *Rispetti e Strambotti* and *Stornelli e Ballate* (1920 and 1923) are, with the *Concertino* for quartet and the *Trois Pièces* of Igor Stravinsky (also of this time), the most notable works produced recently in circles always characterized by the finest originality. Darius Milhaud and Paul Hindemith have made repeated attempts at composition for this instrumental combination; these attempts, however, seem to be focused chiefly on the solving of problems of form and material and are frequently impaired by a notable lack of style (overabundance of material and lack of selection) or by an abstractness in which objectivism results in dryness.

The color, novel effects of timbre, delicacy of the sonorous material of which the quartet is capable beyond the classical pattern seem to have less attraction for young musicians than one would expect. Worthy of mention as attempts exceptionally well realized are those of John Blackwood McEwen (1868) and Eugène Goossens in England. The delicate tonal landscapes of the former find shadings of the most subtle gradations in gray, especially in the composition entitled Biscay. The Fantasy by Goossens is an essay of great novelty which still betrays a youthful hand but his Two Sketches is a little masterpiece. The first composition of Ernesto Halffter known in Spain was also called Two Sketches (*Dos Bocetos*). Refined in its material, subtle in spirit and emotionally intense, it gained little when it was orchestrated. As an example of this type of composition which seeks unusual timbres and a new manner of treatment in the conventional combination of the string quartet, I may be permitted to mention my own series of short fantasies of oriental color entitled Rubaiyat (1924). The suggestion of exotic instruments in this work is effected by a special treatment of each instrument and of all of them together, in harmonic superpositions which convey an impression of the sonorities of an "imaginary orient" (a title which Malipiero gave to a work with a delightful coloring), while its melodic material alludes in various passages to the popular music of Andalusia.

In addition to these aspects, it is in the modern art of the quartet that one may appreciate with unmistakable clarity the divergence that exists between the most advanced extremes of expressionism, emotional as well as tonal, and the most recent efforts to achieve with modern harmonic ideas a form as robust as the classical. These developments of contemporary art are to be found on the one hand in the quartets of the Viennese atonal school of which the *Suite lyrique* of Alban Berg is the best example, while at the other extreme are the last quartets of Béla Bartók. Their respective significance within the tendencies mentioned makes it imperative to study these works when we come to a consideration of these tendencies in their general aspect.

Part
TWO

Chapter THIRTEEN

Debussyism was not the work of Debussy alone but a traditionally logical stage of modern evolution.

CHARLES KOECHLIN

AT THE musical high tide of the new century we can distinguish two vital streams which characterized and determined the future course of music; two currents, springing from distant sources which, as the nineteenth century unfolded, became ever more clearly defined. In the ordinary language of the day the one is called expressionistic, for in it predominates the artistic impulse of the romantic composer who gives to the inherited structure of earlier musical forms an emotional and dramatic content. The other is termed impressionistic, for in it those purely sonorous qualities of color and chord values (by which is understood the *chord* as an independent entity rather than as related to and generating others) stand out from the musical fabric through the composer's primary interest in harmonic combinations. To sum up more concisely, one may say that those composers who are moved by considerations of *expression* in the dramatic human sense, those who write symphonic poems are formalists (in the stricter terminology of the musical critic), while those composers who seek an *impression,* in the purely musical and aesthetic sense, are harmonists.

Both tendencies necessarily possess points of contact. The exploitation of the expressive values of harmony is one of the considerations which impel the formalist composer from within, urging him toward a constant development of the elements of form. Vice versa, the impressionist finds himself continually confronted with problems of form in the effort to give coherence to his experiments in the domain of pure harmony. Nevertheless, the urge toward form (though the forms may change or be entirely new) predominates in the one since he is moved primarily by emotional experiences just as was the romantic composer, while the other is moved by entirely new aesthetic criteria. The latter seeks to exploit the qualities inherent in musical sound, both in their essence and in combination.

We shall see, in fact, that it is this impulse which dictates the experiments of the harmonist or, in popular parlance, the impressionist. Before going further, however, it is necessary to resolve an apparent paradox. If the musical impressionist is guided by sensations of an aesthetic order which awaken in him purely musical reactions (the desire for new harmonies, etc.) how does it happen that impressionistic music, certainly in the beginning, was linked with evocations, more or less concrete, of an extrinsic or literary nature which lie within the field of the emotions? Does that which distinguishes the expressionist from the impressionist composer consist simply in a change in the object which awakens the emotion? Can it be that, while the one is inspired by heroism, tragic love, religious mysticism, the ominous presentiment of death, the other responds to the mystery of nature, the murmur of the woods, the tranquillity of night or perhaps the friendliness or majesty of mountains or the sea, of the fertile plain or the desert? No, the difference is far more profound.

In fact, each moves in contrary orbits. The first case, that of the composer who seeks in music the translation of his emotions, resembles the poet who seeks in the vocabulary of his language words and phrases best suited to express his inner sentiment and who sometimes is obliged to re-discover forgotten words or to invent new ones. When Wagner played on his piano for the first time the chord:

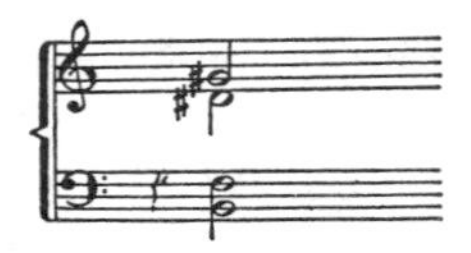

the seed from which *Tristan und Isolde* sprang like a gigantic flower, did he realize the possibility of creating a vast dramatic work from the emotional potentialities hidden in this chord or, on the contrary, did he find that this chord summed up the dramatic impulse which burned within him? Did the chord bring *Tristan* into being or did *Tristan* find musical expression in the chord? We may accept the second alternative. Wagner, then, proceeds like the poet described above. The discoveries of his harmonic idiom are rather a consequence of his desire for expression than the result of the compulsion of sonorous material in search of translation in artistic terms. He himself fought long and hard to make the musical world understand the essential humanness and pathos of his music, its emotional essence in search of a form, its drive which inspired his followers, the creators of the symphonic poem.

The impressionists pursue a contrary path. Beginning with Chopin himself, as the best example, it is the chance discoveries of the keyboard that acquire prime importance. Yet this chance is only relative. The explorer of new worlds is guided by a certain intuition as he equips his caravels. He does not know with scientific certainty what he is going to discover but he knows that he is going to discover something. Chopin did not let his fingers play over the keyboard in a thoughtless or arbitrary fashion. At first his fingers were guided by a fully mastered traditional and classical technique to which his ear responded. But these systematic combinations of sound arrive at last at limits where the average musician halts while Chopin, inspired by the spirit of adventure, risks going forward. Step by step he advances, little by little, always treading with care. This prudence is not calculated but results simply from the necessity of maintaining contact with the realm of the intelligible, while advancing just a degree beyond the point hitherto understood and accepted by the crowd. Now he requests still another step forward which the more advanced minds readily grant. Even if slower spirits cannot follow as yet, it will not be long before the universal frontier of music has advanced to a new line which the restless soul of the musician constantly seeks to extend.

On his voyage of discovery the composer has found a new flower, a rare gem he cannot classify according to the terminology of the science in which he has been trained. These chords, these novel combinations of tone that he hears for the first time with such keen delight, can they be assimilated to his earlier experiences? Can the composer, indeed, classify these new musical sensations in the conventional romantic repertory as of heroic, amorous, pathetic, or pastoral inspiration? Obviously not. All that is outworn. It belongs alike to the repertory of the old-fashioned poets and to the music of their day.

Now while the composer pursues his discoveries on the responsive keyboard, other artists, painters, and poets are seeking similar values in their respective domains in literary or plastic forms. The musician feels himself closely drawn by the common will which impels his brother artists. For example, a painter will put on his canvas a mixture of delicious colors not representing anything concrete, even though they inevitably recall some form. Thus to Claude Monet whether he paints water-lilies or rushes is unimportant; the problem is how to render light and shade.

Similarly, the piece of music which our musician composes of these new ingredients does not have a well-defined form. He experiences something [1] which may be compared to the delight aroused in us by the combination of colors to which the painter gives such titles as water lilies, nymphs, or twilight. Or, again, they may correspond to the vague, sweet resonances with which the contemporary poet evokes a landscape. Is it really *this* the musician wished to translate in sound? And how translate that which has never yet been clearly expressed?

Does it not happen rather that these colors, these verses awaken in the composer a like impression—certain corresponding sensations? To new sen-

[1] "Our observant spirit finds itself confronted with a form for which it possesses no intellectual equivalent, from which it must extract the unknown." Marcel Proust, *Le Côté de Guermantes,* I, 45.

sations of sonority must correspond a new order of plastic or verbal sensations. In order to clarify his process of thought for the listener, somewhat disconcerted by this new aesthetic approach, the composer seeks the aid of the painter or the poet in giving realization to these new sonorous elements. He says that his piece of music is something *like* those "magnolias at twilight" or *like* those "perfumes in moonlight,"—titles which, without malice, we all understand to be mere excuses.

There is one poet, however, who is wholly explicit:

> In Nature's temple living pillars rise,
> And words are murmured none have understood,
> And man must wander through a tangled wood
> Of symbols watching him with friendly eyes.
>
> As long-drawn echoes heard far-off and dim
> Mingle to one deep sound and fade away;
> Vast as the night and brilliant as the day,
> Color and sound and perfume speak to him.
>
> Some perfumes are as fragrant as a child,
> Sweet as the sound of hautboys, meadow-green;
> Others, corrupted, rich, exultant, wild,
>
> Have all the expansion of things infinite:
> As amber, incense, musk, and benzoin,
> Which sing the sense's and the soul's delight.[2]

Charles Baudelaire gives the title "Correspondances" to this poem in which, at the midpoint of the century, the new aesthetic philosophy already stands declared. (*Les Fleurs du Mal,* in which these verses appeared, was published in 1861 but it includes works dating from 1845.) We observe, first of all, that Baudelaire still uses the classic form of the sonnet; his meter is the traditional Alexandrine; his rhymes are regular; his prosody impeccable. Yet the content must have been disconcerting, must have seemed anarchical, even dangerous, to his contemporaries. Perfumes, sweet as hautboys, are green, corrupt, even triumphant. He speaks of echoes melting in the distance in a "profound and shadowy unity"—a unity that is mysterious yet clear as are "confused words" for he is dealing above all with symbols, a word to be remembered. To sum up, he speaks of a correspondence of sensations which appeal equally to the spirit and to the senses and in which perfumes, sounds, and colors respond to each other by virtue of that "vicariousness of the senses" or that act by which, in the phrase of Friedrich Nietzsche, two or three decades later, certain senses momentarily change places with each other.

[2] Translation by F. P. Sturm.

This correspondence between aesthetic sensations is not, however, a discovery of Baudelaire. Strictly speaking it is, indeed, an old problem of romanticism but only as a correspondence between music and poetry. In the early years of German romanticism, Tieck asked: "What, were we not to think in chords, compose music with words and thoughts?" As a result, Tieck endowed his Teutonic idiom with grace and lightness. He employed assonance and alliteration with an onomatopoeic insistence only surpassed by Richard Wagner beginning with the scene of Siegfried's forge and continuing to the death of Isolde.[3] Tieck further wrote directions for his verses such as: "chord in A minor," "arpeggiando," "dolce," and "forte," which imply more than a simple prosodic indication for the benefit of the reader or reciter.

John Field may wish to indicate by Nocturne simply a piece to be played in the night. But, when Chopin calls his pieces nocturnes and Schumann his pages *Nachtstuecke,* they both see in these words something more than music in the night; the titles contain an allusion to their source of inspiration. The relationship between the emotional sensations aroused by different arts, such as those of color and of sound (an interchange which is called synesthesia), interested Berlioz for the "color" which he discovered in each tonality or musical scale and his idea of modulation is to be compared with the art of mixing color tones on the palette.

The orchestrator, likewise, was to follow a similar process the moment he felt that each instrument had a characteristic color: green for the pastoral oboe, heaven's blue for the flute, vibrant red for trumpets and trombones. These elemental synestheses are equivalent to the classical ethos of the Greek modes. After the correspondences of Baudelaire, the more advanced heirs of his symbolist aesthetics, like Jean Arthur Rimbaud, find definite color in the vowels: *"A noir, E blanc, I rouge, U vert, O bleu—"* Poets like René Ghil went so far as to codify this sensorial or sensual vicariousness in a system according to which each sound in the French language, or each vowel at least, could find a translation in the timbres of different orchestral instruments. Thus the sound "ou," according to Ghil, has the color of flutes; the

[3] *"Hoho! Hahei! Blase, Balg."* Alliteration and onomatopoeia are a basic element in Wagner. Recall, for example, *"Weia! Weia! Weia! Wagalaweia!"* of the Rhine maidens; *"Hojotoho"* of the Valkyries; *"Hehe! Hehe! Hieher! Hieher!"* of Alberich; *"Heda! Hedo!"* of Donner. Verses of another type are

Brünnhilde: *"Nicht Gut, nicht Gold,*
Noch göttliche Pracht;
Nicht Haus, nicht Hof,
Noch Herrischer Prunk, . . ."

Sieglinde: *"Was im Busen ich barg, was ich bin*
hell wie der Tag taucht'es mir auf . . ."

French "u," a sound lost since the Greeks, finds its counterpart in the timbre of the treble flute; the sounds "eu" and "o" correspond to trumpets and trombones, and so on.

In Hugo's verse, better than in Tieck's, it is possible to find syllabic motives that act as musical cells. For example:

> On *était dans le* mois *ou la* na*ture est douce* . . .
> *Une* immen*se bonté* tom*bait du fir*mament . . .

The syllabic motifs in *m, n* may be compared to the motif *l* which mingles deliciously with the vowels in:

> *C'etait* l'*heure tranqui*lle *ou* l*es* l*ions vont boire.*

There is something more here than mere classical alliteration which, nevertheless, also responds to the imitative phenomenon on which synesthesia is based. A step further and Claude Debussy will translate effectively into musical tones the song of the brook as it tumbles over its rocky bed:

In romantic music, the invitation to synesthesia occurs on different levels: from (*a*) the employment of allusive values which we already recognize (as the pastoral in the Scene in the Fields from the *Symphonie Fantastique*); (*b*) then to new motives, yet ones belonging to the same category as the first (the use of the supernatural from Weber to Berlioz and Liszt); and, (*c*) to a plasticity in the characteristic motive suggested ordinarily by the gesture (as in Carnaval, by Schumann); (*d*) finally, to new sensations produced by definite musical means—such as the use of unusual chords or by the liberal use of chords little employed in the technique of the preceding period; the linking of harmonies not hitherto recognized as related; licenses of various kinds from exceptional chord resolutions or nonresolutions to free appoggiaturas; vagueness of tonality which comes with chromaticism; hints of a mingling of tonalities which result in the use of arabesques stretched delicately on a harmonic basis foreign to their essential tonality.

We have seen that all this occurs in Chopin and is extended by the pianistic development of the romantic period. We are now, therefore, in the presence of a definitely new phenomenon. Thus, both Chopin and Debussy compose nocturnes. Liszt and Ravel allude to valleys echoing to distant bells whose sounds dissolve in the mist while the harmonies of Chopin and Debussy vanish in the half-light of the dying day. Between them, the phenomenon differs only in degree but it departs radically from that of its classical predecessors. From the romanticism of the first to the impressionism of the others there is the almost imperceptible development of sonorous subtleties which depend for their full appreciation on the listener's musical culture and refinement of taste. Paul Bekker justly says that "the excessive gradation of all essentially romantic qualities leads to their decay." Thus, in fact, one may speak of the decadence of Debussy's music as well as that of the poetic production of more than half a century, from Baudelaire to Mallarmé. Already with Verlaine this "excessive gradation" becomes consciously defined. "No more color, only shading," he says in his *Art Poétique* which, in setting forth the new aesthetics of impressionism in painting and of symbolism in poetry, is the final manifestation of romanticism.

Now a new element—the musical quality—appears in the pictorial and poetic arts, just as music had earlier borrowed poetical and pictorial qualities from her sister arts. "Music before all else," says Verlaine, translating in verse what Walter Pater [4] expressed in philosophical terms when he said "all art aspires unceasingly to become music"; this is certainly true in this period when one could say, to the astonishment of the Encyclopedists of the eighteenth century (could they have heard), that "the Gothic is frozen music, a visible music," just as it would be equally possible to reverse the figure saying, "music is a liquid architecture, an architecture that can be heard."

This dissolution, the melting of the outlines of things in an iridescent mist through subtle chromatic changes as delicately tinted as mother of pearl, this dissolving of the normal harmonic pulsation of the tonic-dominant of classical music and, finally, this relaxing of rhythmic tension is typical of the new impressionistic aesthetics in music.

Similarly, prosody itself will soon dissolve in the atmosphere of pure lyricism as did tonality and form before Debussy.[5] The time for Mallarmé is ripe. In a little-known sonnet of Verlaine, the alliteration possesses a musical quality which can only be described as Debussylike. In it, the poet achieves the quintessence in words, the reduction of language to pure sound values whose poetic images are intelligible only through intuition. This, which we may call—how illogically yet how truly—the abstract image, constitutes the whole poetic art of Stéphane Mallarmé. Verlaine's sonnet to Parsifal begins thus:

[4] "All art constantly aspires toward the condition of music"; and again: "But although each art has thus its own specific order of impressions and an untranslatable charm, while a just apprehension of the ultimate differences of the arts is the beginning of aesthetic criticism; yet it is noticeable that, in its special mode of handling its given material, each art may be observed to pass into the condition of some other art, by what German critics term an *Andersstreben*—a partial alienation from its own limitations, through which the arts are able, not indeed to supply the place of each other, but reciprocally to lend each other new forces." Walter Pater, "The School of Giorgione," *Studies in the History of the Renaissance.*

[5] "In comparison with the pure dream, the unanalyzed impression, a definite, a positive art is blasphemous. Here, everything has the needful clarity and the delicious obscurity of harmony." Charles Baudelaire, *Le Spleen de Paris* (1860).

Parsifal a vaincu les Filles, leur gentil
Babil et la luxure amusante—et sa pente
Vers la chair de garçon vierge que celà tente
D'aimer les seins légers et ce gentil babil. . . .

Abstract image! Toward that abstraction, no longer plastic but musical, all impressionism tends. It is useless and misleading now to speak of the external object as the motive. Claude Monet may paint the shadowy façade of the cathedral at Chartres, showing it in a mist of evanescent colors—light refracted into its primary colors which "melt" in the transparent atmosphere or, again, he may depict the unsubstantial water lilies in his garden. Yet the painter's interest is no longer in a special object as a pictorial motive but rather in the manner in which the light plays on its surface. In the art of poetry, likewise, we find ourselves very far from the simple use of the syllabic patterns which served to support the poetic idea in Hugo. Alliteration, the interplay of the sonorities of language, reach a higher plane which dominates the aesthetic will of Verlaine in the sonnet to Parsifal, as later with Mallarmé. What will be the source of inspiration for the impressionists in music? Will they be content with naïve musical descriptions of romantic landscapes or dancing nymphs? Obviously not. If light for its own sake, if the sonorous interplay of vowels and consonants attract the painter and the poet at this moment in European art, it is evident their contemporaries in music will concern themselves with pure music, with its essential and intrinsic elements. Above all, they will seek independent harmonic sensations for their own sake, for their essential worth, not simply for their function in tonal relationships. Let us leave to the student of the plastic and poetic arts the task of examining how these arts have moved in similar paths. Let us rather follow the stages along which the art of music has passed since we left the romantic composers as they endeavored to resolve into intelligible form the "categorical imperatives" with which, to their surprise, delight, or despair, the material of their art confronted them.

Chapter FOURTEEN

THE HISTORICAL process of European music since the Middle Ages has marked the gradual organization, within a concept of harmonic unity, of the different sounds employed in a composition. Thus, not only the motion within the individual voices of a composition but also the vertical, or chordal, relationships between the voices came to be realized. In time, furthermore, these chordal unities were felt to be linked one to another successively according to that same unifying principle operative in the individual chord. As a result of this new way of "hearing" a complex of different voices, the whole became organized around a central sonorous nucleus, the tonic chord. Through the organization of the succession of consonant and dissonant chords in their relationship to the focal point, the tonic, arises the unifying principle of tonality.

Consonance conveys a feeling of unity, of repose, while dissonance arouses a sensation of unrest, of motion. The tension induced by the interplay of these two factors provides a driving force which impels them toward their goal, the all-embracing tonic chord in which they find repose. The alternate states of tension and relaxation thus achieved through harmonic means have to represent the expression of emotion to the occidental listener of recent times.

From the baroque *opera in musica* of the seventeenth century, down to the final phases of romantic music, musical art appeared to be—for the listener as well as the artist—primarily an art of emotion. This fact explains why the general public remains unmoved by the music of an earlier or later period than the above-mentioned span of some three hundred years. The listener condemns as mere primitivism all music prior to the germination of the harmonic principle, while it estimates as decadent that music of our day in which this principle reaches a state of dissolution or extreme amplification.

Now the evolution of the harmonic processes in music has its basis in acoustical phenomena: in the series of overtones produced above the clearly heard fundamental tone emitted by any vibrating body such as a cello string or the column of air in a wind instrument. Each tone in this series is related according to mathematical proportion to its fundamental. In theory the series of overtones is of infinite extent. It is no accident, however, that those intervals considered as consonants by medieval musicians are those corresponding to the overtones having the simplest ratio to the fundamental; namely, the octave, fifth and fourth. The whole history of western musical development has been marked by a progressive acceptance as consonant of intervals corresponding to overtones having an increasingly complex ratio to the fundamental tone and in consequence ever more remote from it in the harmonic series. The following diagram showing the first twenty-two overtones of the fundamental C will illustrate this process and demonstrate how the harmonic feeling of different historical periods is associated with the gradual extension in the direction of complexity of the combinations of intervals which the ear has accepted as consonant. It will thus be evident that the latest developments in musical thought have followed paths that are not really new but that are actually extensions of the very principles that form the basis of all the music which preceded.

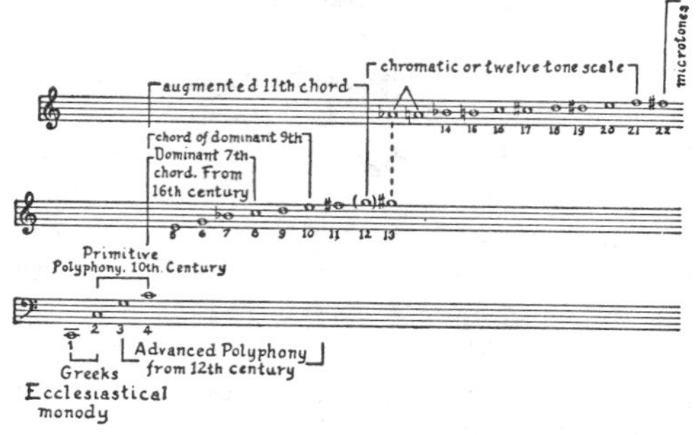

It is clear that the first six notes of this series lie within the tonality of the fundamental note; grouped as a chord, indeed, the notes C, C, G, C, E, G give an effect of magnificent solidity and repose. The next note in the series, however, causes us considerable uneasiness. In pitch, it lies between the notes A and B flat. It is so close to B flat, however, that we may assimilate it to that note without serious misgivings. This gives us a new chord—C-E-G-B♭. This chord, a chord of the seventh, leaves the tonality of C major since the note B flat does not belong to that tonality.

B flat does belong, however, to a tonality very close to that of C, namely, the tonality of F major. The new chord which we have found is that which is born on the fifth degree, or dominant, of the key of F. It is unstable and requires a following chord upon which it may descend, seeking the nearest point of repose. The dominant-seventh chord finds greatest repose by moving directly to the tonic chord in a process which is known as perfect cadence.

So amenable is the human ear that the chord of the seventh, the first dissonance in the series of natural resonance, has long been regarded with as much complacency as the tonic chord itself. We may even, if we so desire, rest on it and consider it as a consonant chord. This kind of dissonance, actually the slightest within the tonal series, is admitted by the romantic ear as another consonance. It is no longer a chord that requires a forward movement or resolution. It has obtained, then, a pure value, a value per se.

The way is marked. The ninth tone of the series is D, that is, a note at the interval of a ninth (eliminating the intermediate octaves) from the fundamental. Thus, we have the chord, C-E-G-B♭-D; this is the chord of the dominant ninth and contains two dissonances, namely, the seventh, B flat, and the ninth, D. If the seventh has lost some of its driving power, the new dissonance arrives to strike even more energetic sparks. The chord of the dominant ninth is the dynamic and expressive element par excellence in the music of the nineteenth century. When this motive force in the ninth has been consumed, like that of the seventh before it, we shall have reached the high tide of the age of Debussy, that in which the chord of the ninth is understood and accepted as an independent chord needing no resolution of any kind.

The eleventh note of the series offers a problem similar to that which we encountered in the approximate note, B flat. This eleventh note is almost halfway between the note F and F sharp. Two solutions are possible: we may either select F sharp, as did Scriabin, or we may decide on F natural. From the first solution results the chord of the dominant ninth with a diminished fifth, since F sharp is enharmonically equivalent to G flat. The second solution gives us the chord of the dominant eleventh. Scriabin wished to consider his chord, C-E-F♯-B♭-D, as a chord of repose. And, indeed, he does end compositions on that chord. What Scriabin does, in effect, is to use a dominant chord in which the fifth, G, is replaced by a contiguous note, or in technical language, an appoggiatura.

In the academic and conservative technique, appoggiaturas have a value that is more melodic than harmonic. It is a note which, inasmuch as it is foreign to the harmonic complex, must be quitted immediately by means of a resolution. The new step forward taken by our present harmonic feeling consists: first, in not resolving the appoggiatura, i.e., in accepting it as a constituent note in the harmonic complex of the chord; and, second, in not resolving this chord, itself a dissonance, to another more consonant one. Thus we see in this first and simplest case of the many ambiguities presented by chords with altered notes how the so-called harmonic vagueness of advanced musical impressionism has its basis in acoustical phenomena. Such instances will become more numerous and complicated as we advance in the series of overtones. Thus the thirteenth overtone gives an A nearer to A flat than to A natural. It may, therefore, form part of a chord of the dominant thirteenth, either major or minor depending on which note is chosen.

Utilizing the tones of the series up to and including the fifteenth note, B natural, we may construct a chord—C-E-G-B♭-D-F-A-B♮—which offers new complications through the fact that it brings together B flat and B natural in the same chord. The first of these two notes belongs to the tonality of F major and the second to that of C major. By this means, among others, we begin to glimpse a very recent idea, one known as double tonality or bitonality.

From the eleventh to the twenty-second overtone a series of semitones appear which are represented in our system of equal temperament by the equidistant semitones of the chromatic scale. Thus all the notes of the chromatic scale may form a dominant chord in a tonality. Can the unifying capacity of harmony achieve more than to embrace in a single chord all the notes of the chromatic scale?

Now, while these series of overtones may be considered in their vertical relationship as chords, they may also be conceived as scales. Thus we observe that the overtones 7 to 13 produce the whole tone scale exploited by Debussy for its impressionistic effect and its evocation of exotic and primitive scales. Similarly, the scale of chromatic semitones produced by the overtones 11 to 22 provides the acoustical basis for a very recent *modus operandi* called usually the "twelve-tone technique." This method of utilizing the chromatic scale lies within the realm of a post-impressionist aesthetics sometimes known as expressionism or atonality, a term open to frequent misconstruction. This new musical style has been practiced especially by Schoenberg and the composers of the Viennese school.

Have we reached the end? No, there is no end to the evolution of music. Beyond the twenty-second harmonic, a new order of things takes place. The sounds no longer appear in relationships of whole and half tones but in intervals smaller than a semitone—in microtonic intervals, with the quarter tone as the most readily perceptible unit. A new music begins. Musicians and theorists are endeavoring to give it an aesthetic meaning which will make it comprehensible, not simply as an acoustical speculation but as a true musical art.

The art of music could not exist if our aural faculty did not have a memory which can preserve or prolong the effect of sounds whose vibrations have faded away. The memory retains impressions of all the sounds of a musical composition and organizes these impressions in such a way that the music takes on meaning for the listener. The organizing principle that we ordinarily look for in our music is that of tonality; one might say that tonality is a prolongation, within our musical sense, of the relationship between consonance and dissonance. In other words, it is the fullest expression in a horizontal direction of those relationships that are summed up in the vertical grouping of the chord.

Tonality is not an ironclad concept, constructed all of a piece like a mechanism. It is, on the contrary, shifting and unsteady. Its consistency is subject to the surrounding atmosphere, like gelatine. In the emotional heat of German chromaticism, it tends to dissolve. The French taste for clear and crystalline form stiffens it. The two great currents in the evolution of tonal feeling in the most recent stages of European musical art originate in those tastes peculiar to Central European musicians or in those on the periphery of this nucleus, from Russia to Paris by way of the countries of the south. This process of evolution of the tonal feeling brings us to a critical point on which the most recent Central European composers base their aesthetics. This phase may be defined by saying that it is that in which the tonal memory loses its cohesive faculty, when the musical magma begins slowly to dissolve; this is what has been known from a very early, and in fact a premature, moment as atonality.

Tonality is neither a natural phenomenon nor a mere artificial convention. From the moment in which tonality becomes a factor in musical art, it has, like music itself, its roots in the natural soil on which man treads. But man carries his head erect in a higher atmosphere, in a loftier spiritual region. Music is an artifice by which the musician operates on man's aesthetic faculty. All the agents which collaborate in this process have a natural principle but the means by which they accomplish their ends, their *modus operandi,* is an arbitrary product of the artistic genius of mankind.

Just as the natural feeling for harmony is summed up in methods of practical application grouped for pedagogical purposes under the title, system of harmony, so it would be worth while for the sake of clarity to call the aggregate of practices which preserves the coherence of the tonal feeling a system of tonality. In this system, the word atonality would occupy a position corresponding to that held by dissonance in the harmonic system. We would have, then, this double interplay of elements: consonance-dissonance and tonality-atonality. The second pair of factors is nothing more than the extension in a third dimension of the first two. The concept, dissonance, is a relative value in respect to consonance; atonality is a relative value in respect to tonality.

Since tonality is born of the functional relationship of the fundamental chords, subdominant-tonic-dominant, and since atonality begins to develop precisely at the instant in which the modulatory process relaxes these basic relationships, it would be useful—in order to avoid the confusion which the word atonality induces—to introduce a change in the current terminology. The classical concept of tonality might be called the *functional system.* Its final phase, that which begins at its point of dissolution and which has been called atonality despite the vehement protest of its purest cultivators, might be termed the *nonfunctional system.* Starting from this premise, it may be easier to explain clearly the evolution of tonal feeling in the course of the nineteenth century and during the early decades of the twentieth.

In the same way that the tonal sense is the horizontal extension of the vertical harmonic sense, so there exist two ways in impressionism to give meaning to the sonorous shape: one of them is the touch of color in a dissonance applied in the form of a vertical chord; the other is the continuous brush stroke, color spread on the tonal horizon. We have, then, an impressionism of the chord in the one case, in the other, an impressionism of the tonality. Even though there exists no line separating the two and even though composers everywhere employ them simultaneously, there is a marked preference for the first procedure in French impressionism; Central European expressionism leans toward the second procedure. In both cases the vertical tonal feeling is considerably weakened; but, in exchange, the general feeling of tonality is proportionately amplified. In the first case, the frequently diatonic and modal melodism produces for the listener a much more definite feeling of normalcy than in the case of the accepted atonalists, such as the Viennese composers; in the latter, the chromatic melody is broken up into successions more nearly comparable to the functional chromaticism of *Tristan* and its immediate successors—the works of Mahler, Wolf, and the like.

For this reason, the atonalist music appears more vague and incoherent than the impressionist, while at the same time one easily recognizes its Tristanesque derivation, since these composers for the most part place this nonfunctional system at the service of expressive intuitions which belong wholly to the romantic repertoire. For this reason, their music may seem old to us, since it only carries to a more extreme degree that which Wagnerianism and poematic symphonism had already expressed. The French, on the other hand, use their more functional system to express intuitions derived from French poetic symbolism or from French pictorial impressionism; these are intuitions of a much less hackneyed order than those of the Wagnerian school.

During the space of a generation, new political, artistic, and aesthetic programs have arisen. The development of our auditory faculty, the "education" of the musical ear, the broadening of our artistic concepts, of our capacity for comprehension and acceptance—not only in music but in painting, sculpture, and poetry—have progressed so rapidly that those early works of Arnold Schönberg, so disconcerting when first heard, appear perfectly logical and clear to us today.

If nonfunctional chromaticism arrives, through Schönberg, at the stage known as atonalism, vertical dissonance will suggest to the French composers after Ravel another class of experiences—namely, the superposition of tonalities expressed in a combination currently known as polytonality. The following chapters will endeavor to explain both points of view in the light of the achievements of their respective authors.

Chapter FIFTEEN

WE HAVE observed how the evolution of the harmonic sense led certain romantic composers, notably Chopin, to explore new possibilities of the sonorous material and how, as time went on and the discoveries advanced, these ideas must needs find an explanation of an aesthetic order. Thus, while inspirations of a specifically musical character brought about, for example, the use of series of consecutive seconds, as early as 1865, by Modest Mussorgsky, or series of parallel chords of the ninth in *Pelléas,* or progressions of every kind in Fauré and Debussy, or the chords of the eleventh in parallel motion used by Erik Satie beginning with *Le Fils des étoiles* in 1890, or of tonic thirteenth chords in Ravel, as in the final measures of "Le Martin pêcheur" (*Histoires naturelles*)—they are all linked to a specific poetic allusion.

This is no more than a redundancy to which the musician has recourse in order to see if, by this means, he may succeed in producing on the listener an acoustico-musical sensation similar to his own. This way of evoking the impression is rendered valid by the vicariousness of aesthetic sensations, according to the philosophy of the artists of impressionism. Yet, when all is said and done, the effect produced on the listener will depend solely on the purely musical authenticity with which it appeals to the aural sense.

In order to clarify the most significant stages in the process of the evolution of the harmonic sense [1] it is indispensable to point out historically, if only

[1] See also the studies of Charles Koechlin, "Évolution de l'harmonie: Période contemporaine," *Encyclopédie de la Musique,* II, 678, 688.

in a summary way, the various elements which composers have utilized in this process of the evolution of the harmonic sense.

NATIONAL OR POPULAR COLOR, MODAL AND EXOTIC COLOR

One of the most suggestive and richest sources of stimulus to the composer's imagination and also one of the most exploited since the beginnings of the romantic epoch is that of national song or popular song—in its sense as the direct expression of the spirit of the people of each country. Being traditional, it may have a very great antiquity. It may therefore happen, and frequently does, that the melodic, harmonic, and rhythmic structure of this song will differ more or less widely from that of "art music." On the one hand, some popular songs, whether purely melodic or proceeding from the dance, offer rhythmical peculiarities which require a modification of the habitual rhythmic-harmonic pulsation of classical construction. Melodically, they may present reminiscences of the modal scales which formed the nucleus whence sprang a melody which became modified by the musical taste of each epoch. The harmonization of such types of melodies, or of melodies newly created by composers at a more advanced stage of nationalist musical art, may suggest liberties in the treatment of the harmony (or harmonizations close to the medieval modal successions), especially in connection with cadences, such as the dominant-tonic cadence without the leading tone, in paraphrase of those cases in which the final of the medieval mode is preceded by a note more than a minor second away.

Unmistakable examples of modal feeling can be found already in Berlioz (*Enfance du Christ; invocation à la nature* in *La Damnation de Faust*) and in certain piano works of Chopin, already mentioned, which owe their origin to the popular song that inspired them. The modal color in the *Christus* of Liszt is more directly owing to the religious spirit of this oratorio, as is also the case in the final chorus of Gounod's *Faust,* or in the agreeable *Pas d'armes du Roi Jean* (1852) by the young Saint-Saëns, where the melody is harmonized in parallel fifths, probably in order to give an archaic feeling. Modal color is not frequent in Wagner; yet it is the basis of the funeral march of Titurel in *Parsifal*. In the same opera, on the other hand, passages seeking to describe the exoticism of the enchanted garden of Klingsor recall instead certain melismas of Andalusian song, as does also another passage in the scene of the forge in *Siegfried*. Russian composers, who have frequently had recourse to the religious chant of the Greek church, fall naturally into this modal color—Mussorgsky above all, especially in *Boris Godunov*. This coloring extends to the other works of the great Russian musician, such as his songs, "*Sans Soleil,*" "*Chants et dances de la Mort,*" and "*Enfantines,*" in which the realistic melodism, according to some critics, links itself with great preciseness to the spoken Russian language, to the normal prosody which governs most of the popular songs that are not derived from the dance.

The ecclesiastical modes which seem to have been used with the greatest success by modern composers are (*a*) the Dorian or first authentic mode (*b*) the Mixolydian or seventh mode (fourth authentic) and (*c*) the Lydian or third authentic mode which has its dominant on the fifth degree of the scale and which was used by Beethoven in his famous "song of thanksgiving" in his Quartet No. 15. Yet, needless to say, composers who use modal color are not guided by archaeological considerations, but use it for its evocative effect or else they seek a certain melodic originality and, hence, are not preoccupied with the dominants appropriate to each ecclesiastical mode. Their modern ear obliges them to maintain the relationship of dominant-tonic, while the novelty consists in avoiding the leading tone in the chord of the dominant or in employing the minor chord on the fourth degree of the scale.

Special characteristics of the modal scales induce harmonic successions entirely different from those of the classical technique; as a result, a multitude of attractive effects are produced. These have been used sometimes to evoke a certain religious atmosphere and, at other times, as by Saint-Saëns in *Samson et Dalila* to allude to Hebrew choral songs; by Fauré, in many cases, for exotic effects; by Massenet and by Ravel (*"Chansons Grècques"*) for similar reasons; by Debussy (*"La Damoiselle élue"; "Le Martyre de Saint-Sébastien"*) to suggest remote and mysterious atmospheres or poetic sensations of the pre-Raphaelites or of d'Annunzio. It will be readily understood, therefore, what interest this class of nonacademic harmonizations can offer in its intrinsic musical value.

Now the music of oriental countries is fundamentally monodic. Its evocations will be effected above all by recourse to incomplete scales, especially the pentatonic, so common in the Javanese gamelangs which Debussy heard with much pleasure in the Exposition of 1889. Combined with this exotic melodism, composers employ authentic percussion instruments or those capable of suggesting the rich combinations of interlacing rhythms. Nevertheless, the general effect is frequently subject to the prevailing mode concerning what is thought to be the music of China or Japan or the Indies or the African Congo or of the Africans transplanted to the Antilles. The exotic chords conceived to accompany these melodies (rather than to harmonize them) are frequently realized as a tuned percussion: they are employed with a special effect which suggests, whether in the orchestra or in the keyboard—where impressionism has developed this idea most fruitfully—a percussive chord, as distinguished from the gliding, superimposed chords which are a favorite orchestral device. Certain modifications in the classical chords served the Russians in their search for oriental color effects; for example, they frequently use alterations of the fifth, especially in descending motion.

Exotic effects have been sought in music since the seventeenth century when Lully, inspired by the visit of an ambassador from the shah of Persia to the court of Louis XIV, used oriental *agréments* to add novelty to his music for some of Molière's comedies and ballets. Gluck, Mozart, Beethoven, Weber, Wolf, Cornelius, and—at the high tide of romanticism—Mahler, in his "Song of the Earth," constantly renewed exotic themes, accenting or diluting them in accord with the taste of the times. Supposed Arabic and Moorish exoticisms were a commonplace of Spanish and French nineteenth century music, as we have seen. A more authentic Moorish flavor occurs in a passage of Rimsky-Korsakov's Shéhérazade, that entitled "Ya lil," which is taken from one of the collections of *ghernatas* made in Algiers.[2] Oriental color is achieved by the introduction of melismatic phrases, arabesques, of which the perfect example is supplied by the chromaticism of the song of the king of the seas in *Sadko.*

A new exotic flavor, this time primarily rhythmic, was added to the fascinations of Andalusian music by the popular dances and songs from the Spanish Americas. Folklorists have attributed a Mexican origin to the fandango, although not even the word itself is known in Mexico; it is said, moreover, that the habanera is based on an African rhythm. The habanera invaded all the music of the later nineteenth century in the final stages of a Spanish exoticism which had been in vogue from the early years of the century. The folia, the chacona, the passacaglia, and the saraband passed into the French ballet of the seventeenth century and thence into instrumental music, where they were divested of their local color; the bolero, however, which spread throughout the Europe of romanticism, became an unpardonable musical commonplace. Even Beethoven contributed his bolero; Chopin produced another, and the cycle closes with that of Maurice Ravel. Ravel, like Debussy, honored the habanera as a type of Andalusian music; Manuel de Falla repays this compliment by recalling in his *Hommage à Debussy,* for the guitar, those rhythms which the great Frenchman had used in his subtle and perfumed evocation of a garden in Granada.

CHROMATIC RICHNESS AND COMPLICATION OF TEXTURE

The influence that oriental chromaticism exercised on the development of modern music is little more than superficial.[3] Its deceptive aroma penetrates only slightly the threads of which this music is woven. Exotic evocations do not combine well with complications of texture (except in rare examples like the preceding), but prefer an accompanied melody or one surrounded with

[2] The *ghernatas* are traditional songs preserved by the descendants of the Moors who were expelled from Granada in the sixteenth century.

[3] Later we shall encounter another result: that a concept of music, in a certain sense oriental, will lead to a type of atonal heterophony in the sonorous texture.

a suggestive atmosphere, more heterophonic than harmonic in the most advanced cases, instead of a richly woven counterpoint. In this complication of the weave there intervenes the rather strictly harmonic chromaticism of *Tristan*.

Harmonic chromaticism, one of the most outstanding achievements of the work of Richard Wagner, constitutes the climax of romantic harmony just as the ninths of Debussy constitute that of impressionistic harmony. But the complication of the texture, of the polyphonic weave in which the expression of the different voices is enriched through the alteration of the melodic lines, provokes a chromaticism of a different sort—a contrapuntal chromaticism which, strictly speaking, may be supported by a diatonic harmony. An enriching of the texture by means of melodic alteration will lead to consequences of unlimited perspectives because, when the resulting, dissonant successions are considered separately for their own sonorous value, we shall have encountered a whole field typical of modern harmony: that of altered chords with their sequels of unresolved appoggiaturas, elisions, anticipations, suspensions without preparation or resolution, *échappées* (notes arbitrarily added to the chord), and other procedures which classical harmony considered simply as means for enriching the texture. In the new logic of harmony, limits are set only by the individual composer and these rhetorical procedures are changed into real harmonic effects with their own peculiar value.

Harmonic chromaticism was the field in which romanticism first established itself. The dramatic expression of the melodic line was favorable to it and the harmonic background, the sentimental landscape, widened its horizons with harmonies laden with a mystery derived from chromatic alterations which, like the augmented fifth, the augmented sixth, the diminished seventh, rapidly became commonplaces of the style. The feeling for nature, which is the sentimental disguise to which composers betake themselves to justify the new shadings of their harmonic sense, differs essentially from that of the classics. The evocations of night of Schumann and Chopin, even of Mendelssohn (who enjoyed daylight more than the others), are quite a different thing from the Pastoral Symphony, for the same reason that the serenity of Debussy's ninths is quite a different thing from the demoniac quality of the dominant major ninth in *Der Freischütz*. The essential difference lies in the fact that the harmonies of Weber, like those of Wagner, are conceived orchestrally. Those of Debussy, like the series of chromatic chords produced by conjunct movement, are first discovered by the fingers on the keyboard and thereafter by the ear, which gives its approval.

These sliding chromatics can have two kinds of terminations: they can either return to the point of departure or else, remaining at a point tonally distant from it, they will inaugurate a modulatory process of ever greater amplitude. The tonal landscape widens limitlessly, as if we were to open a photographic lens with which we are focusing. A point will be reached at which the landscape will dissolve in blobs of vague colors; all form is lost in the "unfocusing" which is the road to atonality. So long as the chromatic modulations pass in rapid succession coming to rest on tonal supports, nothing is endangered. But if these points are suppressed or are replaced by others having no connection with each other, and all this with excessive rapidity, the feeling for tonality will tend to disappear, dissolving itself into a web of many amorphous colors.

The continuous alteration of the chords may weaken the tonal feeling but the danger in this case is not so imminent as in the other. Its dissonances enrich the harmonic complex in a manner far more effective and richer in color than when they occur polyphonically. In this respect the touch proper to the piano has contributed to the acceptance of the purely percussive dissonance in a way similar to that in which "writing" paved the way for sliding dissonances with their tendency toward atonality. I do not believe it is necessary to elaborate further what has been said concerning the altered chords which enriched romantic harmony and behind which impressionism was waiting. Nevertheless it seems to me necessary to say something concerning the road that leads from romantic harmony to impressionist harmony, a road that consists in the increasing endowment of chords of the seventh and ninth as harmonic complexes with such a feeling of unity that they may be termed semiconsonances.

CONSONANT FEELING OF THE SEVENTH AND THE NINTH

As regards the dominant seventh, its consonance is so far beyond doubt that some theorists call it the "perfect chord of the dominant seventh" but the sevenths known as those of the second class remain behind in their degree of acceptability, to which are added those built on diminished chords (third class), so typical in Wagner. Major sevenths, the most difficult to accept, are already used by Bizet and Mussorgsky. Ravel uses them freely: in root position, which is the place of their greatest harshness; disguised in inversions, which are in evidence everywhere in pre-Debussy French music (just like the diminished sevenths whose variety and charm are increased by the great quantity of exceptional resolutions to which they are particularly susceptible); and together with daring and unexpected modulations.

What is characteristic of the sevenths is emphasized in the ninths. "The land of the ninths," it was said of *Pelléas* and if, indeed, there is a composer who has known how to penetrate the magic enchantment of the sonority of these chords and their many derivations, he is without doubt Claude Debussy. The examples are so abundant and spread themselves in such a way throughout the whole panorama of contemporary music that it is scarcely necessary to insist on details which would turn this book into a didactic treatise. There is, nevertheless, one case on which it is necessary to pause for a moment.

It was always possible to place a chord of the dominant seventh upon the tonic. This produced, as a chord, two dissonances of the second (C-D and C-B, in the key of C major). Nevertheless, the absorbent capacity of the tonic disguised these shocks. If we place a chord of the dominant ninth on the tonic a new interpretation arises: namely, the possibility of understanding it as a harmony of seven tones or as a chord of the thirteenth, which would suggest that the previous superposition of the dominant seventh on the tonic was a chord of the eleventh. Both superpositions would present a major seventh which means that it is no longer a question of chords of the dominant but of several tones with independent value and without the expectation of a resolution on the tonic (which lies latent in the chord). The third of the chord does not appear, which conveys an additional shading, a modal indefiniteness to these chords, all of which makes them susceptible to different kinds of treatment. For example, let us assume the minor third: enharmonic change will admit of such devices as will allow the chord to enter various keys (preserving or rejecting from the complex some of its constituent intervals), a game which may be prolonged like Chinese solitaire by making use of enharmonic change in other intervals.

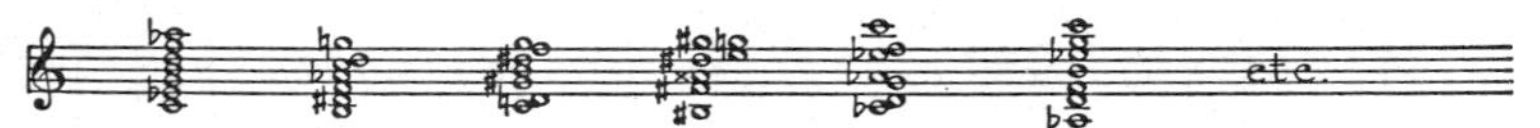

The principle of building a chord on a pedal point will, in turn, bring about incalculable consequences which have been enormously extended, and even viciously and abusively so, in contemporary music. It will be more appropriate to speak of them, since they are connected with limits, in the chapter devoted to polytonality and its close relative, atonality.

Chapter SIXTEEN

IF IMPRESSIONISM is the logical continuation of romantic harmony, it follows that, with Debussy and Ravel, there comes to an end a cycle of European music which began in France—but not for France alone—with Hector Berlioz. We have already referred to the epic significance of the sudden appearance of Berlioz' powerful and original genius joined, furthermore, to a technique which seemed almost superhuman to his contemporaries.

In the earlier nineteenth century, French comic opera and the symphony were two antagonistic poles. Berlioz declared himself for the second; this led him by the way of the most ebullient romanticism to romantic opera. His destiny was tragic. Meyerbeer was on the point of initiating the *grande opéra française,* of which Gounod became the apostle; Berlioz was left behind. And when the French romantic movement felt the impact of Richard Wagner, the last romantics (with Baudelaire at their head), were so stirred and enthralled by the emotional intensity of this novel art that they abandoned Berlioz to the most complete obscurity. In the *Mémoires* of Berlioz, says Romain Rolland in an article on *Le Renouveau* in French music, we can see what enthusiasm, what tears, what passion the performance of Gluck and Spontini provoked but it can be clearly observed, too, that this enthusiasm lasted only until 1840. Thereafter, it died down little by little, and an almost complete apathy succeeded it for twenty years. The incredible impoverishment of musical feeling in France between 1840 and 1870 is strikingly apparent in the romantic and naturalist literature of that era.

Nevertheless, fine music continued to be cultivated in France as an art of performance and interpretation. In the first years of the century the interpretation which the orchestra of the conservatoire gave to the symphonies of Beethoven had achieved such renown that Beethoven himself thought of going to Paris to hear "how they sounded," for in his own country his symphonies seem to have sounded pretty badly, to judge from contemporary testimony.[1] After the death of Beethoven, some of his music ceased to have

[1] G. Prodhomme, *Les Symphonies de Beethoven* (Paris: 1907).

an influence; the romantics of the Schumann-Chopin generation are not those most directly nourished by it and it had no influence on French composers. His quartets, particularly, fell into oblivion. However, in the year 1852 the French violinist Mauren and the Belgian violoncellist, Pierre Alexandre Chevillard (father of the orchestral conductor, Camille Chevillard) formed the Chevillard quartet. Its mission consisted in performing for a Société des derniers quatuors de Beethoven the quartets of the great composer, completely forgotten at that time. (Curiously enough, there was founded in England, in the same year, a Quartet Association whose most authoritative voice was that of the violoncellist, Piatti; its purpose was to make known the last quartets of Beethoven as well as recent works of English composers.) The snobs profoundly disdained this French society which undertook to perform an incomprehensible and extravagant music but the group included, on the other hand, such enthusiastic listeners as Berlioz and, in the year 1853, Richard Wagner and Franz Liszt.

In this year, when the German musical world began to hear talk of a young composer in Hamburg called Johannes Brahms, musical as well as political Europe was passing through some exciting moments; events were stirred by the recent coronations of two emperors, one in Germany and one in France. Still fresh was the *coup d'état* of the second Napoleon, that Napoléon le petit who was destined under the pernicious influence of his empress, a Spanish countess of rags and tatters much in the style of Mérimée, to bring his empire to disaster. The other emperor and his war lord, Bismarck of the iron fist, were to foster aspirations of hegemony whose musical culmination, Wagnerianism, formed the triumphant finale of the imperialist battle.

Napoleon—whose profoundly Germanophile minister (at least as regards love and music) Emile Ollivier was the husband of Blandina Liszt, oldest daughter of the great musician—brought about the performance of *Tannhäuser* at the Paris Opéra, defying the anti-Germans of the Jockey Club and the traditionalist and reactionary group of high French society. The spectacular failure of *Tannhäuser* is an episode known to everyone. Berlioz, a royalist in politics whose *Roméo et Juliette* had suggested to Wagner the road to *Tristan und Isolde* (at least as regards the romantic color of its chromaticism), was the first to throw a stone at the author of *Tannhäuser.* But the war cry had sounded in the hisses, the stampings, and the catcalls of the nobility, and the army of Wagnerophiles rode to the lists to fight for one whom, despite the incompatibility of his genius with the French spirit, they recognized as representing at that moment in 1860-61 the highest point in European symphonic-dramatic art. Such a defense on the part of French poets did not seem incongruous since Berlioz had, after all, prepared it but these same poets had not felt moved to honor their great compatriot, scorned, embittered, and resentful as he was.

As much as a year before the unfortunate catastrophe, Baudelaire wrote Wagner a letter in which he declared his passionate admiration for music which was to him "the greatest joy that I have ever experienced," music in which he finds "the solemnity of immense sounds, of the grand aspects of nature and the solemnity of man's great passions." He wrote this on February 17, 1860, one week after the appearance of Berlioz' pamphlet on the Wagner concerts of the Théâtre Italien.[2] Baudelaire, who turned to Berlioz to justify his enthusiasm for the Prelude to *Lohengrin,* took good care to forget the lines which he had just read on the Prelude to *Tristan und Isolde,* lines which could not have fed his enthusiasm. "It is strange," wrote Berlioz, "that the author has included this work [the Prelude] in the same concert with the Introduction to *Lohengrin* because he follows the same plan in both. Again we have a slow work, beginning pianissimo, which increases little by little to fortissimo, to fall away again to its starting point, without other theme than a kind of chromatic sigh full of dissonant chords whose appoggiaturas, which replace the real note of the harmony, only add to its cruel effect. I have read and reread this strange work [which Wagner had sent to Berlioz in printed score with an autograph dedication which read, 'To the great and beloved author of *Roméo et Juliette* from the author of *Tristan und Isolde'*]; I have listened to it with the most profound attention and with a great desire to discover its meaning. Yet, I am obliged to confess that I have not even the slightest idea of what the author has intended. . . ."[3]

But the program of this concert contained some explanatory notes capable of rousing a poet to fever pitch: they spoke of "infinite spaces" in which the soul is submerged by "a miraculous cohort of angels" who carry the Grail; of the increasing beatitude and of the "luminous apparition" of the magic and divine cup after which the world "sinks in ecstatic adoration." This playing with words, appearing a long time after the real *Parsifal* (not simply that announced in *Lohengrin*), reaches the extremes of a verbal mysticism which Liszt anticipated in masterly fashion in speaking of *Lohengrin* and *Tannhäuser* in 1851.

Baudelaire desired to translate these ineffable reveries, these supreme ecstasies, into his own words, and returning to one of his favorite themes—"things always being expressed by a reciprocal analogy"—he quotes the two quatrains of his now famous sonnet "Correspondances" (which we have already reproduced in our turn). Its origin is to be found in certain lines of the "Kreisleriana" (1846) of E. T. A. Hoffmann which Baudelaire quotes and

[2] Nevertheless, Jules Claretie says that on one occasion Baudelaire said to him, making a wry face: "I like Wagner but the music I prefer is that of a cat hung tail downward at a window and scratching the glass with its claws." (Quoted by Huneker, *Essays,* p. 170.) Wagner had written Baudelaire thanking him for his criticisms and later he made his acquaintance. Baudelaire also was personally acquainted with Liszt. (*Ibid.,* p. 196.)

[3] In *À travers chants,* ed. Calman-Lévy (Paris), p. 310.

which have their interest here: ". . . when I hear music I find, even though quite wide-awake, an analogy and a union between colors, sounds, and perfumes. It seems to me that all these things have been engendered by the same ray of light and that they must unite in a marvelous ensemble. . . ." Baudelaire adds, on his own account, that, "in color, one finds harmony, melody, and counterpoint. . . ."[4]

Harmony is the basis of the theory of color. Melody is unity in color or general color. Melody requires a conclusion: it is a combination in which all the effects contribute to the general effect. The reader who has properly understood what has preceded concerning the meaning of harmony and tonality will see how Baudelaire, through his intuition, followed German romanticism and came to discover the feeling of unity in the tonal sensation through the same complementary forces of consonance and dissonance which he had found in the two tones of color. "Color is, then, the chord produced by these two tones: the warm tone and the cool tone, in whose opposition consists the whole theory, without its being possible to define it in an absolute sense because they exist only relatively." And anticipating the dissolving forces in dissonance, in the chord now understood as an entity with independent value, as in the beginning of the Prelude to *Tristan,* Baudelaire adds, with the intuition of genius: "The lens is the eye of the colorist."

Pointillism might find its starting point in this phrase. For the present, it should be observed in following the historical thread, that the Wagnerianism of the French artists of that moment is less a passion for the artist Wagner and his art than a way of reacting favorably to the stimulus of certain sensations whose vast horizon and intense power belong to that stage in the evolution of musical aesthetics in which Europe found itself at about the middle of the century. Is it not clear, then, why it was the artists, and not the politicians or the aristocrats, who saw immediately—in the Bacchanal of *Tannhäuser*—that Faustian meaning which music assumed in the final period of romanticism? This sentiment had its counterpart in the poetry from Baudelaire to the symbolists and in impressionistic painting. And it is not strange that, while musicians allowed themselves to be ensnared in the magic nets of this Klingsor-Wagner, as he has been called,[5] Wagnerianism should continue to increase in France until the final years of the century when, as in 1885, *La Revue Wagnerienne* included among its contributors the most advanced spirits of the day, from Verlaine and Villiers de l'Isle-Adam to Mallarmé and Huysmans, from Fantin Latour to Jacques Blanche and Odilon Redon, besides the keenest minds among critics and philosophers of music.

But d'Indy, while recognizing the influence—beneficent for the reason

[4] *Curiosités esthétiques,* Salon de 1846 (Paris: edition of I.N.R.F.), pp. 69-70.

[5] Vincent d'Indy, *Richard Wagner et son influence sur l'art musical français* (Paris: Delaparc, 1930).

stated yet pernicious for reasons of style and technique—which Wagnerian art exercised in the second half of the nineteenth century, looked back to the most ancient French composers to find in them already alive and unequivocal the lyric soul of France. Berlioz, too, had sensed in them the essence of his meaning when, in 1860, he pronounced himself partly for, partly against, Wagnerianism. It is the first warning cry. At the end of the century arose another profoundly French spirit, Claude Debussy. He had felt deeply in his adolescent years the fascination of Wagnerianism (more than that of the music itself); he had been loyal to the aesthetic sense of his age, a sense expressed in impressionist painting and in symbolist poetry; he understood clearly, at last, that the way of Wagner led in the end to a fetid swamp in which the "flowers of evil" lay decaying, and that it was urgently necessary to tear oneself free from the amorous arms of the flower maidens of the enchanted garden; finally, he comprehended the Tolstoyan phrase, "salvation lies within ourselves" and turned his back on the Medusa to salute the pale yet smiling countenance of the ancient French tradition. This was the Debussy of Villon, of Charles d'Orléans, of the *Hommage à Rameau,* the Debussy in whom the disconcerting promises of his years in the conservatory and of his Wagnerianism at last find their form.

Claude Achille Debussy was still a child in 1870,[6] when France, brought to her ruin by the rivalry of the two recently manufactured emperors, knew the bitterness of defeat and the pseudoimperial throne crashed to the ground. In those twenty years the old France, that of the first half of the century, had changed profoundly and new seeds of every kind, spiritual as well as scientific, political as well as technical, were maturing in her soil. The shock of 1870 gave them a vigorous forward impulse. One of the new phases, partly an expression of resentment and repressed revenge, partly a healthy sign of a new orientation, was that of nationalism. In the field of music, the founding of the Société Nationale (which ended some decades later by becoming reactionary and conservative, the fatal course of all nationalisms) had consequences of immense importance. The musical atmosphere, in any case, was changing radically. The extremely timid cultivation of instrumental music now took on first importance. Now composers were not ashamed of being harmonists nor were professors bashful about teaching *la symphonie.* The difficulties which Pasdeloup placed before young French musicians disappeared; these youngsters were called César Franck, Camille Saint-Saëns, Ernest Guiraud, Gabriel Fauré, Henri Duparc, Jules Massenet—and along with them such savants as Bourgault-Ducoudray, who began to teach Greek

[6] He was born at St. Germain-en-Laye near Paris, August 22, 1862, of modest family.

music in the conservatory, and Charles Lalo, who expounded the first outlines of scientific musical aesthetics in the Sorbonne at the same time that other incipient musicologists began talking about a marvelous and forgotten art, that of the old baroque opera.[7]

A trio of César Franck, still imbued with a Beethovenlike feeling, inaugurated the Société Nationale. Later, the Société took all young France to its bosom. Franck, Saint-Saëns, d'Indy, Chabrier, Lalo, Bruneau, and Chausson preceded *La Demoiselle élue,* the *Prélude à l'après-midi d'un faune,* the quartet, the pages for piano. These men were the precursors of the new day. Dukas, Magnard, Ravel, Florent Schmitt, Roger Ducasse, Albert Roussel, Sévérac—these were Debussy's contemporaries: Debussy, axis and center of the new day, of the new French music. When the Société Nationale became restricted, it was supplemented by the Société Musicale Indépendante and its moving spirit, Maurice Ravel. The symphony orchestra, founded in 1873 by Edouard Colonne with the title Concert National, amplified the work of the first society and soon became one of the first orchestras in Europe. The music which it cultivated as daringly advanced was soon, with Claude Debussy, to recover the prominent place it had lost for a long time.

An international, youthful brigade of Germans, Austrians, Russians, Bohemians, Scandinavians, and Spaniards sat at the desks of Colonne's orchestra and afterward at those of the orchestra of Lamoureux. Another group which was to seek the pristine fount of lyric inspiration in the past and to open vast perspectives to the musical spirit of the generation of the *fin de siècle* was the Schola Cantorum, which had had illustrious predecessors. At the death of Franck in 1890, his first disciples wished to preserve the spirit of his teaching; the Schola was a kind of illustrious monument which filial piety raised to him. Another series of names appears in its lyric shade: Duparc, Alexis de Castillon, Vincent d'Indy (who became the high priest of this shrine on the Left Bank, still living in the heart of the Latin Quarter, rue Saint Jacques), Chausson, Pierre de Bréville, Augusta Holmès, Charles Bordes (who had founded in 1892 the Association des Chanteurs de Saint-Gervais), Guy Ropartz, and the short-lived Guillaume Lekeu—a Belgian like the venerated and vanished master—who followed Franck to the grave in the same year, 1894, in which the Schola Cantorum officially initiated its labors.

In that unhappy year of 1870,[8] Claude Achille was placed in the hands of a teacher of piano who was—fortuitous or symbolic accident—a direct disciple of Chopin; this was Madame Mauté de Fleurville who had known Wagner, Musset, and Balzac and who was, furthermore, the mother-in-law of Paul Verlaine. The little Claude was beginning to link himself with his age.

[7] In 1890, H. Expert began to publish "Les maîtres musiciens de la Renaissance française." In 1894, Romain Rolland wrote his "Histoire de l'Opéra en Europe avant Lully et Scarlatti."

[8] According to Ed. Lockspeiser; in 1872 according to L. Vallas.

At eleven, after three years of preliminary study, Debussy entered the conservatory under the direction of Lavignac and Marmontel, two classics of pedagogy. At fourteen, his youthful talent began to disclose itself; as a student of harmony under the severe eye of Émile Durand, he set to music some poems of Théodore de Banville: a brief effort, modest but sensitive. The strange chords, the watery arpeggios, the translucent harmonies which surprised his classmates would later have a perfect structure. For the moment they disconcerted his teachers and drew down upon Debussy both sympathy and scorn, causing the boy "to retire into himself," as the saying goes, so that he became reserved, taciturn, not a little eccentric. Debussy's youth revolved between two poles: that of his temperament, whereby nature was to lead to art, and that of his absorption in the lyric atmosphere which shone with most luster at the time—Wagnerianism. An old teacher, Auguste Bazille—ignored by the dictionaries but a sympathetic example of generosity, gentleness, and understanding, tempered by an "official" respect for pedagogy—observed the first expanding of the tender genius of his pupil. Surprised at first by his singularities, he soon realized that they were not the result of chance but responded to something struggling within the youth. He tried to explain and give them meaning and let Debussy pursue his way. In 1880, he gave Debussy first prize for reading score; this enabled the student to enter advanced classes in composition. Meanwhile Debussy produced the first results of his meditations.

Chapter SEVENTEEN

AT THE threshold of his advanced studies, Debussy was still only a boy of eighteen, without clear-cut personal convictions; yet, even while he reflected the light and superficial musical atmosphere around him, he possessed one striking characteristic which never changed—his inalienable French feeling. Marmontel had introduced him to the Overture to *Tannhäuser* but Debussy's inclinations leaned first of all toward Berlioz, Saint-Saëns, Lalo, Delibes and toward a young composer of light comic operas which delighted the young Debussy, Émile-Louis Pessard (who, two years later, was to replace Savard in the chair of harmony in the conservatory); above all toward Massenet. This admiration must surely have been more a result of what he heard Massenet explain in the class in composition (to which Massenet had been appointed in 1878) than for his comic operas for in 1880 Massenet had only produced *La Grand' Tante, Don César de Bazan* (with its *sevillanas*), and *Le Roi de Lahore,* with its orientalisms, so much liked in its time. Yet Massenet was also known among his contemporaries for his orchestral pieces; his picturesque suites of every variety, with their nationalistic coloring ranging from that of Hungary to Naples, and his patriotic overtures figured on the symphonic programs of the day.

An unexpected event now (1880) intervened to provide the incipient talent of Claude Achille with a series of experiences which were to contribute much to the formation of his character and his musical tastes. This was his acquaintanceship with the famous friend of Peter Ilyitch Tchaikovsky, Nadejda von Meck, an episode well known and frequently misinterpreted. Madame von Meck, the rich widow of a Russian industrialist, who alleviated her bereavement by traveling through Europe with her eleven children and writing interminable letters to the "immortal beloved"—the author, at that time, of the Fourth Symphony—applied at the Paris Conservatory for a young pianist whom she desired in the capacity of house musician to play four hands with her and to read to her at the piano. Marmontel, who was fond of Claude Achille despite his "defects" and who valued the qualities of his budding though not well-disciplined personality, recommended his pupil. During several months of travel in Switzerland and Italy as one of the Russian lady's entourage, Debussy came to know well the works of Tchaikovsky, the chief deity in this restricted musical environment, and also those of Liszt and Wagner. It appears that the lady and the young musician visited Wagner in his melancholy Venetian palace. Later, when a scholarship student in Rome, Debussy became personally acquainted with Liszt.

On the occasion of a visit to Mme. von Meck at her residence at Brailov in the Ukraine, in the summer of 1881, Debussy spent several weeks in Moscow. There he discovered the dances and songs of the Russian gypsies with their modal turns, their free harmonies, and their sensual rhythm. His acquaintance at this time with the music of the "Mighty Five," so badly received in Mme. von Meck's circle, was reflected in some of his music of this period in which may be seen a certain influence of Borodin, whom he came to know personally. The songs of Balakirev pleased him especially. Debussy was able to convince his generous patroness of the reasons for his taste and she was not slow to recount the discovery of the *jeune parisien* to Tchaikovsky. The lady had already submitted some of Debussy's compositions to the authoritative judgment of the recluse of Kamenka. Tchaikovsky commented favorably, though not without making some observations which appear to have been just but which evidently did not much please the budding composer. In any case, Debussy made no attempt to see Tchaikovsky nor does the young composer's music show the slightest trace of his influence.

On his return, Debussy brought with him not only the recent scores of *La Demoiselle d'Orléans* and *Roméo et Juliette,* presented to him by Mme. von Meck but also an opera of Rimsky, whose orchestration impressed him greatly in its relationship to that of Berlioz, as well as several songs of Borodin. At that time Debussy knew of Mussorgsky, apparently from Mme. von Meck's lips, only that he was "finished." Neither Mussorgsky's music nor that of his companions of the "Mighty Five" was much appreciated or performed in Russia. A hearing of *Tristan und Isolde* in Vienna on his way home impressed Debussy far more than all the Russian music he had heard up to that time.

Subsequently, the score of *Tristan* was Debussy's refuge during his stay as a scholarship student at the Villa Medici, for lack of more stimulating incentives. Debussy had won the Grand Prix de Rome with a cantata, the conservative sentiment of which was already at variance with the new aesthetic perspectives he was discovering through his friendship with a highly intelligent couple, the architect Vasnier and his young wife. At their famous gatherings, in the rue de Rome, Debussy came into contact with the most advanced poets of the day, Stéphane Mallarmé and Paul Verlaine among them. Madame Vasnier was a singer of exceptional talent and, in the warmth of the artistic and sympathetic atmosphere which she and her husband offered him, Debussy wrote his first significant works, such as the music to the *"Fêtes Galantes"* of Verlaine. In the months with Mme. von Meck, Debussy had written some pages—a trio and sketches for a symphony—in which the influence of Massenet seems to predominate. Nevertheless, an already unmistakably Debussyist page is the Mandoline of 1880. Debussy visited Mme. von Meck again in 1884, the year in which he began to set to music a comedy of Théodore de Banville, *Diane au bois,* and the new official cantata *L'Enfant prodigue,* which won him unanimous applause and in which original traits are mingled with the dominating influence of Massenet.

His stay at the Villa Medici did little more than nourish a desire to escape. The memory of Mme. Vasnier pursued him but, instead of stimulating his creative faculty, it depressed him. Perhaps his enthusiasm for *Tristan* in those empty months reflects the anguish of that absence. The Diana of the wood did not progress nor did successive attempts at that French pseudo orientalism which left its mark on the first Spanish orientalists: a *Salambó,* a *Zuleima,* an *Almanzor,* the artificiality of which he promptly recognized. In the long days of melancholy meditation, Debussy was changing his earlier tastes for new decisive influences. With his fellow scholars, he played the works of Bach for four hands, the Ninth Symphony of Beethoven, which had somewhat increased his meager interest as a conservatory student in the great symphonist. But Palestrina and Orlando di Lasso, whose works he heard in the Roman churches, opened vistas until then unknown to him and drew him from the religious music of Gounod and his like. A composer, who had recently appeared in print, excited Debussy's interest with the novelty and unexpectedness of his harmonies: it was Emmanuel Chabrier in his *Valses Romantiques.*

From Italian art he acquired, above all, a feeling for ordered harmony, as simple and transparent as that in Botticelli, whose *"Primavera"* inspired the suite, *Printemps.* This work, as an accomplishment of the obligations of his fellowship, was received by the academic tribunal with less severity than the earlier *Zuleima,* although not without some reproaches. In all justice, it must be said that these reproaches show a keen critical sense on the part of the judges but not an aesthetic sense because what they considered failings are precisely the prime qualities to be noted in the style and talent of Debussy. In effect, what startled the worthy gentlemen of the institute and made them fearful for a talent "which certainly does not sin either through vulgarity or frivolity" was Debussy's tendency toward a strange "feeling for musical color, an exaggeration of which readily causes forgetfulness of the importance of preciseness in line and form. It is much to be desired [they added] that he should put himself on his guard against this vague impressionism," which they found endangered "truthfulness" in a work of art. The magic word impressionism thus appears for the first time in music. Although Debussy might protest it and the abuses which it was to bring about in connection with his music, it was not to abandon him in his entire career nor was it to cease to characterize him in the history of music, despite all the vagueness and lack of precision which that term may possess and which is indeed its essence.

Another work in which the tendencies initiated in *Printemps* are emphasized and defined is the music for solo and chorus on the poem of Dante Gabriele Rossetti, whose refinement and delicate originality moved Debussy to the depths of his being. *La Damoiselle élue* is already the purest Debussy. It is also a musical work in which the symbolist poets of Mallarmé's groups found embodied their aspirations toward a poetry of musical essence. And this work is to such a degree a faithful translation of the maturing talent of its author that, when Debussy reaches his apogee in *Pelléas et Mélisande,* the gentle, translucent harmonies of the Blessed Damsel sound again from the opera's first measures.

At the end of his artistic life, Debussy in *Le Martyre de Saint Sébastien* is still as near the Blessed Damsel as Wagner in *Parsifal* is to *Lohengrin.* This lyricism, a poetic vagueness which the first Wagnerian commentators had understood so well, endures in the d'Annunzian poetry translated by Debussy into music which the gentle wind of his inspiration wafted from certain pages of Franck as well as from the last ones of Wagner.

The charm of harmonies in fifths produced in Debussy a kind of supernatural ecstasy which he was never to abandon. The tenuousness of incomplete scales, with tonal ambiguities already used in *Printemps,* will go on defining itself in brush strokes similar to those which, in Monet, are like tiny flakes of color capable of evoking a form. In this work, as in the *Fantaisie* for piano and orchestra, the modal indecisiveness is one of the reasons for its vaporous charm, for its tonal mobility into which slips, like fleeting apparitions, the scale of whole tones. Successions of chords of the seventh and ninth introduced into the orchestra, in these works of the prize scholar, the ornamental melismaticism which was one of the characteristic discoveries of Chopin in the field of the piano; of course, Debussy uses this effect on the piano too, considerably amplified by the possibilities of new sonorities and poetic effects hitherto unexploited. His manner of treating the voice is a prolongation of that art, of an effectiveness and good taste undiminished by hypersensitivity. Yet, in vocal ensembles, Debussy knows how to produce new effects which he probably sensed from the time of his visits to Russia and in which the undulations of the Wagnerian Rhine maidens are not far distant.

Debussy was struggling in those years with the principles of form. The thematic and tonal alternation of the sonata seemed to him too conventional a framework, and in the *Fantaisie* he tries to substitute cyclical procedures which belong to the Franck school. Although Debussy was not long in abandoning the features of a system he defined as "a heavy structure," he nevertheless did not fail to retain some of its principles and utilized them in such works as the Quartet, which was necessarily based on an abstract plan in contrast to brief pages freer in feeling. The shadow of Franck, dimmed by distance, is perceptible in Debussy's last works, like the Sonata for violin and piano, in a form now given utmost amplitude and elasticity. The determining ideas in the rest of his production are those unmistakably apparent in the works of the scholarship student. Debussy never deviated from them; he treats them, he revises them, he formulates them in different ways throughout a production exquisite and intense in its refinement. Thanks to them he selects a musical vocabulary, a syntax which, while it gives an unmistakable definition to his personality, separates the musical language prior to his time completely from his own. His imitators precipitately attempted to adopt it without realizing that this language, which corresponded to individual and highly original ideas, was by its very nature inimitable. But musical feeling at the end of the century found it to be so appropriate a translation of the point which the evolution in acoustical perception had reached that it proclaimed Debussy the discoverer of a new epoch in European music.

Those perspectives which became the guiding thread of Debussy's aesthetics and technique from the time he started work on *La Damoiselle élue* have been synthesized by Debussy's friend, Maurice Emmanuel.[1] These principles are: (*a*) the extension of harmonic relationships, (*b*) independence in the use of dissonances without preparation or resolution, (*c*) the free employment of notes foreign to the chord, (*d*) the formation of an arbitrary scale or of an oriental or modal coloring with the resulting successions of chords, and (*e*) the use of enharmonic change as a means of modulating to distant tonalities whose modality rests uncertainly between major and minor. We are very far, in this year of 1887, from the aesthetics of romanticism or even of Wagnerianism. Nevertheless, Wagner still had much to say and Debussy, the *Damoiselle élue* still unfinished, went to Bayreuth to hear *Parsifal* and *Tristan* (1888-89).

It is in the latter year that a score which had reached the hands of Saint-Saëns and certain performances of exotic music were to give the final touches to the formation of Debussy's personality. That score was the *Boris Godunov* of Mussorgsky. The other music was that of Spanish *cantaores* and guitarists, that of the Javanese gamelangs and the popular music of other kinds which could be heard every afternoon in the pavilions of the International Exposition in Paris in 1889. The *Cinq Poèmes de Baudelaire* which Debussy finished in that year show him completely formed. Nevertheless, his literary tastes still fluctuated between French romantic poetry and the poetry posterior

[1] Maurice Emmanuel, his excellent study of *Pelléas et Mélisande.*

to it. Thus, he sketched the composition of lyric dramas like *Rodrigue et Chimene,*[2] with libretto by Catulle Mendès, redolent with that romantic Spanish air which we have already observed. Although much of it was completed (as far as the third act), it never was finished. An incident which was to have an enduring influence occurred to lead Debussy in paths much nearer to his own sensibility and to that of the age. In 1892, Debussy saw a performance of the drama, *Pelléas et Mélisande,* by Maurice Maeterlinck. The musician was then involved in the composition of a *Prélude, Interlude et Paraphrase* for Mallarmé's eclogue *L'Après-midi d'un faune.* The performance of Maeterlinck's drama excited him to such a degree that this triptych remained reduced to only one of its parts, the *Prélude.* But Debussy's series of masterpieces begins at this point with the Quartet, first performed in 1893 in a recital of the Société Nationale, together with *La Damoiselle élue* and the *Après-midi,* which appeared on the desks of the same society in the following year (without causing more of a sensation than the other works). A first version of Nocturnes was sketched in the shape of three compositions for violin and orchestra which Debussy had planned in honor of the Belgian violinist Eugène Ysaÿe, so closely linked with the memory of Franck and of Lekeu and, furthermore, a countryman of the author of *Pelléas.*

The Nocturnes, first performed in their definitive version in 1900 by Camille Chevillard, mark the first of Debussy's great triumphs. *Pelléas* was at the point of being finished (after a first version which was destroyed). Its first performance in 1902 was to mark, like that earlier Parisian first performance of *Tannhäuser,* a decisive date in the history of contemporary music. Debussy had reached the high point of his career. The next few years constituted his period of plenitude with: *Estampes* in 1903; the symphonic triptych, *La Mer,* finished in 1905; in 1906, Ibéria. The *"Chansons de Charles d'Orléans"* (for chorus), in 1908, mark the point of subtlest refinement in Debussy's literary taste. For many years his glance had turned to the past to find in the poetry of the French Renaissance the unmistakable accents of the spirit of his country; he wished, at one time, to render even greater homage by bringing a French Tristan to the stage in Joseph Bédier's edition. The music with which Debussy between 1904 and 1910 enhanced the rondels of Charles d'Orléans, of Tristan l'Hermite, and the ballads of Villon constitutes, perhaps, the moment of greatest delicacy and refinement in expression and in harmonic color which the European music of impressionism reached in its last period. The *Préludes,* which carry music for the piano to the same height, extend from 1910 to 1913. In between appear, with scarcely any warning, *Le Martyre de Saint Sébastien* (1911) and the ballet *Jeux,* written for Nijinsky (1913).

[2] Based on the *Mocedades del Cid* of Guillén de Castro.

Pianistic impressionism already appeared in a colloidal state in the Études of 1915. Debussy was very ill. He intended to write a series of six sonatas, for various instruments which, conceived during the war, were to have been signed, "Claude Debussy, *musicien français.*" Only three were finished: one for harp, flute, and viola, and another sonata, for piano and violoncello, in which are found some echoes of the most recent enthusiasm to stir the musical world: the Russian, Igor Stravinsky. Finally came the Sonata for piano and violin, Debussy's last effort, which dates from 1917. The following year, Paris was bombarded by long-range German guns. The ominous rumbling faintly reached the mansion where Debussy had lived since the period of *La Mer.* The muffled vibrations of this distant thunder offered a sinister pedal note to accompany the transcendent journey of Debussy's spirit—freed of the earthly wrappings that had been emaciated by cancer—on the fifteenth of March in the historic year, 1918.

The second trip to Bayreuth, in 1889, produced in Debussy something more than disillusionment regarding an art which he knew represented an admirable moment in the last days of romanticism: he realized its lack of universality. Now that his individuality as a French musician had crystallized, Debussy could appreciate that the enthusiasm which Wagner had awakened in France forty years before had been motivated, among artists, by reasons other than purely musical ones. With the death of César Franck there disappeared the last authentic example of a postromantic art that had been engendered half by the German tradition, half by the French spirit. Now Debussy saw clearly that French music could rise of itself alone, without direct contact with foreign sentiment just as was happening in French painting and poetry. As a matter of fact, his last journey to the mecca of Wagnerianism coincided with the course of opinion which, despite isolated cases such as that of Vincent d'Indy, tended to depart further and further from the Germanic concept of music. Yet, in fairness to the objectivity of Debussy, who had attacked Gluck and who did not revere Beethoven exaggeratedly (unlike certain mystics of the nineteenth century), it must be said that while he considered d'Indy, Chausson, and Dukas the most notable French composers of the time, he had a serious critical respect for the work of Richard Strauss; this opinion, however, did not influence those who, in other respects, were Debussy's followers.

This last journey to the land of German ultrachromaticism lay between two affirmations of the pure French spirit: the *Ariettes* with a text of Verlaine, which date from 1888, and the *Cinq Poèmes de Baudelaire,* which are of 1890. The Parisian musical environment still was little prepared, and so these works played the role of precursors, for Debussy re-edited the ariettas years later under the title *Ariettes Oubliées.* The first performance of *Pelléas et Mélisande,* with the accompanying emotional excitement and clash of opinions which belonged to the theater at that time, was the clarion call which decisively raised the banner of an anti-Wagnerianism; this movement was shortly to be converted, to its author's disgust, into a wildly exaggerated Debussyism. Since then, almost all the labels which have been used for the different schools or groups arising in the new century, such as Stravinskyism, atonalism, objectivism, as well as superrealism, have actually denoted the extremes of musical hero worship rather than any truly aesthetic attitudes. Debussyism then, like impressionism in general, closes its cycle in the first decades of the new century, as we shall see in speaking of the culmination of Maurice Ravel's production. Meanwhile, let me endeavor to complete this sketch of the figure of Claude Debussy and of the general scene which served as his background.

"*Pelléas et Mélisande* of M. Debussy," wrote Romain Rolland, speaking of its first performance, in an article which is a model of intelligence and detachment as well as of penetrating criticism, "seemed to announce, in 1902, the date of the true emancipation of French music. From that moment, French music felt itself definitely freed from its apprenticeship and set out to found a new art which should reflect the genius of the race with more flexibility than Wagnerian art." And in commenting on the rapid extension of this point of view among Debussy's commentators and followers who thought they had discovered a superior art, this critic asks: "Is this conviction justified?" If such superiority is understood to be in comparison with the musical art of other European countries between 1890 and 1920, one can agree with it. If it is to be understood as referring to the art prior to that period, one must disagree for a multitude of reasons. But if one considers what was to be the future of music from impressionism on, one must recognize that the stage of Debussy and Ravel was a magnificent period of contemporary music, ineffaceable and unforgettable; it was a period which did not prolong itself beyond its own setting, despite the weak repercussions which it had beyond its own confines, and which vanished in the lyric atmosphere like the volatile substance it was.

One of the reasons for the effect that *Pelléas et Mélisande* produced on its French audiences lay, as has been explained to us repeatedly, in its fatalism, in which was reflected the weariness of a European intellectual aristocracy. This opinion was upheld by the German critics, even those of such independent judgment as Adolph Weissmann, who found in *Pelléas* a typical example of a decay of the French spirit which had been in process since *Les Fleurs du Mal,* in the year following the fiasco of *Tannhäuser.* Weissmann, who was a Jew, saw clearly the episodic character of impressionism, and as all German Jews are even more German than non-Jewish Germans, he believed he saw in the opposing element in Germanic countries—in the expressionism of Schönberg and his group—a vindication of German art. Weissmann died before being able to confirm the fact that this impressionism of tonality, so-called atonalism, to which the composers of this group address themselves, had not produced an art of more permanence than the French. In point of fact, is it not a question of a dissolution of European culture in its entirety? It is stupid to talk of a "German culture" which has never existed independently but rather as a component part of the European cultural complex, despite certain effects that strive toward an appearance of autonomy. And, in truth, after the best pages of Maurice Ravel, European musical art seems to fall into the abyss which the struggle of the masses for the recovery of their social rights has been preparing while their leaders, plebeians for a hundred generations, paraded an instant as the "leaders of the people": leaders to the abyss, for whom Berlioz prophetically wrote his famous march in *La Damnation de Faust.*

Chapter EIGHTEEN

WE ARE very far, at the end of the nineteenth century, from the endless polemics aroused by the reform whence opera was born in the first years of the seventeenth century. Then, certain men of genius in Florence devoted themselves to giving to the Italian language, when sung, the prosodic naturalness of speech (following the poets of the French Renaissance who, led by Baïf, had applied themselves to a like task in that Parisian Académie de Musique et de Poésie created by Henry III) in such a way that monody, timidly accompanied by lutes and theorbos, might be a kind of musical speech. All beginnings are imperfect. If Monteverdi, the greatest lyric genius who existed before Gluck, Mozart, and Verdi, had not written his *opera in musica,* the effort of the musicians of the group led by Giovanni Bardi, Count of Vernio, would probably have come to nothing. Or maybe not, since reform was in the air. For, after this art spread throughout Italy, it invaded neighboring countries.

The first national opera to rise outside of Italy, albeit created by a native Italian, was the French *tragédie lyrique* of Lully. The name itself demonstrates that this genre resulted from a fusion of French literary precepts with the new musico-dramatic spirit coming from Italy. Lully first, Rameau later, joined together Parisian and Florentine ideals in the search for a natural language which, now, was harmonized in the sonorous setting of the orchestra, a background against which moved characters whose emotional conflicts provided the poet with his argument and the musician with its translation: the translation of emotional conflicts into musical terms which the French recognized as a new dramatic form, hence *tragédie lyrique,* as this opera first was called. Lully, who attended performances of Molière's comedies in order to note the inflections in the accent of the great actresses like Champmeslé, took the first step toward the sought-after naturalness of the dramatic musical accent.

Rousseau, a better grammarian if not a better musician, went a step further. He said that the spoken language is one thing and the musical another and that recitative in the style of *opera buffa* brought the language of everyday with a more specific—that is, musical rather than spoken—naturalness to a theater which derived its plots from the petty intrigues furnished by everyday life. The Spaniards of the eighteenth century knew this well but their sphere of action was too limited and they were overruled by an aristocratic society that was convinced of the superiority of Italian opera. The French tradition of Lully and Rameau declined after the death of the latter and, as the Italian muse was taking possession of the field, certain people of traditionalist spirit found in a distant European capital the man capable of giving French opera the nobility of mien and the air it had lost. Paradoxically, this man was far from having French blood in his veins or the French language on his tongue, for he was a German musician of Bohemian descent. Thus the reform of French opera was initiated by Christoph Willibald Gluck and was later continued—O, shades of French art!—by Gioacchino Rossini and Jakob Liebmann Beer, called Meyerbeer.

Claude Debussy, who considered the native tradition lost with Rameau, refused to admit that Gluck was the one who continued it; in an open letter to the other world, he reproached Gluck for having filled French music, especially in the theater, with pedantries and vocal artificialities. Let us leave to him the responsibility for these assertions and hear his suggestions for endowing with music the drama of Maurice Maeterlinck, *Pelléas et Mélisande,* possessed of such obvious lyric substance despite its dramatic weaknesses.

After his passionate pilgrimages to Bayreuth, he tells us, he realized that Wagnerian music could only serve the individual purpose of Wagner himself; this individuality of style is also true of Debussy: fanatic Debussyists agreed with him less than did Wagnerians with *their* inventor. Wagner, he adds, was a great collector of formulas and he put them together in a single formula which seemed highly personal only because music—and, he might have added, the history of music—is badly understood. "Without denying his [Wagner's] genius," he continues, "one may say that he put the final mark of punctuation to the music of his time, more or less as Victor Hugo absorbed all previous poetry. We must, then, look *après Wagner,* not *d'après Wagner.*" This is very well said but one cannot deny that Debussy saw in the Saxon a final beacon light, a shore line beyond which the open sea beckoned adventure. A Mediterranean sea, this, quickly traversed. The welcoming beacon might be called Claude Debussy: *Parsifal* on one shore and *Pelléas* on the other.

What attracted Debussy in the first place was the malleableness of a language which could lend itself, with a freedom until then unsuspected, to musical intonation in such a way that it gave vital color to a humanity which seemed to him far more real than all the "documents of life" realism or naturalism advocated. But this was exactly the vulnerable point through which the enemies of Debussy found it easy to attack him. The characters sing (as he thought) like real people and not in an arbitrary idiom imposed by tradition. Caccini, Cavalieri, Monteverdi, Metastasio, Ranieri di Calzabigi, Father Arteaga, Gluck himself spoke in the same terms. Reformers in art, like politicians, think they have found the philosopher's stone, the solution for tomorrow. How does Schönberg think his soprano sings, sliding and wavering in imprecise intonations in the oriental manner in his *Pierrot Lunaire?* And Alban Berg in *Wozzeck,* in *Lulu?* Debussy, like Lully, still believes that the evocative emotion of his characters can find "extension in the music and in the orchestral setting." This is the point of divergence between *Pelléas* and *L'Heure espagnole* of Ravel and those Viennese works we have mentioned. In the former, the music, realistic this time (that is to say, realistic in the opinion of Ravel), is what provides the dramatic value by virtue of the sonorous expression which does not now emanate from a motive, but which appears concentrated in the harmonic power of the unusual chord; in the Viennese, the music, transformed into atmosphere in which the dramatic feeling is diluted, is now expressive per se, for which reason the composers of that group considered themselves well described in the word expressionists, although in point of fact, the resulting fusion is what Wagnerian chromaticism thought it had achieved.

If Debussy makes use of the characteristic motive in *Pelléas,* he uses it less in the sense of a leading motive, like Wagner, than in the sense of presentation or a calling to mind, like the *idée fixe* in Berlioz and the reminiscence in Liszt or in Verdi. The symphonic possibilities of the leitmotiv scarcely exist in the faint and gentle apparitions of the motive in *Pelléas;* here the motive is a discreet reminder to the sensitive memory of the listener: a certain timbre in the orchestra, a specific dissonance, a simple, elemental rhythmic turn, subtly suggested, may have a reminiscent value and, at the same time, a constructive purpose.

The crux of the problem of the musical theater lies in the fact that it has to do with two actions, the dramatic-vocal and the musical, which move in parallel lines without ever becoming fused. It must be confessed that the musical theater consists in a superimposing of two currents which may have the same, the identical purpose, but which in reality proceed apart from each other: the one illuminated by the footlights on the stage, the other in the semidarkness of its mystic abyss. Each theatrical composer has tried in his own way and in accord with the norm of his age to solve this problem, insoluble though it may be. Wagner thought he had definitively achieved the fusion of these two physical elements which, by their very nature, can never aspire to more than a mingling. At least, so Wagner must have thought, it is possible to achieve a fusion of spiritual elements: the human voice and the instrumental voice. This ideal is, in any case, that toward which composers ceaselessly aspire.

Debussy saw the same goal: "It has been my intention that the action should never be held back but that it should be continuous, uninterrupted. I have tried to avoid parasitical musical phrases. In listening to an opera the spectator habitually experiences two different kinds of emotions: the musical emotion on the one hand, the human emotion on the other. Ordinarily he experiences them successively. I have endeavored to fuse these two emotions perfectly in their simultaneity." Illusion, as in the case of his predecessors! Indeed it is the contrary which occurs in *Pelléas*. As has been explained, the evolution of the romantic-impressionist harmonic system brought about a musical interpretation of the independent chord, according to its sonorous value per se. But this verticality of the chord, requiring neither preparation nor resolution, gives by its very essence an impression of tranquillity and repose. Impressionist music is above all soothing, restful, and tranquil. If ever there was theater without movement, without external action, it is *Pelléas*. In saying that melody is "almost antilyric" because of its inability to translate the mobility of the soul and of life, Debussy reaches the point of positively denying the existence of the lyric theater. Debussy believes that this mobility can only be expressed in song, that is to say, in melody of concrete form; this is equivalent to saying that the true musical theater is that of Alessandro Scarlatti and the composers of late baroque opera.

At the opposite pole is the "infinite melody" of Wagner, or "indefinite melody" (which is what Wagner really means) but this is transcendent melody: it cannot be made concrete within the limitations of a human emotion and, for this reason, in order to confine the melodic stream which flows unceasingly, the author must have recourse to expressive devices which will restrain it a little—these are his leitmotivs. In the drama, the specific emotion which song translates does not exist. The souls of Maeterlinck's characters are, as has been said, "soft, evanescent creatures" of protoplasmic substance, which impressionist harmony translates marvelously in its indefiniteness, its lack of preciseness, its exquisite delicacy. What is it that Debussy saw—the possibility of translating the soul of Mélisande in the eddying harmony of impressionism or, on the contrary, did he see in Mélisande the human shadow capable of embodying (in what pale hues!) the sensual flood of impressionist harmony? In short, is *Pelléas* a cause or an effect? To all eternity artists will believe the first; the second is the truth. The real process is that which Schopenhauer describes in the simile of the stone which, when hurled, believes it is moving of its own volition.

But art by nature is dynamic. If a point of repose is reached at which the emotions enjoy tarrying, the elements which impel the musical sense onward will not be long in applying new stimuli. It was such stimuli that Maurice Ravel was to bring to the music of the new century, after Debussy.

The first consequence of the breaking-up of the chordal complex into small dissonant fragments, fleeting sparks of sound which vanish once their stimulating effect is accomplished, is dissolution of classico-romantic form which, based on the firm coherence of tonal relationships, becomes relaxed with the weakening of these very bonds. From the early days of romanticism, its composers, immediately following the Ninth Symphony and the grand, yet loose symphonic constructions of Schubert, found themselves (like Schubert himself) obliged to lay chief stress on the small forms, in which it was easier to achieve the principle of coherence within the new harmonic terms then in process of rapid evolution. The grand form, with these composers, was a problem to be solved not in conformity with the harmonic feeling which dictated the small works but by means of rhetorical and academic devices. For this reason the symphonic works of the romantics play a subordinate role and when, at the end of the movement, there was a desire to return to a grand form of adequate coherence and unity, as with Brahms and Franck, one had to look back to Beethoven.

The series of pieces, like the Carnaval of Schumann, for example, based their unity in the general poetic sentiment, in their character; or else, the composer had recourse, as Mussorgsky in Pictures at an Exhibition, to the artifice of joining together unrelated pages with a connecting passage like the brief and malleable measures called Promenades. Chopin never intended, it would seem, that his Preludes or Études, written at different times and in different circumstances, should be played as a series. Nevertheless, the general character of his inspiration, style, and harmonic sense and the unmistakable personality of their author lend them a unity which makes the continuity feasible, provided the performer makes certain adjustments of key and of tempo.

Debussy's works of grand dimensions share in the formal dissolution to be observed in the large impressionist canvases, like the water lilies of Claude Monet. It is well known that this vast series of paintings in which Monet painted the water lilies in his garden (as well as other similar series) at different hours of the day are like colored fragments which follow one after the other with scarcely a break, somewhat as if the painter had had the intention of presenting as a cinematographic series (or "vanishing pictures" as they were called at that time) the constant and insensible change of atmospheric color with the passing of the hours. Seen individually, not in succession, the difference between two canvases may seem as sharp as that which separates the morning light from that of twilight; seen progressively, as they are installed in the little oval salons of the Orangerie in the Parisian garden of the Tuileries, each fragment seems a luminous transformation of the previous one. Each scene, of course, has its own life and expression: their continuity is simply a further idea on the painter's part, but is not indispensable to each picture. Debussy's symphonic pieces, such as *La Mer*[1] or *Images,* produce a similar effect on the listener and it is above all the effect received on hearing *Pelléas et Mélisande.*[2]

This effect of dissolution is no more than the consequence of the slow extension of the harmony and the tonality which projects itself upon the form. From the day of its first performance such a writer as Romain Rolland, in a just, thoughtful, and objective article, wrote: "From the point of view of the stage *Pelléas et Mélisande* is quite opposed to the ideal of Bayreuth. The vast, almost unlimited proportions of Wagnerian drama, its compact structure, the tension of will which supports these enormous works from beginning to end, their ideology frequently developed at the expense of the action and even of the emotion are all as far as possible from the French taste for clear, logical, and sober action. The little scenes of *Pelléas et Mélisande* are brief and well knit, each of them marks without insistence a new stage in the evolution of the drama, and have an architecture totally distinct from the Wagnerian theater."[3]

"Clear, logical, and sober action" is the center, constantly emphasized, which marks the transformation of the impressionism of Debussy to that of his successors, of whom the most eminent, for his profoundly original personality as for his individual technical means, is Maurice Ravel. If one compares a work of each composer belonging to the same type of composition: the Ibéria of the one with the *Rhapsodie Espagnole* of the other; the prelude *L'Après-midi d'un faune* with certain scenes from *Daphnis et Chloé;* piano pieces like *Estampes* with the scenes of *Gaspard de la nuit;* or *Jardins sous la pluie* and *Jeux d'eau;* the toccatas of both composers; their respective Ondines; one can easily appreciate the increasing keenness of the harmonic and expressive procedure, of the stylization which, within the same general aesthetic category, leads from Debussy to Ravel. When Debussy gives concrete outline to his motives and tightens his form (as for example in the first movement of the Quartet or in Iberia), one might say that he presages Ravel in his formal works with a greater degree of clarity than the impressionistic works of both would suggest. For in these, what is atmosphere in Debussy tends to become outline in Ravel; the splotch becomes design; and what in Debussy is an arabesque aspires to be, with Ravel, the motive, firm of line.

The comparison (aside from the dimensions of each) between the only dramatic compositions of the two great Frenchmen, between *Pelléas et Méli-*

[1] See especially From Dawn to Midday on the Sea, the first of this set of three symphonic sketches.

[2] ". . . that charm spread fleetingly through a verse, those fluid and ever-changing gestures, the successive scenes, all this was the intangible result, the momentary aim, the shifting ideal which the theatrical art set before itself and which destroyed—in the very effort to capture it—the attention of the overwhelmed spectator." M. Proust, *Le Côté de Guermantes,* I, 47.

[3] R. Rolland, *Musiciens d'Aujourd'hui,* 1908.

sande and *L'Heure espagnole,* is especially revealing. What stands out immediately with the greatest sharpness is the increasing accentuation of outline and accents in the declamation. The true and fecund theory of Paul Bekker, that opera is a musical work based on the genius of the language,[4] illuminates with great clarity the development of German opera, from Gluck, as a construction rooted in the spirit of instrumental music, in the spirit of the symphony. In contrast, French opera (whose purest essence is *opéra comique*), with the Italian, from the classical opera of the baroque to *opera buffa* and the verismo of our own time, is a type of lyric theater in which the spoken language is the nucleus which engenders the plan and development of the work. The instrumentalization is subordinate and takes the form, in the classics, of simple harmonizations or else aspires to provide a lyric atmosphere for the action, as from Lully to Debussy. At the same time the action seeks to express itself according to the norms of the language.

I have remarked that Lully attended the *haute comédie* to note the inflections in the recitation of the great actors of his day. It has also been observed that Jean Jacques Rousseau justly criticized this method because, as he said, if opera proposes to bring the language of everyday life to the theater, it is clear that that language is not to be found in the grandiloquent, affected, and conventional speech of the actors of the seventeenth and eighteenth centuries (who followed a stylistic convention which produced a special kind of singsong still preserved at the Comédie Française for the classical works of Corneille, Racine, Molière, etc.). Very different is the French language of daily life in its "connected accents, so simple and so discreet," far from the "shrill and noisy" intonations of the recitative of French opera, for the natural language proceeds as if "it revolved within narrow limits, without great risings or fallings of the voice, with little sustained sounds, never bursting out in brusqueness, still less in shouts; nothing which resembles *song,* neither the inequality in the time and value of the notes nor in the degrees on which the recitation is produced." And Romain Rolland, who records these passages of Rousseau, adds with perfect truth: "This is an exact description of the recitative of Debussy." [5]

Verlaine had said that one must wring the neck of eloquence. No one could be less "eloquent," certainly, than the characters of Maeterlinck. In the sobriety, simplicity, even monotony of their manner of expressing themselves with little, short paragraphs and frequently repeated words, Debussy found already realized his ideal of an anti-Wagnerian lyric idiom. "Anti-Wagnerian" means, in this instance, "antisymphonic," far from the dramatic dilations which are induced by the expansion of the harmonic sense concentrated in the chord, the fount whence sprang the poematic symphonies of Bruckner

[4] P. Bekker, *Musikgeschichte als Geschichte der musikalischen Form.*

[5] *Op. cit.*

and Mahler, as the cosmic consequence of the dramatic symphonism of Wagner.

Let one wring the neck of eloquence to the point of strangulation and, obviously, expression will be reduced practically to inarticulate sound, to phrases no longer than the strangler will permit, to expressions startling in their form, incisive in their prosody, harsh in their accentuation. In the poetic text, the epigram will succeed the arietta of Verlaine whose brevity succeeded the Baudelairian sonnet. A poetic language will appear like that of Mallarmé, which seems to dissolve the bonds of syntax and the caesura of the verse, closely approximating a versification which might be called melopoeic, like the language of the eclogue *L'Après-midi d'un faune*. Such an art, in words, would correspond marvelously to the aesthetic sense of musical impressionism; tonal ambiguities and sonorous complexes, hitherto untried and unsuspected, would correspond in a certain way to the obscurity of symbolist poetry, to that of Mallarmé above all, who by successive distillations of the first versions of his poems so veiled the original meaning as to make it recede into indefinable distances.[6] Ravel, later on, discovered a new type of poetry, most seductive to the musical translator, in the brief, caustic epigram of Jules Renard.

In the *Histoires Naturelles* of Renard, where all lyric emotion has seemingly been replaced by an amiable irony clad in an unadorned, laconic language built with simple verbal touches, the musical essence of Ravel found a center in which it might concentrate itself. When Ravel asked permission of the poet to translate these poems into musical terms, the latter, who was not the least musical, was dumfounded. Indeed, what is there in his zoological epigrams capable of inspiring a musician? Neither Renard nor Ravel himself could know the reason; the fact was sufficient. A music born of the genius of the idiom, eager to express itself vocally in a sonorous medium of equivalent brevity, with a conciseness of musical syntax which, at the moment of Ravel's writing, was capable of concentrating in one or two chords the substance diluted by his predecessors in several pianistic or vocal pages, had no need of more words: the fewer the better.

A single chord suffices to underline with a kind of compressed expression the brief and isolated rhythm, the melismatic segments or fragments of arabesque which frame the musical epigram of Ravel. With it comes neither the operatic song, the recitative of Lully, nor the succinct declamation of Debussy; rather, the "song of the street" which Jean Jacques had advocated. Indeed the "musicalization" of the verse in Ravel avoids, most opportunely, the conventionalities of "sung" French, with its mute-but-

[6] Mallarmé said of the Prelude of Debussy that the music "extracted the emotion of the poem and gave it a background more glowing than color." (Letter to Jean Aubry, quoted by Lockspeiser.)

sounded vowels, its diphthongizations; far better seemed the elisions of Parisian speech, the frequent intersyllabic suppressions: *"ell' avait un' jamb' en bois,"* etc. Yet, nevertheless, a refined sensibility could not fail to perceive a subtle poetry within these epigrams in prose. Their apparent coldness surrounds them with a protective zone that separates them from the vulgar mind. As if in a kind of latent state, there is in them a feeling for landscape, for the enchantment of the hour, the love of little things; fine shadings of poetic sentiment tending toward a quality of the spirit that is only fleetingly suggested, but which the subtle observer grasps instantly.

All Ravel's art is enclosed within this family of blended colors. His music reveals the hidden meaning that lies within the shyness and discreet reserve of Renard's poetry. Dissonance takes on a special value in this music of Ravel and translates the poetic quality into purely musical terms.

The flowering hawthorn may at intervals lose its short-lived, intensely perfumed flowers yet it is then no less decorative, with its finely etched branches bristling with hard and prickly needles. It is said that this manner of expressing himself in his art was of a piece with Ravel's personal character. This is only relatively true, for in that case *Daphnis* would seem less typically Ravel than *Ma Mère l'Oye,* and no one would have the temerity to say so. Those who knew Ravel know that, beneath his courteous smile reminiscent of Voltaire, shone a cordiality which never spent itself in effusiveness because the self-restraint which Ravel imposed on himself (and on his music) as a style of conduct was the social manner he preferred. In any event it must be agreed that it was a style purely French in form and essence. It is also said that the epigrammatic, sententious manner is French par excellence. It is true that there is a noble literature in this style, from La Bruyère and Chamfort to Jules Laforgue and Jules Renard but it is not less true that amplitude is just as French, in Balzac and Zola, in Victor Hugo or Marcel Proust. Hector Berlioz is no less French than Claude Debussy or Maurice Ravel.

Chapter NINETEEN

MAURICE RAVEL was working on his *"Histoires naturelles,"* which had already taken shape on paper or in his imagination, when he discovered in a "burlesque" of Franc-Nohain, entitled *L'Heure espagnole,* the type of theatrical piece which, in its brevity, its sprightliness, its freedom in expression and manners, somewhat crude for bourgeois susceptibilities, could carry to the more ample atmosphere of the stage the designs of the pianistic-vocal music suggested by the epigrams of Renard. These last, appearing in 1906, were followed, therefore, in 1907 by a *comédie-musicale* with the original title, to which was added a qualifying phrase which indicated that Ravel considered it little more than a *conversation musicale*. These two works mark the central point of Ravel's production, of which the most remarkable period includes the five years from the *Miroirs* for piano (*Noctuelles, Oiseaux tristes, Une Barque sur l'océan, Alborada del gracioso, La Vallée des cloches*), appearing in 1905, to *Daphnis et Chloé,* a *symphonie chorégraphique,* begun in 1909. Although *La Valse, poème chorégraphique,* appears in 1920, its gestation dates from many years before and it is, therefore, to be grouped with the compositions of the central period.

To this central period belong the *"Histoires naturelles"* (*"Le Paon," "Le Grillon," "Le Cygne," "Le Martin-pêcheur," "La Pintade,"* 1906); the *Rhapsodie espagnole* (1907), the comedy *L'Heure espagnole,* in which he brings together his experiments with the French language of everyday, as we have said, and combines them with those which, from 1895, he had been making with the melodic and rhythmic motives of popular Spanish song. Ravel, like Debussy before him, was to utilize the Spanish element allusively for the sake of its novel possibilities in both rhythm and melody as well as for the harmonic suggestions which Andalusian song, accompanied by guitar, stimulates in the musician's ear. Ravel, who in 1889 was a boy of fourteen,[1] fre-

[1] Ravel was born March 7, 1875, in the little village of Ciboure, near Saint-Jean-de-Luz, in the French Basque country. His mother was a native of this land, locked between France and Spain, and Ravel knew the ancestral tongue although he did not speak it fluently. The maternal surname was Delouart, in its French form, but Ravel sometimes liked to sign him-

quented the same pavilions of exotic music at the International Exposition referred to in connection with Claude Achille Debussy, who was then a young musician of twenty-seven. This was the year when Debussy, recently entered in the Conservatory, came to know the score of *Boris* and to set to music the five poems of Baudelaire.

The musical atmosphere, in which an oriental picturesqueness, the Russian, the Spanish, and the most quintessential French mingle in a strange and admirable synthesis, is the same for both men; their likenesses become closer while the differences widen between these two artists who move on the same aesthetic plane and in the same historical moment. Ravel's method of procedure quickly announced itself; in some ways it is based on Debussy's acoustics as, for example, in his feeling for the chord of the ninth, in his inversions and in other dissonances. At the same time, Ravel rapidly discarded other characteristic Debussy features, such as the whole-tone scale, after he had used them to the point of satiety in some of his early compositions.

At the risk of seeming exaggerated in the aesthetic interpretation of Ravel's dissonances, one might attribute a certain symbolic value to his way of understanding the old romantic chord of the augmented triad (F, A, C♯) which, in Debussy, suggests the whole-tone scale. We have noticed a tendency, in romantic harmony, toward the breaking-up of the chord into its component parts; the final expansive-expressive phase of this movement is to be found in *Tristan,* where the melody is the emotional consequence of the shattering of the harmonic forces concentrated in the chord (and from this centrifugal movement is born the post-Wagnerian poematic symphony). Now Ravel, on the other hand, initiates a reverse process, such that the dissonance implicit in the melody, which has a predominant value in Ravel as in Debussy, tends to project itself downward toward the base of the harmony in such a way that the augmented fifth drops to the consonance of the perfect fifth. Thus, in *"Le Grillon,"* from the *"Histoires Naturelles,"*

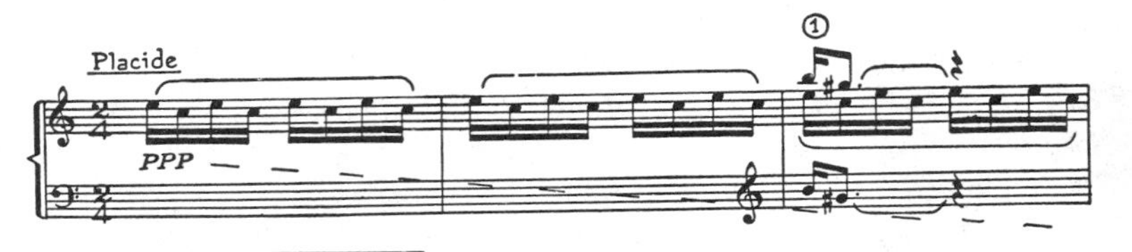

self (as he did in his letters to me) in the Spanish fashion: Ravel y Deluarte. The paternal surname is of Swiss origin, of the canton of Savoy, and its spelling by the musician's ancestors in the second half of the eighteenth century was Ravex or Ravet, changed to Ravel by his grandfather.

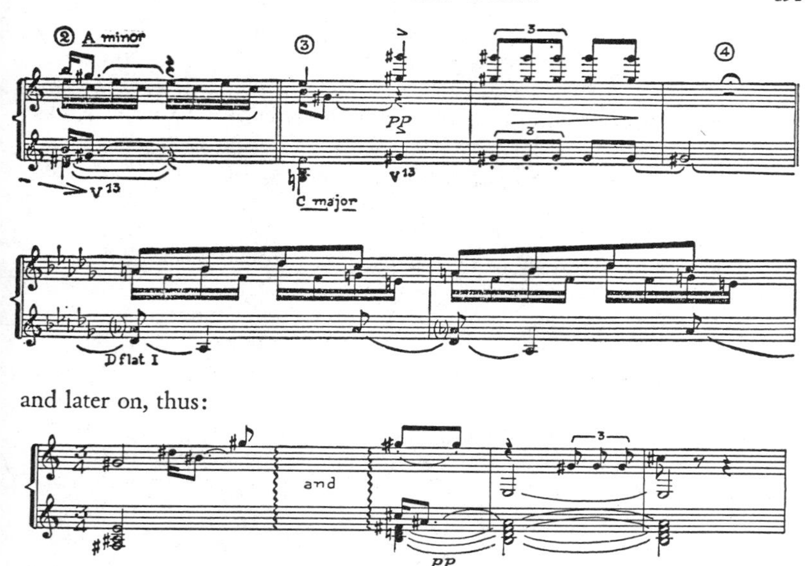

and later on, thus:

The first period of Ravel's production begins with his *Sérénade grotesque* of 1893, for piano. The title alone indicates the suggestive stimulus which plastic expression (here, the musician with his guitar at the window), particularly that with a burlesque flavor, exercised on Ravel from the beginning of his career as composer. His technique, perfect from his first work, shortly reached a point which it would seem impossible to surpass. The *Habanera,* first number of *Les Sites auriculaires* (for piano) of 1895, is the same which, orchestrated, was included twelve years later in the *Rhapsodie espagnole.* The second number, *Entre Cloches,* although in no way connected with *La Vallée des Cloches* of 1905, indicates at least a propensity in Ravel for certain resonances produced by the use of inner pedals and a nebulous material of pure impressionist stamp, likewise evident in other pages, very like the last-mentioned work, such as *Noctuelles, Oiseaux tristes,* and *Une Barque sur l'océan.* However, he tends to dissipate these sonorous mists beneath a crystalline light which shines with a dazzling and gemlike brilliance as in the *Alborada del gracioso,* belonging to the same collection as the composition last mentioned, and above all, in Scarbo, the third "poem" for piano in the series inspired by *"Gaspard de la nuit"* of Aloysius Bertrand, written three years after the *Histoires naturelles.* Two of these, Ondine and *Le Gibet,* still belong completely to impressionism and to Debussy's style. But while Ondine offers a telling point of comparison with the work of the same title which appears in the second collection of Debussy's Préludes (1910-13), as proof of how a vague impressionism tends to define itself in cleanly modeled lines, it may be said, on the other hand, that *Le Gibet,* with its delicious sonorities of bells lost in the morning mist (like *Cloches à travers les feuilles* in Debussy's second series of *Images,* of 1907), marks the final phase of impressionism. Only the beginning of *La Valse* is impressionist, this time in orchestral timbres, but we have already pointed out that this work dates from many years before its definitive version.

Ravel's impressionism, in its evolution beyond that of Debussy, appears perfectly defined in the five pieces, *Miroirs,* which appeared in 1905. No better definition of this new phase of impressionism could be found than that of Ernst Hello:[1a] "Art has as its essential element the preparation of the harmonies which have not as yet taken shape within our consciousness, presenting us with their image as in a mirror." This, in musical terms, is the equivalent of poetic symbolism. "All nature," says Lanson in describing this movement, "is but a blind image, a veiled and indefinite symbol of the conditions which determine it." And the same noted historian of French literature adds, in completing his definition of the expressive purpose of the symbolist poet: "To paint the scenes I see in the tints with which I see them." The verb "to paint" had an unfortunate connotation in musical romanticism after Beethoven's Pastoral Symphony—"more an expression of feeling than painting." Nevertheless, the impressionists (who followed a long and illustrious tradition in France in the representation of scenes, things, and persons from the days of the clavecinists) were not deceived by words for they knew that feeling and painting, in music, are interchangeable terms. Ravel, undemonstrative, reserved, and taciturn as he was, never permitted himself any lyric effusions in his art; his manner of feeling never took on a sentimental quality. Debussy was free of sentimentality, although he was not without softness or sweetness. This was entirely opposed to Ravel's temperament, methods, and concept of art. In the titles I have quoted, there is as much painting as in Couperín or Rameau, in whom the sentimental appeared with the greatest discretion despite some of their titles which may be interpreted as having a certain irony. Ravel had no prejudice, however, against painting. Painting and sentiment were resolved in music of the purest sort in which the titles are no more than a "documentary" clarification.

Between his first work in 1893 and *Miroirs* are included some, like the Quartet in F Major (1902-3) and the Sonatina for Piano (1905), which give an idea of the elasticity the classic form acquired in Ravel's hands. The Sonatina continues along the line of *Jeux d'eau* (1901); both works carry to a point of extreme perfection the idea, the writing, and the piano style set by Liszt in his *Jeux d'eau de la Villa d'Este*. At the same time, these compo-

[1a] R. Manuel, *M. Ravel* (Paris: 1938), p. 66.

sitions typify impressionist harmony in the field of keyboard music. Yet Ravel took pains to point out to a critic, who saw in this sparkling page a result of Debussy's influence, that the *Jeux* appeared at the beginning of the year 1902, when only Debussy's short pieces *pour le piano* were known. (*La Suite bergamasque* of 1890 did not appear until 1905; these other pages which date from 1896 appeared in 1901, and the first of Debussy's great series, *Estampes,* with his *Pagôdes, Soirée dans Grenade,* and *Jardins sous la pluie,* belong to 1903.) The Quartet—which Ravel submitted to Debussy, who earnestly begged him not to modify it—is the formal work of greatest poise and at the same time the least rhetorical in all chamber music following Debussy's Quartet. The first movement is considerably superior to the others and, as Ravel himself told me, was rewritten despite Debussy's admonition. The thematic development is unique in Ravel; its exoticism, of a color which defies analysis, has no counterpart in any contemporary music of the kind.

The elasticity of traditional forms acquires as great ease as breadth in the formalist works of Ravel's final period, from the *Trois Poèmes de Stéphane Mallarmé* of 1913, the Trio in A minor (1914), the Sonata for Violin and Cello (1922), and the Sonata for Violin and Piano (1923-27) to the two piano concertos of 1931 and the songs, *"Don Quichotte à Dulcinée."* These songs (1932), which were to have formed a part of the music for a film in which Chaliapin was to have been the protagonist, were the final inspiration of his genius. In 1935, his memory already lost in the mists of oblivion, Ravel journeyed to Spain and Morocco in the hope of alleviating the illness which periods in a sanitarium had failed to cure. His condition was hopeless, however, and after an unsuccessful operation, he died in Paris in December, 1937.

Painting, expression of emotion, idealism, realism, objectivism, subjectivism, impressionism, symbolism, naturalness, artificiality—all these are provisional terms whose use is unavoidable because they and similar words belong to the vocabulary of art criticism; we accept these terms despite their relative character and their lack of mathematical exactitude.

Of Ravel, it has been said that his art has a "natural artificiality."[2] Ravel protested this critique, although he did not think it necessary to deny it. And, indeed, since everything in nature is natural, and everything in art artificial, why not admit an artificial naturalism and a natural artificiality? If one reflects for a moment, one will see that this is a phase through which each art passes. The art of Ravel seemed to his contemporaries less natural than that of anyone else, even that of Debussy himself, simply because it was based on experiences which the taste of the time still did not recognize. When these experiences cease to be unusual, then the art based on them will seem the most natural thing in the world.

[2] "ordered complexity, that is, beauty"—M. Proust, *Le Côté de Guermantes,* I, 46.

All artists are proud of their originality and they cultivate it consciously. Rather like Gaspar Hauser, the famous impostor of romantic times, it amuses them to pose before the ignorant public as the descendants of a legendary race rather than of the humble stock of those of us who are not blue-blooded. If, in the artistic family tree, a Debussy or a Ravel cannot claim to be the proudest of blue bloods, who indeed can? To be the pupil of musicians as humble as Henry Ghys, Charles-René, Anthiome, Émile Pessard, and even Charles de Bériot was not unusual; the disconcerting originality of the young Maurice Ravel could not proceed from these everyday sources. Ravel, who never denied his masters, obscure though they were beside his own renown, and who remembered them in several dedications, liked to say that his art flowed from three fountainheads: from Emmanuel Chabrier, from Erik Satie, and from the *Mireille* of Gounod. Yet it was really André Gédalge and Gabriel Fauré who prepared the ground on which the art of a Ravel, however original it might be, could find firm footing. Ravel recognizes, in his autobiographical sketch, that he owed his technique to the discipline in counterpoint which Gédalge insisted upon; to Fauré he is grateful especially for "his advice as an artist."

But it was not mere caprice which made Ravel allude to those other three French minds of such diverse qualities. He emphasizes in this way his descent from the various phases of the French genius, from three different stages, three generations of musical art during the second half of the nineteenth century. The most recent influence, Erik Satie, Ravel's senior by ten years, was that of a meticulous, rare, extravagant type characterized by extreme irony and sensitiveness. "Whenever he sees me he repeats how much he owes me, and so I believe it to be," wrote Satie in 1911 to his brother Conrad. Each of them, the musician of Honfleur and the musician of Ciboure, thus paid their respects to each other with double irony for Satie knew that people wanted to make him a kind of precursor even of Debussy because (as early as 1887, in the Second Saraband) Satie made liberal use of chords of the ninth and (in *Le Fils des étoiles* in 1891) of formations of thirteenths in parallel motion. It is only fair to give credit to Satie as well as to the melancholy Ernest Fanelli (1860-1917) for the priority of these inventions since, although never integrated into a personal aesthetic idea, they provide examples quite close at hand.

The technique of Satie was as precarious as his realizations. His personal character was extremely curious. He had a humorous vein very similar to that of the English "clowns," which he explained by his descent from a Scotch woman; yet, on the other hand, this humor had the strongly local characteristics of the region of Calvados whence came his father's family. And, in recognition of Satie's personality, so gracefully reflected in his compositions for piano, Debussy and Ravel were his life-long friends and even orchestrated some of his slight pieces. Satie dazzled his ingenuous listeners in the Café Nouvelle Athènes and in the Auberge du Clou in Montmartre, where Debussy met him in 1891. One of the habitués of that revivified Hellenic metropolis was Ravel's father who, as the inventor of interesting mechanisms, felt a curiosity for novelties of all kinds and who, discriminating lover of music that he was, did not fail to recognize the interesting character of Satie's experiments. Ravel was at that time fifteen or sixteen years old and was studying his harmony and counterpoint in the class of Émile Pessard. The young Ravel was feeling the prick of an inner rebellion; this unrest, prudently turned into tractable channels, was the origin of his artfulness, his keen yet good-natured sense of humor, and that *blague à froid* and *pince sans rire* so often cited in appreciations of his work. Yet perhaps even these most important aspects of Ravel's art owed something also to Satie, along with his elevenths and thirteenths. Two songs (*"Un grand sommeil noir"* and *"Sainte"*), one with text of Verlaine, the other of Mallarmé—which date from 1895 and 1896, the period of Ravel's visits to the café where Satie played the piano to earn his daily bread and cognac—may be pointed out as marking Satie's influence on his harmony.[3]

Satie's melody, with its quiet and gently swaying rhythm, may be seen reflected in some of the pages of Ravel's *Ma Mère l'Oye* (1908). This series, so characteristically Ravel, of pieces for piano four hands, displays in both the orchestrated and the original version that same unadorned, effective simplicity of means already present in Satie.

The influence of Emmanuel Chabrier on Ravel is of a deeper kind and is not limited to such titillations of the ear as the splashing of the water in

[3] The influence of Satie on *"Sainte"* is mentioned by Roland Manuel in his book on Ravel. *"Sainte,"* based on a poem by Mallarmé, is dedicated to his daughter. Its final measures have been cited above as a clear example of the transition, in every respect, from Debussy to Ravel.

Ravel's *Jeux d'eau.* By way of Chabrier, Ravel linked his adolescent dreams in the enchanted wood with the first romantic impressions he heard in Weber, Chopin, Liszt, and the Russians—especially Balakirev. (It was Ravel's ambition to surpass the finger technique required by Balakirev's virtuoso Islamey.) Borodin's melodism is suggested in Ravel's fondness for a singing line, eloquent in its restraint, and Rimsky-Korsakov is felt in some of his iridescent orchestral passages.

What was to interest the young French musician in Wagner was not his declamation or his passion, something to which Ravel was always refractory, but rather certain orchestral pages in which Wagner shows his connection with that romanticism of the supernatural, that sense of the enchantment and mystery of the hour in nature, that feeling which Weber had admirably transferred to the orchestra, and Chopin and Liszt to the piano. If Ravel studied the prelude *L'Après-midi d'un faune*[4] at this moment it was for this feeling in it rather than for its properly Debussyan qualities. (This feeling was reflected in the pale afterglow of such music as that to which Ravel later set the poems Shéhérazade [1903], in some passages of the Quartet, where the powerfully suggestive orientalism of those songs is continually transformed into the highly original melodic substance of this work.) Ravel found in the *Trois valses romantiques* of Chabrier the same repertoire of fascinating dissonances in a highly original pianistic writing that Debussy had already appreciated there.[5]

The romanticism of these waltzes of Chabrier exercised on Ravel a profound fascination that lasted throughout his life. His *Valses nobles et sentimentales* (1911), which mark the culminating point of his harmonic system, are also impregnated with a soft Schubertian aroma which, in *La Valse* (1919), is intensified with the intoxicating perfume of the waltzes of Lanner and Strauss of imperial Vienna. Chabrier, too, had used these models with an orchestral verbosity in combination with the rude wholesomeness of the Aragonese jota. The result was his rhapsody, *España,* of 1883, followed two years later by a *Habanera,* which had its influence on that of Ravel, of 1895—a composition already so well defined in thought and technique that it could be included with no other change than the sonorous medium (from piano to orchestra) in his *Rhapsodie espagnole.* It was the *Pavane pour une infante défunte* with its typically Ravelian melody which brought Ravel his first public triumph (1899). This work made him secure with his first admirers just as the Bolero did with his later enthusiasts. Yet, if the last is a work which demonstrates the height of Ravel's knowledge of orchestration, such mastery is scarcely glimpsed in the orchestral version of the first (1912).

[4] Ravel made a transcription for two pianos of this work which he always proclaimed, in so many words, to be the masterpiece of music. Roland Manuel, *op. cit.,* p. 55.

[5] On Chabrier, see J. Chantavoine, *De Couperin à Debussy* (Paris: 1921), VI.

Orchestration in Ravel, as in Debussy, is surpassing art. The clever orchestration of certain dissonances gives those dissonances a value which they would not possess of themselves alone as simple sonorous shocks. This feeling for dissonance color comes, in Ravel's early works, from the palette of the Russians but it soon simplified itself until it acquired the incisive clarity characteristic of his mature works, whether in the sober harmonic lines of *Ma Mère l'Oye* or *Le Tombeau de Couperin,* or in the rich splendor of *Daphnis* or *La Valse.* The precision with which Ravel writes for instruments —and this is especially evident in the way he reproduces the sound of the various mechanisms of the watchmaker Torquemada, the hero of *L'Heure espagnole*—is of another type and has a sonorous effect different from the orchestra of Debussy, however precise and exact the latter may be. In Debussy, the orchestra is always poetic; in Ravel, it is always mechanical. In Debussy, all is picturesque and evocative; in Ravel, the predominant trait is a specific feeling for the instrument. Ravel obtains his shading within the normal register of the instrument in such a way that the performer need never force his playing. The conductor does not have to balance the sonorities according to his own judgment or understanding; Ravel has done it all and, as in the case of Stravinsky's music, the conductor need only "play" what he has before him in order to have Ravel's thought appear, perfectly clear and transparent.

This is especially true if one understands Ravel's tempos and rhythms. The music of Ravel, never sentimental, and less poetic than acoustic, derives its instrumental rhythm from the dance first of all. That exquisite vagueness, "where the imprecise to the precise is joined," begins to disappear rapidly with his first compositions, giving way entirely to the precise. The dance is always a model of precision and a dance title appears frequently in Ravel, indicating the author's desire to the interpreter with that brief eloquence toward which Ravel constantly aspired. The same brevity determined the evolution of his form, carrying it ever further away from impressionism and ever closer to the pure forms, to such a degree that Ravel did not hesitate to take Saint-Saëns, Mozart, or even Scarlatti for his model.

The clarity of the rhythmic constitution, which proceeds from the dance, always has in Ravel the firm guiding thread of a melody that is as perfect, as elegant, and as well cut as that of Chopin himself. But the harmony of Ravel, after the atmospheres in the style of *La Vallée des cloches* or *Le Gibet,* tends to accentuate the verticality of the chord in which dissonance affirms its pure value and along with this comes a clarity in the rhythmic subdivisions. The result contributes to the clear, cold, impassive hardness with which Ravel treats his harmony [6] and which reaches the peak in *Valses nobles et*

[6] His music was branded as *perce-oreille,* after that little insect which we call earwig and which, quite inoffensive (as the music of Ravel), never pierced an eardrum. One will also

sentimentales (1911). Ravel was perfectly aware of this but his logic was rigorous and not to be weakened. In consequence, the motive acquired a definiteness of contour and outline which was to separate it from the arabesques of Debussy. It proceeds more directly from the "gesture" (as in some of the Germans) and from the declamatory, energetic, even interjectional, phrase than from the emotion. The power of stylization in this plastic sense is notorious in Ravel but it is a power typically French, capable of imposing order (as it did in the seventeenth and eighteenth centuries) on the tumultuous rococo into which the baroque dramaticism of line and mass declined.

His writing incessantly "strengthens the harmony and sharpens the outline" as Ravel himself said, and stands at the opposite pole from German contrapuntism and from that tonal amorphousness which leads in its expressiveness to Schönberg and to Alban Berg. Like Satie, Ravel sometimes indicates at the beginning of a work: *Placidement, Liturgiquement, On ne peut plus lent* but its character, making itself felt promptly, does not encourage digressions.

The Germans dissolve the tonality within the classic modes; and modal feeling suggests to Debussy enveloped harmonies, singing of themselves (*"une harmonie harmonieuse,"* he said aptly of his own, in the sense of a singing harmony). In Ravel, however, whose melody is frequently built on the Dorian or first ecclesiastical mode (D-D without altered notes) and on the Phrygian or second authentic mode (E-E diatonically), it is the characteristic melodic phrase, based on the mode, which suggests the harmony. As a typical example, one may recall the first phrase of the Quartet built on the chord of the eleventh of D Minor with its modal-harmonic feeling on which Ravel insists throughout the Quartet, no matter what may be the play of harmonies which unfold below it or what the thematic transformations.

The Quartet (1902-3) is the work of Ravel at the age of twenty-seven. It is robust of form and, although based on the French tradition of which Franck was the most recent exponent, it nevertheless belongs to a different period, tc a time different also from that of the Quartet of Debussy; if the latter work is more romantic than impressionist, that of Ravel is neither the one nor the other but is classic in its modernity. A like quality, understanding the word "classic" to mean a "value" beyond what is purely stylistic, is observable in Ravel's other chamber works, such as the Trio and the sonatas, whatever may be their melodism (so sharp in the Sonata for Violoncello and Violin, so gentle and popular in the Trio) and the harmonic play on which they

remember the famous caricature of Gill, in *L'Eclipse* (1869), in which Wagner hammers an eighth note into an enormous ear.

are based. Thus it happens that the form and content of these works possess such sureness that Ravel becomes in them an exponent of the classic, a quality that is increasingly accentuated until it culminates in the Concerto for Piano and Orchestra in G major, which was received as academic by the advanced standards of 1931. At that date, his manner of treating popular material could not be understood in any other light, even when this popularism was jazz, as in the Sonata for Violin and Piano, in the theatrical piece *L'Enfant et les sortilèges* or in the concerto for left hand alone, any more than could his manner of focusing the exoticism of the *"Chansons Madécasses"* or the extreme Spanish quality of the songs of *"Don Quichotte à Dulcinée."* Yet it is an academicism comparable in a sense to that which informs the classicism of the "Odalisque" of Ingres, the exoticism in literature of the African scenes of Guillaumet or of Benjamin Constant, or the descriptions of India by Besnard or of Algiers by Fromentin.

Everything was precipitated, distilled by the astringent properties of Ravel's genius. The impetus of renewal in French music which began approximately in 1870 brought its cycle to a close two generations later in these concertos of Ravel. The movement had obviously revitalized all the music of his country; but, in truth, it had renewed it too in the whole world. The musical feeling at work in the course of half a century, between Paris, Andalusia, and Vienna, signified an aesthetic concept of a new type whose origins go back to Berlioz, Chopin, and Liszt, and whose specific, sonorous basis is the fruit of long gestation. This fruit carried within it seeds which need to germinate in a different soil, in a neighboring land beyond the frontiers of tonality. A new period is about to open in European music but its principles have not yet been reduced to concrete forms. It lacks a Ravel to crystallize its aims. Let us undertake with caution our observations of this new world in its struggle to be born.

Chapter
TWENTY

IN A COMPOSITION that is organized according to tonal relationships, the cohesive power of tonality binds the musical whole together in such a way that the vertical meaning of the chord is fused with the horizontal meaning of the counterpoint. The fusion of the two constitutes tonal harmony or, in other words, the functional system of the harmony. The polyphonic writing remains subject to the laws governing the sequence of chords and, in its turn, the harmonic movement progresses as a result of the movement of the voices, of the texture. The composite whole comes to assume a new role, more like melodic homophony than polyphony. Debussy insisted, like his critics, that his harmony was melodious, "singing." Paul Bekker very justly terms "univocal" this polyphony which is conceived harmonically.

The apogee of the tonal-harmonic concept as a homogeneous sonorous mass occurs during the seventeenth and eighteenth centuries with the *basso continuo* or thoroughbass which strengthened the functional linking of the harmonies and the polyphonic movement of the different instrumental voices. After two centuries of the thoroughbass, the harmonic sense asserted its independence at a moment of transformation of styles which, supplanting the contrapuntal writing of the *canzone* and of the *sonata da chiesa,* came to prefer the predominating air, homophonically accompanied by instruments with repeated chords in a more or less rapid movement. It is the moment when, with Telemann at the head, German music was revolutionized and left behind Johann Sebastian Bach and the contrapuntists.

But Bach's polyphony had become harmonically enriched through the repeated use of the dominant seventh (as the best examples I would refer to his sonatas for solo violin), which dynamically impelled the contrapuntal complex. In the semihomophony of the new arioso style, the expression is dramatic rather than harmonic, and is achieved by means of the appoggiatura (which the French school even terms expressive). The instrumental homogeneity is satisfied by the string quartet, where the predominating style is semihomophonic but which Haydn and Mozart tend soon to construct polyphonically. Its dynamism is now brought about by the increasing richness of the intermediate harmonic sections and to alternations and substitutions of the constituent notes of the chords.[1] An eloquent example is the opening of the Mozart Quartet in C major (K. 465), in which three chromatic phrases are superimposed one above the other, causing the tonality to waver despite the solid support of the repeated tonic note:[2]

This is symptomatic of the growing Germanic feeling for chromaticism of which one might cite numerous examples, although it is sufficient here to recall the beginning of the Quartet, Op. 133, of Beethoven (the Great Fugue in B-flat major), where a phrase with indecisive tonality—

shortly takes on the plasticity of a motive.

In it we find two details which maintain themselves until recent times when atonalism has become a system. These are its (*a*) broken rhythm and (*b*) its leaps of a seventh, both of them details which assume a special meaning in the theme of the fugue.

It is useful, from this point of view, to compare this with a passage of Op. 11, No. 1 of Schönberg.

[1] P. Bekker, *op. cit.*, p. 218.

[2] Other interesting examples are: the finale of the Symphony in E flat (Breitkopf, No. 12) of Haydn, a passage of Jommelli's Vologeso, and others of Gluck and Méhul, quoted by G. Abraham in his book, *Chopin's Musical Style* (New York: Oxford University Press, 1939), p. 21.

In this passage it is important above all to remark Schönberg's desire that his basses possess harmonic independence and are not to be confused with the simple harmonic bass. Very well, is it not a similar desire that prompts Beethoven when, in his fugue, he presents us for the first time with three voices which separate themselves from one another harmonically, rhythmically, dynamically, and in instrumental timbre?

The constant law in the evolution of music seems to be that no sooner is the realization of a long maturing desire reached than one flees immediately from the satisfaction which it produces to seek new adventures. Scarcely is tonal and instrumental homogeneity achieved in the classical quartet than Mozart himself begins to eschew it or at least to suggest a future where such an evasion will be a *desideratum*. The process is typical of German art but is more moderate among the Latin nations. Is it due to the romantic character of German art? It matters little; what is important is to discover why Wagner became incomprehensible to Berlioz; the expressionists to the impressionists; Kandinsky, in painting, to Monet. Within their respective limits, Stravinsky and Ravel may find a point of contact with the *Pierrot Lunaire* of Schönberg: the first in his *Poésies de la lyrique japonnaise,* and Ravel, in his *Trois Poèmes de Stéphane Mallarmé.*

The desire, ever more clearly manifest in German composers, to differentiate the lines that make up their polyphonic texture has led them, since Max Reger, to separate the lines from each other first melodically and next harmonically, avoiding points of meeting which would recall the earlier consonances and finally eliminating groupings which might produce a tonal sensation on the ear. Schumann's *Bunte Blätter* indicates the method: first we have the normal successions tonic-dominant-tonic, more or less altered. The alteration becomes more and more accentuated as the process becomes more elastic and the references to the tonal support drift farther and farther away. A modulatory process becoming more rapid each time dissolves the harmony-tonality, just as a group of colors in motion, tends to become a single color which may be the synthesis of them all.[3] The peak of functional chromaticism, which is still a chromaticized diatonicism rather than a true chromaticism, is achieved in *Tristan*. In its successors this chromaticism tends to become valid per se, making itself independent of the fundamental diatonic

[3] Ch. Koechlin, *Traité de l'Harmonie,* II, 262.

base. (The process of rapid modulations, without reference to a tonic, touching in passing on many tonalities, had already been used in a moderate way by Beethoven in his Two Preludes in all the major keys.)

A period of decline set in; it has been called polytonality. It is really not necessary to give it a name. As long as the tonal feeling has not disappeared, the functional system continues in force. When it does disappear, we shall have reached a new continent. The Viennese who commented on Schönberg's first works described them as atonal. He and Alban Berg maintain that a certain tonal feeling exists since there is an ordered arrangement in their works, as is proved by the fact that the ear rapidly becomes accustomed to the new order of things; so much so, that as soon as an element from the previous system slips into the nontonal fabric its presence acquires the explosive quality possessed by dissonance in the old harmonic system.

Harmony has broken the vessel which held the substance of the chord as a painter might empty all the tubes of color on his palette, producing a kind of sonorous pandemonium, in reality, nothing more than the simultaneous mingling of all the resonances of the natural series. The chromaticism of the new school is no more than the indiscriminate use of the tones 11 to 21 of the natural resonance, usually made independent of the fundamental note. The polyphonic texture retains all the cleanness of line one could wish and each of two lines can safely mingle their sounds which are separated from each other by their dissonant character. The dissonance prevents the harmonic fusion of these lines for our ears but, in the tonal complex, the dissonant character is lost because of the lack of any basis of comparison with the consonances which have been carefully avoided. The leaps of chromatic sevenths and ninths, traditionally unvocal, give the contrapuntal line an unmistakable appearance, yet one not unusual in German melodism. Freed from the rules regulating the classico-romantic system, the artists of this new turn taken by musical art are subject only to those restrictions that their feeling, their taste, and their sense of style impose—it is the liberty of the bird in the cage, the liberty of man "who cannot outstrip his shadow." In point of fact they will remain true to themselves, that is, to Germanic romantic feeling, and this will give an initial sense of unity to the new music.

Arnold Schönberg was his own teacher. In reality, and notwithstanding the teachers of their infancy, composers of exceptional worth have always been their own teachers. The example of the masterpieces, not the instruction of the conservatories, was the teacher of Bach and of Mozart, of Beethoven and of Schubert, of Schumann and of Chopin, of Berlioz, Wagner, Liszt, Mussorgsky, Mahler, and Wolf. The linking with the traditional chain is effected under the stimulus of the works of genius, without the superstition of the letter. The letter, if taken literally, kills the spirit. But the spirit has wings. By way of the masterpieces, contemporary or of the past, the spirit of the young composer seeks its lineage, the family tree of which it feels itself a branch, free in the light and air, yet wholesomely bound to the trunk of historical continuity. The first experiments of Schönberg, like those of so many of his contemporaries, proceeded from a contact with Wagner, Brahms, and Mahler. Schönberg's guiding instrument, to strengthen still further his roots in the German tradition, is the string quartet and a work for this medium is the first to come from his pen; all his initial essays are pieces of chamber music. Next to them stands the lied, that other characteristic musical aspect of the German soul.

In Schönberg's youth, his ardent and silent spirit made its way in the solitude of poverty. An understanding friend, Alexander von Zemlinsky, gave definition to the gropings of the young Schönberg and put him in contact with those young musicians of the day who, in the Viennese cafés, were struggling to find the sequel to the broadening movement implicit in the chromaticism of *Tristan* and in postromantic emotionalism. Schönberg sailed that stream from whose depths the song of all the Loreleis sounds changelessly and whose surface is rippled by the *wagalaweia* of all the Germanic Undines. In the warm breezes of Wagnerian harmonies which swelled the sails of all the lyric barks of Central Europe, melody is dissolved in extended melopoeias, vague of outline and laden with the opium of dreams. Form constantly aspires to mount to a mystic, ecstatic height, expanding around its inner centrifugal forces.

Schönberg's first significant work, the *"Gurre-Lieder,"* dating from the early years of this century, is the visible result of this postromantic movement. This is a masterwork of hypertrophy from a youth who gave his aspirations great amplitude but whose driving force is the emotional intensity of Germanic tradition: an emotionalism which had found its appropriate language in the increasing role of dissonance, in the incessant flow of modulation and chromaticism. Its orchestration is of such colossal size as to relegate Wagner to the position of a mere beginner (four piccolos, four flutes, three oboes, three English horns, three clarinets, two bass clarinets, two treble clarinets, three bassoons, two contra-bassoons, ten horns, six trumpets, a bass trumpet, alto trombone, four tenor trombones, bass trombone, double bass trombone, bass tuba, six kettle drums, big drum, snare drum, cymbals, triangle, glockenspiel, xylophone, gong, four harps, celesta, iron chains, strings in proportion, five solo voices, three male choruses, and a mixed chorus of eight parts). The gamut of its expression is so Wagnerian [4] and so Mahlerlike (the latter

[4] Compare it with the death of Isolde:

> *"Doch dereinst, beim Auferstehen des Gebeins,*
> *Nimm es dir wohl zu Herzen:*
> *Ich und Tove, wir sind eins."*

above all in the part for voices) that the auditor of this drama-without-action comes to feel a certain impatience, even though he cannot help but admire the laborious talent of this artist of twenty-seven. With all the copious abundance of instruments, the expressive tone is always discreetly veiled, wrapped in a sonorous half-light which was to be found, a year before the *"Gurre-Lieder,"* in the sextet *Verklärte Nacht,* a moonlit poem with a texture not to be confined within the limits of the string quartet.

So-called intellectual curiosity is a sign of spiritual unrest which seeks new means of expression. If the intellectually curious individual is of a contemplative temperament, he will be content with the satisfaction his spirit derives from attuning itself to artistic forms. The creative artist, for his part, requires a higher satisfaction. His curiosity brings him stimuli, incentives to create or, again, to mold the dynamism of his spirit in new-born forms. The vitality of these beings is of first consideration, their originality comes later. Viennese youth in the last years of the century sought in music, in painting, in poetry, new modes of expression which would answer alike the need for a transformation in art and for what is characteristic of German genius. From Paris came stirring words which spoke eloquently to the consciousness of these young artists. But their response could not simply be to fling wide the door. The German artist could not feel poetry in the terms of parnassians and symbolists; the painter was not satisfied to adopt methods not suited to his feeling for art or to the kind of material he was accustomed to handling. Similarly, in the case of the German musician, the musical impressionism he saw dawning in France aroused alike his amazement and his inquietude in his sincere desire to emulate it.

When Arnold Schönberg composed his First Quartet, in 1897, Claude Debussy, twelve years his senior, had already presented to a startled world his prelude to *L'Après-midi d'un faune,* his pre-Raphaelite poem on Rossetti's *La Damoiselle élue,* next, the Quartet, so different from the traditionally German ones for this medium, and finally, the *"Chansons de Bilitis"* (also 1897). At this time Debussy had solemnly abjured his adolescent Wagnerianism. After nearly ten years, the crisis had been precipitated by his contact with the exotic music at the Exposition of 1889 and his reading of *Boris Godunov.* These are the years of the solitary, ardent, and poverty-stricken adolescence of Schönberg. In his eagerness to find types of poetry that would coincide with his need for expression, the young Schönberg turned to the more or less famous poets of the day; Lentzov, for his first lieder; Richard Dehmel, who provided such vivid inspiration for *Verklärte Nacht* that Schönberg finished this work in three weeks; Jacobsen, for his series of poems on the loves of Waldemar and Tove, a Scandinavian saga in which Schönberg was to gather the twilit splendors of Wagnerianism for his *"Gurre-Lieder."*

At the same time a crisis was approaching. While Schönberg was working on the prolix orchestration of the last-named work (which was to occupy him for another ten years), a drama, *Pelléas et Mélisande,* written in French and bringing to the theater the vague sentiment, the mystery, the delicacy, and the exquisiteness of poetic symbolism came to him. Its accents were touched with shadings entirely new to him yet very close to German post-romantic sentiment, which delights in this kind of fusion of human emotions with a transcendent cosmology in which the personal feeling seeks a beyond and which finds its most adequate poetic, musical, and metaphysical realization in the death of Isolde. Ten years earlier, this dramatic work of a Belgian poet, as we have seen, had been discovered by a French musician who during this time was engaged in translating it into music. Curiously enough, the first performance of Debussy's *Pelléas et Mélisande* occurred in Paris at the Opéra Comique in 1902, the year in which Schönberg began his poem *Pelleas und Melisande,* on the same plot by Maeterlinck.

Debussy's opera, long meditated, is the summit of French musical impressionism. The technique and expression of Debussy's art reached in it their final and perfect definition. The composition of Schönberg's poem required little more than a year but it marks the beginning of a new path which opened broad perspectives.

Whither would he have been led by the path of the Wagner-Mahler tradition of his earlier *"Gurre-Lieder"?* The expansive force of this art clearly struggled, from Schönberg's first composition, to achieve concreteness of texture and a painstaking definition of expression for every sonorous moment. The poetic sentiment of German postromanticism may be as vague and formless as one likes; in Schönberg's music of this period there is evident a constant effort to confine this volatile substance in the well-marked limits of an expression which seeks a contour defined by form. Over and above the impracticability of execution which the enormous instrumental masses such as those of *"Gurre-Lieder"* present, such a system must have appeared without future possibilities to a composer like Schönberg. He undoubtedly realized that such an inflated form was simply the consequence of the past, of the symphonism of Bruckner and Mahler, but not a way toward the future which would have to be attained by the concrete, by the clearest possible definition of a new harmonic feeling. The independent value of chordal dissonance appeared, in impressionism, as the antidote for the tonal dissolution induced by the ultrachromatic polyphonic texture.

The reaction between the two systems might prove shocking to sensibilities like those of Schönberg which were rooted in native German art; yet, perhaps the universal mindedness of his Jewish descent, incompatible with ideal or political frontiers, made him so much the more open to every lyric inspiration. That which reached him from the West fitted well, for the reasons mentioned, Schönberg's natural tendencies but at the same time it incited him to explorations he was soon to carry out: adventures which, without losing contact with the native soil of German art, were to aspire to a new order of things in which all that was customary in former creations was to be dissolved in order to attain a limitless freedom.

In his journey toward atonality, Schönberg threw overboard all excess baggage; he restrained his eloquence, shortened his forms, restricted his sonorous medium to the limits of the quartet or chamber orchestra, and accepted the restriction of movement imposed by dissonance per se, no longer subject to the laws of the functional system of tonality. Yet, faithful to the exigencies of Germanic musical feeling (whose expressive norm lies in the polyphonic texture), he imposed strict systematization upon this harmonic-polyphonic material which threatened to overflow and to dissolve every limitation of form, every idea of ordered arrangement. Unlike the sorcerer's apprentice of the old ballad which Goethe adapted from Lucian as an example and warning to German artists, Schönberg knows how to direct into a narrow channel the tumultuous flood of sonority freed from the restraining walls of the rhythmic-tonal system. How? The answer cannot be given in a word but here is a preliminary indication: by the age-old power of melody. A melody to be sure, which is not subjected to the unifying principles of homophonic melodism nor to those of polyphonic tonalism but which, as in both of these systems, derives its power from the expressive feeling that fills it. Thus we see that, if Schönberg approaches the new continent of atonality, he is carried thither by the changeless winds of expression.

Before reaching these new shores, Schönberg had passed through a considerable experimental period from his *Pelleas und Melisande* (Op. 5) to the music for the songs of Stefan George, the German poet most akin to the symbolists, which date from 1908 (Op. 15). Five years and ten works had been accomplished. In them and by them Schönberg was carrying out the transmutation of his genius: the stage of the chrysalis, between Op. 5 and Op. 15, after the larval stage of his first thirty years.

The orchestra of *Pelleas und Melisande* is still a massive group (four of each of the wood-wind instruments, eight horns, four trumpets, four trombones, a treble trombone, a bass tuba, in addition to abundant percussion, and a corresponding body of strings), yet the prolix thematic treatment in the polyphonic texture leads Schönberg at moments to make the necessary instrumental selection in order that the intricate combination of the motives may be heard with a degree of clearness. Very soon Schönberg was to become convinced of the error of using a texture which only exhibits on paper, but not to the ear, its lengthy counterpoint of phrases, all of them possessed of a striking dramatic intention. For the moment, he reduces the orchestration to groups of threes and avoids using the violins in certain passages where he wants to give the orchestra the somber coloring of the scene of the action or of the spiritual state of the characters in Maeterlinck's drama.

In this work, for the first time in German music, appears—so Debussylike—the whole-tone scale (presented as a series of major thirds, in the instruments with high register), which Schönberg was to use, moreover, abundantly in the *Kammersymphonie,* the last of his works in which the functional system still exists. This work, in its turn, marks a crisis in Schönberg's thought for here, in his search for the concrete and the well-defined shape, he renounces the great orchestral masses (which as a matter of fact, he had used less as such than for the possibility they offer for breaking up the whole into fragments capable of very special coloring as in the case just discussed). The orchestration of the Chamber Symphony, Op. 9, includes fifteen solo instruments, the quintet of strings among them, although for performance in a large hall it seems advisable to double them. In this work Schönberg still writes the definite key signature of E major, but from the very opening theme, with its structure in fourths, the tonality is in peril. Curiously enough (be it said in passing) this theme is no other than the succession of intervals produced by the strings of the guitar.

It has already been remarked that the resonance produced in the body of the guitar, a series of fourths (in Schönberg, D, G, C, F, B♭, E♭), had already acted as a keen stimulus on the first impressionist musicians. A certain impressionistic way of looking at things—which such analysts of Schönberg's art as Egon Wellesz have not hesitated to associate with pictorial pointillism—exists in the breaking up of the constructive phrases into short thematic motives, as occurs in Schönberg's Second Quartet in F-sharp Minor, Op. 10; this composition may be considered, at least in its meaning, as a work prior to the *Kammersymphonie* and, like it, demonstrates eloquently the transition to Schönberg's new manner, now definitely atonal.

This quartet which, like all the music of Schönberg before it, endeavors to give a highly concentrated expression to dramatic emotions, uses the voice, united with the four strings, to sing (or rather recite) a poem of Stefan George. The poem is symptomatic of the German romantic and postromantic cosmology: *"Ich fühle Luft von anderen Planeten"* (I breathe the air of other planets). Mahler had been content to breathe the perfume of the linden trees in blossom: *"Ich atmet' einen Linden Duft, Im Zimmer stand ein Zweig der Linde"* (in his music to the poems of Rückert). The swelling current of those last moments of Germanic postromanticism, which proceeds from Rückert to George and from Mahler to Schönberg, could not be content with less than imbuing the star with that humble perfume!

In order to reach such lofty spheres, the musical prosody in use, including the Wagnerian with its highly characteristic intervals, will need a corresponding amplification and intensification of its accents. In some cases Schönberg renounces the timbre of the singing voice which follows only at a distance the musical inflection of the intervals which compose the melody: as, for example, in the final pages of the *"Gurre-Lieder,"* whose passage, *"O' schwing doch aus dem Blumenkelch,"* will lead to the sung-recitative of *Pierrot Lunaire.* In other cases the singing voice is subjected to a disintegration, as in one of the *"Acht Lieder,"* Op. 6 (*"Traumleben"*).

Intonations such as these had already caused difficulties in instruments and, indeed, caused no little trouble in the performance of the *Kammersymphonie* but Schönberg demands them because they will come to be his normal method of melodic construction once he has definitely abandoned functional tonality.

It is in a series of songs with orchestra (still functional, like those of Op. 6) in that transitional period of Schönberg's art, in the *"Sechs Orchesterlieder,"* Op. 8, that the composer bids farewell to the aesthetics of romantic orchestration as well as the impressionist, and translates the harmonies by appropriate orchestral timbres to provide a poetic background—either as an atmosphere which surrounds the voice or as a sonorous atmosphere expressive in itself. Schönberg tends to a concentration of the motive which even reaches the point of enclosing in simultaneous sound what is now no longer a chord but a motive compressed into a sonorous unit which, heard after the horizontal exposition of the same motive, may perhaps remind us of its expressive meaning. Such a method may be used in purely instrumental works like those in which the voice is united with the orchestra; it is evident that in such a case the instruments will concentrate, in a single quintessential drop, the melodic phrase sung by the voice.

But when it is a question of lieder with piano, Schönberg pushes Hugo Wolf's manner, already described, to an extreme. The piano concentrates the poetic idea expressed by the voice in motives which unfold independently of it yet which have, as regards the musicalization of the poem, identical ends; such is the case of the "Six Lieder," Op. 3 (on poems of Dehmel, G. Keller, Friedrich Nietzche, Kurt Aram and others), and in the later lieder already referred to.

From the moment in which tonality no longer supplies the inner bond that gives unity to the melody, this melodic line, always dominant and leading in Schönberg, ceases to be conceived according to the style appropriate to song, even when it is confined to the human voice. The melodic line is composed of little thematic fragments, very brief, but with an intonation so characteristic that, like certain motives in Wagner and Strauss, it is sufficient to give an unmistakable feeling to the motive group. In the phrase, *"Es ruht auf meinen Munde"* which we have just quoted, there may be observed the procedure which has the purpose of making the leading motive recognizable even within a dissonantly complex texture, above all if it is linked to a definite orchestral timbre (as in Strauss). Each motive is conceived as apt for treatment according to all the classical procedures of the variation, including those to which medieval counterpoint so fruitfully repaired. With it we approach the new technique which, announced thus in his works of transition, Schönberg will continue to employ systematically (and which his followers like Křenek will carry to a formalism devoid of all musicality) in the works of his last period.

Such a method in the treatment of the motive seems to be derived directly from the purest Germanic symphonism. Nevertheless, since the motives from now on lack tonal feeling, they are not able, as before, to originate the great periods leading from one tonality to another on which classical symphonic architecture was in large measure based. It seems that in the first years of the present century German musical youth considered the post-Wagnerian symphonic vagueness as liquidated and, as in the case of Schönberg, flung themselves into the search for new methods of construction and of unification. According to Egon Wellesz in his brief and authoritative study of Schönberg, the influence of César Franck and his school was decisive as regards this constructive concept in process of formation, for the cyclical method of Franck (in its turn having such profound Germanic roots) was a system capable of being followed with modifications and adaptations appropriate to the new tonal feeling, still also in a nebulous state. In the three works that inaugurate Schönberg's decisive period, the composer affirms his motivic treatment and his linking of the motive to the inner expression which he desires to translate into musical terms. These three works are the fifteen songs of Stefan George (Op. 15, 1908) belonging to *"Das Buch der Hängenden Gärten,"* the Three Pieces for Piano, Op. 11, 1909—which are to find a kind of summing up in the Five Orchestral Pieces (Op. 16)—and the monodrama, *Erwartung,* Op. 17, belonging also to the year 1909. In order to discuss with clarity this latest period of Schönberg's art, having once sketched that which has to do with tonal considerations by themselves, we shall give an idea of the meaning which the concept of expression assumes in Schönberg; a meaning peculiar to him, which thus obliged him to seek ways as yet untrodden (yet which were found not on another planet but in his own Vienna) and whose beginnings have been described.

Chapter TWENTY-ONE

IN THE same way that the music of Debussy has been linked to the post-romantic style of French painting known as impressionism, the music of Schönberg and of his pupils and friends has been brought under the rubric of German pictorial expressionism. Today we understand, much better than in the time of Debussy or Manet himself, what impressionism is; for this reason we can accept the term without risk and even disregard the protests of musicians who, like Debussy, have come to represent the essential substance of the term.

We cannot, however, say the same thing of expressionism, at least outside of Germany and in circles of music and painting as distant as ours from those in which expressionism was born and fostered. It seems indispensable to explain briefly what this word contains within it from the point of view of the will of expression and of the form for those artists who subscribe to it. Nothing defines it better than the lines written by Vincent Van Gogh, the great Dutch painter (1853-90) who was so closely linked with the modern movement in French painting. "There exist colors," he says, "which, while false according to the criterion of the realists, may deceive the eye, but which possess a suggestiveness capable of expressing the impulse of a burning emotion." [1] If it is recalled that in the old musical terminology, in the age of the Renaissance, dissonances were termed "false," these lines of Van Gogh will take on a most precise meaning in terms of music. In fact, what seems to convey best the musical idea of Schönberg is that power of suggestion which a note or group of notes possesses to express an emotional fervor in his music.

It is undoubtedly true that certain dissonant groups of notes, in impressionism and expressionism, have an analogous power of suggestion. What differentiates the two movements lies in the different nature of the impulse in

[1] Quoted by Peter Thoene in his little book, *Modern German Art* (London: Pelican Books, 1933). Not to mention more detailed recent works on this art, the brief study of Thoene may be extremely useful to the reader. Little critical and biographical sketches are to be found, with abundant illustrations, in C. J. Bulliet, *The Significant Moderns and Their Pictures* (New York: 1936). See also: J. Rohlfs, *El Realismo Magico* (Madrid: 1930) and Sheldon Cheney, "Decline in Paris. Resurgence and Eclipse in Germany," *The Story of Modern Art* (New York: 1941), Ch. xvi.

each: the musical sound has a value per se in the French aesthetics, which alludes by poetic and symbolic means to a specific pictorial or poetic impression; in German aesthetics, it is expressive of an impulse of the soul (to put it in the idealist terminology of the Germans) which seeks its exteriorization in these musical terms. Two things immediately become apparent: the latter art maintains close connection with what has been traditional in music since the beginning of romanticism, while French impressionism has scarcely any contact with that tradition but rather seeks a contact with the related arts.

In order to pursue a similar path, since impressionism rapidly acquired an immense prestige in every country, Germanic artists (and I include in the term Scandinavians like Munch and Slavs like Kandinsky since they collaborated decisively in the movement of the renewal of Central European art at the end of the last century and the beginning of the present one) sought this indispensable interchange between painters and musicians. Painters such as Kandinsky and Paul Klee thought they were composing music instead of painting objects since, strictly speaking, they were painting linear or coloristic abstractions rather than objects. Contemporary musicians appropriated the name expressionists, which certain painters had invented for themselves. Indeed, Schönberg himself took up painting in 1907, at the time when the word expressionism reached Berlin (where Schönberg was living). The high point of expressionist painting under its new direction of transcendental objectivism, of *Sachlichkeit,* which converts its motives into plastic symbols, now far from the reality of the object (or as it has been aptly termed in Spanish, *realismo magico,* magic realism), was reached in the Improvisations of Kandinsky in 1912. Now improvisation is a favorite term with musicians and, precisely in 1912, Schönberg composed his *Pierrot Lunaire;* this work is the culminating point of expressionism, although it is no more improvised than the series of paintings of Kandinsky with this title.

In the one case as in the other, musician and painter "construct" their respective works. The painter, following the example of Picasso, uses those elements of form with which real objects provide him not for the sake of recalling objective reality but for the purpose of composing his picture from such elements (without reproducing the appearance of the objects themselves). There is then a kind of remote realism which the painter minimizes and an abstraction of the object's formal elements (line, color, mass, values) which the painter stresses. Realism and abstraction are, then, terms relative to one another just as were consonance and dissonance, tonality and atonality.

Schönberg proceeds with an equivalent parallelism as far as the means appropriate to musical art permit. For the painter, an apple, a bottle, a nude reclining on the grass beside a stream may serve as the initial "motive" which the painter's faculty for abstraction forthwith transforms. But, for the composer, what apple, what bottle, what nude can provide him with his abstract elements? The expressive phrase in former music, which has become a commonplace (for example, the succession A, F, E, D♯ of the prelude to *Tristan*), may give, as in extract, some of those elements which the expressionist composer will utilize with a constructive purpose, more or less remote from their original dramatic feeling. This is the regular process in the formation of artistic styles; the leaf of the vulgar acanthus was used in Corinthian architecture, the skulls of sheep in Baroque ornamentation. Gothic art from earliest times proceeded in a similar way: stylizing animal forms geometrically or in arabesques. And it is precisely the continuation, in modern Germanic artists, of the Gothic spirit to which one must refer in order to establish in them a plastic tradition lacking since those early times.

German art, indeed, must go back to the early period of the Gothic in order to find a native vitality before that style, in the plastic arts as in music, was supplanted by meridional influences. Romanesque art, emphasizing the line and its density, or mass, has its musical equivalent in the chant of the Catholic church, in monody; Gothic art, on the other hand, combines elements which, independent of each other, collaborate in a homogeneous whole. Its musical counterpart is the art of polyphony. Polyphony and the Gothic were born, in all probability, in that vague region which in the centuries following the first millennium were Nordic or Scandinavian countries. But its molding into an art took place in a cultural zone included in the north of France, the east coast of England, and the Low Countries: the zone understood as belonging to French culture, whose center was a Paris illumined by the approaching dawn of a new millennium. This culture took root in the Germanic countries and became their strongest tradition. When a German painter wants to feel his historic past he turns to Gothic stained glass, Martin Schongauer, Bartholomaus Zeitblom, Burgkmair, Wohlgemuth, Lucas Cranach, or Matthias Grünewald.[2]

The Renaissance and the baroque brought into Germany new forms in music as in the plastic arts. These were shaped in the native mold and imbued with the Gothic spirit of the race at the hands of a long line of talented and original musicians—from the work of such men as Senfl, Bruck,

[2] The first school of German painters appears in Bohemia (Prague about 1360) and is inspired by Italian models. The German Renaissance, born under the influence of the Flemish in the fifteenth century, is Gothic in feeling. The Rhenish school is a branch of the art of Dierick Bouts and van der Weyden. Martin Schongauer (1450-1491) founded the school of Colmar. The sculptors of the Nuremberg school, Veit Stoss, Adam Kraft, and Peter Vischer, belong to the end of the fifteenth and the first half of the sixteenth century. To this period belong the three great painters of the German Renaissance: Albrecht Dürer (1471-1528), Hans Holbein (1492-1543), and Lucas Cranach (1472-1553), in whom the Gothic basis is intermingled with more or less strong Italian influences. Matthias Grünewald, an Alsatian, flourished in the sixteenth century and, like Hans Baldung, his pupil, tends toward a realism which is reflected in the German expressionists.

and Stoltzer, contemporaries of Josquin and Isaak, through the production of the three *S*'s, Schein (1586-1630), Scheidt (1587-1654), and Schütz (1585-1672), in the seventeenth century and developed in the work of the great organists, Tunder, Buxtehude, and Pachelbel, to culminate in the art of Johann Sebastian Bach. Thus when, with romanticism, German musicians in their turn felt impelled to seek within their own tradition and history (returning by way of Viennese classicism based on the Italian arioso and by way of the art of the variation in the organists of the baroque), they find no better symbol than Bach himself; to him they impute a dramatic feeling, a romantic sentimentality which he entirely lacked but which they project on him like a reflected light.

Thus a new cult arose in the rediscovery of Bach, the final phase of which proceeds from Max Reger to the young atonal school. And if one takes into consideration the fact that functional harmony and tonality are phenomena of postpolyphonic music which developed primarily in non-Germanic countries—while sentimentality and polyphony are the focuses between which German art, past and present, is established—one will comprehend the profound logic of the evolution of a modern German musical art. It has proceeded from Wagner to Mahler to Schönberg in an uninterrupted process: from: (*a*) expression, (*b*) dissolution of classic forms, (*c*) polyphonic texture, (*d*) chromaticism-atonalism.

While German romanticism created a new world for music, German romantic painting is distinguished for its technical weakness and for a sentimentalism that is half ingenuous, half simple-minded. Doubtless it has its charm, especially in periods like our own where candor is an unknown quality and when the hurried pace of life leaves no time for domestic dallyings in the style of Ph. Otto Runge or for the melodramatic landscapes of Friedrich (*"Über allen Gipfeln ist Ruh'"*) or the bourgeois sentimentality of Ludwig Richter or the decorative Hellenism of Moritz von Schwind. This type of nineteenth century German painting finds one of its favorite manifestations in the ironic and provincial genre painting of Karl Spitzweg.

The romanticism whose fairy tales, mythological woodland creatures, and water sprites peopled German opera ever since the time of *Freischütz* continued in painting from Schwind to Boecklin, to Feuerbach—with his pseudo classicism in the style of Thorvaldsen and Hans Thoma—in the second half of the nineteenth century, when French pictorial naturalism of the landscape painters of Barbizon and the *pleinairisme* of Courbet had flowered in the impressionism of Manet, Degas, Renoir, and Monet. Adolf Menzel was an important figure during this period when German art was seeking a solidity which it found for the moment in Hans von Marées, while the liberal spirit in painting appeared in Max Liebermann, who incarnates German impressionism.

Holland and France gave Liebermann the lofty tone of his painting; his art progressively assimilated the impressionism of Degas and Manet and gave Germany a really modern painting as early as the first years of the present century. But even when German impressionism realized notable achievements, the native artist who felt deep within himself the Gothic tradition viewed it disparagingly as an art of essentially foreign origin. A "secession" took place in 1894 among the traditionalists and the youth, the defenders of the Young Style, as against the conservatives of the Crystal Palace in Munich. Beside Liebermann figured the fine, restless spirit of Max Slevogt, a Bavarian, and Louis Corinth, a Prussian from the north who gave this stage of German art a solid basis preparing the way for new generations. These three painters had been born in the middle years of the century (1847, 1858, 1868).

Those who were to follow them like Emil Nolde, the Swiss, Hodler, and the Scandinavian, Munch, were approaching their fortieth year with the beginning of the new century. Munch and Hodler had worked along the lines of Cézanne, Van Gogh, and Gauguin with the purpose of surpassing impressionism by giving painting, based on its principles, a solid construction. Hodler is considered a symbolist although his painting is full of Wagnerian feeling well understood by youthful Germans. Full of dramatic complexes, Munch approaches, according to Peter Thoene, the literary concepts of Strindberg and Wedekind. In Nolde appears explicit the idea of pictorial expressionism.

This idea started and reached formulation with a transition group, appropriately called Die Brücke (the bridge), in which the influence of Hodler and Munch dominated. But the poetic German spirit demanded its rights, seeing in impressionism an antiobjective attitude or a subjective manner of feeling, the "data" offered by nature. Impressionist poematicism was to lead, very shortly, to a new creed which held that what the artist sets himself to express is no other than the fruit of an impression on the pictorial sensibilities —by means which may already have lost direct contact with the object, whose impression on the painter is simply his point of departure not his goal. Between these two points lies the realization, the technique.

Nolde, on seeking within himself the impression produced by an external object, observed that the motives basic to impressionism left him cold. He found it impossible to express anything pictorially according to a set of ideas that seemed foreign to him. Pulsating strongly within him was a distant echo, the native echo of the Gothic tradition. Brilliant coloring applied in clearly delimited masses placed one beside the other but never mixed, the sharply cut line which bounds planes in two dimensions without perspective to give depth (just as early polyphony lacked the third dimension to be supplied by harmonic feeling)—this is the art which deeply moved Nolde:

an art which finds its model in Gothic stained glass. But there are also windows without figures, great rosettes where colors dance in gay rounds as in a kaleidoscope. This aspect of Gothic art comes later. Ernst Barlach was to be Nolde's counterpart in sculpture, both in his figures with their violent gestures, their rigid garments, and in those pieces of a contemplative nature, so inexpressive in gesture yet so intense in soul.

Other artists figured in the group of Die Brücke when Arnold Schönberg found this movement at the height of its fervor on his second arrival in Berlin, 1911. In 1907 he had taken up the brush in order to "clarify" his musical ideas along a similar line of thought. What has been said of one of these artists, Ernst Ludwig Kirchner, whose Gothic quality dissolved in a lyric atmosphere deeply moved his generation, may also be said of the Schönberg of the first years of the century: "the ethic content serves him as a point of departure for formulating the inner dissonance produced by the dynamism of the spirit" (Thoene, *op. cit.,* p. 50). The German soul shines through the most commonplace motives.[3] Like Monet, Kirchner paints a railway station. In Monet, the locomotive, the smoke escaping from it, the two-plane surfaces of the glass roof tend to dissolve in the delicate gray tones of the atmosphere. In Kirchner the lines converge like the tops of the trees in a wood; they flower; they break up into a thousand tiny branches and the station, its trains, and the passengers miraculously become a German forest in the spring. Other artists accentuated the romantic German tone, eternal in its infinite transformations.

We need not mention all of them here but at least we must refer to two who made the group triumph and carried it to the other side of the bridge. They are the Saxon, Max Pechstein, and an Austrian of the Danube, Oskar Kokoschka, who saw in the portrait the goal of expressionist painting because all the aforementioned circumstances are to be found in it as well as the character, the living being, the dynamism of the spirit. Among his most successfully realized portraits is that of Schönberg. But between the two what a great difference in the concept of the material and of the form! The brushwork of Kokoschka is dense, thick, and greasy yet gay and luminous. The musical material of Schönberg is complex, composed of minute details for the purpose of producing a whole that is somber, sad, agonized in its aspiration toward cosmic planes which are indifferent to Kokoschka. The Austrian is satisfied only with the intoxication of the light of our planet on clear days not with the crepuscular half-light of impressionism or of contemporary German poetic symbolism.

"Perfection," said the landscapist Eugene Boudin, a precursor of French impressionism at about the time the first impressionists were born, "is a col-

[3] "Expressionism thereupon developed into agony, the painters scraping the sensitive depths of their subconscious material for their pictures." C. H. Bulliet, *op. cit.,* p. 171.

lective work." The war of 1914-18 burst upon this work of collaboration among German artists and those neighboring artists who were attuned to German sensibilities. Among the most gifted was Franz Marc who fell at Verdun—having scarcely succeeded in enunciating with notable clarity the principles of the most advanced phase of expressionism (which was integrated from 1911 by the Muscovite, Wasili Kandinsky, and the Bavarian, Paul Klee). Marc, born in 1880, wrote—between 1912 and 1916—some "Aphorisms" in which may be found expressed in philosophical terms the motivating idea of Kandinsky and Schönberg.

Each of these men had already tried to formulate his ideas, though not so freely nor so clearly; the first in his essay entitled "The Art of Spiritual Harmony" (1912-13) and the second in his "Treatise on Harmony" (1910-11, although not published until much later). A phrase written by Marc in 1915 seems to me decisive as regards the art of Schönberg: "The coming art will be the concretion in form of a scientific conviction." We shall see this conviction arising in Schönberg, beginning in 1908-9 with his poems on texts of Stefan George and his three pieces for piano, Op. 11. It is a "scientific" conviction whose most fully achieved realization is to be found in vocal settings of the little poems (originally in the French language) combined with a few instruments entitled *Pierrot Lunaire,* contemporary, as has been said, with the most advanced realizations of Kandinsky.

These paintings, like those of Paul Klee, have often been compared with the art of Schönberg for the purpose of providing the public with an explanation, good or bad, by intuitive means. But, as a matter of fact, the paintings of the new expressionist group, called Der Blaue Reiter (The Blue Horseman, perhaps because of Marc's fondness for blue horses arranged in harmonious combinations), which followed the early expressionism of Die Brücke, goes further than the art of Schönberg. The latter always worked, whether in *Verklärte Nacht* or in the Five Orchestral Pieces with short, well-defined motives; he combines them with each other and develops them within the "scientific" technique of so-called atonality, which he, like other artists of his time (Josef Mathias Hauer, for example), preferred to call simply *technique in the twelve tones,* in short: a nonfunctional chromaticism.

Some pictures of Kandinsky and of Klee consist in juxtapositions and combinations of plastic motives clearly drawn as straight lines, zigzags, circles, protoplasmic matter, shooting stars, polyhedrons, and brilliant spots scattered here and there; but there is in these pictures no development or leading of the plastic feeling equivalent to that brought about by an inner dramatic action in Schönberg's compositions; that is, by a romantic principle of which not a trace exists in the paintings referred to. On the contrary, the linear, the circular, the geometric elements in Kandinsky and Klee are fixed forms nailed to the canvas, at the opposite pole to French impressionistic painting, so restless and dissolvent, as also to that of early expressionism.

From his origin, Schönberg seems to me to be an impressionist who proceeds in German style from chromatic, ultramodulatory technique to the final dissolution of the tonal functions which are definitely separated from one another in the works of last-mentioned dates. In this period he proceeds more in accord with the "postimpressionist" German expressionism of Die Brücke, in my opinion, than with the Improvisations of Kandinsky [4] which Percy Scholes cites in his article on the Viennese musician in the fifth pamphlet of Columbia History of Music through Ear and Eye. The musician, who collaborated in the review which bore the name of the group,[5] perhaps felt himself nearer to them than to the former Die Brücke, but this seems to me to be a mistake in perspective. At this moment, when impressionism, expressionism, atonality, and polytonality are essays surpassed by a new constructive and tonal sense, it seems to me that the tapestry work of Klee and the wrapping-paper art of Kandinsky lack any relationship to the music of our time.

Can it be that these painters went too fast? Is it that music is not satisfied with compromises and substitutes? Undoubtedly one can find a concept of musical utility in *Gebrauchsmusik* (utilitarian music) which we shall mention in speaking of Hindemith. But this music, devoid of strictly musical inspiration, that is, lacking any purely musical reason for existence, cannot provide any sense of musical fulfillment.

The music of Schönberg, of Alban Berg, of Webern is deeply nourished with intuitions which are derived from romantic symbology as regards the dramatic episode which they endeavor to express; at the same time, it is derived from the polyphony of Gothic music, so far as the character of the material employed, its form, and its manner of expression is concerned. This expression, then, is specific, in contrast to its purely sentimental and literary predecessor. But in this case, just as in impressionism, the two moving forces are added to one another in order to integrate the aesthetics and the technique of the artist. From this union a new value is born; a value specifically musical as well as ethical because it concerns the activity of the artist's soul in its intimate relationship with the material manufactured. This new value, which characterizes Debussy as well as Schönberg, Ravel as well as Alban Berg, is quality. From the first moment of contact with French or German music, the listener, even one who is badly prejudiced, experiences at least an unmistakable sensation that commands his respect. His own intuition responds to the quality of this art. To be sure, he does not comprehend it as yet nor does he even appreciate it. Nevertheless, he suspends judgment.

[4] See the famous "Prophecy of War" (1913) in C. J. Bulliet, *op. cit.*, plate 240.
[5] In the volume for 1912-13 of *Der Blaue Reiter.*

The first decade of the century was decisive for the German painters whom we have passed here in rapid review and for the musicians of the same countries who were spurred by similar impulses. It was the painters who took the decisive step which led from the first group of Die Brücke to the ultrarevolutionaries of Der Blaue Reiter. Schönberg, who in 1902 found Richard Strauss disposed to protect his audacities, encountered in Mahler, the following year, that cordial and intelligent support without which the most solid expectations often meet disaster. In that same year, 1903, on his return from his first stay in Berlin, Schönberg began to teach harmony and counterpoint. In the Institute of Musical History of the University of Vienna, directed by the great musicologist, Guido Adler, the last symphonies of Adler's friend, Mahler, were being rehearsed. Under the latter's influence the young musicians were seeking new horizons in which they might find new ideas in contrast to official teachings.

Schönberg was discovered and promptly there formed around him a group in which were Alban Berg, Anton von Webern, Egon Wellesz, Heinrich Jalowetz, and Erwin Stein. Primarily for them, Schönberg systematized his ideas and began to comprehend that a method or theory existed in them. The first stage in this methodization, in this way or *Vorversuche* (preliminary experiments) as Schönberg called it, was his *Harmonielehre* (theory of harmony). It dates from 1910-11 and its text, often diffuse, was later made more succinct (1922).[6] The theatrical piece entitled, *Die Glückliche Hand* occupied him at the same time. Schönberg wrote both text and music, neither of which received definitive form until 1913, on the eve of the war. Meanwhile he composed Six Short Pieces for piano, Op. 19, and wrote various articles on the teaching of music. The *Sechs kleine Klavierstücke* belong to 1911.

In the following year, *Pierrot Lunaire* on short poems by the Belgian, Albert Giraud (in the German translation of O. E. Hartleben), Schönberg's decisive work, was finished: twenty-one pieces for instruments and voice *quasi parlato*. These were to be followed by Four Songs with orchestra, Op. 22, between 1913 and 1914. It was at the end of this latter year, of such historical importance, and in the first months of 1915 that Schönberg discovered the definitive *Vorversuche* in his atonal practice—while he was working on the composition *Jacob's Ladder* (*Die Jakobsleiter*) which turned out to be in fact the chromatic scale or series of twelve tones whose tonal idea and technical system will be described in detail in the next chapter. For his own part, since 1912, Joseph Mathias Hauer was making experiments in atonalism and the series of twelve tones which led him to results of a rather different kind from those of Schönberg, as we shall see hereafter.

Die Jakobsleiter never reached its final step, any more than has Schönberg's

[6] On Schönberg's method of teaching, see Egon Wellesz, *Arnold Schönberg,* Third Part (London: J. M. Dent, 1925), English translation by W. H. Kerridge.

production so far. But after the last-mentioned works and the Quintet, Op. 26, for wind instruments in 1923-24 it would seem that the composer had reached his definitive stage. In this year Schönberg was fifty; his birthday was celebrated by his pupils and followers by the founding, in his name, of a library of modern music. Shortly after, he was made professor in the Prussian Academy of Fine Arts in Berlin to replace Busoni. Before ten years had passed, the national socialist minister of the Third Reich demanded the resignation of artists like Schönberg and Franz Schreker (the latter, from his post in the Hochschule für Musik).

Arnold Schönberg left Germany in 1933. On arriving in Paris he made solemn profession of the Jewish faith and, in October of the same year, he embarked for the United States where a conservatory in Boston had opened its doors to him. Some months later he went to California, seeking—like Igor Stravinsky and Darius Milhaud—a less rigorous climate than that of the north. After 1930 (as before, between 1915 and 1920), Schönberg passed through a sterile period. His last works before this crisis were of Hebraic character, like the sketches for the theater, *Der biblische Weg* and *Moses und Aron,* and like his Jewish liturgical music. In 1936 the wand of Moses again put forth shoots and Schönberg finished, among other less important works, his Fourth String Quartet (first performed by the quartet led by his brother-in-law, Kolisch), a second *Kammersymphonie* (1940, begun in 1906), and a Concerto for Violin, Op. 36.

Meanwhile, he has been meditating on his nonfunctional system of composition in *Tonreihen* (tone rows in the technical language of his adopted country), the most perfect application of which is demonstrated in the Suite for Piano and Sextet of winds and strings, Op. 29. These meditations are soon to appear in a volume which Schönberg is completing or may already have completed as we write. It is a treatise to be entitled "Fundamentals of Musical Composition." Pending the appearance of this volume of aesthetic meditations as well as a summary of his technical experiences, let us leave Schönberg to the weaving of his tone rows and turn to observe at what point atonal technique and its most clearly characterized successors stand at the present moment.

Chapter TWENTY-TWO

THE THEATER is the touchstone of musical aesthetics. In its realm all the factors that make up the art of an epoch confront each other in decisive manner. And when this theater has absorbed in itself all the lyric currents of its time and grows old, the aesthetic age of which it is the synthesis may consider itself in its turn worn out. An examination of the baroque theater—of the *opera in musica* in connection with accompanied madrigalian polyphony (which disappears with the new concept of the "chorus"), the solo madrigal (which was to be absorbed by the new concept of the aria) and then from the point of view of harmonic accompaniment, the height which the art of the lute achieves—is a fruitful study to prove the thesis which I merely suggest but will not develop here. At present, it is interesting to recall how *Pelléas et Mélisande* embodies impressionist aesthetics, the art of Debussy in its fullest sense, just as *L'Heure espagnole* sums up an art like that of Ravel which derives from the prosodic exactness of everyday French speech or, so to speak, from the expressive genius of the phrase translated into musical terms.

By its very nature, expressionism had to enter the field of the theater, and it is only natural that it should do so in original terms, in the subject matter as in the technique. There are three planes in the theater which Schönberg and, after him, those disciples most closely linked to his thought were to attempt to resolve jointly. The first plane is that of the action: sung, declaimed or spoken. The second is that of the music proper: divided into vocal melody, harmonic setting, instrumental color. The third consists in the conformity of the theatrical setting with all that has gone before so that the stage effect may attain a lyric value equal to the expressiveness sought on the other planes.

An art like that of Schönberg, so closely bound to the plastic feeling of his age, could not be content, when approaching the theater, with ordinary scenic realizations but must proclaim the necessity of introducing the kind of new effects corresponding to the musician's need of expression. We shall see in a moment what Schönberg and, later, Alban Berg succeeded in drawing out of the technique of stage craft and of theatrical design, arts which developed so rapidly in the intensity and novelty of their effects in the German and Russian theater. First, it is necessary to examine everything related to the other points which are the indispensable premises of the lyric theater.

In contrast to Italian verismo, which proclaimed itself an *arte di stupore,* impressionism did not set itself to "impress" the audience. This kind of immediate effect was very far from the refinement, the distance, which the artist placed between the first impression received on reading a poem, on contemplating a picture or a landscape, and the realization of that impression in terms of art. The commonly accepted term, symbolism, explained this double perspective, this distance between the inspiring motive and the work. The characters in the *Pelléas* of Debussy are like expressive symbols of lyric emotions whose anguish, as a reality, has moved very far away from what had been the original impression.

The expressionist theater of Schönberg presents us with a similar separation, but in another sense. In a manner analogous to that which has been described in the case of impressionism, which never sought to "impress," expressionism never set itself directly to "express" the dramatic action (as did the romantics). Rather, expressionists sought to fashion the sonorous material in musical terms which were the equivalent of what the composer felt in his innermost being. Those imponderable elements which the artist revolves in his subconscious, in what has been called his somnambulism, have given the art of every epoch those indefinable shadings which sensitive minds know how to discover and which are the impalpable grain of musk perfuming certain works of art from the archaic Apollo of pre-Hellenic art with his Ravelian smile to the sculptures of Lehmbruck; from the exoticisms of Andrea Vanni and the old Sienese painters to Turner and to Whistler; from the monsters who engender the dream of reason in Patinir and in the elder Breughel to El Greco, to the "black" Goya or the surrealists.

In the modern German art of the theater and of the dance, one feels conscious of this kind of lyric somnambulism (especially if one is a Latin) which has points of similarity with the Russian novel, as with the characters of Dostoievski. Maeterlinck's characters move through the pages of the book or across the stage in this somnambulant way, especially when translated musically by Debussy. An extreme somnambulism seems to be contagious in the musical works of expressionism and especially in the theatrical works of this school. Its roots are to be found in Schönberg's monodrama entitled *Erwartung* (Op. 17, 1909) and in the "symbolist" drama (I use this term here in the sense of expressionism par excellence), *Die Glückliche Hand* (Op. 18, 1910-13). Its culmination up to the present seems to be the *Wozzeck* of Alban Berg and his semiposthumous *Lulu.*

Returning to the first of the above-mentioned planes on which the lyric theater rests, that of the musical translation of a dramatic action, Schönberg himself has explained the manner in which he conceives the lied or, more accurately, the dramatic scene. His theory, expounded in an article entitled "Das Verhältnis zum Text" (The relationship between music and text)—published in 1912 in the review *Blaue Reiter,* edited by Kandinsky and Marc—is tinged with that nebulous quality characteristic of German metaphysics. Yet, when one studies it closely, one recognizes that it is valid not only for Schönberg and expressionism but equally so for all romantic art.

In fact, Schönberg takes Schubert as his example. If one reflects, it will be easy to see—after the "Erlking," after "Margaret at the Spinning Wheel," after Wagner—that the process of musicalization of a text is the fruit of an unconscious or, rather, subconscious elaboration of a text and that its explanation is as valid for those romantic composers mentioned as for the impressionists and for the expressionists. The process is fundamentally different from that of the formalist composers, who limit themselves to framing a poetic phrase within the architecture of the musical phrase. Yet, after all, this formalism was never so rigorous as to exclude entirely the subconscious faculty, which sometimes injected its grain of imponderable substance into the constructive rigidity of the form.

What Schönberg says in this article, as I understand him, is that the music of a lied could not clarify for him the inner meaning of the text nor could the text alone with its dramatic episodes make him understand the music. He felt the two as separate things which he wished to unite (this, I believe, is constantly the case in opera, although to the detriment of the text, which is too often disregarded by the listener). But when he considered well the musical content of the first phrase whose poetic expression is easily caught (for example when we hear *"Meine Ruhe ist hin, mein Herz ist schwer"* ["My repose is gone, my heart is heavy"], or *"Wer reiset so spätz durch Nacht und Wind?"* ["Who rides so late in the wind and the night?"]) simultaneously with the purely musical sense of the notes to which the words are sung or with which the piano accompanies the song, it was sufficient for him to abandon himself to the music in order that the meaning of the lied, both musical and poetic, should become clear to him. It is unnecessary to adhere closely to the specific development of the dramatic episode; one need follow it only at a distance, as when the thread of Margaret's spinning wheel breaks or when the voice of the child is heard in dialogue with the father in the "Erlking." The double content of the lied arises from the continuity of the spinning-wheel motive, in the one case, or of the galloping horse, in the other; in both instances, the continuity is due to the musical content of both motives not to their distant imitative effect.

Yet this is true of all music, even formal music—sonata, rondo, or passacaglia—and to an even greater extent of dramatic music. All *Tristan* is implicit in the four first notes of the Prelude. All the Symphony in C minor lies latent in the four notes of "fate knocking at the door." "Then," says Schönberg, "I understood clearly that the same thing occurs with a musical work as with a perfect organism." (It is curious, incidentally, that until "then" Schönberg had not discovered the "organic" quality of all symphonic music.) When one has understood the dramatic force contained in the first notes of a lied or in the sound of the first syllables of a poem (as when we hear: "Full fathom five thy father lies" or "Season of mists and mellow fruitfulness" or "She walks in beauty like the night" or "The curfew tolls the knell of parting day"), all the rest included in the "external accord" between music and text in its aspects concerning declamation, tempo, tonal intensity, etc. appears of secondary importance because the essential part of the expression, poetic as well as musical, has been captured by the listener.

The musical prosody of Schönberg does not come from the spoken language but adjusts itself to the melodism of his atonal system. Beginning with *"Das Buch der Hängenden Gärten,"* of Stefan George, and the Pieces for Piano, Op. 11, the atonal process became intensified until Schönberg saw its systematization clearly in his duodecimal series or the twelve-tone technique, when working in 1914 on his still unfinished oratorio, *Die Jakobsleiter.* This new musical prosody, however amelodic or unvocal may be its structure according to his earlier aesthetic technique, nevertheless shows a close connection with the melodism of the first works discussed.

The new atonal melody is born directly from Schönberg's original melody, even though nourished by Wagnerism and Mahlerism but, in proportion as it becomes more expressionist, it loses its human quality. While Alban Berg proceeds in conformity with this and even accentuates the instrumental quality of his characters in *Lulu,* Schönberg apparently tries to avoid this loss of the human quality by appealing to a special method which consists in the quasi-speaking style, in the *parlato* with a measured semi-intonation, already suggested as early as the *"Gurre-Lieder,"* and whose perfection and systematization is achieved in *Pierrot Lunaire* after the essays for spoken choruses in the *Glückliche Hand.*

In the prologue to *Pierrot,* Schönberg explains his intention and the effect he wishes to obtain from the singer-narrator. Although the melody of the voice is written in notes (the conventional notes are replaced by little stars), the interpreter must neither sing nor declaim exclusively, even when passages from this melody are used in the accompanying instrumental fabric. Of course, the performer must follow the rhythm strictly and even begin each syllable on the tone that corresponds to it but he must immediately abandon the musical intonation, raising and lowering the spoken intonation in accord with the line of the phrase (or whatever else indicates the sense of the interval). The interpreter is obliged to divine Schönberg's intention of "transforming the melody" in this way and at the same time must avoid the effect of humming and of a sliding up and down. Those who have heard, at least in gramophone recordings, oriental singers with their semi-glissandi and their characteristic indecisive intonation will better understand what it is that Schönberg wants to avoid. Only a few artists with special coaching have been capable of interpreting this kind of sung declamation to the author's satisfaction; gramophone editions of *Pierrot Lunaire* will make this method widely known but perhaps one may find a successful realization of Schönberg's invention in the Façade (1922-26) of the English composer, William Walton.

The role played by instruments in this example of *Pierrot Lunaire* or in Schönberg's two theatrical pieces, or, again, in the singing voice in his Lieder with orchestra, Op. 22 (1913-14), or with piano, beginning with the Stefan George songs, is as far from the traditional one as is the function of the piano in the lieder of Hugo Wolf from that of romantic accompaniment. The best-organized realization of this concept is to be heard in Schönberg's theatrical works in which the color of the instrumental combinations underlines the change in position of the chordal combinations, giving a distinctly new value to the same chordal entity. In short, the role of the orchestra or of the piano comes to be a kind of expressionist accentuation (that is, a subconscious echo), in the instrumental realm, of the vocal turn of phrase.

The piano produces isolated sounds, little phrases, chordal groups, while the voice unfolds its part: there is no effort toward form, rhythmic unity, or accompanying motives. It is an indeterminate flowing of sound—sometimes complex, sometimes very simple—in a succession which neither doubles the voice nor harmonizes it but which collaborates with it in that mystery proper to the subconscious and the superreal. If one is disposed to accept it, it must be admitted that the effect received is wholly convincing and, sometimes, unquestionably beautiful. The effect is analogous to that produced by impressionist harmony in its accompaniment of the voice in Debussy's songs. We are dealing with a phenomenon of poetic suggestion (rising from the meaning of the text or, better, simply from the title of the page or the emotional direction indicated by the first phrases) produced by the color of the instrumental sound—"beautiful dissonance" in impressionism, a special non-harmonic combination in expressionism—concurrent with the human voice.

Similarly, Schönberg's orchestration beginning with the Five Orchestral Pieces, Op. 16 (contemporary with the Piano Pieces, Op. 11, and with the monodrama, *Erwartung*), will take on a new aspect, within an order of ideas canalized in the direction already described. The key to the Five Orchestral Pieces appears in the third one of the group, which bears the title *Der Wechselnde Akkord* (the Changing Chord), in which a single chord or chordal agglomeration (C-G#-B-E-A) changes its color and even its meaning incessantly through the mere change of instrumental combination. Examples are C, viola; G♯, two bassoons; B, clarinet; E, A, two flutes; these notes are immediately afterward played by a double bass, a horn, a bassoon, a muted trumpet and an English horn. Any thematic idea has completely disappeared in this piece while the orchestration avoids the instrumental contrasts and combinations proper to the usual technique. The instruments are treated as soloists, that is, each one stands out individually (without any idea of virtuosity, of course) somewhat as if the orchestra were a grand piano in which each note were endowed with a special timbre. These features were to be taken up later by Schönberg's disciples, especially by Anton von Webern, who has carried this analytical criterion and a corresponding minuteness of detail to an extreme which results in the surprising brevity of his pieces, even of those called symphonies.

The first of Schönberg's Five Pieces is constructed on a basic motive, which serves no expressive intention whatsoever but which is subjected to such transformations as augmentation, diminution, and canonic treatment. In fact, the twelve-tone technique reduces itself to a perpetual variation of the fundamental series, or tone row, which is the "scale" of the atonal system. This thematic manipulation to which the new atonal technique finds itself reduced makes a virtue of necessity and seeks an escape from its impasse by pretending that the composer has returned to medieval times, when the construction of forms was carried out empirically by an artificial handling of the sonorous materials at hand.

It was, in fact, the mechanical procedures of augmentation and diminution which led to the baroque forms of the passacaglia and the chaconne, with their incessantly repeated nucleus subjected to the ornamental variations and contrapuntal devices already mentioned. If the motive is treated rhythmically, as in the old dance suites of which the different sections are based on an identical succession of notes (for example, the Variation Suite, No. 7, of Paul Peuerl [1]), we have according to the rhythm and measure a pavan, an intrada, a dantz, a galliard, etc. Thus Schönberg, in his Suite, Op. 25 (1923), derives his Praeludium, Gavotte, Musette, Intermezzo, Minuet, and Gigue from a fundamental series in the twelve tones—E, F, G, D♭, G♭, E♭, A♭, D, B, C, A, B♭—the series may be inverted, may change its rhythms and time values, may be treated in *ostinato* (like *Das Obbligato Recitativ,* which is the fifth piece of Op. 16), in short, may be broken up into the inevitable fugue on the notes B-A-C-H (B♭-A-C-B♮). This treatment is not objection-

[1] Quoted as an example in Guido Adler, *Handbuch der Musikgeschichte* (Frankfurt am Main: 1924), "Instrumental-musik von 1600-1750" by Wilhelm Fischer, p. 506.

The custom of basing all the sections of the suite on a single theme varied rhythmically became general about the middle of the sixteenth century. See H. Prunières, *Nouvelle Histoire de la Musique* (Paris: 1934), I, 235.

able: in our time it may be practiced, if the composer deems it advisable, in the tonal as well as in the atonal system but it is curious to find Alban Berg utilizing it as the basis of the dramatic scenes of *Wozzeck*. That tiny closed forms may seem appropriate for a somnambulistic, dramatic symbolism like that of the characters of this lyric drama is surprising.

Nevertheless, if one has understood sufficiently clearly the idea Schönberg explains in regard to the accompaniment of a poetic text, one will understand also that the principle remains the same, whether this accompaniment lacks form of any kind (as in the songs, Op. 15, of George) or whether it adopts the form of a pavan, passacaglia, gigue or, as Erik Satie said, a *"forme de poire."* In the instinctive necessity of giving some kind of structure to the sonorous fluid, musicians strongly rooted in the German tradition, like Schönberg and Alban Berg, find a certain relief from the natural amorphousness of atonality in constructing something which distantly recalls the forms of the pavan, passacaglia, or gigue. Yet, without a previous analysis of the score or without the program notes, the ear perceives absolutely nothing of these forms. The role of the orchestra in Berg's *Wozzeck* is like that of the piano in the "Songs of the Hanging Gardens of Babylon" in which, of course, there exist neither Babylon nor hanging gardens. But that is of no importance. No China, either stylized or symbolical exists in *"Das Lied von der Erde,"* even though it purports to follow a Chinese poem supposedly reworked by Hans Bethge. Yet this does not prevent the work from being perhaps the most notable of Mahler's production.

The minute combinations characteristic of this art reach their climax in the "three times seven" songs of *Pierrot Lunaire,*[2] where the symbolist texts—full of ailing moons (*Der kranke Mond*), moonstruck souls (*Mondestrunken*), and lunar radiances from the protagonist's face (*Der Mondfleck*)—were translated into German by Otto Erich Hartleben from the original French of Albert Giraud, a Belgian poet. In these pages Schönberg carries his technique to its extremes, in a writing meticulously prolix and in the instrumental combinations for a group composed of a piano, violin (alternating with viola), violoncello, flute (alternating with a piccolo), and clarinet (alternating with bass clarinet). Above the delicate combinations and juxtapositions made by the sonorous brush, like an harmonic-instrumental pointillism, glides the speech-song (*Sprachgesang*) of the reciter of the poems. Schönberg gathers into this work all his experience in writing for the theater, in *Erwartung* and *Die Glückliche Hand,* as well as his ideas regarding this kind of sung-declamation and its instrumental accompaniment, whether in the closed forms above referred to or in free form. As a matter of fact, *Pierrot*

[2] Published by Columbia in 1942 on four records, Album M461 after two hundred rehearsals, as is there stated by the author himself who directed the work. The singer is Frau Erika Wagner-Stiedry.

Lunaire could be performed on the stage with at least as much reason as *Erwartung*. As these works of Schönberg lead to those of Alban Berg and since atonal music (before its systematization in tone rows) reaches its culmination in them, I have felt it advisable to discuss them last.

Schönberg's *Erwartung* (*Waiting*), directly follows the Five Orchestral Pieces and belongs to the same year, 1909. The descriptive epithet, monodrama, signifies that it is a play with a single character. It is the story of a woman who seeks everywhere in the solitude and the obscurity of night for her lover, of whom another woman has robbed her. In her search she comes upon a corpse, that of her lover. She refuses to believe that he is dead, even when day dawns with its unambiguous light. She prefers to descend to self-deceit: "Ah! it is you," she exclaims. "I was waiting for you." And the curtain falls.

The work is short and, in kind, belongs to those essays at chamber theater which were performed in Berlin in the first years of the century, in theaters or in cafés with an intellectual atmosphere. Schönberg worked in one of them in 1901, the Buntes Theater, of Wolzogen. The idea for his monodrama is his own but the realization is the work of an authoress, Marie Pappenheim, who arranged the episode in short scenes which pass from the edge of a wood in moonlight into the wood itself and then to the high road in full daylight. The orchestra follows the song of the protagonist closely with the idea of expressing in color the meaning of each word. Written in a few days, this work is full of passion and most effective, according to Schönberg's commentators, although they consider it an error to have staged it, apparently because it is impossible to carry out the expressive mobility of the diction and of the music.

Schönberg believed, in view of his experience with the performance of *Erwartung,* that a revolution in staging was necessary in order to achieve this rapid succession of shifting, emotional scenes. In *Die Glückliche Hand* (the *Lucky Hand*), he was to attempt this process by means of the play of lighting, a little in the manner of Scriabin's Prometheus, which is of precisely the same epoch as Schönberg's work. (The *Lucky Hand* dates from 1910-13 and Prometheus from 1909-10.) The succession of colored lighting effects in Scriabin's poem corresponds to that of the tonal episodes derived from his "mystic chord." In Schönberg's work the changes of color occur as the result of the dramatic episodes. The plot is Schönberg's and is a mixture of symbolism, somnambulism, frustrations, and Wagnerian complications with grottoes and anvils, subterranean workers in precious metals, monsters, etc.

A curious detail (also used in the little scenes written for the artists' cabaret in Berlin, the Blue Bird, after the style of the little theaters in Moscow—the Distorted Mirror, the Bat, and others—beginning in the last years of the past century) [3] consists in the fact that only the heads of the actors who take the part of the chorus are visible through holes in a dark backdrop, the only scenery; the actors' bodies remain concealed and motionless in contrast to the mobility of their facial expression. This chorus (six men and six women) expresses its sympathy for the protagonist in the kind of song-speech described above, while the latter sings in more definite manner in phrases with the chromaticism and leaps characteristic of Schönberg's melodism.

The action opens with the struggles of this character in the darkness with a monster who bites him in the neck. In a succession of different lightings a woman appears pursued by a knight (both are mute) who symbolize vulgar love, as indicated by the trivial accompanying music. The man who had been attacked by the monster tries to approach the woman without success. In other episodes, reminiscent of *Siegfried,* the woman issues from a mysterious grotto and the man shatters an anvil. From the anvil comes forth a diadem of precious stones which seduces the woman but she pushes a rock in the path of the man and the rock assumes the shape of the monster of before. Everything returns to the first scene and the chorus of heads repeats its lamentations.

"Each measure," says Egon Wellesz, "represents an incident" in the development of the action. Each chord coincides with a lighting effect. The culminating scene reaches a height of great intensity—a rising hurricane is translated by a succession of luminous tones from red to sienna and dark green, then to dark blue that changes to gray, and thence to a deep red turning to orange and finally a brilliant yellow—which is constructed musically on a motive of three notes in two distinct positions:

an idea analogous to that of the changing chord in the Five Orchestral Pieces. The effect of the orchestration is likewise analogous, developing by brushstrokes of color in solo instruments or in subtle combinations of instruments.

The work was performed in a hall of the Volksoper of Vienna in 1924 under the musical direction of Fritz Stiedry and under the stage direction of Eugen Steinhof. The experiment was very successful and called forth lively expressions of admiration for Schönberg whose brief symbolist panto-

[3] These attempts at miniature theaters are derived from the Moscow Art Theater, founded in 1897 by Stanislavsky and Nemirovitch-Dantchenko. The Blue Bird ceased to exist in Moscow in 1920 and was reborn in Berlin in 1921, afterward traveling all over Europe.

mime achieved, according to the critics, as great an effect as an entire drama of Strindberg. Because, they added, this time it was not a question of projecting upon the audience the dramatic aura which the author exhaled, but "of a highly personal form of expression made real by means of dramatic representation." [4]

[4] Egon Wellesz, *op. cit.*, p. 138.

Chapter
TWENTY-THREE

WHEN Schönberg came to know those who were to be his most fervent disciples: Alban Berg, Anton von Webern, the future conductor, Heinrich Jalowetz, Erwin Stein, and later Egon Wellesz, he had scarcely set foot on the new continent of atonality. Their meeting took place when he was giving his course in composition at the Institute of Musical History of the University of Vienna during the winter of 1903 and 1904. Schönberg had just finished the composition of his poem *Pelleas und Melisande,* Op. 5, which, as has been said, marks a moment of spiritual crisis; the attendant reflections on musical technique were undoubtedly communicated by Schönberg to his future followers.

Among them, Alban Berg, a young Viennese of Bavarian family, was at that time nineteen years old. The son of a middle-class businessman, Berg's youth recalls that of Hugo Wolf and of Schönberg himself in its inclination toward an art which, in Vienna, one absorbed spontaneously from the classics to the ultraromantics. There were fleeting attempts at self-taught composition carried on simultaneously with an effort to earn his living in a government position. Then occurred a strong spiritual shock: Berg met the master who was to set down the norms for a whole artistic life in an atmosphere of a reviving mysticism which was mingled with ethics, sociology, proselytizing enthusiasms, and an abnegation illuminated by faith. Faith is much talked of in the letters of these musicians [1] but a psychoanalyst in the Viennese style, a contemporary of all these inventions of tonal art, would have seen in this feeling simply autosuggestion or collective suggestion among a group of disciples. "The soul," "abstraction," "intensity," "the inner self" are words constantly interwoven in this faith which, in the musical species as cultivated by the young Viennese school, impatiently bears the name of atonality. From those boyhood years, Berg was to be one of the most important of its faithful and he lived in its faith until he died in his fiftieth year.

During those years a portentous figure—full of a mysterious attraction for Germanic sensibilities, an audacious figure, great in his strength as in his

[1] See Alban Berg in *Music since 1900* by N. Slonimsky, p. 565. See also, Schönberg on the quartets of Webern in *Cobbett's Cyclopaedic Survey of Chamber Music,* II, 571.

weakness and admired by young Viennese musicians both for his achievements and for his mistakes—cast his shadow over the German musical world. That figure was Gustav Mahler. The composers who raised their banners against the old musical spirit, which had tenacious roots in Vienna, banded themselves together in a Vereinigung schaffender Tonkünstler or Society of Creative Musicians, made Mahler their president, and caused his works such as the *"Kindertotenlieder"* to be performed as well as the Domestic Symphony of Strauss, well regarded by the group, the *Nereid* (*Seejungfrau*) of Zemlinsky, and the *Pelleas und Melisande* of Schönberg. The reputations of some of these "creative musicians" have spread beyond the German frontiers: those of Zemlinsky and Hausegger, one of the great German conductors, while those of J. von Wöss, Posa, Karl Weigl, or Rudolf Hoffmann would be scarcely known to us except for the fact that Egon Wellesz mentions them in his monograph on Schönberg.[2]

Beneath this shadow of Mahler, which sheltered the Germanic musicians born in the last years of the century just as Wagner's shadow had fostered the two preceding generations, blossomed the tender sensibilities of Alban Berg in his early songs (1907) on texts of Lenau, Storm, Rilke, Hauptmann, and others. In the following year appeared a Sonata for Piano, his Op. 1, in which the Tristanesque harmony endeavors to mold itself in a Brahmsian idea of form. But the seed dropped in the receptive soil of Alban Berg's sensibility (a pliancy of character, even a peculiar physical softness characterized this musician throughout his life which he passed, with the moonlike pallor of a passing phantom, in the streets and gardens of Florence) by Schönberg's teaching matured slowly through these years, finally to come to the surface in a quartet—in two movements—which had taken shape during the period of World War I but which did not appear until 1924.

This slowness of production is typical of Berg and, aside from being simply a personal idiosyncrasy of the composer, seems to result from a highly developed faculty of self-criticism, from scrupulous selection, from reiterated meditation, and from the refinement of his craftsmanship. His art is very far indeed from being parsimonious (like that of Anton von Webern) and, although few in number, his productions have an ample eloquence, a richness of material, and are endowed with a communicativeness which seems to me to surpass that of Schönberg himself. It is a highly intellectualized art, as is that of all the group (although they may wish it to be something else) but in Berg at least it has a certain reflection of human emotion, even of romantic inspiration. Berg admits this quality without embarrassment in the directions for the movements of his works as, for example, in the *Suite Lyrique* (for

[2] The name of Karl Weigl is familiar because he now resides in New York. Josef Venantius von Wöss is associated with Bruckner, whose works he revised and about whom he published some personal reminiscences.

string quartet, 1926), his most fully realized composition and the one of most accessible beauty; this is perhaps his definitive work, and perhaps even the definitive work of the young Viennese school.

Before reaching in this work the plenitude of his talent and of his mature technique, so closely linked to that of his master, Berg tried his meticulous weaving in some miniatures for clarinet and piano, Op. 5, contemporary with the preparatory studies for the Quartet, Op. 3. The Four Pieces, Op. 15, may be compared with Anton von Webern's Bagatelles, Op. 9, for quartet—works which both musicians were composing simultaneously in 1913. About this time Berg carried his miniaturist's technique to the orchestra in his Three Orchestral Pieces, Op. 6 (1913-14).[3] So detailed is the composition and so meticulous the author as regards its performance that he had to invent a new system for indicating the orchestral planes which he desired should dominate the rest.

An occidental composer well versed in orchestration would not but express doubt at this invention of a young composer who was writing for orchestra for the first time. Yet Schönberg himself, who begged conductors not to take it upon themselves to interpret him by altering the degree of sonorities that he himself had carefully determined, follows a system similar to that of Berg in order to "help" the conductor in his understanding of what is of first and what of secondary importance in his compositions. Perhaps a musician belonging to the group would not need such indications nor would a proficient conductor need them if concerned with traditional music, but undoubtedly these clarifications were useful in an art that was still so nebulous.

What preoccupied Berg above all in these pieces was the exact shading and movement of each note or little group of notes. Such meticulousness is nothing new. One has only to glance at the score of *Pelleas und Melisande* to see how prodigal it is of "mutes on" and "mutes off," of simultaneous directions for different shadings, "G string," harmonics, "in two parts," "tremolo near the bridge," "in four parts," etc., and all this not for phrases or passages of a certain dimension but for single notes set in the air like precious stones. This is a technique of goldwork, of marquetry, of Mechlin lace which Webern carries to such a point that he leaves a note isolated in process of dissolving, that he makes a chord not a chord but a simultaneity of three, four, or more timbres in which the intonation of the tone ceases to be the base but becomes one more element of color.

Immediately after these Three Pieces for Orchestra (Prelude, Rondo, March), Alban Berg began his composition of the music for Büchner's drama, *Wozzeck,* to which he brings the same point of view, both as regards orchestral technique and as regards the structure of the pieces in whose

[3] His Op. 4 (1912) are five little songs for "post cards" with verses by Peter Altenberg.

preclassic or baroque forms he thought to symbolize the personalities of his characters, their emotional conflicts and even whimsies.

Following this criterion, Act I of *Wozzeck* consists of five characteristic pieces in closed forms; Act II is a so-called symphony in five movements; Act III, six inventions, a kind of technical homage to the author of the *Art of the Fugue* which is ever present with this school in its methods of writing. As regards the voice parts, Berg does not make use of Schönberg's *parlato* but the melody, sung by the voice and deprived of all connection with what until then was considered vocal melody, is a categorically instrumental melody. And in this Berg simply follows a fundamental German tendency.

But when all is said, there remains to be ascertained whether, within these technical methods and aesthetic intentions, there exists that prerequisite for the realization of all works of art, musical or otherwise: I refer to artistic intuition or, in music, to musical intuition. In what way and to what degree does musical intuition intervene in the compositions of the young Viennese school? The artistic intuition which moves the creator of a work of art is only perceived by the spectator-listener to the extent to which he feels or comprehends that type of intuition. The attempt to measure the intensity or quality of Schönberg's musical intuition is childish. It would be equivalent to putting oneself on a level with the romantic audiences who did not understand their Beethoven at all when they listened to the Great Fugue, Op. 133.

Latin audiences may remain cold at hearing the works of Schönberg or of his disciples; Central Europeans, Germans, Slavs, on the other hand, respond profoundly to this music. The composers' musical intuitions speak to these peoples in a language strange to others. It is reasonable to suppose that if we understand sufficiently *Verklärte Nacht* or *"Gurre-Lieder"* (although they may be far from filling us with enthusiasm, a type of emotion which Schönberg does not seem to solicit) and if we appreciate in these first works an intuition traditionally German and romantic, we may assume that a similar type of intuition will continue to dictate later works although the technical vocabulary, unfamiliar to our auditory habits, blurs our perception of the intuitive element. *Wozzeck* serves precisely to convince us of this because, despite its atonalism, its construction in closed forms, the antivocal character of its vocal melody, and other circumstances, this work, when we see it performed, "reaches" us profoundly, excites us dramatically, reveals itself to us clearly, if inexplicably, in its dramatic and musical values. Is the musical intuition of Berg more intense than that of Schönberg? I make the suggestion for purposes of comparison. I neither affirm nor deny it but it seems certain that no one would take the negative stand if the comparison were with Webern rather than with Schönberg.

The convincing effect of *Wozzeck* and, for me, the unconvincingness of its technical system has preoccupied me during entire years. My solution, which perhaps may be provisional, consists in the belief that *Wozzeck* makes its impression musically in a way analogous to the effect produced on us by a film accompanied by music "which we do not hear" or which we hear with an attention very much subordinated to that which we fix on the screen. The ear, in this case, is no more than an almost passive collaborator of the eye. In *Wozzeck* the ear is a collaborator of the dramatic sense which receives the sonorous atmosphere, the height and the intensity of emotional tone, the atmosphere of musical color, all these as musical intuitions which surround the nucleus of the human action. Professional musicians may perhaps be indignant at such a conclusion. As for me, I see it simply as an extreme example of what is the permanent phenomenon of the musical theater. In the disjunct music drama, never resolved in a perfect union, one hears the music in the degree in which one does not see the action (but rather follows it within the emotions) or, on the contrary, the visualness of the spectacle eclipses in direct proportion the hearing of the music. *Tristan* is the best proof of the first; the ballet of the second.

Alban Berg spent six years in the composition of his lyric drama *Wozzeck*. The first performance of *Wozzeck* occurred in the State Opera House in Berlin, December 14, 1925. In the meantime the twelve-tone technique had reached complete maturity with the group of Schönberg and his friends. As has been said, Schönberg clearly saw this technique which was to put order and system into his free use of the tonal function when, at the end of 1914, he was working on the symphony of his oratorio, *Jacob's Ladder*. In that year, Berg began the composition of *Wozzeck*. This work, therefore, still does not reveal an exact knowledge of the twelve-tone technique although, as in earlier works of his and of Schönberg's, the system was on the point of appearing.

In 1924, Berg finished a Chamber Concerto for violin, piano, and thirteen instruments which, conceived and worked out entirely within the new technique, is dedicated to the master of the new idiom, Arnold Schönberg, who had just completed his fiftieth year. In the duodecimal series Berg found various notes which, in German *solfeggio,* correspond to letters included in the three names of Schönberg, Webern, and Berg. This succession came to be the key theme of the work and of the group, and its treatment is that suggested by the variations and devices of writing of medieval composers. If the Concerto is a little dry, the work which followed it was to affirm the system amid musical intuitions richer in inner feeling: the *Suite Lyrique* of 1926. Official recognition of Berg's merits came in 1930 when he was named an officer of the Prussian Academy of Fine Arts.

Ten years after the first performance of *Wozzeck,* the most advanced Berlin audiences were offered a suite composed of five pieces from the new opera on which Berg was working and which he left unfinished at his death. It was Wedekind's drama, *Lulu,* the work into which Berg had put his whole heart; complex in its dramatic development, the play nevertheless has an essential theme which is easy to explain, although not so easy to interpret musically. Lulu is the "eternal feminine manifestation of evil," the eternal *femme fatale* who, from one degrading depth to the next, leads men to suicide, herself commits a crime, and finally ends in prison. The plot of Wedekind, like a great part of the contemporary German theater, is full of the complexes involved in sexual perversions, with a marked weakness for morbid individuals and for acts of frustration or of triumph; it is antipathetic, not to say repulsive, like other dramas by Arnold Bronnen or K. Bruckner.

But the important point is to know whether Alban Berg succeeded, on bringing it to the musical stage, in achieving the same triumph that he had in setting musically the drama of Büchner. Ultraromanticism reigns in the latter case, crude realism in that of *Lulu,* somewhat in the style of the drawings of George Grosz. The incomplete performance of *Lulu* (with the orchestration of some passages finished by Schönberg) took place in Zurich in 1937. The beginnings of the European deluge had cast many of us from its shores. My own impression was obtained at a performance of the orchestral pieces (Prague, 1935; Barcelona, 1936) with a result less favorable for *Lulu* than for *Wozzeck,* parts of which were also played at the festival of the International Society of Music in Barcelona in 1936. I am sure, however, that the fact of having previously heard and seen the opera on the stage must have contributed to the more convincing effect of the fragments from *Wozzeck*.

The entire drama of *Lulu* is constructed according to the system which Schönberg terms simply, "composition in twelve tones," a system which is simple in itself (like Columbus' egg) but whose capacity for exploitation is surprising if one takes into account that not only short instrumental works have issued from this technique but also the *Suite Lyrique* and *Lulu.* This latter work is, of course, the apotheosis of the system and will serve us for the purpose of explaining the system in the simplest way possible. Its didactic analysis has been made by musicians like Webern himself, the still younger Ernst Křenek, Willi Reich, and many more who, in my opinion, carry their proselytizing enthusiasm to extremes in aesthetic and historical theories of a somewhat exaggerated kind.

In its general lines, the system (according to Willi Reich, it is not a system but a means of facilitating the work of the atonal composer yet, for Theodor Wiesengrund, it is not even an expedient but "the true historical preformation of the material with which the composer is to work") is based on the following consideration. Now that there is no scale properly so called, but a series of twelve chromatic semitones without the functional offices of a tonic, dominant, etc., it will be necessary to arrange these notes in such a way that their succession will present our ear with the same definite value that the scale once offered. And since there is no tonal principle which gives a feeling of unity to the notes we are going to use, it will be advisable to arrange the twelve-tone series, in a manner optional for the composer, in such a form that the ear may sooner or later end by recognizing it, and in a way which succeeds in bringing about a feeling of unity. Both objects will be achieved (up to a certain point) if the arrangement of the twelve notes becomes the basis of the entire composition through constant repetition in the original order; the series may be varied in a thousand ways, as long as the fundamental order remains undisturbed. This series, which in the last analysis has a fundamental thematic value, is called a tone row by American musicians.

Let us observe the twelve-tone series, ascending or descending (enharmonic change loses its purpose in this system and we may use interchangeably any desired way of writing a sound or its enharmonic).

Such a series, which by itself sounds like old-fashioned chromatic music, will only serve to disturb us just as occurs with those intervals or successions of notes that may remind us of turns of phrase proper to the old music. This starting point becomes inflexible in the pedagogy of the system as explained by Ernst Křenek in *Studies in Counterpoint* (New York, 1940) but was not yet absolute in the first works of Schönberg and Berg, who utilized successions more or less similar to the motives of good old-fashioned music. This similarity, it must be remembered, was of enormous help to the poor listener who clung to it with all his might in order not to lose himself in the semitonal fluid.

The theory of the *Grundgestalten* or fundamental series was set forth for the first time in the Viennese review, *Anbruch,* by one of Schönberg's pupils, Erwin Stein.

First: Every phrase of a composition must refer to a series of twelve different notes. This series, an arbitrary arrangement of these twelve notes in accord with the composer's preference, is the *Grundgestalt* or basis of the entire work.

Second: It does not matter in what region or octave the *Grundgestalt* appears for the first time and all its transpositions are permissible but the composer is obliged to present the twelve notes *always* in the same order in which they appeared in the *Grundgestalt.*

Third: The *Grundgestalt* is valid not only in its original position (as it first appeared) and in its twelve transpositions but also in its inversion, read backwards (from right to left or cancrizans), and in the inversion of this reading, and in *their* twelve transpositions. There are, then, forty-eight versions of the *Grundgestalt,* all or only some of which may be used in the composition of the entire work.

In Schönberg's Suite for Piano, Op. 25, the basic *Grundgestalt* and its inversions appear in the following way.

First: Grundgestalt in its original form

Second: Inversion (by intervals)

Third: Read backwards (cancrizans)

Fourth: Inversion of the above

The *Grundgestalt,* or fundamental series or tone row, merely presents the series of twelve tones without any indication of rhythmic or harmonic values. The introduction of these is what gives the *Grundgestalt* thematic value.[4] Here we have the fundamental series from which all of Alban Berg's *Lulu* will proceed.

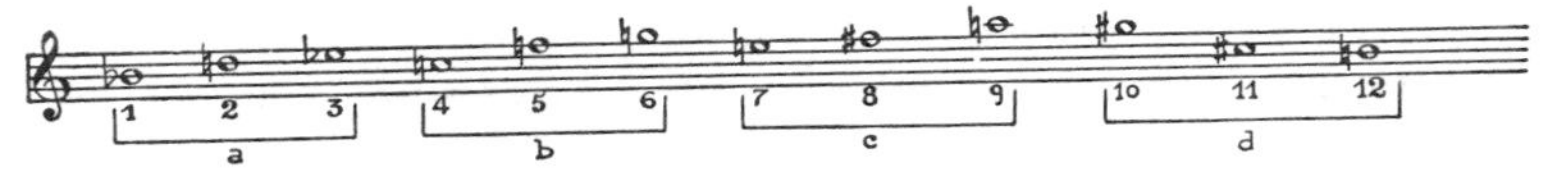

In this series we clearly discern four successions of notes which have a certain motivic color; they are marked in the tone row with the letters *a, b, c,* and *d.* Berg goes further; he unites them in four chordal groups of three notes.

Now if we dissect these chords analytically in three horizontal planes, we shall find a succession of notes having something of the form of a scale.

[4] See Willi Reich, "Alban Berg's *Lulu,*" the *Musical Quarterly,* October, 1936. In the same number appears an article by Hans Hollaender on Berg. On the twelve-tone technique of Schönberg and Berg see in addition, Richard S. Hill, "Schönberg's Tone Rows and the Tonal System of the Future," the *Musical Quarterly,* January, 1936.

Berg exploits this thematically in Lulu's motive in $\frac{3}{4}$. Without seeking further, it is possible to select within the fundamental series different ones of its component notes: every third, every fourth, every fifth, every seventh, etc. In this way Berg obtains new successions, which may be said to be derived from the fundamental, thus.

There is nothing further to do now but to combine these derivative series, complicate them rhythmically, place them head-to-tail or tail-to-head, do with them whatever our combined genius inspires us to do, and above all to treat them contrapuntally with no other restriction than that indicated of *not altering the order in which the notes appear in the fundamental series.* Let the novice, who aspires to become one of this *cénacle,* give no thought to the vertical combinations which result by chance from the superposition of the secondary series; dissonance is the rule. Above all, he will carefully see to it that two or three notes shall not be found to produce a consonance, which would be a dissonance in this system, and which would paralyze the flow of the duodecimal stream. I leave it to the curious reader to ascertain how Berg succeeds in constructing, according to this method, themes like the following and others much more complicated—for complication, also, is basic in this art.

Nevertheless, and despite its panegyrists, it is an art of calculation, of patience, like a Chinese puzzle, like solitaire, or like the thematic guides to Wagner's dramas.[5] It must be "injected" with truly musical intuition.

[5] The puerility reached by some of Wagner's commentators in their eagerness to assign thematic motives to simple objects is well known—from the sword of Sigmund, the lance of Parsifal, the magic helm of the Nibelungen to the coffer of the love philter in *Tristan.* It is

Do all succeed? It seems to me that Berg does, and Schönberg sometimes, as in his Variations, Op. 21, 1928. Webern perhaps tarries on the way, enchanted by the beauty of each note in itself, by each individual timbre, in its constant *pianissimo expressivissimo*. Křenek, who has carried the theory to its highest point of schematism and to its lowest point of musical quality, has at least the merit of demonstrating how extreme futurism in the art can be made academic and how whimsical pieces can be composed, such as his Dancing Toys, Streamliner, and A Boat; the last-named, reflected in the lake and described by the medieval method of a "mirror canon," an exact inversion of the model, becomes a "Sailing boat reflected in the pond," etc., etc., Op. 83. The curious music lover may hear this work on gramophone records at the same time that he studies its method and its tricks in the little book *Studies in Counterpoint,* which Křenek wrote for his students at Vassar College. Very amusingly, Křenek says in his book—and it seems also to be the opinion of the other members of the group—that the listener ought not to be informed of such procedures, which are in full course of evolution and at the mercy of whatever the most recent comers may bring to it of talent, of calculation, and of mystification. After all, what the listener gathers from these pieces is the sensation of a blurred photograph, of an unfinished drawing, of a splotch of color; guided by the timbre of the piano, his familiar friend, the listener assimilates, for better or worse, this final impression to his most recently received and comprehended musical experience.

It is not surprising that atonalism made rapid progress and that it has enthusiastic adherents. In this chapter I shall discuss only three of its most important followers: two belonging to its beginnings, Anton von Webern and Josef Hauer, and the other to its most recent phase, Ernst Křenek. These men have already appeared in the course of these pages and I shall leave for the following chapter other composers with whom atonalism is not an exclusive method but a road to further experiments.

Anton von Webern, as has been said, was one of Schönberg's disciples from the beginning. Two years older than Berg (1883 and 1885 respectively), he shares with him his predilection for a refinement in writing. In Webern,

amusing to observe that a similar objectivity is to be found in *Lulu,* applied to objects of such lyric quality as a stethoscope-revolver, legal medicine, bottle of capsules, cholera bacilli, hospital shirts, prison corridors, judges, doctors, jurymen, students, nurses, police, etc. See Willi Reich, article mentioned. The majority of these passages occur during a silent-film scene which serves to describe the events of the year in prison, which Lulu undergoes before she escapes in disguise.

Alban Berg died in 1935, the year in which he reached his fiftieth birthday. His work immediately prior to *Lulu* is Concert Aria for soprano and orchestra (1929) based on the translation which Stefan George made of the three poems by Charles Baudelaire, on *le vin.* Berg's last work is a concerto for violin and orchestra, In Memory of an Angel, finished in 1935, in honor of a daughter of Alma Maria Mahler who had just died. The work was first performed in Barcelona at the festival of the International Society of Music in 1936.

this refinement consists above all in the succession of pure, almost isolated tones which attain value through their qualities of timbre (among which intonation is no longer a melodic or harmonic value but a kind of color) and through qualities derived from juxtaposition and contrast. Webern demonstrates the extremes which "the harmonic dispersion of the tone" had reached, in the phrase of Paul Bekker, who adds: "the movement of reflux [now] seeks unification. The tone is no longer to be felt as a part of the harmonic complex but as an independent unity in itself."

Bekker finds that this movement of reflux toward the tone as tone, which led in Germany to an idea of the resurrection of classical art, had its starting point in the work of the Italo-German composer and pianist, Ferruccio Busoni. Better known in his character of virtuoso than in that of composer and scarcely appreciated in this latter capacity outside certain Central European circles, Busoni achieved in his opera *Doktor Faust* the most complete realization of his creative work. This opera, however, remained incomplete at his death in 1924 and was finished by his disciple, Philipp Jarnach. Other operas, in one act, *Arlecchino* and *Turandot* (1918), gave Busoni some reputation as a composer. In another connection, as the promulgator of the use of the thirds of the tone (which he explains in his little book entitled, *Entwurf einer neuen Aesthetik der Tonkunst,* 1907), Busoni will be discussed later.

As for Webern, the economy inherent in his works is demonstrated in the meagerness of his production which does not amount to thirty compositions, all of extremely restricted proportions. A few lieder with orchestra, settings of George and Rilke, and some *a capella* choruses sum up his lyric production. His preference seems to be for chamber groups, the quartet above all, of course. In his orchestrations are to be found some curious combinations. For example, one of his Five Pieces for Orchestra (Op. 10, 1911-13) is for clarinet, trumpet, trombone, mandolin, celesta, harp, drum, violin, and viola; instruments, be it understood, treated as solo voices. This pointillist technique is illustrated by measures like the following from the Six Bagatelles for String Quartet, Op. 9.

Another of Webern's works combines, in three songs, the human voice, the guitar, and an E-flat clarinet. Other songs of a sacred character are written for voice, violin, clarinet, and bass clarinet. Webern entered the fraternity of the twelve-tone technique with these three songs, of popular origin, as his Op. 17 in 1924. Webern possesses two further claims to originality. Up to the present he has composed little for piano [6] and one of his orchestral works (that referred to for its unusual orchestration) holds the record for brevity: nineteen seconds.

Ernst Křenek, a Viennese with a Czech name, was one of the sensational discoveries of the period after the last war, a little like the Parisian *Les Six,* with some of whom he may be compared: with Milhaud, for example, for his abundance, his versatility, his lightness of touch, and sometimes for his apparent indifference, and for his cold cerebralism. Born with the century, Křenek became known at various Central European festivals and at twenty-four he had his first opera, *Zwingburg,* performed. With a libretto by Franz Werfel, the work is really a scenic cantata since Křenek appears to be dissatisfied with the older term opera. He classifies as *Bühnenwerk* his last and most important scenic work, a drama on the history of the Austro-Spanish emperor, Charles V. Orchestral and chamber works, compositions for piano, for voice alone, for chorus followed each other with irrepressible fecundity as Křenek assimilated the technical procedures in vogue, from the neoclassicism in Busoni's style to atonalism and, finally, the twelve-tone technique which he applies conscientiously—though not without original contributions —in *Charles V.*

On adopting it as his definitive method (up to the present) Křenek has become its theorist. He has become its simplifier, too, in respect to his schematism, bordering on triviality—although this cannot be said of his writing.

[6] Shortly before his death he wrote some Variations for piano, Op. 27.

Indeed, a simplifier is needed, for the combinatory maze of the system (explained by Křenek in the little book mentioned above, which may serve as a key to the comprehension of the mysteries of this music and especially of his own) has reached its culmination in the dizzying tangle which the art of musical composition seems to have reached. It is sad to think of the kind of composers the system can produce; composers who, thanks to cheap international politics in the art world, appear for a moment in the limelight and then give place to the next comer.

Křenek's reputation became fabulous throughout Europe with the first performance of his opera or operetta *Jonny spielt auf,* Op. 45, in Leipzig in 1927. Perhaps the negroid type of its protagonist, his jazz saxophone, and the plot in "film" style affected the public as a startling novelty. At the present time Křenek has doubled the number of his works. The most important, the aforementioned drama on Charles V, was written between 1931 and 1933. The complete work was first performed in Prague in the fateful year, 1938.

If the musical technique of this work belongs to the most advanced stage of the twelve-tone technique, its theatrical technique (from what I could deduce from the concert performance in Barcelona) is far from equaling it in audacity. There are long speeches in which the principal characters tell their troubles to a patient, decorative character; narratives and political discussions between the emperor, his sister Leonore (the wife of his rival, Francis I of France), and Francisco de Borja, destined to sainthood, etc. The heart of the drama lies in Charles's ambition and his downfall brought about by the multiple forces that opposed his imperialist ideas in Rome, in Germany, in France, in Spain, in the Near East, and in the young America—a good theme at the moment of the Munich "peace." "All is one in its innumerable diversity," reflects the former emperor as he listens to the striking of his twelve clocks, which mark the hour in the twelve semitones of the twelve-tone scale. And he leaves to time, less dissonant, the responsibility for his acts: a convenient attitude for all makers of history.

Beside the commotion produced in the musical world by the productions of the young Viennese school (more on account of its theories and experiments in the field of dissonance and tonality than for its expressionist ideas which, when all is said and done, are simply the ultimate consequence of Germanic romanticism and, therefore, have a local significance), the figure of one of the pioneers in the twelve-tone technique, the Austrian, Josef Mathias Hauer, has passed almost unnoticed outside his own country. His point of departure was completely different from that of the composers of Schönberg's group; it develops from a consideration of the tone in relationships a little like those of the colors in the spectrum, that is, the white light of the chord divided by the prism into its component elements.[7] It is said that Hauer based his first experiments on Goethe's theory of colors, which the musician developed in his treatises *Über die Klangfarbe* and *Vom Wesen des Musikalischen,* published in Vienna in 1920.

But on proceeding by a juxtaposition rather than a combination of tones, Hauer found himself led, with considerable logic, to a conclusion diametrically opposed to that of the Schönberg group: Hauer's music, neither tonal nor atonal, completely disregards simultaneous harmony, tracing its completely linear way in a melopoeia which brings him to seek a point of contact with oriental monody, particularly that of the Chinese. Hauer saw clearly that atonal simultaneity is no more than a kind of heterophony in the fashion of the music of the Orient, that is to say, it is a sonorous simultaneity unregulated by any concept of harmonic unity. Other essays at this type of simultaneity in Europe will indeed lead to a heterophonic concept of music, as will be explained in the following chapter. Thus, as in the music of the Far East, Hauer seeks a constructive principle in the use of little thematic groups derived from the twelve-tone scale (which he calls the "tropus"); the principal value of these groups consists in the latent force of their characteristic intervals.[8]

The idea which Hauer developed in his works *Vom Melos zur Pauke* (1925) and *Zwölftontechnik* (1926) as well as in his earlier compositions, does not lack a certain similarity with the first phase of atonalism, when Schönberg was seeking support and structural aid in the use of well-defined melodic formulas which are not as yet the fundamental series or rows of the twelve-tone technique. Yet, while these motives or series lie at the base of the construction, as on the foundation above which rises the complicated fabric of dissonant writing, with Hauer they have a different function, closer to oriental repetition, as a species of concretions or solidifications which tend to regulate the formless, dissipated sonorous flow.

[7] For this reason Hauer commends the *true* or *untempered* intonation of the tone as produced in the natural resonance, and which is "not transferable" to another octave (a tranposition which is at the base of all European musical systems) than the one in which it is produced. See Chapter XXVI.

[8] The doctrine of the tropus is related to atonalism in that it renounces tonal relationships and that the components of the twelve-tone series may be grouped horizontally as well as vertically. But while Schönberg (like Scriabin with his series of resonances) considers that the twelve tones may compose a vertical formation in fourths, Hauer distributes the twelve tones in four triads. Different methods of *harmonization* may be derived from the one or the other criterion, if one wishes.

The precept, mentioned above, according to which it is desirable to avoid, in atonal music, successions which may recall harmonic music[9] carries along with it the idea of a melody of nonvocal character, antivocal if you wish, with leaps which immediately give a special color to this type of music as well, indeed, as a monotony of expression which is correlative. This nonsimilarity with earlier music is logical but it comes about that the more systematic the avoidance of such a contact is, the narrower the range of atonal expressive color. Scarcely having enunciated this principle, its own cultivators renounced it explicitly, and not only that but they seek, like Alban Berg in his Concerto for Violin (posthumous), significant approximations to Tristanesque expressivism, already announced in the *Suite Lyrique*. The *Grundgestalt* which Berg employs in this concerto admits an alternation of major and minor chords, followed by a group of whole tones[10]

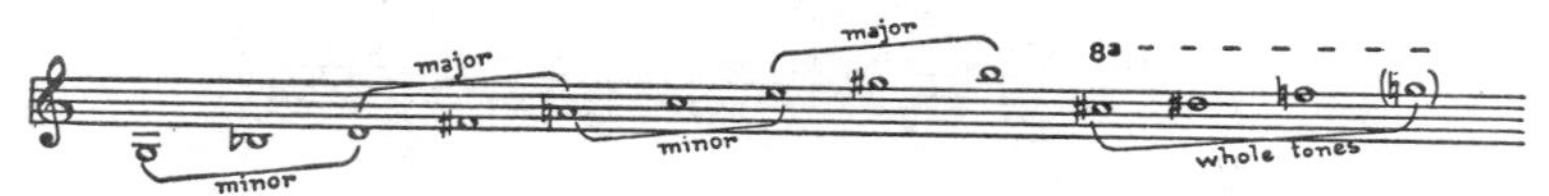

which Berg presents insistently, constructing little motives based on these successions in such a way that the harmonic feeling of the *Grundgestalt* is manifest from the beginning of the work when the violin announces the fundamental succession of tones. Now, this *Grundgestalt* of Berg is extremely near to the succession of the natural harmonics which (with the omission of repeated notes) is as follows.

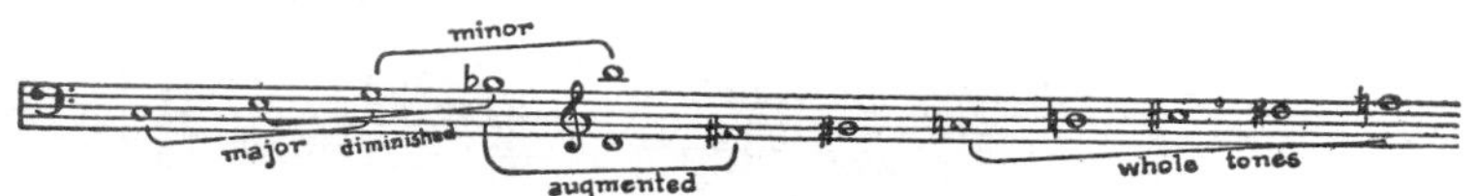

Furthermore, Křenek in his theoretical work referred to above disposes the natural intervals in a *Grundgestalt* which includes them all, major, minor, and perfect, an idea which he was to develop at length in his opera, *Karl V*.

The result in these cases is a music much nearer to what we consider ordinarily as normal than that constructed on the rigid system of the *Zwölftontechnik* following the precept of nonsimilarity. Nevertheless there does not exist in this manner of constructing atonal music the least trace of tonal func-

[9] See Ernst Křenek, *Studies in Counterpoint* (New York: 1940), Ch. i, No. 2.

[10] Successions also, as a matter of fact, of chords of the seventh and the ninth of different kinds.

tion nor of implicit harmonic relationships. Thus it is possible for Berg to quote phrases from *Tristan* in his *Suite Lyrique* (measures 26-27 of the sixth section). On the other hand, the melodic constructions in the twelve tones correspond so perfectly to the spirit of German music that composers as little guilty of atonalism as Schubert write phrases, such as that which opens the Minuet of his Fourth Symphony, which may be converted into a *Grundgestalt* with very slight modifications, although it is obvious that it never occurred to Schubert's imagination to treat them according to the principle of constant rotation. The phrase to which I allude is as follows

which we may transfer to *Zwölftonmusik* in this way.

Other arrangements may accentuate even more the external similarity to modern music based on points of view prior to atonality. Indeed, by using that freedom in whose light the *Zwölftontechnik* was born we can arrange the *Grundgestalt* as a scale

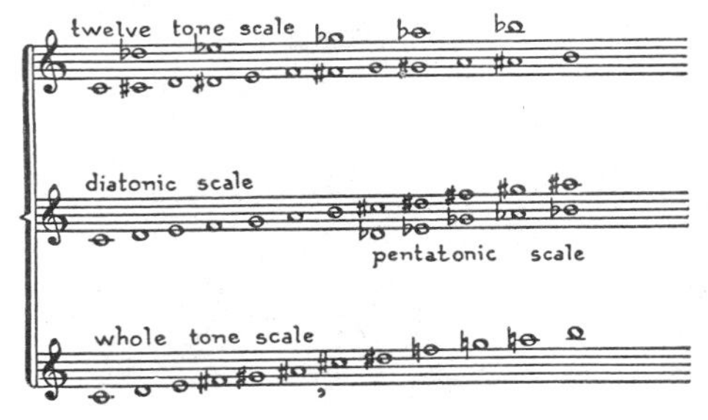

or again, in the form of successions of chords, such as Berg proposes but with another arrangement.

This arrangement is that which Josef Mathias Hauer terms a tropus, as we saw a moment ago, and is fundamental to his theory. With it a new state of things presents itself: atonalism tends to disappear in such ways of arranging the twelve-tone series, arrangements in which it is possible to preserve the tonal feeling; furthermore, we now find formations upon which may be superimposed others, also tonal. Thus we shall have arrived at an entirely different situation, even one opposed to the atonality of the Viennese group, namely, at polytonality or the superposition of different keys. This may be effected in two ways: either without a functional linking between the chords occurring in each line or, on the contrary, by preserving such a relationship.

We observe, then, an extremely important result: that, in so far as the rigid principle of systematic repetition of the *Grundgestalt* is broken, we turn back in our course to Tristanesque chromaticism or else we look ahead to a new kind of tonalism, multiple this time. Composers who began practicing atonalism gradually separated themselves from it to the degree in which they wished to obtain a greater freedom than that which the *Zwölftontechnik* permitted them. We find this turning back in Hindemith, while in Milhaud we shall see the art of polytonality flowering with a gentleness of manner appropriately corresponding to the traditions of *la douce France.*

Chapter TWENTY-FOUR

THE YOUNG Viennese school considered Johann Sebastian Bach its highest divinity (just as its direct predecessors, Bruckner and Mahler, looked upon Beethoven and Wagner as apostles) and the *Art of the Fugue* its gospel. For one reason or another there are many schools or theories that turn to Bach as an excuse for practices to which they think to give legitimacy in his name, but which would have greatly astonished him. Reger, Schönberg, Busoni, Stravinsky, Hindemith, and Milhaud have seen in Bach a way out of their respective blind alleys: either in the name of the objectivity of their ideas, foreign to all emotion or in the name of pure tone and its material combinations, uninspired by the breath of the spirit, or because Bach is regarded as the absolute model for contrapuntal writing (as if Bach had been the only contrapuntist of his time) or, again, for the freedom which this texture suggests in the treatment of dissonance, not categorically harmonic, and even for certain tonal ambiguities which, in Bach's time, did not result from a sharpening of the tonal sense but, quite the contrary, were a residue of modal habits.

Thus it comes about that if instead of seeing these aspects of the art of Bach (and of his non-Italianized contemporaries) as a reminiscence of the Gothic past—which was dissipated by the definitive triumph of the classical Viennese school with its affirmation of the formal principles of the sonata and symphony—they are understood, instead, as embodiments of a future which never occurred historically, it is possible to make Bach a precursor of doctrines which, eclipsed by the adventure of romanticism, have only been understood or have only been heard again in our own day. In any case, such a view implies that what in Bach is an exception must be considered the rule and, by establishing oneself firmly on the universal foundation of texture as the desirable end and aim of music, one will arrive at the extremes reached by Busoni in his Contrapuntal Fantasy, by Schönberg and his friends in atonality, and from another less rigorous point of view at the methods practiced by the young German musicians, by Paul Hindemith, as the most important both for his technique and his talent.

Yet, if one reflects for a moment, the texture in Schönberg, Berg, and

Webern is not strictly speaking contrapuntal. A mere glance at one of Schönberg's scores reveals that this texture resembles rather minute mosaic or inlay work. Small fragments devoid of motivic character are superimposed and interlaced, without forming either a line, properly so-called, or a definite rhythmic structure. Just as certain pianistic harmonies came to have the value of "notes with a certain timbre," Schönberg's orchestra differs from the traditional idea of the orchestra as a synthetic instrument; it becomes converted into a kind of grand keyboard in which every note possesses an individual instrumental timbre and each small combination or agglomeration of notes has an effect somewhat similar to that of the dissonant chord in impressionism with a value per se.

With all its pretensions of following the path of the traditional German spirit, Schönbergian expressionism was a result (by action and reaction) of French impressionism, practiced, however, not with the idea of the "beauty" of dissonance but for its supposed expressiveness. Thus, since it expressed definite inner states, it was thought inappropriate to develop color for its plastic effect, for its aesthetic value because, as we shall see, this school (and the youngest composers form part of it) rejects the type of intuitions traditionally thought of as beautiful. The word "beautiful" and all that is associated with it was an idea foreign to this stage of German music and, to a lesser degree, to the music of other countries; although it was quite well known as regards the art of painting and even of sculpture, it was still to be experienced in music. As far as Schönberg is concerned, to say that his music is beautiful, ugly, or even horrible (as has been said most frequently) represents a reaction as incongruous as to say, for example, that it is high or low, blonde or brunette, green or yellow.

Schönberg's texture, then, using contrapuntal devices (augmentation, diminution, inversions of the motives or of the intervals, etc.) divorced from Bach's melodic line, consists rather in abstract procedures than in those really derived from the practice of the polyphonists and is as remote from the old polyphony as opium is from the poppy. His pretension to compose in closed forms (like those of the suite and pieces for organ of the baroque period) is also no more than an abstraction related to a constructive principle, not a sonorous reality; the listener receives impressions very different from the intended effect—in the cases where he receives any at all. And the principle that constitutes the foundation of Schönberg's system, that is, nonfunctionalism, the absence of tonal relations, has nothing to do with Bach nor yet with the art of the fugue which is, on the contrary, the most solemn affirmation of the tonic-dominant function.

There remains the burning problem of texture: a problem pre-eminently German, even though without texture no music of any kind exists. Just as romanticism was, at bottom, simply an exaggeration of all that had survived intact down to the classical Viennese period so likewise the most recent personalities of German music base their art on an exaggeration of the polyphonic weaving of the parts, texture thus being understood as that process which had already reached a degree of extremism in Max Reger. From this extremism diverge those German musicians who, like Paul Hindemith, apparently desire to form a sect apart from Viennese atonalism even though at times they may meet it accidentally since they also start from Bach as the pristine fount of truth.

To avoid confusion a term has been found which, although not wholly precise, is useful in the musical vocabulary: *linear counterpoint* signifies a musical texture whose basis is categorically melodic, not merely a layer-by-layer breaking-up of dissonant molecules; each line of the contrapuntal texture aspires toward complete independence. For indeed, while it is true that in the real fugue and in some of Bach's canons the theme in a given key is answered by its transposition at the fifth above or the fourth below, in order to present it in the key of the dominant, it is also true that Bach modified the answer in such a way that the superposition of the two lines produces an effect of tonal harmony on the ear. Considering the two lines individually, however, we find ourselves concerned with two actually different keys; it is possible to go against the grain of tonal unity and accentuate this tonal duality. Thus, we enter one of the doors which lead to a new state of things, to bitonality, and thence to polytonality.[1] We shall soon see that there are other doors: this one, at least, may claim to be that of the greatest antiquity and may even claim to represent a tradition which, it should be emphasized, is a false tradition.

The accentuation of tonal differences between two or more lines may result from the chromatic working-out of each line. Departing from a normal beginning, each voice can be continued in an independent modulatory process which promptly brings about a polytonal state of affairs. Then too, within the polyphonic web, dissonance can be looked upon as an accident of melodic writing, without entirely losing the original tonal feeling; we have seen early examples of this balancing of opposing forces in Mozart. This use of a very rich texture, continually modulating and producing dissonances—never resolved as dissonances but considered as independent superpositions eventually ending in less dissonant, and more tonal, passages (the frequency or rarity of which makes the work seem more or less tonal)—this is one way of understanding linear counterpoint. The extreme limit of this viewpoint is atonality but the process and actual result are different from those of Schönberg's art. As has been said, one of the most conspicuous advocates of this process is Paul Hindemith.

[1] In the real fugue there occurs, strictly speaking, a double tonality ending in the final predominance of the tonic; here, then, we do not have a true bitonal effect.

Another type of contrapuntal writing, in which each of several independent lines asserts itself tonally without any regard to the vertical groupings that may arise with the other voices, leads to another type of polytonality, one that is more to the taste of the younger French composers like Darius Milhaud. These two tendencies, then, find expression in the work of Hindemith and Milhaud: in the horizontal polytonality of Hindemith, with its consequent atonality; and in the vertical polytonality of Milhaud, with its consequent heterophony. The former approaches Germanic ultraromanticism; the latter is closer to the nonharmonic combinations of oriental music. Coincidentally, the former presents a rhythmic-melodic dissolution somewhat invertebrate in character; while the latter, the French, presents a crude rhythmic-melodic affirmation which may reach a mild form of cacophony.

It has truthfully been said of Paul Hindemith—born in south Germany, in Hanau near Frankfort, in 1895—that he is a musician "by race." Hindemith is also one of those German artists of whom it may be said that "a certain kind of music" is as natural to him as his own language. Beginning with his earliest works, Hindemith fluently speaks this musical language so closely akin to the German soul; his first compositions are, likewise, the type most appropriate to the German artist: chamber music and lieder. They show the spontaneity of the born musician and a technical fluency and a freedom in writing that reflect a thought unwilling to confine itself in concrete ideas, in profound opinions, in an aphoristic style. The result was a verbosity which soon threatened to become excessive and a technique in which freedom might reach indifference.

But in spite of all, this music is entirely devoid of one trait so completely German that one can scarcely conceive of German music without it: namely, romantic feeling. Hindemith is less concerned with what he says than with the words in which he says it. He is guilty of euphuisms in his contrapuntal texture and, while he claims to base his expression on specifically sonorous elements, he weaves a network which attracts the eye and the analytic interest of the technician—a network from which all truly musical intuition has vanished. Thus his works frequently produce a disillusionment in the listener which does not occur in the reading of them.

That criterion according to which music is expressive in and for itself inevitably leads to an excessive regard for "writing" which has been expressed in various ways: sometimes it is called neoclassicism (in form, not in essence) a movement whose patron saint is Johann Sebastian Bach; at other times it is called objectivism. If by subjectivism is meant the dramatic sentiment indispensable to romanticism, Hindemith would by definition be an objective composer.

Yet, taking things in the sense they have today, it has been said that impressionism is objective to the degree that expressionism is subjective. But if one compares a page of Debussy with one of Schönberg it will be easily seen that the music of the French composer, despite its "delicious dissonance," is all within. The music of Schönberg, on the other hand, however intensely expressive it may be, is complete on paper, complete in the care lavished on the texture and on the perfect craftsmanship; this would be quite adequate if art were only handiwork and not also headwork. Again, in the work of Hindemith, one is not sure whether the head directs the hand or is simply content to approve what the hand displays.

From the vantage ground of his second series of *Kammermusik,* between 1924 and 1925, Hindemith apparently underwent a crisis. What he saw behind him was gratifying. In the first place, he saw the futility of an art that was facile for him and that was at the same time difficult for the listener, an inversion of the truly classic aphorism—so often recommended by Bach—"true art is to conceal art." He saw something more, namely, his character as a German musician reflected not in an art of the future, which never grants its inventor freedom, but rather in an art of the past. That past, as was explained in a previous chapter, was for German postromantic painters the Gothic past. The painters found their Gothic in the German Renaissance of Cranach, Dürer, Holbein, and Grünewald. Musicians like Hindemith found it in the musical renaissance of German songs of the fifteenth and sixteenth centuries.

Spanish composers of today have found it likewise in old Spanish songs. The *Liederbücher* of Locham and of Oeglin were to the Germans what the Cancionero de Palacio and that found at Upsala were to the Spaniards. Wenzel Nodler and Adam of Fulda provided for the former what Juan del Encina or Salinas furnished to the latter; so the *quodlibets* of Melchior Franck compare with the *villancicos* of Juan Vásquez. And if the influence of the *villancico* gives a tang of rosemary and marjoram to the Concerto of Falla, the *quodlibet* adds a much-needed, popular aroma to Hindemith's work. While Falla may find an ideal in the asceticism of Berruguete or of Pedro de Mena, Hindemith finds it in Grünewald, in Matthew the painter. Indeed, *Mathis der Maler* is perhaps Hindemith's best work and one which, at the present time, affords him well-considered admiration as compared with the frenzied enthusiasms accorded it when first performed in 1938.

The comic opera, *Sancta Susanna,* in 1922, and the opera *Cardillac* (1926) represent, each in its respective field, Hindemith's most important and significant work prior to *Mathis der Maler,* of which a first version was presented in the Symphony-suite of 1934. The term comic opera given *Sancta Susanna* refers to the genre; in species it is a violently tormented, expressionistic work, even though its author is not one of the expressionist group. Its intensity is achieved by means of a contorted, extremely complex texture and by a dissonance bordering on exasperation; yet the work is not without a certain wordy dramaticism. Cardillac, like Susanna, is a pathological case: he is a kind of French Benvenuto Cellini of the seventeenth century; she is a type of mystic sadist. The character of Susanna has been termed "irreverent and bestial" by one of Hindemith's favorable commentators, Guido Pannain. It is Pannain, too, who says amusingly that the true protagonist of *Cardillac* is not the goldsmith of the title role—jealous of the purchasers of his works, a kind of Polyphemus of a lower category, passionately enamored of his creations—but rather the counterpoint. And it is in truth the counterpoint as much as Cardillac that kills the audacious beings who desire to possess the gems it has carved. Pannain points out that, when the climax of the work is reached with the spectacle of Cardillac being drawn by his artist's narcissism to the perpetration of a new crime (the last, destined to be discovered and to destroy him), the passage in the music is based on a low orchestral theme whose fundamental phrase appears in the piano part of one of Hindemith's chamber works (*Kammermusik,* Op. 36, No. 1).

In itself this is little worth noting; what is strange is that it occurs with a composer as fecund as Hindemith, who has a superabundance of ideas and of ways of treating them. On the other hand, some of his *Kammermusik,* such as Op. 24, possess a certain dramatic content, not always carried out in the movement of the voices. The logical leading of the parts and the stylistic feeling of Hindemith can be appreciated in this work in which, while the wind instruments expound a tearful lament in shameless chromatic accents, a trumpet bursts into a fox-trot-like tune.

The *Kammermusik* of Hindemith includes works calling for very diverse instrumental combinations. *Kammermusik,* Op. 24 (1922), is composed of two separate compositions: No. 1 is for small orchestra; No. 2 for a quintet of the usual wind instruments. *Kammermusik II* (1925) is a concerto for piano and twelve instruments; *III* (1925) another concerto for violoncello and ten solo instruments; *IV* (1925) for violin and chamber orchestra; *V* (1927) for viola—an instrument on which Hindemith is a fine virtuoso and for which he has written various works—and chamber orchestra; *VI* (1930) is a concerto for viola d'amore and chamber orchestra; *VII* (1929) is for organ and chamber orchestra. To the year 1930 also belongs the concerto for viola and large orchestra; in 1935 appeared another concerto for viola and small orchestra, bearing the title *Der Schwanendreher* (based on old popular songs of the fifteenth and sixteenth centuries); finally, in 1936, a *Trauermusik* for viola (or violin or violoncello) and string orchestra.

Other chamber-music compositions of Hindemith (to 1938) are separately numbered, such as those for piano (four sonatas, suites, and pieces in series) and other concertos and compositions for orchestra, for organ, for solo voices and chorus, and so forth. As regards the theatrical production of Hindemith, there exist, in addition to the works already mentioned, various short pieces such as that entitled *Mörder, Hoffnung der Frauen* in one act (1920), which presents the unusual circumstance of being composed on a libretto of Oscar Kokoschka; the entr'acte for Burmese marionettes entitled, *Das Nusch-Nuschi* (1920); the sketch *Hin und Zurück* (1927) the second half of which reproduces, in reverse order, the episodes and music of the first—as if time, returning on itself, could undo its mistakes, putting things back as they were at the beginning; and the musical comedy *Neues vom Tage* (1929). More recently, there is the ballet composed for the company of Léonide Massine, *Nobilissima Visione;* although this is ostensibly an evocation of the life of Saint Francis of Assisi, the music—first performed in London and later in Washington in 1938—is so German in temperament that it but poorly interprets the warm-hearted Latin saint.

Other minor works of Hindemith bring us to a certain branch of music which was much talked of in the years before World War II—years during which, in reality, there was little to talk about except Negro painting, jazz, cubism, expressionism, surrealism, all of which were on the inclined plane of decadence. I refer to the so-called *Gebrauchsmusik,* a term which came to be equivalent to a type of utilitarian or occasional music, music which goes all the way from that which accompanies a film to the music written for special events.

As a matter of fact, this type of music has existed since *Tafelmusik,* the dining-room music in the German provincial courts, which romantic bourgeois society turned into music for the grand hotel, for restaurants, or fashionable bathing resorts on all degrees of the social scale. *Gebrauchsmusik* is, strictly speaking, written for concert players of every sort and description and includes all music written to order.[2] It is possible, as in the case of Ravel, that such music may be of first rank but this is not usually the case. It would be interesting to study the complex which has prompted Hindemith to attach an exclusive name to this bric-a-brac music, as if music of this kind, furbished with the trappings of high art, could take on the noble quality of art for art's sake.

Hindemith, still a comparatively young man, has developed his art under the influence of the two poles between which contemporary music moves. After his first propensities to the atonality toward which his dissonant counterpoint was leading him and after his later consideration of the oldest tradi-

[2] *Gebrauchsmusik* is also called *Gemeinschaftsmusik,* community music, music for sociable gatherings. It began to appear in the catalogue of the publishers Schott, at Mainz about 1927 with compositions by Hindemith, entitled *Das Neue Werk.* See N. Slonimsky, *Music since 1900,* pp. 572-3.

tions of German art, Hindemith seems to have taken refuge, in a sense, in the functional feeling of harmony or, in other words, in tonality. The return journey was made by the most effective way for the idea, namely, by the modulatory flow which, before the appearance of atonality, had taken on an aspect of "pantonality," as the composers of the Viennese school preferred to call it. The Sonata, Op. 35, of Hindemith, dated 1935, although highly modulatory, presents a definite tonality which bears out the key signature of E major. In this work, as in impressionism, dissonance has an independent value as harmonic color, even though Hindemith's feeling and general aesthetic attitude may be far from impressionism and from its way of understanding that color which Hindemith, with keen observation, defines as a "harmonic gradation or harmonic tendency." Following this path we approach, in fact, a new aspect of our present day music.

Chapter TWENTY-FIVE

IF ONE analyzes works like the Serenade, Op. 24, of Schönberg (1921-23) or the *Chôros* No. 8 of H. Villa-Lobos (also a kind of serenade, 1925) one finds that below the complicated contrapuntal weaving and the mixture of tonalities in the upper parts, the lowest part proceeds as if the work were written normally in the key of C major. This would seem to signify that neither composer had forgotten that the series of natural harmonics, numbers 11 to 22, starting from a fundamental, C, for example, gives the chromatic scale. It is true that a composer, if he so wishes, can break the whole series of resonances up into sections and, by filling out these sections with intermediate notes, can write in different superimposed tonalities.

Despite their radical appearance, all these tonalities may be related in greater or less degree to the fundamental key of C; the greater or less degree will depend on many circumstances, principally on whether the different tonal currents will coincide on vertical points of support which are functionally related to one another. The situation would be somewhat comparable to oriental heterophony in which some consonant leaps (ordinarily of the fourth and fifth) have the function of a cadence, while the intervening notes are not heard as notes with harmonic value but as passing notes: thus a German theorist, Erich Schumann, proposes very justly in his *Akustik* a distinction between the two kinds of melodic intervals, calling one *harmonic interval* and the other *distance interval:* the one possesses an implicit harmonic feeling; the other is simply a mechanical aid in the horizontal movement of the voice.

Schönberg's technique consists, as we have seen, in not admitting for his scale of twelve semitones any other value but that of distance intervals whether this distance occurs melodically (horizontally) or vertically (which would be understood as harmony in ordinary practice). Even when using various melodic lines in different keys, a composer can cause them to come together in a tonal relationship at certain cadential supporting points and can take the intermediate notes as simple passing notes. This is one of the routes which leads, empirically, to so-called polytonality. Enharmonic writing can produce very strange tonal combinations particularly when one voice stands out not only in its volume and timbre but also in its melodic leading. The ingenious composer can so arrange his music on paper that he really appears to be handling various tonalities simultaneously. A case notable for its skillful writing and for its fine effect to the ear is to be found in the Concerto (for harpsichord and various instruments) by Manuel de Falla, which we shall use as an example.

A few measures after the beginning when the tonality of D major has been clearly affirmed the flute and the oboe announce a motive, very clear as to melodic line and very conspicuous for its timbre in B major (the third below the fundamental), while the keyboard sounds harmonies which seem to combine the tonality of A minor (right hand) and B-flat minor (left hand), the latter tonality being emphasized in the violoncello.

But if the reader will take the trouble to replace the flatted notes with their enharmonics he will become aware, without much effort, that this triple polytonality reduces itself to a simple chord of the dominant ninth of the key of B major, a chord which, in the fourth measure, is resolved on the dominant ninth of E major and, after proceeding melodically from the leading tone to the tonic, returns to the former interplay of tonalities.

This procedure would be little more than puerile if it were nothing but tonal camouflage. However, as a matter of fact, the moment that various tonalities are superimposed on one another, a new auditory effect results comparable to that resulting to the eye from the pictorial procedure known as velatura. In velatura, various colors are superimposed with a transparency such that the individuality of each is perceptible and does not form a synthetic color of two or three components. This synthesis had been obtained in the earlier painting technique by the juxtaposition of colors which, as in certain paintings of the French artist Delaunay, produces a kind of prismatic refraction that is very pleasing in effect. The correlative procedure in music consisted in rapid modulation or pantonalism. Now, this succession seems to become contracted or telescoped by placing one period above another in the same way that the appoggiatura, whose primitive form was the mordent of fleeting duration, came to take on a harmonic value through its more extended duration.

In the afore-mentioned work of the Brazilian composer Villa-Lobos, we see how the composition seems to fluctuate between the tonalities of C major. the fundamental one, and E-flat minor, a kind of "relative in reverse": a play of tonal relationships (not simply modal ones) at the interval of the third which, as we have seen in earlier chapters, interested romantic composers[1] for the new constructive possibilities it offered. The classical technique had reduced its architecture to the tonal relationships of the fourth and fifth (that is, of the first two harmonics after the octave), while the harmonic immediately following presents the interval of the third.

If the development of the harmonic feeling consists in expanding the simple melodic relationships which brought about the origin of tonal feeling, it becomes evident that this process of harmonic expansion, which causes a single note to engender a chord and a chord to engender a tonality, will eventually lead to the superposition of two tonalities, first in the relation of fifth and fourth and afterward in the relation of the major third. In other words, the natural chord of C major *has an immediate resonance* in that of G major; that of G major in that of C major, and, a third above, that of C major in that of E major. Let us see what are the natural harmonics of C, next of G, its first harmonic (after the octave); that of its second harmonic, C, and that of E, the third harmonic.

The present state of our perception of various simultaneous keys does not seem to have passed this point in the series of natural resonance.[2] But contemporary composers who are interested in the effects that music may acquire by tonal superpositions or polytonality do not stop with this succinct method of reasoning; since history shows that the evolution of harmony and of tonality has been an empirical process, these men consider it their right to experiment in their practical treatment of tonal combinations. Another fact authorizes them to assert that in so doing they do not proceed arbitrarily, namely, that the germ of double tonality (bitonality), or even of polytonality exists in romantic and impressionist harmony and that those suggestions should

[1] And specifically Beethoven, even in his first quartets and sonatas. We also see it occasionally in Haydn.

[2] Taking *b* as the seventh diatonic note in the key of *c*, we shall now obtain tonal relationships of the dominant, *two by two*, taking as a basis the successive harmonies which form the chords of the seventh, the ninth, and the eleventh.

therefore have further development. We describe here, very briefly, how this process of harmonic polytonality is begun.

The prolongation or superposition of harmonies which continue sounding in the ear after a new harmony has been heard produces the effect of a superposition of tonalities. We find in Beethoven very simple cases of this apparent prolongation yielding poetic effects that cannot be analyzed as dissonant chords. For example, note the well-known passage from the Pastoral Symphony in which

obviously, there is not even a remote question of an incomplete dominant ninth chord in B flat. Simply, but boldly for its period, and with an impressionist feeling of distance and landscape, the key of F major slips under that of C as the latter softly dies away. It is a case similar to that of the Farewell Sonata in which a motive, heard as an echo, slips over or beneath itself; it is impossible to analyze the resulting agglomerations (G, E♭, B♭, F or B♭, F, G, E♭) as true harmonies.

Chabrier and Debussy have used this effect of sonorous perspective with similar means (Chabrier's *Le Roi malgré lui; "De fleurs,"* in the first *"Proses Lyriques"* of Debussy). But what the theorists consider as an initial suggestion of two superimposed tonalities results from ornamentation, with appoggiaturas or chromatic passing notes, presenting a changing tonal significance in the classics from Bach to Haydn and Mozart. The passing note may bring about, according to the liberties which the composer takes with it, certain ambiguities from which fine effects may be derived. Charles Koechlin, a subtle master in the analysis of the most daring harmonies, has written an entire essay on "Notes de passage" [3] which every professional musician should know.

But in this book we are not writing for professionals and it is impossible to multiply examples or insist on explanations of a technical nature. It suffices to point out that the horizontal independence of two tonalities remained

[3] (Paris: 1922.)

related, in the classics, to a dominant harmonic feeling. In Bach, accidental bitonalism through imitation is frequent; in Mozart, this effect is reached through his very expressive use of appoggiaturas; in Haydn through passing ornamentation which—like the use of retarded resolutions, resolved and unresolved appoggiaturas—constitutes a large part of the romantic repertory.

To these devices must be added another procedure, dear to romantic composers, which the impressionists converted into one of their favorite formulas: that of pedal notes, rapidly changed into pedal chords and pedal figures, and into motives repeated with pedal effect. When whole chords are used as a pedal, as if reinforcing this pedal's bass note, we shall have reached a point at which it may be said that two simultaneous lines in two distinct tonalities can be harmonized individually and independently of one another: bitonality will then definitely appear. Similarly, an appoggiatura may be completed by the chord which it implies in such a way that it is no longer a mere grace note but a complete "appoggiatura chord." Thus arise chordal agglomerations which have not lost their functional meaning and their dependence on the basic notes of the key. This fact makes it clear that bitonality —and later, polytonality—need not be atonal if the composer does not so desire, no matter how dissonant and complex the superposition may be.

It is possible to subdivide these high, dissonant chords and treat them on two or more planes, as when the chords of the eleventh and thirteenth are considered as superpositions of several chords belonging to different keys. For example, the chord

can be considered as a superposition of

This method is especially applicable when dealing with altered chords or chords with appoggiaturas. If, in effect, we consider a minor thirteenth chord with a minor ninth and without the seventh, we may say that it is not an agglomeration with the feeling of the dominant but, rather, two different chords in two widely separated tonalities, C major and D-flat major, placed one upon the other. Darius Milhaud, pursuing this line of reasoning, proceeds to establish a harmonic and vertical polytonal technique which corresponds, in France, to the contrapuntal and horizontal atonality of the twelve-tone technique in Germany. This polytonal technique is as simple in principle as the other and can be summed up in the following way.

On a perfect chord taken as a pedal point there can be superimposed a whole series of consonant major and minor chords (as the first step toward polytonality) built on each degree of the chromatic scale.

It is obvious that these chords can also be superimposed on a minor chord (C minor in this series). This implies four classes of possible combinations.

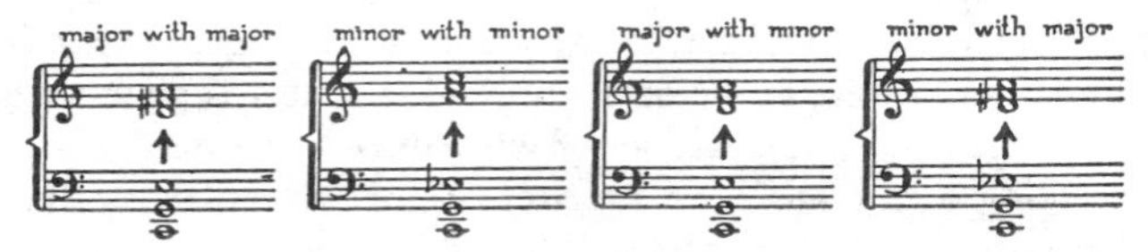

In accord with traditional practice, each one of these chords may be arranged in as many positions as there are notes in the chord; the first of these four bitonal types can therefore be written

Amazingly enough, it is perfectly possible, when convenient, to consider the second position of this series of inversions as an ordinary chord of the dominant eleventh. Imagine the combinations that can result from the superimposition of seventh chords, ninth chords, and all the rest! Then there are the altered chords, chords with appoggiaturas or substitutions—all of which can be related, if one so desires, to a more or less distant tonic.

A step further will unite three chords with all their possible combinations; with a little more complication in the writing we shall have approached atonality, if the melodic lines do not have a clearly defined tonality. At this point we reach polytonality in full development. For the ear it will seem more like a kind of heterophony within tonal limits. The superposition of three perfect chords, major or minor, makes possible no less than fifty-five groups (instead of eleven), each one of them in nine positions while the four combinations [4] *M-M, m-m, M-m, m-M* will have been doubled. Sometimes, as in the Serenade (Third Symphony) by Milhaud, the twelve notes of the chromatic scale are to be found simultaneously.

Nevertheless, two principles to which the polytonal composers, Milhaud above all, seem to attach the greatest importance offer no possible analogy with the twelve-tone technique. These principles may be stated thus: (*a*) each line has a definite tonality; (*b*) each retains a very marked diatonic character, and the melodic leading seems to avoid the use of notes foreign to the tonality.[5] This method of procedure is, however, no more than personal: the whole result consists in the fact that the ear catches a sonorous conglomerate in which diatonic feeling is outstanding while in atonality the ear perceives a chromatic effect. In all truthfulness the ear probably appreciates nothing more than the manner peculiar to a familiar style. The publication in gramophone records of music of this type (like the above-mentioned Serenade of Milhaud) permits of a repetition as often as necessary to verify what the ear perceives. Undoubtedly we come to grasp more at the end of a certain number of hearings than at the beginning. But it is a matter of practice, of an adjustment of the ear, not of what the ear can normally perceive. The same thing occurs when we hear records of oriental music: the heterophony becomes clear and appears to be more or less systematized, thanks to the repetition of a motive which serves as the axis of the piece; around this axis is woven a heterogeneous combination of reiterated rhythms, made to stand out by their timbre.

In the Milhaud Serenade, a clarinet announces the motive which is perceptible to us most directly in the key of E major. A bassoon harmonizes it in D major, without being too disturbing. The double tonality is then repeated by the bassoon and the violoncello. The ear rests on C major in three instruments three octaves apart. Then a new melody in F major appears;

[4] But this abundance is neither a merit nor an advantage. On the contrary, it is raw material from which selections must be made. In the eighteenth century when composers codified the repertory of usable chords in a tonality, they chose three, which they employed almost exclusively over a long period: they were the so-called "good degrees." Chords of the second, third, sixth, and seventh degrees were at best "ambiguous chords" and their use was secondary and subordinated to that of the *fundamental* chords.

[5] It is still better if the rhythmical structure is not complicated. The following passage from Holst in which a C-major chord is heard every third note illustrates the point. See *Cobbett's*, p. 43.

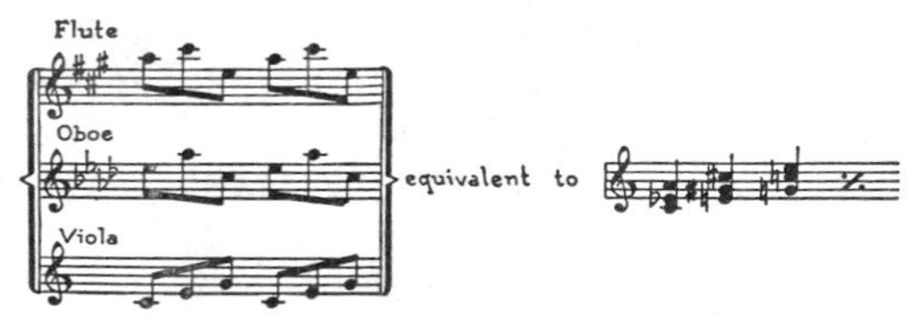

finally, the clarinet and bassoon reappear in the relation D-E. The keys of C, F, and D appear together in a certain passage; in others we find the following superposition: flute, B flat; clarinet, F major; bassoon, E major; violin and viola, B flat; violoncello, D major. A melody like that which is heard in the cello

seems as if it might govern the construction. But if this line were to be eliminated, the bass in E major of the bassoon might serve as well; to sum up, there is no real governing theme. The tonalities are arbitrarily superimposed to suit the taste of the composer.

An amusing experiment which Charles Koechlin relates in his *Traité d' Harmonie* seems very significant in this connection. One day, Koechlin was rehearsing his Third String Quartet with the artists who were to perform it. The work is extremely modern and in it the composer employs all the procedures described above. It occurred to him to propose to the players that they each should play a different movement at the same time: the first violin, the introductory adagio; the second, the scherzo; the viola, the following movement; the violoncello, the fourth. The result, says Koechlin (who knew the work very well and could hear all the themes and their melodic and harmonic continuity), was in no way shocking. The ear—that of the composer, at any rate—was capable of following that polytonic and polythematic combination; but the general coloring was a grayish mass, without differentiation, in which no plane stood out. The interest, says Koechlin, promptly disappeared.

True, "the interest." What do the polytonal composers offer us? Is it an experiment, more or less curious, or a work of art? "That is the question."

The revolutionary composers, explorers of aesthetic and theoretical novelties, bold travelers to more or less virgin islands and continents, have always left an extensive, a written record of their labors. Musicians and poets of the early baroque from Galilei to Peri, Caccini, and Monteverde, explained in their prologues, minutely and at length, their findings in the field which was to become opera: song, recitative, harmonic and instrumental accompaniment; technique of the score, aesthetics. The most celebrated artists of our day, celebrated more for their inquiring spirit than for the popularity of their works (Stravinsky said to me recently, "the public is more interested in my name than in my music," alluding naturally, to his most recent production) have covered reams of foolscap, although in a more restrained manner than they use on scored paper. The *Harmonielehre* of Schönberg is a monument for kindred spirits, even though it may lack the stature of his most mature compositions. We have already mentioned Křenek's summary of the twelve-tone technique, which serves as appendix to Schönberg's treatise. A recent volume by Křenek, *Music Here and Now* (New York, 1939), discusses at length such timely subjects as the decline of tonality, atonality, the new constructive criteria, and music in relation to mathematics. From the last-named point of view, the brief and solid little book by Carlos Chávez, *Toward a New Music* (New York, 1937), is one of the most important contributions (by an Hispano-American) to the collection of musicians' literary efforts in English. The translation, in 1939, of Hindemith's *Unterweisung in Tonsatz,* written two years before, appropriately balances the work of Křenek. For his part, Darius Milhaud caused a sensation in 1923 in the Latin musical world—a world as yet little aware of questions relative to tonal taboo—with his article on "Polytonalité et Atonalité," which may be described as the personal manifesto of the Provençal musician.

Milhaud, Hindemith, and Křenek can be considered in one group (especially for their investigations in tonality) because of the many similarities in their art. The first two especially display a like fecundity and facility in writing; both possess agile and alert minds, free of any doubts concerning the purity of their material or of the style with which it is treated. Both men display an unevenness, a fluctuation in their work despite their sureness of touch and their spontaneous handling of the closed forms.

As regards genres, Hindemith and Milhaud are united in their preference for chamber music, for the small orchestra, and for brief theatrical pieces with rather free plots—a preference which does not prevent them from proceeding to grand lyric creations: Milhaud with his *Christophe Colomb* (two acts, with text by Paul Claudel, first performed in Berlin in 1930) and *Maximilien* (written in 1930 and first performed at the Opéra in Paris in 1932). Many of Milhaud's pages for piano, for orchestra, and for the theater could be included in the category of *Gebrauchsmusik* (*Cinéma-Fantaisie sur le Boeuf sur le Toit, "Machines agricoles," "Catalogue des Fleurs"*) while others reflect the passing European vogue for the jazz band (*Le Tango des Fratellini, Caramel Mou, shimmy, Trois Rag Caprices*) to which the muse of Ravel and of Stravinsky did not fail to do homage.

The café-concert air of some of these inspirations may be traced to the carefree gaiety of the postwar years in Paris, while in the similar accents of Hindemith has been seen a sarcastic desperation produced by defeat, inflation, and the other calamities in contemporary Germany. It is easy to blame the environment; but it is difficult to discover an inner, spiritual crisis allied with the crisis in technical methods. The crisis of words and ideas which produced the Dada movement in Paris and, in Germany, the pictorial Dadaism of Klee and Kandinsky had results reflected less in the French than in the Spaniards. If Picasso was one of the apostles of the new art, Joan Miró and Salvador Dali (to mention only the most outstanding) mark a zenith in the art of the peninsula which has not yet been matched by parallel figures in music.

In 1935, at forty-three, Darius Milhaud had to his credit nine string quartets, various sonatas, sonatinas, and suites, five symphonies for chamber orchestra, and various other orchestral compositions, among them two symphonic suites, two concertos for violin, and one for piano. His production for piano and for voice, although not so extensive in numbers, is still considerable; and what with operas, incidental music, and ballets, the number of stage works reaches twenty-one, all of great diversity in meaning, style, and spirit. Throughout his works, Milhaud's personality is unmistakably individual; his manner of working, despite the mentioned carelessness, is likewise distinctive: sureness of thought and technique mark this artist as perhaps the most fully developed figure among the young Latin, as Hindemith is among the young German, musicians.

The end of Milhaud's first, adolescent period was marked by a trip to Rio de Janeiro during the years of the last world war. There Milhaud met Paul Claudel, who must have helped him set an artistic goal for himself. Then, after the armistice, came the happy reunion of *Les Six* in the carefree, sparkling, witty doctrine of Cocteau. While that subtle writer prepared his "return to order," musicians like Milhaud had put order, in every sense, into their music. This seriousness of concept and of realization appears above all in Milhaud's chamber music, which perhaps occupies first place in his work. An English musicographer, Edwin Evans, says that there are three factors in Milhaud that determine his place in the musical scheme: (*a*) his vehemence, which is attributed to his Israelite ancestry; (*b*) the minute preciseness of his technique; and (*c*) his approach to it as to a problem in chess, also attributed (as in Schönberg?) to the same ancestral influences. Yet an identical approach is to be observed in Berg, in von Webern, and in Hindemith, none of whom, I believe, possess this ancestral strain. Finally, there is to be noted a great simplicity in fundamentals, which is authentic and not simulated, as in so many composers who espoused *dépouillé* aesthetics then so much in vogue. To sum up, Milhaud displays clarity, simplicity, and an ample eloquence without garrulousness—qualities which, so it seems to me, typify the Latin.

The meridional luminosity, which always shines through the most tangled growth in Milhaud's music, is to be observed in his First Quartet (1912), with its somewhat Schubertlike reminiscence. It is a juvenile work like *La Brébis égarée* and has an early-morning freshness that only begins to absorb the warm sunshine in the Second Quartet (1915) with its spicy, polyphonic atonality. This first period ends with the Third Quartet (1916), and the second era begins in 1917 with the first chamber symphony, the one entitled

Le Printemps and dedicated to André Gide. (Springlike and pastoral themes —as a basis for distant stylizations—are dear to Milhaud along with others, especially a mocking tone and the short, wittily sketched caricature.)

The earliest hints of polytonality *à la* Milhaud appear here, to be confirmed in the Fourth Quartet (1918), one of those most frequently performed. The next one, dated 1920, belongs to the year following Milhaud's return to Paris from his sojourn amid the opulent Brazilian landscape with its enormous butterflies, its tiny multicolored birds with their gruff voices. Milhaud was then generously and enthusiastically devoting himself to the task of making Schönberg's *Pierrot Lunaire* known in France, and the Fifth Quartet is dedicated to the Austrian in testimony of the French musician's admiration. As can be imagined, problems of texture appear in this work in a high degree of complication. This complexity is not repeated in the first symphonies of 1921. At that time jazz made its appearance in the Sonatina for flute and piano, in a stylized suggestion of a "blues." The work is dedicated to one of the musicians who made the most important contribution to the popularity of this American music in Paris: Jean Wiener.

Milhaud now tries melodic simplification, a tendency which, in addition to the fact that it is natural to him, is especially favored by the Parisian group. It is happily achieved in the Sixth Quartet which Milhaud, the senior member of *Les Six,* dedicated to the junior member of the group, Francis Poulenc. It is said that some passages of this composition seem to be inspired by *Mouvements Perpetuels,* the short, charming, early work of Poulenc but the slow movement is a piece of polytonal polyphony which is once more confronted by the problem of complicated texture. The texture is simplified again in the Seventh Quartet (1925) a work whose gracious quality of purely meridional inspiration is aided by its delicious, rocking rhythm.

Milhaud's production from this time on, whether it aspires to the lofty heights of his *Christophe Colomb* with its daring rhythmic and polytonal construction and his recent work, *Bolivar,* or moves in the intimacy of his sketches for piano and chamber music, does not contain essential novelties. Milhaud has now attained his "way" and he follows it tranquilly in alternate abundance and moderation. The catastrophe, both moral and physical, which France suffered in 1939, sent Milhaud into exile. And since 1941 Milhaud has found refuge in the tranquil shelter of an American college in the temperate California sunshine, near Schönberg and Stravinsky and not far from Hindemith and Křenek.

Chapter
TWENTY-SIX

IT HAS been repeatedly pointed out in this book that the art of music, like all the creations of the human spirit, has two aspects: one consists in its quality as a natural phenomenon, the other in its character as an invention of the human fancy. The material peculiar to music, the tone, is subject to a multitude of physical conditions as regards its fundamental nature as sound and to physiological conditions as regards its effect on our auditory sense: it is physical in so far as concerns its vibratory essence; physiological in reference to the manner in which these vibrations react on our ears.

The history of music marks in every stage that slow, selective process by which our musical sense has come to recognize musical values where once it only perceived crude and uncertain sounds. The final phase of musical art, the aesthetic response to music of the human being, is incapable of codification. The effort to apply to art norms based on physiology or physics is pure foolishness and, almost without exception, originates with people who are neither artists, physiologists, nor physicists.

The history of music offers, nevertheless, a multitude of instances in which the theorists have attempted to lay down the laws of the art. Unfortunately, the theorists have ignored the practical realities of music and have often overlooked that intuition which is the keystone of the artist's sensibility. The result has been that the theorists have drawn up lists of rules which, once codified, have no further meaning for a living, growing art.

The most extensive part of theoretical speculation has been concerned, through the centuries, with the nature of the tone. Particular emphasis has been given to the vulgar sophism that perfection consists in a servile adherence to nature and that, therefore, a work of art will be perfect in so far as its sonorous material most nearly approaches the natural phenomenon. To state the matter more specifically, the work of art will be perfect if its consonances and dissonances are adjusted in exactly the same way in which the tones occur in nature. The natural adjustment of the tones is discovered by the use of analytic instruments in a physical laboratory where consonances and dissonances exist, not as the ear hears them, but exactly as physical mathematics defines them.

Such pseudoscientific and pseudomusical childishness would not deserve mention were it not that, in addition to constituting a large section of the history of music (with which we shall not concern ourselves here), it appears frequently in our own times and defends its existence by an appeal to one of the fundamental aspects of classico-romantic music, the so-called tempered system. Even worse, similar mathematical-acoustical disquisitions (which differ considerably from one theorist to another) actually pretend to revolutionize this ancient art. Among these theories, however, there is one rational idea which merits examination, namely, the concept of microtonalism.

Microtonalism is a practice which has been observed in all ages among certain non-European peoples (and even among some European people, as will presently be shown, although not within the types of music understood under this concept). Using the natural production of intervals smaller than our traditional minimum unit (the semitone) as a basis, it seeks to establish the composer's right to utilize extremely small intervals. In describing this attempt and in examining what has been achieved along this line, we shall confine ourselves to the serious present day work and experimentation in this field. We shall disregard the charlatanism and the absurd messianic attitude of some who pretend to redeem the ancient art of music from the original sin of temperament.

The unification of the two so-called enharmonic tones (such as C sharp and D flat) into one was a step taken during the eighteenth century. The necessity for it had been felt more or less acutely for some time past, when practical musicians saw the impossibility of extending the dimensions of the keyboard instruments and of modulating to keys much altered by sharps and flats. They found, on tuning their instruments by true fourths and fifths from a given fundamental, that the octaves at a distance from the central notes were noticeably out of tune with respect to those that composed the central octave. The impossibility of increasing the dimensions of the keyboard was obvious, as well as the difficulty of modulating to greatly altered keys (with more than five sharps or four flats) clearly conflicted with the material needs of musicians and the spiritual needs of their works. Both required greater freedom in modulation and instruments of greater capacity and of richer possibilities, with a keyboard practically as extensive as the total gamut of a chest of viols, from the lowest to the highest. Since the Renaissance, a great variety of solutions to the problem have been proposed. The adoption of double keyboards was frequently suggested, on one of which could be played (for example) C sharp and on the other D flat, in other words, keyboards separated from each other by the extremely small distance of a comma, a Pythagorean interval which is more mathematical than perceptible to the ear. Much simpler and, above all, far more feasible was the suggestion made at the end of the seventeenth century by the German organist and mathematician, Andreas Werckmeister, which consisted in the construction of a central octave in which, by slightly lowering the C sharp and raising the D flat a little, both tones would become identical and might be used interchangeably. This model scale was then to be repeated exactly in the successive octaves above and below.

The procedure known as equal temperament was adopted definitively by the approaching eighteenth century. Johann Sebastian Bach, emulating the example set by J. C. F. Fischer, erected a monument to equal temperament in his *Well-tempered Clavier,* forty-eight preludes and fugues in all the major and minor keys. In addition to all the arguments of a technical nature that may be adduced concerning the convenience of the Werckmeister system, there is another of a general character. It is that the ear is not so critical nor instruments in general so carefully tuned that the difference existing between C sharp and D flat can be perceived in practical performance. As a matter of fact, all instruments in actual use are, at best, only moderately well tuned and, according to the repeated testimony of persons of the period, the organs and claviers of earlier epochs were horribly out of tune. Why such prudish scruples? Werckmeister and Bach must certainly have said to their contemporaries (and continue to say it to the reformers of our own day): "Enough of farce! The music which you make and which you hear disagrees by more commas than those adjusted by equal temperament. Don't be so squeamish!"

And, indeed, those of ultrasusceptibility can be accused, if not of hypocrisy, of being the reformers of our times. I base this statement on the friendly confidences of performing artists (singers and violinists) who were congratulated by the originators of microtonal systems and by famous orchestral conductors, upon performing works of this character, for being artists of a highly refined taste and technique capable of rendering with violin or with voice not only quarter tones but sixths, eighths, twelfths, and even sixteenths of a tone. Yet, confidentially, the artists told the present writer that while they were performing such prodigies they were dying of amusement because they limited themselves purely and simply to performing "out of tune!" So much for the charlatanism connected with microtonal reforms. We shall now turn to the elements of truth which microtonalism contains.

All students of the monodic music of the Moslem or Asiatic Orient know that its singers emit intervals in their melodies which do not coincide with the tempered scale. Oriental instruments, too, produce consonances different from one another: since orientals do not understand their music *harmonically,* they are not concerned that there may be a discrepancy between two notes (which ought to be in unison or at the octave) emitted, one by a wind instrument and another by a plucked instrument. On the other hand, the oriental singer is so sensitive in his listening habits that he can systematically and accurately intone intervals that are but a minute fraction of a semitone in span. Andalusian interpreters of *cante jondo* frequently intone intervals of less than a semitone; Greeks, Bulgarians, Hungarians, peasants of the Transylvania in Rumania, not to mention the Chinese, Japanese, Malayans, Hindustani, and, in general, the inhabitants of the Polynesian Islands—all base their melopoeia on similar intonations.

But it must be pointed out promptly that, in their musical system instead of what we call the scale, there are special groupings of notes that form melodic patterns called *maqamâts, rāgas, patets,* etc. When we speak from the point of view of our analytical system of the multitude of scales which must be formed in oriental music, based on a systematization of microtonal intervals, we are greatly in error. The fact, for example, that in one of these songs is to be found a fourth, an eighth, or a sixth of a tone does not mean that the native possesses a musical system made up of as many scales as may be formed by the division of the tone into two semitones, four quarter tones, eight eighths, etc. The peculiar intonation is connected with a specific note in a specific *maqamât* and has nothing to do with systematization in scales. To base a reform of the tempered scale on the practices in oriental music—to say, for example, that Arab or Indian music is richer than ours because therein exist all the scales which our combinatory method might produce—implies a lack of information because, in point of fact, no such scales exist.

The altered note in an oriental melody is self-sufficient. The alteration occurs in *it* exclusively and the singer is not obliged to give the same alteration to the corresponding note in a different octave. In fact, the concept of "octaves equal to each other" is not a rigorous convention in oriental music, which has never required that each note of an octave maintain the relation of two-to-one to the same note of the next octave. This idea of the octave, so natural to us, is a convention of occidental music which does not actually exist in nature.

The scale which serves as the basis of our harmonic music was born centuries after the modal art, as a consequence of the harmonic evolution of the ear (of musical feeling) on the foundation of traditional melodic customs. The scale starts from the intuitive principle which continuously made equivalent to each other all the audible sounds which form octaves with each other, next the fifths and fourths, later the major and minor thirds, sixths, and the other intervals. Our musical perception says that one octave is equal to another, one fifth to another fifth, one fourth to another fourth: thus, for example, the series C, F, C is always equal (as to structure) to the series D, G, D. All this, speaking from the point of view of acoustics, is false: as false as art itself.

Neither the example of oriental musicians, with their variable intervals of less than a semitone, nor the pretext of the lack of trueness or of perfection (!) in the intonation of the unscientific intervals of which Western music is composed can serve as the basis—thank God!—for reforms in a system which has produced countless masterpieces. Those who promulgate the idea of a new music based on intertonal relations of less than the semitone or who include them in the present chromatic complex start out from much clearer and more positive reasoning. They start, in fact, from the practical evidence of hearing, from the development which the auditory sense, as a result of its experiences with tonal or atonal chromatic music, has succeeded in acquiring in our day "within the habits appropriate to our musical system" (of course, the ear always perceives infinitely small sonorous relationships, even those not as yet integrated in a musical and artistic systematization).

In occidental music we normally have two ways of dividing the octave into equal parts: (*a*) *A scale of whole tones:* six notes (from C-B flat) in the relationship of whole tones. (*b*) *A chromatic scale:* twelve notes (from C-B) in semitones.

Both scales have appeared in the natural series of harmonics, the first between the tones 7 and 13, and the second between the tones 11 and 22. Starting with tone 22, there begins a new series, in intervals smaller than the semitone. Shall musicians employ this natural series with its highly prolix succession of intonations? It seems preferable to follow the path pursued by those musicians who employed the whole-tone scale or the twelve-tone scale by accommodating them to the practices of equal temperament. This path, the simplest and closest to the experience of the ear, consists once again in dividing in half the intervals of the twelve-tone scale already considered.

We shall thus obtain a scale in quarter tones, composed of twenty-four notes which, according to the belief of the composers who employ it, can fulfill: (*a*) the tonal functions of the normal scale, (*b*) the impressionist successions of the whole-tone scale, (*c*) the atonalism of the twelve-tone scale. According to the first criterion, music in quarter tones can have the character of a functional ultrachromatic, that is to say, harmonic phenomenon. According to the second criterion, this music can be purely monodic and, in this manner, two ways of using the quarter tone may result: as augmentation or diminution of the normal semitones, and as appoggiatura or substitution or as a skip. The experiments so far made in this field indicate that, as in oriental music, microtones are easily perceptible when heard in succession one after another. When the microtone is introduced by a skip, our ear seems not to perceive it as such but assimilates it to the nearest normal sound. Within the third criterion, that is in atonal music, it appears that the microtone may be used quite freely, both as a monodic leap and in chordal groupings. There is, then, a certain development from the closest proximity to traditional practice to the greatest divergence from it.

In the majority of experiments up to now the microtone is employed as an appoggiatura or passing tone to a normal note, that is, the progression.

To the untrained ear, the first progression seems just like the second except for the fact that it sounds a little out of tune. Ultrachromaticism is thus heard as an exaggerated, expressive accentuation of the attractive force of adjacent notes (as in resolutions of dissonances or in the leading-tone cadence to the tonic), an extremely common practice with violinists and also with singers, for the purpose of emphasizing, sometimes injudiciously, the dramatic character of a passage. Thus conceived, ultrachromaticism can, with a certain effectiveness, result from intervals smaller than a quarter tone. The auditory effect is simply that of an indefinite sliding or gliding between notes; in other words, it is like an excessive portamento, something which was an infallible sign of bad taste in the music of the preceding periods. We shall have to dismiss this prejudice if we are to listen, at least calmly and dispassionately, to this type of music.

In his essay entitled "Entwurf einer Aesthetik der Tonkunst" published in Trieste in 1907, the Italian-German composer, pianist, and theorist Ferruccio Busoni proposed the division of the semitone into three parts, as that intonation seemed to him easier for the ear to catch than the quarter tone. But the problem does not lie in the difficulty of perceiving these microtones for the ear rapidly accustoms itself to recognize them with a little practice, and does not consider them as tones whose intonation has been forced in an upward or downward direction. The difficulty consists in the one case as in the other, in recognizing microtones in a "leap," and this difficulty does not seem to have been overcome as yet by the various contemporary musicians who have worked along these lines.

Among these men, Alois Hába (1893), the Moravian composer, stands out for his theoretical work as well as for his achievements in composition. It is said that Hába realized the necessity of rejecting the tempered system because the popular songs of his native region fall frequently into microtonal intonations. But these intonations fall within accented melodism and do not appear to affect their tonal character. However, Hába felt the need of studying acoustics thoroughly and did so in the Hochschule in Berlin. After studying the exact constitution of the scale, Hába thought of the possibility of using quarter tones contrapuntally and harmonically in the constitution of the chord. His first essay was a quartet, Op. 7 (1921), in which microtonic intonations occur below the normal semitone when descending and above the semitone in ascending. That is to say, the quarter tone or three-quarter tone resolves itself on the nearest semitone. The effect, then, is that of ultrachromaticism without further technical or aesthetic implications.

In 1927, Hába unified his ideas in a treatise entitled "Neue Harmonielehre des Diatonischen, Chromatischen, Viertel-, Drittel-, Sechstel-, und Zwölftel-Tonsystems" where, as can be seen, he studies the possibility of using thirds, quarters, sixths, and twelfths of a tone. His practical application of the use of intervals smaller than the quarter tone appears in a quartet, Op. 15, in sixths of a tone. Hába has made use of the quarter tone in choral works, as in his "Merry Rhythms" for women's and children's voices, and in two operas—*Die Mutter,* Op. 35 (1931), and *Die Arbeitslosen* (in the last-named work, political theories of a somewhat revolutionary tone are to be observed, as seems only natural). In a suite, Op. 37, for strings or harmonium, Hába returns to the use of sixths of a tone. Other works carry his microtonal system to the piano, a piano, however, adequate for his needs.

The construction of instruments capable of producing microtones is, of course, an imperative necessity. Among the various attempts which will be mentioned in detail in a moment, the piano or double piano which the firm of August Förster constructed under Hába's direction is the one which seems to have stood up most satisfactorily under tests, while many other similar ones were rapidly abandoned. Hába's piano is a kind of double piano in which one keyboard is tuned at a distance of a quarter tone from the other. In the work above mentioned, Op. 37, Hába employs a harmonium tuned in sixths of a tone and, in his operas, he includes clarinets and harps which produce quarter tones.

A prime necessity, in these systems, appears in the reform of musical notation. Reform, even for our traditional system, is an ancient mania; various attempts have been carried out, so far without any future use. In the first place, reformed notations are good, at most, for a single melodic line but they lack the clarity and admirable plasticity of our traditional notation both for polyphonic and orchestral writing. Under the present system, a musician of only moderate technical ability is capable of understanding at a glance the instrumental arrangement on a page as well as the harmony and the march of the voices. The effort to replace the work of hundreds of years with an expedient devised, more or less laboriously, by the brain of some generous contriver has systematically met with failure. And even were it not for this fact, it would be sufficient to point out the expense of having to re-edit, according to a new system, the total number of musical editions in the world.

But a reform of notation for the purpose of making it adequate for the microtonal systems is, naturally, quite another thing. Hába, who in his first works employed a kind of half-flat for the descending quarter tone and a kind of half-sharp for the ascending quarter tone, later devised another sign to indicate the three-quarter tone, ascending and descending. Recently he has invented other signs, distantly related to the sharp and the flat, with which he indicates the twelfth of a tone, the value of five-twelfths and even of eleven-twelfths of a tone, both ascending and descending.

Inspired perhaps by his investigations in microtonalism, although the two are not directly related, Hába proposes an "athematic" system of composition; that is to say, a composition in which the melodic line cannot be subdivided into phrases, motives, or periods. In other words, it is a kind of fluid melopoeia, a truly infinite melody (undefined) in the Wagnerian sense—although Wagner never used it. This indefinite and vague melody or melopoeia, which Hába advocates and employs in his quartet in quarter tones, Op. 12, carries with it another implication: that of never repeating itself nor any of the fragments of which it is composed. Undoubtedly the procedure is convenient and it is not to be wondered at that Hába has had numerous disciples. The quartet mentioned is composed of six sections, obviously independent of one another; the unity of the composition is founded on the melodic feeling, accented by the peculiar color of the microtonal turns of phrase, while contrast is provided by the carefully calculated difference between the character of each part, their movement or tempi, and their rhythms.

Aside from Hába and his pupils in the official Conservatory of Prague (1923), another of the most notable cultivators of microtonalism seems to be, at present, the German, Hans Barth (1897), who had a piano constructed with two keyboards of quarter tones for which he wrote a concerto with string accompaniment (1930). Silvestre Baglioni, professor of philosophy at the University of Rome, had a harmonium similarly constructed which he called "enharmonium." The idea of untempered enharmony, but with a division of the intonation by commas made perceptible to the ear, inspired the construction of another harmonium by Don Juan Domínguez Berrueta, professor of geometry in the University of Salamanca as well as a notable literary critic and the writer of various essays on the tempered scale (whose divisions "like a thermometer" provoked him to many sarcasms).[1]

A young Valencian, Eduardo Panach Ramos, constructed a kind of *citarina* in thirds of tones which had (like the harmonium of Berrueta) a singular tendency to get out of tune; for this reason, one never could be sure whether one was hearing the comma, the point under discussion, or its closest relative.

[1] In Mexico, Augusto Novaro has carried out interesting experiments in the tuning of instruments (especially in pianos of his own invention) based on the acoustic phenomenon of "beats." Beats are the pulsations heard when two series of sonorous vibrations do not exactly coincide with each other. The acoustical definition of dissonance (Helmholtz) is based on the greater or lesser number of beats produced by two simultaneous tones. (See "Beats" and "Consonance" in the article, "Acoustics," in Grove's Dictionary.)

Two Russians, Ivan Vyshnegradsky and Georg Rimsky-Korsakov (grandson of the author of Shéhérazade), have each founded societies for the study and dissemination of the good news concerning the quarter tone. Vyshnegradsky (1893) wrote several works for violin, clarinet, and piano in quarter tones as well as a *Manual of Harmony* (in two volumes, Paris, 1923), and founded at Paris a Groupe Estival which included Nicolas Obouhov and the American, Katherine Ruth Heyman. The piano they use is the same Förster invented by Hába while that of Barth was constructed in New York by the Baldwin Company on the basis of two keyboards, in equal temperament, divided in quarter tones.

The rejection of temperament as a prerequisite for microtonal theories is, then, fairly ephemeral and temperament comes into use again in connection with that very system when the keyboard is in question. An English composer, J. Herbert Foulds (1880), has written some quartotonal works for orchestra and his countryman, John Appleby, has attempted to decipher microtonally the inflections of the speaking voice. A native of Halle, R. H. Stein (1882), has written pieces for violoncello and piano in quarter tones and others for a clarinet adapted to the new system whose peculiarities he has described in various pamphlets since 1909.

Finally, last but not least, since his experiments in this field cover no less than thirty-five years, the Mexican composer Julián Carrillo (1875) has written copiously on the use of the sixteenth of a tone (in his so-called "theory of the tone 13"). He has constructed a guitar in quarter tones, an octarina in eighths of a tone, a harp-zither and a French horn which produce sixteenths of a tone. In 1926 the League of Composers in New York presented his Sonata quasi Fantasia in which Carrillo employs quarter tones; his orchestral poem, Cristóbal Colón, also quartotonal, can be heard on gramophone records. In 1927, Leopold Stokowski performed in Philadelphia the Concertino in which Carrillo uses eighths and sixteenths of a tone.

Microtonalism goes hand in hand with the continuous tone, the emission of a tone that has no fixed interval divisions,[2] no matter how small, but is rather a sliding tone (as in oriental music). Intonations which might be called micrometric and which, heard as gliding tones like those produced by a siren, may have a certain charm. Such music is closely related to certain theosophical ideas which seek in this art a spiritual region whose sonorous translation is to be found in the mystical and sometimes exquisite vagueness of the music of the spheres: a kind of musical Orphism which reproduces the most ancient oriental concept of music and whose steps consist in the

[2] Recall what was said concerning Josef M. Hauer in Chapter XXIII.

multiplicity of scales or supposed scales (since they are a series of sounds arranged in conjunct order) such as can be formed by microtones.

Busoni prided himself on the fact that with his system of thirds of a tone he could construct no less than one hundred and thirty-three of these so-called scales. Hába surpassed that number and arrives at no less than five hundred and eighty-one, which go all the way from scales of five tones to those of twelve. It is evident that systems based on the sixteenth of a tone will considerably increase the number of scales. Shall we not, then, be nearer to this indefinite and indefinable ideal with the uninterrupted flow of musical sounds, ascending and descending in imperceptible glissandi? We can take an affirmative or negative position, since the production of such types of musical sounds is offered us by electromagnetic contrivances which reproduce, more or less satisfactorily, the timbre of different instruments from the violin to the ocarina or the violoncello as well as entirely new timbres.

The engineers—Leo Theremin (1896) of Russian origin and the Frenchman, Maurice Martenot—have devoted themselves to the construction of such instruments. Theremin began his experiments in Leningrad with an electric organ and so far has constructed ten different instruments that he uses together as an orchestra to which he adds effects of lighting—an old aspiration, this, from the days of a Jesuit in the eighteenth century, P. Castel, who invented a color organ, to Scriabin and his Prometheus. Theremin, who had studied music in his youth, has made a number of essays in music, some of which have been given relatively practical form by Henry Cowell (1897), composer and theorist, who has proposed *New Musical Resources* (1930) to young composers. Joseph Schillinger has taken up some of these suggestions, according to such musicographers as Marion Bauer, in a work entitled Airphonic Suite for RCA Theremin with Orchestra.

"All of this is very fine," replied Candide, "but let us continue to cultivate our garden."

Chapter TWENTY-SEVEN

ONLY that which is forgotten is dead. This idea, which belongs in the permanent repertory of the poets, is a fundamental principle of aesthetics and one of the bases of style. As long as an art has vigor and actuality in the stylistic formations of a period, it is a living art. To speak of an art of the future means to express the hope that an art of the present may enter into the stylistic formations of an art as yet unborn. The history of art teaches us that not every artistic style survives the period of its birth.

Thus it happens that certain stylistic elements which in their own time were considered old came to belong to subsequent arts while those which aspired to the category of newness, presenting themselves as newly created elements, never acquired a long-lasting existence. As an example, the well-known case of Bach and Telemann is in point. Bach was the *vieille perruque,* the provincial musician, the good builder of fugues; his own son, Johann Christian, denied him in the name of the young melodist school of Telemann and of the composers in Italian style. Yet the elements of style of Telemann and his colleagues have disappeared while those of the old Bach have been revived to a certain point. They have acquired actual substance in the sensibilities of certain composers of our time as we have had occasion to see in previous chapters, even though Bach lives only as a symbol. Only a short time before Richard Wagner devoted himself to the construction of a *Zukunftsmusik,* Felix Mendelssohn had resuscitated Bach's shade from the past. These two musical forces have been pulsating in a dramatic struggle through a large part of the music of our times; both aesthetics have taken shape as elements of style. In these elements the idea of the future seems to predominate over the idea of the past among those composers who passionately practice linear or dissonant counterpoint, while the stylistic practices of others may be traced quite easily to original sources in the Gothic or the baroque, in the musical anthologies of the Renaissance or in Palestrina, Bach, Vivaldi, Pergolesi, or Scarlatti—in Rossini or Tchaikovsky.

By this time the reader will have grasped the end toward which the discussion is pointing. As is well known, Igor Stravinsky, in the works of the second period of his musical production, frequently used elements typical of the style of past composers. Just as the painter conceives his models—not as a "bottle" or an "apple"—but as value and form so, likewise, musicians like Stravinsky or Falla conceive their objects—Pergolesi, Scarlatti, or Tchaikovsky—as stylistic elements of form and value possessing a higher degree of spirituality than simple material elements such as harmonic or instrumental color or motive gesture, rhythm, etc.

Such use of another composer's personal property has been a subject frequently discussed in modern criticism under the pretext of discussing the so-called *retours à*. Other, more perspicacious writers, however, have considered this reminiscence as *retours de*. Given either emphasis, such *retours* may achieve no more than the category of a pastime or of rather attractive and intelligent caprices. Yet they may have a far deeper meaning. They possess such importance that I see in them the easiest way of understanding what is meant, in the summary of the present chapter, by a passing beyond the experimental period in contemporary musical art. The employment of motives or of stylistic elements from the art of the past is here nothing more than an allegorical means by which is presented a new stage in the art of our century, a stage wherein musical values are lifted from their former, subordinate role to one of independence. This ascending movement is the process whereby all the sonorous elements of music have attained, in the course of time, an autonomous value.

It is not enough, however, to leave these harmonic, tonal, and stylistic features in the state of glorious self-assertion which they have reached in the various phases of impressionist and expressionist music. These scattered, individual elements must assume definitive, formal meaning as integral parts of an art that passes beyond the tentative experimentation of recent decades. I believe that, in the work of some present day composers—of whom the most significant, in my opinion, is Igor Stravinsky—there is to be found that crystallization of artistic purpose for which we seek.

A new period is at hand; in the light of its achievements, such procedures as atonality, polytonality, polymodality, ultrachromaticism, and polyrhythm will be seen as simply intermediate, experimental phases of contemporary musical thought. In the same way that impressionism, in order to make itself understood, alluded to poetic features easily recognized by the listener, the new music alludes to stylistic elements (melodic, harmonic, rhythmic, or coloristic) which derive now from the field of folklore or again from a pseudo-popular source; now from the classical field, or again from a pseudo classicism. It may allude to such widely divergent fields as Debussy's highly typical harmonic procedures, Tchaikovsky and his romantic turns of phrase, Chinese pentatonic music, the Andalusian *cante jondo,* the harpsichord, the guitar, the ecclesiastical modes, the vague recitatives of the Japanese *No* dramas, the cymbals, or the *ḳanûn,* etc., etc.

This popularism, folklorism, classicism, medievalism, primitivism, or what will you, are not, I repeat vigorously, anything more than allegorical or symbolic means of working with harmonic and tonal elements which aspire to find a form and style in which earlier musical experiments (almost inoperative on the aesthetic conscience of our time) may be filled with unmistakably vital force. It is in this sense that I speak of a passing beyond. In so doing I express my personal point of view, well knowing that the partisans of those composers or schools previously studied will violently oppose to this their own points of view, esteeming the art of Schönberg to be as vital as that of Stravinsky, that of Hába as that of Falla, that of Alban Berg as that of Bartók. They may be right but I, who am without a party, who have no contact with any group, only aspire to comprehend the meaning of our present day art and to make it comprehensible to the reader of these pages. I proceed, then, according to my sincere knowledge and belief, but I do not pretend to establish incontestable axioms.

As a preliminary step, let us examine the specific elements of the musical art of Igor Stravinsky. Later, I will discuss his works from the listener's point of view, considering them as successive stages in Stravinsky's artistic development and creative evolution.

In one of the early chapters of this book, we spoke of the bonds that make a given type of culture the most profound expression of a particular race. This expression is, in a certain sense, unconscious on the artist's part, for it takes on its particular shape in accord with the personal reaction of the artist to his cultural environment. We may, however, accept the current belief that a musician of a particular race or national group works along stylistic norms which we conventionally consider to be characteristic of that group.

I believe we may affirm that Stravinsky, Falla, and Bartók take their point of departure from a national basis. The profundity of this national or racial feeling, however, cannot be measured by the literalness with which each man employs a national motive. "Truth without authenticity" has been the constant rule advised by Manuel de Falla. And, in fact, do we not know Spanish and Norwegian symphonies written by Lalo, pieces with a Spanish character by Moszkowski or Ravel?

What is the document which certifies that the music of Ravel or of Debussy is as profoundly French as that of Schönberg or Reger is German, as that of Malipiero or Pizzetti is Italian? The Slavic character of Stravinsky's music, like the Spanish character of Falla's, may be literal or imaginary yet the Russian or Spanish substance of each composer's work escapes no one. In their music we are dealing with an integral nationalism just as in Mahler's or Bruckner's. But here there is an essential difference which has its roots in the stylistic elements that are brought into play. For these Germans, as also for Schönberg and Reger, stylistic elements are based in the tradition of German art-music while for the others the basis is popular tradition.

This is especially important because it explains why peoples endowed with a strong popular feeling in their musical tradition have never assimilated well those forms of art appropriate to peoples with a different cultural character and with strong racial differences. For example, the forms sonata, symphony, quartet, each so typical of German art, have been cultivated in Slavic and Latin countries only precariously and after substantial alterations. Again, the forms of the vocal aria, so characteristically Italian, have to be transformed according to the manner of the popular lied, chanson, or *canción* in the other countries while, furthermore, with Germanic composers it undergoes a transformation dictated by their typical gift for abstraction. In view of this fact, it will be understood why Bach and Handel are profoundly German composers in spite of having systematically employed French or Italian stylistic motives, or why Gluck continues to be German even after having adopted the recitative of Lully and Rameau and their sense of harmonic-orchestral accompaniment (especially when he wrote comic operas!), or, again, why Stravinsky is so completely Slavic, whether he uses motives taken from or patterned on popular Russian tradition, as in his first ballets or whether he uses stylistic elements which it is possible to associate with Bach, Pergolesi, or Rossini.

In either case, popular or classicist motive, the first thing that we observe is that the thematic element is not a motive of inspiration for Stravinsky but a point of departure for his work. This distinction is important for the fact that the first process was typical of the romantic composer, while the other was the method of the classical composer. Schumann, for example, takes his motives as stimuli or incitements whose development consequently produces pieces saturated with dramatic expression (as in expressionism). Haydn or Mozart see in their symphonic motives the material whose melodic-harmonic, rhythmic, and modulatory treatment will bring forth a work of the sonata-symphony type. The process which led Beethoven from his First Symphony to his Ninth illustrates well this passage from classical to romantic art.

When do we find that the artist of our time confronts the material (melodic phrase, harmony, tonality, instrumental color, etc.) he is to use from a point of view equivalent to that of the classical artist? Paradoxical though it may seem, *this change of viewpoint came about in impressionist aesthetics,* where the essential value is in the sonorous material—dissonance and harmonic color modeled into a new style. As has been explained, the titles to which impressionism has recourse are no more than a provisional expedient to guide the listener. The essential value of the material he employs is, consequently, of prime importance to Stravinsky and not the dramatic, picturesque, or humorous theme of his pieces. His art, born by force of circumstance under the aegis of the ballet, forced itself from the first moment to achieve an autonomy of form which would make his music valuable for itself alone and not simply as an illustration of dance episodes. The resulting form grew from the treatment given the material employed; this highly personal treatment endows the works of Stravinsky with a special conviction, an effect of equilibrium between the form and the material. Stravinsky grasps the exemplary unity and parallelism of the classical period that was only achieved by exception in romantic music in certain pages of Chopin, Liszt, and Wagner.

At the time these pages are written, Stravinsky's musical production is enclosed by two symphonies: one in E-flat major, begun in 1905, and another in C major, written thirty-five years later, completed during the year 1940. Between these two works, both of which display a closed form and a definite tonality, is included an immense quantity of music of which the principal characteristics are: (*a*) that of being composed for the ballet, an art whose character requires the motive gesture of well-defined lines, not susceptible to thematic transformations in the German sense of symphonic *Durchführung* and (*b*) works of independent form and of an abstract character, i.e., pure music. The treatment of the sonorous material as regards timbre, harmony, and tonality, motive, and organization of the formal unity is substantially the same in both types. The only differences are those imposed by the transformation and development of Stravinsky's creative genius with the course of time. The unity of idea, in any case, can be recognized even in works so different in their external aspect as, for example, *Petrouchka, Pribautki, Pulcinella,* or the Capriccio for piano and orchestra.

The fact that the works which gave Stravinsky his first reputation, beginning with the first performance in Paris of the *Fire Bird* in 1910, were linked to the ballet was due to the interest excited by the performances of music and dance which Sergei Diaghilev had then been presenting for some years past in the French capital. The purpose of these concerts was to direct the attention of the French and cosmopolitan world to Russian artists of all kinds: painters, decorators, singers, ballet dancers, and composers. The artistico-patriotic propaganda of Diaghilev culminated in the spectacle known as the Ballet Russe (although its antecedents were, above all, French), in which were combined —to the immense delight of the spectators—the academic ballet of opera with the exotic dances and with the music of brilliant orchestral color of the nationalist Russian school.

As early as 1907, the talent of the twenty-five-year-old Stravinsky, "private pupil" of Nikolai Rimsky-Korsakov (as he was presented on the programs in St. Petersburg), had attracted the attention of Diaghilev. A restless spirit, avid for novelty in every category of ideas, Diaghilev asked Stravinsky to compose the music for a popular tale in the Rimsky vein, the legend of the magician Kastchei and the fire bird. (It had been set to music many years before by the amateur composer, Count Cavos.) From that time the musical personality of Stravinsky was closely associated with the development of the Ballet Russe, both in its first period of spectacles of great scenic brilliance and in its later era of performances of more modest size.

For the early period, Stravinsky wrote: the *Fire Bird* (1909-10), *Petrouchka* (1910-11), *Le Sacre du Printemps* (1911-13), and *Rossignol* (1914; a second version in 1920). For the new series of more restrained performances he produced: *Renard* (1916-17), *Pulcinella* (1919-20), *Mavra* (1922), *Apollon Musagètes* (1928), *Le Baiser de la fée* (1928), *Perséphone* (1933), and *Jeu de cartes* (1937). Works such as *Les Noces* (1914-17, first performed in 1923) and the opera-oratorio *Oedipus Rex* (1927 and 1928) seem to lie halfway between these two theatrical styles and, as we shall see, mark critical points in the development of Stravinsky's art. To the type which requires a simple setting (like *Renard,* a burlesque tale to be played and sung, designed for stage performance) may be added the *Histoire du Soldat,* to be "read, played, and danced" which was first performed in 1918.

Because it was destined for the dance, Stravinsky's music emphasized certain features which later were extended to his concert works: clear ideas, rigorously delineated, strongly marked in their character of gesture motive and color motive (this last refers as much to instrumental as to harmonic color and is based principally on the character of the dissonance). There is no attempt at the development of these motives, for such treatment would be incongruous with the dance but, on the other hand, there is a well-defined and closed formal treatment which the dance requires. Stravinsky's technique, as regards form, harmony, and instrumental color, is confined within these basic points. There is an additional characteristic in his music, one which likewise depends in large measure on the technique of the dance: it is the economy, the laconic style, the chiseled brevity of the discourse or, as has been said, the "telegraphic style" of Stravinsky. This succinctness is the more desirable since the expression is so intense and the means of expression so aggressive: an intensity and aggressiveness readily recalled by those who were his first, astonished and rather disconcerted auditors in the second and third decades of our century. These qualities have gradually lost their bite along with their novelty and they have come to be included in the technique generally accepted by contemporary composers.

The psychological means that made Stravinsky acceptable, from the beginning, to the great majority of listeners had two aspects: one, his exoticism, a popularism of more or less authentically Russian origin; the other was his sarcasm, the violence of his musical gesture which overwhelmed a world accustomed to postromantic lyricism, to sentimental German digression, or to the saccharine sweetness of certain aspects of French, Italian, Spanish, and even Russian art. The initial connection of Stravinsky with the picturesque orchestra of Rimsky and with the exotic chromaticisms of Borodin took precedence in the public mind over the concise expression, the harmonic justness—so personal in character—which derived from Mussorgsky. But Mussorgsky was still poorly appreciated in the first decades of the century and what was known of him (in the theater) had undergone the arrangements of Rimsky-Korsakov.

Later, Diaghilev asked Ravel and Stravinsky to orchestrate some pages, today very well known, by Mussorgsky. This task (a reinstrumentation of certain passages from *Khovantchina*) brought together for the first time (in Clarens, Switzerland, in 1913) the French master and the young Russian musician who at that time was finishing his *Sacre du Printemps.* To Ravel's artificiality, to his effortlessly restrained art, indeed to the art of both musicians, was also presented the example of a different but equally artificial and laconic art: that of Schönberg's *Pierrot Lunaire.* This work had direct influence both on Ravel's *"Poèmes de Stéphane Mallarmé"* and on the refined exoticism of Stravinsky's *Trois poésies de la lyrique japonnaise,* which followed the picturesque Slavism of his first works and its more pronounced, rude, and primitive aspect in the *Sacre.* This Slavism, which was no more than a distant echo in the works of Stravinsky's middle period, came to assume, in the final stage of his work, a literalness which conveys the curious and powerfully attractive impression of a popular artistic creation; it reveals that vigorous and original Slavic art which, like that of the old icons, retains expressive inflections of Byzantine origin as intense as the Gothic images whose accents the German expressionist artists wished to revive.

André Schaeffner says very justly in his admirable study of Stravinsky,[1] perhaps the most penetrating among the many critiques which have been written of this composer, "[This is] popular music, infantile or rural, *vulgar* but vulgar in the sense in which all everyday objects are vulgar: a wooden table, the thick glass of a wine bottle; [this is] music based on Russian folklore, not to exploit those motives artificially in works of previously stipulated form, but in order to place itself exactly at the level of that music."

This ruralism appears especially in the small works of the type of *Pribautki* (1914), the "Four Russian Songs" (1918-19), the "Three Little Songs" (1913), and in little works like the Three Easy Pieces and the Five Easy Pieces of 1917. They have a popular flavor now Russian, again Italian, or of the Spanish

[1] André Schaeffner, *Stravinsky,* ed. Rieder (Paris: 1931).

zarzuela type. At times it takes on the familiar color of the middle-class parlor with its polkas, waltzes, and galops and knows how to reduce itself to the narrow limits of the little pieces for Five Fingers (1921) or to expand itself in *Le Baiser de la fée,* this time in Tchaikovsky's vein, or in the final section of the Capriccio for Piano and Orchestra (1929).

The carnival music in *Petrouchka* followed the traditional exoticism of the *Fire Bird.* Yet here already appear the rhythmic peculiarities which constitute the nerve center of Stravinsky's entire production. For with his breathless accents, his violent syncopation, his occasionally delirious rhythms, Stravinsky had discovered jazz long before Ernest Ansermet brought him, in 1916, the first examples from American orchestras. The composer utilized these—as suggestion rather than in imitation, of course—in *L'Histoire du Soldat* (with its Argentinian tangos, two-steps, and carnival music), in the Ragtime of 1918, and the Piano Rag-Music of 1919. Its final traces are still to be found in the Concerto for Piano and Brasses (1924).

The exotic accordion is the magic touchstone whence gushes the music of *Petrouchka* with its diminished fifths. That ballet revived the cold and academic tradition of the classical ballet where everything was subordinated to the a priori figures of the classic dance. In *Petrouchka,* with an intensity of effect matched by a clarity and economy of means, the ancient barrel organ plays its borrowed *savoyenne* for the dances of coachmen, nursemaids, and Russian gypsies. The Hungarian zimbalon plays a corresponding part in *Renard,* and the timbre of the balalaika is recalled in the little pieces for piano. Yet, neither the banjo nor the ukulele nor even the saxophone have left their traces in Stravinsky's music, notwithstanding his evident fondness for unconventional combinations of instruments and his treatment of the piano as a percussive instrument.

The use of the *savoyenne* above referred to, *"Ell' avait un jamb' de bois,"* is a perfect example of how Stravinsky directs his handling of popular song. Sometimes his sources are anonymous, as in some Russian examples: the Lithuanian theme with which the *Sacre* begins; the liturgical theme of *Noces;* the children's songs in *"Trois Petites Chansons"* of 1913, so close to Mussorgsky in spirit; or in the "Four Russian Songs" of 1919; and in the four peasant choruses entitled "The Saucer," which are much like the little ritual or magic phrases of the fortune tellers in the small Russian villages.

At other times, Stravinsky uses themes by a known author, like the fragments from Tchaikovsky in *Le Baiser de la fée,* endowing these borrowings with folkloric character. These themes Stravinsky treats as an object to be used, as material to be worked, just as a wood turner works a piece of wood without injuring the grain. In other cases the author of the popular song is Stravinsky himself and then he uses a motive found, not in the mouth of the folk, but in his own heart as a man of the people. Yet, he uses it in the same way, never to paint an evocative scene like Albéniz, never to create a poetic atmosphere like the impressionists, but always to form a structural part of his composition.

The systematic repetition of a motive, sometimes minutely varied by the displacement of its figures within the measure, is one of the typical formal procedures of Stravinsky. It reached its highest power in the great ballets such as *Petrouchka* and the *Sacre* and in the mixed types such as *Noces.* Although there is no symmetry in these repetitions, they nevertheless give a singular robustness to the form. The form itself is distant from any model, except in the case of those works—symphonies, sonatas, or concertos—which allude to those types whose preconceived plan offers no obstacle to Stravinsky's imagination. Indeed, he enjoys confronting himself with all kinds of formal, harmonic, and instrumental problems in order to resolve them in perfect congruity with the requirements of a particular style.

The repetition of short, clean-cut motives gives the music of Stravinsky the air of a metallic mechanism: cold, exact, purposeful. This comparison has been made frequently and is strengthened, in such works as the *Sacre,* by the powerful, rhythmic, Gargantuan pulsation. As the content of each motive is exhausted, it gives place to another episode with a new motive treated with the same felicity. The method seems clear enough in works of ballet type but even when, as in *Les Noces,* the motive returns for structural reasons, it is inert in contrast with the dynamic meaning which a motive has in the classical symphony. The dynamism of Stravinsky's work derives from other sources, principally from the rhythm. Similarly, the "interval of movement," which according to the academic definition means dissonance, does not serve Stravinsky as a dynamic agent. Dissonance, to him, is a simple color motive, a cutting, cleaving, chiseling instrument and not a harmonic value which determines the interlacing of chords. In my opinion, the so-called polyharmony in Stravinsky, which results from the superposition of perfect chords, must be regarded in the same light as his color motive.

Whether of popular derivation or of his own invention, the motive in Stravinsky is clearly tonal, strongly rhythmic, and always vocal. However, Stravinsky makes little use of the development of the thematic cell as motive power. When he wants to write in the closed forms, as in *Mavra,* he limits himself to reproducing the old, operatic types of aria, duo, or cavatina that lend themselves to the ironic character of his music. In his recent work, the symphony of 1940, Stravinsky has used the melodic cell as a counterbalance to the rhythmic cell, generating the entire symphonic structure from the two elements in a manner not unrelated to Franck's method; nevertheless, his typical construction has consisted in the juxtaposition of heterogeneous elements. He manipulates these with a powerful, premeditated logic which is not only convincing but which possesses all the degrees of fascination from the simply suggestive or agreeable to the obsessive; at times, he carries the listener into uncomfortable territory whose violent perspectives and murky atmosphere are very far removed from what was considered pleasant in the preceding musical repertoire.

These suggestions of ugliness are the aesthetic equivalents of dissonance in the field of acoustics; like it, they are a natural product of the evolution of the artistic sense, an evolution which has been repeated in all the arts. In the course of this development, we have encountered the rhythmic motive from the good old days of the Beethoven symphony; the expression motive from Beethoven's Quartet, Op. 135, to the Symphony of Franck and all the music of Wagner; the gesture motive from Schumann to Strauss; the color motive, which suggested the vast symphonic structures from the Eroica to Bruckner. In Stravinsky we find all these motives together, combined in a special violently dissonant agglomeration: gesture, instrumental and harmonic color, expression at once plastic and dramatic, harmonic suggestion—all resting on a basis of formal construction.

Stravinsky who, according to his biographers, sets down carefully in a notebook the opening of each of his compositions or at least of the most important works, attaches special significance to the task of finding the "first chord" of any composition. This is the germinating chord, so to speak, whence the whole composition will spring and which is its harmonic nucleus. Next comes the plastic motive, to give the work its external form. In *Petrouchka,* in the *Sacre du Printemps,* in *Noces,* or in *Oedipus,* the germinating chord is easy to recognize because it imposes itself on the attention from the first moment. In these works, it is especially easy to distinguish the unity which the harmonic process observes in relation to the initial chord which, it may be truly said, exercises the function of a tonic. As will be shown shortly, tonality in the traditional sense is strong in Stravinsky but, at present, we refer to a spiritual tonic from which radiates the entire meaning of the work.

The expressiveness of the work, whether as gesture or harmonic color, is realized with a solidarity of instrumentation appropriate to each specific case. The setting is different in every work, and is never subjected to a conventional plan of orchestration such as exists in Wagner's style, in Rimsky's style, etc. There is no set plan in Stravinsky's style, either in orchestration or in harmony and, nevertheless, the most insignificant of his works shows unmistakable logic. Personality, with Stravinsky, is the principal factor in the unity of the form and style of his works; form and style vary from one composition to the next but with a sense of such profound logic that each work seems to derive from the previous one. And this is so rigorously true that with few composers can a system of criticism based on chronology be applied with greater success.

The score of *Petrouchka* seemed, in its day, "inextricable and precise." Today its precision seems to us the fruit of a great clarity of thought carried out with a sureness of touch which proves the strong sense of expression and form in Stravinsky. The distinctive harmony of this ballet or its germinating chord may cause some astonishment because it is used with a surprising knowledge of plastic effect, employed for its own dissonant value and a color subtly assigned to different orchestral elements. This chord, sometimes presented melodically,

or again as a simple effect of tremolo,

or again in the aspect of a bitonal superposition,

consists of the apparent superposition of the chords of C major and of F-sharp major. Actually, it is simply our old friend, the chord of the ninth *with* a diminished fifth.

The ninth may be minor (D flat) or major (D natural); in any case, in its complete form we have to do with an augmented eleventh chord which is found in the series of natural resonance, composed of the first eleven harmonics.

This series of independent or tonic value presents so many possibilities within itself and is so rich in implicit harmonics that it will scarcely need other complications than those derived spontaneously from within itself. At first glance there is in it a play of superpositions which Stravinsky will utilize copiously and ingeniously. He contrives, for example, tonal superpositions of the tonic and dominant (*Petrouchka*) or an equivocal fusion of their functions (*Rossignol*) or superposition of tonic and subdominant (Berceuse in the *Fire Bird*) or superpositions of natural, augmented or diminished intervals.[2] He makes copious use of fifths, for example in *Rossignol,* of fourths of different kinds similar to Scriabin's as in the dance of Kastchei, of fourths and fifths in *Renard.*

Or, again, there are the complete chords which ride one above another in *Petrouchka,* in *Les Noces,* in *Apollon Musagètes,* and in the symphonies for wind instruments. These chords are not to be understood harmonically but rather as a filling-in of intervals or gaps proceeding from the harmonic series. The series also supplies superpositions of equivocal chords like the dominant with a minor third or with a major third; on various occasions Stravinsky unites both thirds in a chord which is thus neither major nor minor,[3] but in which one of these notes makes an appoggiatura with the other according to the way the general harmonic context works out, ordinarily giving the effect of major. A similar device results from embroidering the leading tone with the minor seventh; Stravinsky achieves these effects of a subtle chromaticism by the ingenious arrangement of successive series of major and minor thirds.

Stravinsky's chromaticism, as a general rule, has the appearance of melodic successions or passing notes but the effect of rich color and sonorous sensuality[4] is emphasized by the orchestration. The chromaticism of Stravinsky's first works has its origin in postromantic music and it is easy to remark points of contact with Debussy or Dukas. In the exotic music of *Rossignol,* he uses passing tones between the notes constituting the pentatonic scale, a decorative chromaticism not far, as regards timbre, from the orientalism of Debussy. On the other hand, the chromaticism in the *Scherzo fantastique* and in the *Fire Bird* proceeds from the most accredited Russian palette, serving at times to amplify a diatonic motive compressed within a very narrow ambitus as in the *Sacre* while at other times, as in the *Poésies de la lyrique japonnaise,* it appears as a radiation surrounding a chord.

The generating chord of one of the most important sections of the *Sacre*—the Auguries of Spring—is a good example of Stravinsky's criterion of dissonance as percussive color. It appears as a chord of E flat whose notes in the low region are surrounded with appoggiaturas but the later use of the

[2] The *filling in* of which, giving complete chords, forms *harmonic, contrapuntal currents* which have been given the name polyharmony, but it is not, accurately speaking, a matter of harmony.

[3] The chord G-B♭-D-F-A-B♮ is formed by the harmonics 6-7-9-11-13-15 of the natural series.

[4] The chromaticism of some passages, like that of the songs of the nightingale in the second and third acts of *Rossignol,* give the impression of quarter tones to musicians like Paul Collaer. See his book, *Stravinsky* (Brussels: 1931), p. 84.

harmonies which result shows that it is not a question of simple color effect, such as that used at the beginning of *Renard*. In the last analysis, the complete harmony, uniting the chords of E flat and F flat by way of D flat, is simply a dominant thirteenth chord. Later, in the second stage of Stravinsky's production, the chord that presides over the birth of Apollo consists in a superposition of two fourths (C, F, B) and of two thirds (B, D, F♯), a surprising combination at first sight but it is less startling when one reflects that it is nothing more than a chord of the dominant seventh with the fundamental altered downward (G♭, B, D, F).[5]

Appoggiaturas and chromaticisms do not alter the strongly tonal feeling in Stravinsky for the simple reason that neither the one nor the other are taken in a harmonic sense but are used for a real percussive effect or as an adornment beneath which the tonal feeling of the chord pulsates with all its force. An apparently strange case, which can be reduced to simple terms by enharmonic change, is that of the tonal structure of *Noces,* and it may serve as a norm to clarify such polytonal complications as we have already seen in previous chapters. This work, in effect, is composed of four great sections disposed tonally in the following fashion:

1. E minor (predominating tone: E)
2. B-flat major (predominating tones: D, E)
3. A minor and major (predominating tones: A, E)
4. B-flat minor—E minor (predominating tones: D♭, B♮)

Such a distribution, however, is simple, for it consists in the circle: F♭ minor, B♭ major (A) B♭ minor, F♭ minor. The intermediate key of A is a kind of harmonic parenthesis between B-flat major and minor, a procedure dear to Chopin (with whom it derived from the keyboard), as was explained in the early chapters of this book.

To continue further with such analyses does not lie within the scope of this book although they might be developed indefinitely. There are innumerable cases in which the tonality might appear endangered, only to reassert itself triumphantly or to make itself felt from within; these apparent dangers result simply from the habitual procedures of modern technique: appoggiaturas, pedal tones, and changing of notes are the means most favored. Modal color appears now and again in Stravinsky's work, sometimes as a reminiscence from the stock of old popular or religious Russian songs or, again, from an exoticism whose refinement goes far beyond the chromatic coloring of the national masters.

As for the rhythmic nervous system of Stravinsky's music, its powerful pulsation appears with the syncopations of the *Fire Bird* and is present

[5] Or also a chord of the seventh degree above a diminished fifth of the tonic.

throughout his entire production, whether in the gigantic breathing of the *Sacre* or in the minute subtleties of many other works, above all in those of small dimensions. Stravinsky's polyrhythm, when it appears, tends like his polyphony to reduce itself to simple units. Even though it is possible to give to the complex succession of irregular measures the down-beat accents they require, it is more proper on occasion to apply the simplest unit of measure, that of one beat: the *tac, tac, tac* of which Stravinsky himself speaks when, in referring to his music, he compares its regular and incessant pulse to the dripping of water.

In contrast to the absolute, yet tempered, chromaticism of Schönberg, it has been said that that of Wagner is a chromaticized diatonalism. In further contrast to the chromaticism of Schönberg, essentially dissonant and nonfunctional, we find that the music of Stravinsky starts out from a dissonant complex which has no function in itself yet which tends to find a reason for existence in a diatonic and functional melody. The melody serves as a vehicle which carries to the listener the feeling of the nuclear dissonance. The general effect of Stravinsky's music, then, may be expressed in the term, dissonant diatonicism. It is nonfunctional in essence, although it does utilize the tonal and functional melody as a constructive medium.

Rhythm, in classical-romantic music, is a powerful agent at the service of tonality; in Stravinsky, on the other hand, rhythm is an independent value which may or may not collaborate with the tonal function. The rhythmic power absorbs all the elements of classical music and fuses them into a new compound which preserves the essence of each ingredient. Here, Stravinsky's music differs from Viennese atonalism, where rhythm and all the other elements remain dissolved in protoplasmic matter.

All the features that make up European music, from the Italian-French-German baroque to romanticism, impressionism, and expressionism, appear in Stravinsky as "adjectival" elements that qualify the personal essence of his style. The mineral quality of Stravinsky's music, an art made up of metals and crystals in a state of fusion, immediately attracted the attention of critics for its departure from every sentimental suggestion, its nonromantic aspect. It carries to extremes that dryness, objectivity, and sonorous idealization which had been started in Debussy, accentuated in Ravel, and made essential in Schönberg. Stravinsky has gone a step beyond these men, and this at a time when the disciples of Debussy, Ravel, and Schönberg are reverting to romantic expressivism.

Strictly speaking this process of dehumanization, as it has been called, appears in European music immediately after the first great romantic period of Beethoven, Weber, and Schubert. It is plainly visible in Schumann whose Pierrot-Arlequin are the sharp, "metallic" contrast to his Florestan-Eusebius. From that moment, the kingdom of the marionette extends to include the

Russian Pierrot or Petrouchka and Schönberg's mad Pierrot—who still has a heart yet a heart which is an opal or a moonstone—and to the Pulcinella-Polichinelle of Italian tradition, born again in Picasso and Stravinsky. Meanwhile, if Strauss's Don Juan and Zarathustra had not yet broken the bonds of romanticism, Tyll Eulenspiegel took leave of this old world with a cold grimace which was re-echoed in all modern music. This echo reached not only to Salomé, Elektra, and the barbaric wife of Theseus but also to Boris, Mimi, Butterfly, Manon, Igor, and Shéhérazade.

Stravinsky's production may be divided into two periods, separated from each other by a pair of compositions: *Le Sacre du Printemps* (1911-13) and *Les Noces* (1914-17).[6] *Le Sacre* marks the point at which the art of the novice reached a crisis; *Les Noces* is the first fruit of that crisis and looks forward to the entire later creation of its author. Between the two there is no interruption. Both are offspring of the same father and both are linked by the will power of an artist who renounces the glamorous success which his first works achieved for him in order to follow a more ascetic path.

The various unsuccessful orchestrations of *Les Noces* and its final instrumentation for chorus, four pianos, and percussion bear testimony to the inner struggle of Stravinsky, following the exaggerated sensibility of *Le Sacre.* It was obviously impossible for Stravinsky to continue along the road on which *Le Sacre* marked an impassable point. To go back, furthermore, to the type of successful works like the *Fire Bird* or *Petrouchka* would have seemed immoral to an artist of such caliber.

A new art was born after *Le Sacre du Printemps.* In its extreme economy of elements, this new style parallels a change in Diaghilev's criterions. The choreographer, too, turned from the spectacular effects of the grand ballets of the type of *Pavillon d'Armide* and Shéhérazade to a chamber art.

The new art of Stravinsky and of Diaghilev appealed to the narrow circles of an ultracultivated society, but it did not derive from the art of chamber music. One type of chamber performance was that of the literary cabaret, so popular in Germany; from that theater-in-miniature sprang spectacles like the Bat and the Blue Bird. However, the later ballets of Diaghilev and the music of Stravinsky's second period were not merely miniature works; in them the two men were trying to purify their artistic ideals. These ideals may belong to a classic, literary line as in *Pulcinella, Oedipus Rex, Apollon Musagètes* or to a popular line as in *Renard, L'Histoire du Soldat,* and even *Mavra.* In both these groups, Stravinsky brought to bear the same objective intensity which he had exercised in dealing with the primitivistic popularism of *Le Sacre* and *Les Noces.*

In the period prior to *Le Sacre,* Stravinsky rarely turned to works of the

[6] The definitive instrumentation of *Les Noces* dates from 1923, the year of its first performance in Paris.

concerto type. The early works in this category include: the First Symphony; the songs with orchestra entitled "*Le Faune et la bergère*" (in which certain flute passages suggest a reminiscence of Debussy); the *Scherzo fantastique*—in which may be found traces of the Sorcerer's Apprentice; the orchestral piece, Fireworks; various pieces for voice; and an unknown work, *Le Roi des étoiles,* which Stravinsky dedicated to Debussy and in which there seem to be interesting suggestions of the Russian's later art. The *Fire Bird* and *Petrouchka* are the great landmarks in this first stage of Stravinsky's career.

From 1911, the year in which Stravinsky began the composition of *Le Sacre* until 1917, when he finished *Les Noces* (although not with its definitive orchestration), other short works began to appear. They are the seeds of Stravinsky's musical future: the *Trois poésies de la lyrique japonnaise* (1912-13); the three pieces for string quartet (1914); the *Pribautki,* or Pleasant Songs, of the same year; and the "*Berceuses du chat*" (1915-16), in which reminiscences of Stravinsky's childhood are tinged with popular touches which, freeing themselves gradually from their character of sentimental reminiscences, aspire to an increasing objectivity. In *Renard,* which appeared at that time, this objectivity in the treatment of a popular motive is achieved. It is realized in such terms of emotional coldness or dryness that, as if there was need for a declaration of principles, it led Stravinsky to write a piece for pianola (1916); an act incomprehensible to the critics of the day, who were left as open-mouthed as they were when Stravinsky announced his fondness for jazz.

The very notable difference, in *Petrouchka,* between the orchestra and the piano has led some writers to say that Stravinsky intended a kind of dialogue between these two elements or a refutation on the part of the orchestra of the extravagances perpetrated on the piano by the typical virtuoso musician. This is undoubtedly an invention based on the information that Stravinsky first conceived the work as a concerto for piano, which was to have begun with the part now entitled In Petrouchka's House. The projected concerto was destined, so it is said, for the pianist—much esteemed by the French musicians of the *Renouveau*—Ricardo Viñes, who was never a "long-hair."

But, however this may be, the contrast or at least the alternation between two elements—the first, purely mechanical, appropriate to dolls or fantoccini, the other more human, represented by the flesh-and-blood charlatan, maidens, *nounous,* and coachmen—really does exist in *Petrouchka.* It exists also in *Le Sacre,* between the stony venerableness of the ancestors and the youthful flowering of the chosen maiden; again, in *Rossignol,* between the music belonging to the living bird and the mechanical one, between that belonging to the emperor and the fisherman and that of the courtiers, those little mechanical figures with their tiny gestures. It is likewise this desire for contrast which caused the turmoil in Stravinsky's spirit and obliged him to rewrite the instrumentation of *Les Noces* several times until he found a clear method of setting the percussive element off against the wind element. Stravinsky finally assigned the latter factor to the voices; the former to four pianos which, following the method initiated in *Petrouchka,* are conceived in terms of percussion instruments exactly like the other noisy or seminoisy instruments included in the orchestra for this composition.

Such a coexistence of the two elements, human and mechanical, gradually tends to resolve itself into a new order of things as Stravinsky goes on to give ever greater clarity to his thought. The best example of this tendency as an exercise are the Three Pieces for Solo Clarinet, in 1919—the year of Piano Rag-Music and of the "Four Russian Songs" and of *Pulcinella.* It can be understood that, however strong the petrifying and dehumanizing power in Stravinsky's music might be at this time, something would persist of a music such as that of Pergolesi, even though it might undergo in Stravinsky's treatment a kind of distorting transformation. Yet, in spite of all this, neither in this period nor later, has Stravinsky been an unfeeling artist. It is only that he wrote music in an unusual style and likewise intended to express in it the unhackneyed.

Stravinsky's dramaticism expresses itself, one might almost say, in nondramatic or, at least, in nontheatrical, nonconventional terms. But in *Petrouchka* as in *Le Sacre, Les Noces, Renard,* or *L'Histoire du Soldat,* there is a strong and implicit dramatic feeling since all these works present a dramatic situation which the composer must resolve in musical terms. For this resolution he makes appeal to accents as obsolete in the first decades of the twentieth century as were those of the Carnaval of Schumann nearly a hundred years before. Similarly, Stravinsky's commentators point out, not without justification, the feeling of nostalgia, of gentle sadness, of tenderness which, either in effects of harmony or of musical timbres, pervades certain of the works not intended for the stage. This is true even of his pure music, as in some of *Pribautki,* in the Serenade for piano, and in many another passage. Whatever may be the emotional sources of his music, however, Stravinsky considers them a personal matter and leaves them in the subconscious depths of his work, as did Johann Sebastian Bach when writing the forty-eight preludes and fugues of the *Well-Tempered Clavier.*

The quality of self-contained reserve in the painting of dramatic situations reaches its maximum in *Oedipus Rex.* Here, the composer desired to avoid so completely the external aspects of the dramatic—in order that his music might refer exclusively to the inner situations—that he asked his collaborators to present the Latin text in such a way that the words should have value exclusively as sounds, independent of their emotional content. The request might seem to trespass on the dignity of the librettist, whether he be Sophocles, Danielou, or Jean Cocteau. Most intelligently, however, Cocteau considered the thing perfectly natural. After all, what did Offenbach do with personages as respectable as Orpheus, Helena, Odysseus, or the Grand Duchess of Gerolstein? Offenbach, however, was poking fun, and Stravinsky, if he is recalcitrant to dramaticism, is impermeable to sarcasm. The biting irony, the *blague à froid,* the *pince sans rire* of a Ravel are shadings entirely foreign to this profoundly serious composer. There may be a bitter humor, a sarcastic mockery in Tyll Eulenspiegel. In *Petrouchka* there is only drama. The hero's gesture is not a grimace, as with Tyll; it is unmistakably a sob, the sob of a sawdust doll.

The permanent difficulty in the lyric theater comes from the fact that the development of the dramatic action has a tempo different from that of the development of the musical action; each has its own laws, completely distinct from those of the other; each a different psychological action; finally, both actions are different arts, incapable of parallel handling, impossible to synchronize. In the lyric theater of all periods, they have never been more than superimposed one on the other, without ever being fused. When artists have clearly understood this problem, they have adopted one of two courses: they have frankly renounced the idea of fusion, composing pieces in closed forms, as in Italian opera or, instead, they have renounced the representation of action in order to pour drama into the symphony, which was thus converted into the poematic symphony. On occasion, this symphony made use of the voice; it even added a kind of stage representation which is, strictly speaking, unnecessary, as in the case of Wagnerian drama. Arriving at the point of *Rossignol,* Stravinsky noted with amazement that, while music for voice accompanied with instruments seemed as natural as pantomime set to music, the musical drama seemed incongruous. Thereupon, he refused to continue his opera along that line.

Ballet, in itself, is a plastic action in which the dramatic feeling is expressed by means of gestures; its plastic form may be fitted to music just as a glove is fitted to the hand. If the music is rhapsodic, the ballet may admit of an expressive theme but then it loses much of what is proper to it: its form. On the contrary, music with very free motives and with a development as independent as in a symphony may be danced in a more abstract manner and may be represented plastically on the stage with a completeness of form which matches that of the music. This is the basis of the classic ballet but such ballet possesses a conventional, academic technique which converts it into a mannered art. It is only necessary to suppress these mannerisms in order to obtain a new type of ballet, whose music will no longer be ballet music. There results a music of concrete expression with motivic forms capable of being translated by forms of gesture equally susceptible of receiving architectural structure. This is the ballet of Stravinsky, the ballet created under the suggestion of Diaghilev.

Gradually Stravinsky shirks the stage to concentrate his attention on the music. But as his inspiration is predominantly concrete, he has retained the scenic representation (even though in certain cases it has been thought that the real reason was his commitment to Diaghilev rather than an unchangeable, aesthetic conviction), as in *Le Sacre du Printemps* and in *Les Noces*. To what degree is scenic representation inescapable in this work or in *Oedipus,* where the actors and the chorus are admitted to the stage on condition that they do not move? To what extent is there really action in *Renard* and in *L'Histoire du Soldat?* If we try to suppress the action, the content of the music becomes clouded and appears unintelligible. This is no paradox, for the stage, however arbitrary and schematic it may be, corresponds intimately to the integration of the music in Stravinsky's idea and is as necessary as the gods in *Rheingold*.

Nevertheless, this road will lead Stravinsky unfalteringly to works of closed form, to pure music. All his music has within it the capacity to exist independently. The stage setting for *Les Noces* is as unnecessary as it would be in the Symphony of Psalms or in the *Perséphone* of 1933 with its long passages of verse. Indeed, can it not be said that the setting is an encumbrance, included only by arrangement in *Le Baiser de la fée* and in *Jeu de cartes?* This question, naturally, may be answered by an abundance of arguments, pro and con. Nevertheless, it is true that Stravinsky has come to regard abstract construction as the most important aspect of his compositions.

His Symphony in C (1940), with which for the present we may consider the cycle of his activities closed, consists simply in the development of two cells, one melodic,

the other, rhythmic.

The interplay of these units constitutes all the argument of the symphony. The work does nothing more than extend the thematic cells into distinct, yet closely related, motives and arranges these motives into ample phrases. The total architecture, then, resembles more closely the Italian symphony or concerto of the seventeenth century than the type of classical symphony; it is certainly far from the symphony in *Durchführung* style.

In this work, Stravinsky seems to have achieved, in an admirable serenity of thought and technique, a kind of summary of what had always pulsated in his previous works: a maximum simplicity in the motive and in its treatment; a form whose perfect clarity and logic are achieved by an austere elimination of everything but the essential. It might really be said of this Symphony in C Major that it is a skeleton of a symphony, the crystallization of a symphony: transparent, cold, hard as a diamond, aloof, and pure. Beside it, any other music seems stained, poisoned with futile intentions, congested with superfluous material.

In the *Symphony in Three Movements,* completed in 1945, Stravinsky in a sense sums up the preceding stages of his musical career.

Chapter TWENTY-EIGHT

DURING the first two decades of our century, the leading currents in contemporary music in Europe crossed and recrossed each other with significant and reciprocal infiltrations. Nonetheless, these tendencies did not lose their distinctive characteristics; on the contrary, their individual qualities became ever more sharply defined and the personalities of their authors took on increasingly definite outlines.

An examination of certain important dates in this period brings out these relationships: (*a*) Debussy and Ravel, the two leading impressionists, were born thirteen years apart in 1862 and 1875 respectively. (*b*) There is a difference of eleven years between the outstanding figures of Viennese expressionism; Schönberg was born in 1874 and Alban Berg in 1885. Schönberg, with whom expressionism comes into being, was born one year before Ravel, in whom French impressionism reaches its climax and takes a new direction. (*c*) Those musicians who, after starting from a popular-national tradition pass fleetingly through impressionism and expressionism to enter a new phase in which formal construction again sets itself on tonal foundations, follow immediately after Schönberg and Ravel; they announce the new generation which appears in the last decades of the century.

Of these the Spaniard, Manuel de Falla (1876-1946), provides the transition from the French and German masters of the preceding groups to Béla Bartók (1881-1945) and Igor Stravinsky. In Bartók, traditional nationalism, the final vestiges of postromanticism, and suggestions of atonality and polytonality appear transcended in the powerful architectonic meaning of his final period. After these three men follow directly Alfredo Casella (1883-1947), the Italian, and Alban Berg (1885-1935), the Austrian, who provide a connecting link between their predecessors and the youngest group, among whom are Sergei Prokofiev (1891), Darius Milhaud (1892), Eugène Goossens (1893), and Paul Hindemith (1895).

The creative periods of the artists who have led the most recent phases in musical art may be compared as follows: the preparatory period of Schönberg falls prior to the year 1909, which is that of Five Pieces for orchestra, Op. 16; the Three Piano Pieces, Op. 11; and the monodrama, *Erwartung*. The analogous period for Bartók reaches to 1908-10, the years of the First Quartet and

Allegro barbaro. The corresponding period for Stravinsky extends to *Le Sacre,* composed between 1911 and 1913. Falla's preliminary phase under the influence of the French impressionists is marked by the Four Spanish Pieces of 1908. His works of universal significance, such as *El Retablo de Maese Pedro,* do not appear until 1919 (the same year as *Pulcinella*), while the Concerto for Harpsichord and five wind instruments dates from 1923 to 1926, about the period of Stravinsky's Concerto for Piano and Brasses (1923-24). Bartók's Second Sonata for violin and piano, which marks the climax of his atonal stage, belongs to 1923.

Something common to the four artists just mentioned must be pointed out: it is their quality of being less European; there is in them a certain element which acts as a differential principle or germ of fermentation within their traditionally European cultural organism. This something is a deep root that unites them with the man of the Orient—so different from the classic man, the Greco-Roman, from the medieval man, the Germano-Roman, and from the romantic man, the Central European. Stravinsky carries in his veins the blood of Slavic peoples; Schönberg is of Israelite descent; Bartók is Hungarian, that is to say, there are within him certain distant Mongolian strains; and of Falla it has been said that he possesses the leaven of the gypsy race. The reader may take this statement with a grain of salt; yet perhaps it will help him to understand with what a profound difference the sonorous fact resounds in the consciousness of these musicians as compared with a César Franck or a Debussy in France; a Verdi or a Puccini in Italy; a Strauss, a Sibelius, a Schreker or a Pfitzner, in Central or northern Europe.

Bartók came from a region of eastern Europe in which a multitude of languages and races are intermingled. His native town, Nagy Szent Miklós, was at the time of Bartók's birth a Hungarian village. After the changes following the last war it became a part of Rumania. He passed his childhood in different Hungarian localities which afterward became Czechoslovakian, Ruthenian, or Rumanian territory. The popular music of these peoples of such varied stock possesses a strong accent and color and an interesting instrumental tradition; such instruments, in addition to the well-known Hungarian zimbalon or dulcimer, the *duda* (a kind of bag pipe), *tárogató* (a sort of double oboe), *furulya, tilinkó, kanásztülök* (pastoral instruments), and the *tekerö* (hurdy-gurdy). The influence of this popular music, combined with the academic tradition, from Liszt to Brahms and Strauss, dominated Bartók's musical youth. This period came to an abrupt end, however, when the young musician reached the conclusion that neither the a priori form of Brahms nor the poematicism of Strauss could translate his original thought; at the same time, he suspected that what he had taken for traditional, folkloristic music was no more, in many cases, than art music, debased and popularized.

To a certain extent this same doubt concerning the authenticity or the contamination of folkloristic sources caused contemporary Spanish composers to question the traditional in Andalusian music—music which, in Spain, plays the same role as that of Magyar or gypsy music among Hungarians. If a considerable part of Andalusian music is not really popular but derives from the stage or the popular theater not much before the nineteenth century, there does exist within it a portion of gypsy music which is thought to be truly antique and native. It still remains to be determined with scientific accuracy, however, whether the gypsy does not adapt the "native" music to which he sings and dances, exactly as he does his vocabulary.[1]

Bartók, at any rate, along with Zoltán Kodály with whom he shared his ideas and his work, set himself to sift the musical material called Magyar; together, they gathered a rich collection of authentically Hungarian, Rumanian, and Slovakian dance melodies and songs, which Bartók analyzed carefully. The analytical method which he developed is today one of the most solid procedures known to folkloristic research, still so full of lacunae.[2] His study published in English with the title *Hungarian Folk Music* (Oxford, 1931) is, like those of Cecil Sharp, indispensable to the folklorist of today.

The works of Bartók's youth, in which can be found traces of that popular music which had not as yet been sifted, have remained unpublished. Nevertheless, the rhapsody, burlesque, and Suite for Orchestra (Op. 1, 2, and 3), which date up to 1905, give an idea of the nationalism that Bartók, then in his early twenties, was cultivating. The influence of that music on his future was decisive: greater, certainly, than that of the academic or postromantic teachings of Erkel and Thomán in the official Conservatory of Budapest or than the early counsels of Dohnányi. The popular songs with their harmonic suggestions hidden beneath the charm of their modal accents, with their peculiar rhythms, with the capricious, unusual, biting quality of their phrases stimulated Bartók's invention in various directions and remained latent in the depths of his personality and at the basis of his technique. If his most happily realized compositions differ so markedly from those of any other

[1] There is more legend than truth in the origin of the gypsies. The bibliography on the gypsies is very large but the reader may refer to a recent publication, Martin Block, *Mœurs et coutumes des tziganes* (Paris: 1936). C. J. Popp Serboianu, *Les Tziganes* (Paris: 1930) is a more scientific work, dealing with the history, ethnography, and linguistics of the gypsies.

[2] Some of Bartók's folkloristic studies are: *Chansons populaires roumaines du département de Bihar* (Bucharest: Akademia Română, 1913); *150 Transylvanian Folksongs*, with Kodály (Budapest: 1923); *Volkmusik der Rumänen von Marmaros, Sbd. f. vgl. M.-W.* (Munich: 1923), IV; *2600 Slowakische Volkslieder, Slovenska Matica* (Turciansky-Sväty-Martin, 1928-29); *Das ungarische Volkslied* (Berlin: 1925); *Die Volksmusik der Araber von Biskra und Umgebung, Zeitschr. f. M.-W.*, II; *Die Volksmusik der Magyaren und der benachbarten Völker* (Berlin: 1935). Among his collections of songs, taken down by ear or recorded on gramophone records, are included some 2,700 Hungarian songs; 3,500 Rumanian; 200 Arabic; and more are prepared for publication. At the time of his death, Bartók was preparing an important work on Yugoslav folksongs.

composer, past or present, it is due in large part to that leaven of popular inspiration, full of its own peculiar characteristics, which Bartók's talent and keen analytical sense enabled him to use in building a highly original personality.

There are in this personality, nonetheless, features which Bartók has in common with his contemporaries and which prove that he is in tune with the color of the times. The most outstanding characteristics are his rich rhythmic vein, the percussive nature of his harmony, his systematic indifference to considerations of consonance or dissonance in his chordal agglomerations, and his independence in regard to the functional values of these chordal groupings (he was led, for a time, to atonality). Then too his writing, at times cold and crude in its clarity, changes in style according to the instrumental medium; sometimes it is polyphonic—with all the variations in modern technique inherent in this concept of texture—and, at others, it is vertical, as when he writes for the piano. Finally, his so-called insensitiveness is another symptom, no less characteristic of his age. His emotional coldness is combined with an objective severity which, indifferent to the idea of symphonic development, determines a form appropriate to the motive and to the treatment it suggests to a composer unhampered by preconceived ideas. The resulting form is powerfully logical in its freedom, and so robust and satisfying that it is perhaps this which the listener perceives with the greatest conviction on the very first hearing of one of Bartók's works, above all, in the last quartets.

What the youthful generation of his listeners admired [3] in his early work was its strong originality and the exoticism of its rhythmic, modal, and harmonic treatment, and especially of its pianistic color. The works of his first period up to Allegro barbaro were astonishing in the variety of their turns of phrase, their rhythmic ingenuity, and their somewhat mysterious effect of unity. This effect, sometimes natural, sometimes capricious, was always convincing. Whether the construction had a traditional symmetry or a surprising irregularity, it was attractive and supremely pleasing just the same.

Bartók's next works in the orchestral field included those entitled Two Portraits (Op. 5, 1907) and Two Paintings (Op. 10, 1910), along with rhapsodies and suites of Hungarian songs. The public's impression of this music did not seem to measure up to the effect created by Bartók's earlier compositions, probably because of the enormous attraction which Stravinsky's orchestral works offered at that time. The theatrical works of Bartók's second period of production are not so widely known. But a little later, a new Bartók appeared—a personality transformed—in his chamber music, from the first

[3] See Adolfo Salazar, "Kodály, Bartók, and the young Hungarian School" (Madrid: Sociedad Nacional de Música, February, 1917).

sonatas for violin and the first quartets up to the Sixth Quartet (New York, 1941).

Bartók's critics find that his ballet pantomime, the *Wooden Prince* (1914-16), surpasses in scenic interest his first work (the *Castle of Duke Bluebeard,* 1911) in which Bartók, perhaps influenced by the vogue for the theater of Maeterlinck (who had also written an *Ariane et Barbe Bleu,* 1907), seems to follow a system of declamation after the model of *Pelléas.* Less well received than the *Wooden Prince,* the *Marvelous Mandarin* (1926) falls, to a certain extent, within the manner of the expressionist theater and its text is said to be a "horrible mixture of macabre, grotesque, and perverse elements."

Like much of the music of our day, Bartók's chamber music may seem macabre, horrible, and perverse to the uninitiated listener; yet, as happens in the case of all truly great music, the new listener will not delay long in exchanging his first bewilderment for a most intense delight. In the First Quartet, 1912, the emotional unity in which the work is established is brought about by a thematic homogeneity, almost cyclical in character, which does not extend much beyond the conventional. Yet in the Second Quartet (1920) the new Bartók appears, freed from the tyranny of major and minor modes, with a melodism of folkloristic derivation which gives it a strong individuality. Furthermore, this melodism, with its pentatonic phrases and its harmonic-modal material of an intense exotic coloring, brings about a nonfunctional system which, although it may be as free as the twelve-tone technique, does not have the fluctuating vagueness of Viennese atonality chiefly because the energy of its melodic accents absorbs all the dissonance. But in this quartet, as in those which follow it, what is especially remarkable is the astonishingly powerful sonorous effect, the gigantic amplitude an instrumental medium of such restricted proportions is capable of achieving. A great richness of timbres is obtained through skillful treatment of the dissonance, as well as through the elasticity of the writing. The texture is open to the maximum degree yet is capable of shrinking into a single line of scarcely whispered intimacy.

The sensation of tonal equilibrium in these works is as decisive as their architectural and rhythmic security. The more fragile structure of the sonatas for violin and piano maintains itself safely within the expressionist musical throbbing. This music, although it uses the twelve-tone scale and concedes tonal autonomy to each chromatic degree, must still be expressionist in a different way from that of the strict Viennese school. In the sonatas of Bartók, the rhythmic pulse is steely; the dynamic contrasts and the percussive dissonances are shrill. The violin passes from a velvety caress to the disturbing, gypsylike accents on the low string and colors the Schönberglike intonations with an expression, not hushed nor whispered, but lacerating. "Fortresses of sound," Cobbett calls these sonatas in his *Cyclopaedic Survey* and they were, indeed, impregnable fortresses in the year 1929—the date of the encyclopedia. Since then, many seemingly impregnable fortresses have fallen—atonality among them. And, profiting by his past experiences, Bartók again sought a terra firma where he might plant his foot firmly.

One of his later works, Contrasts for piano, violin, and clarinet (1938), is typical of his mature way of thinking and working. (This work, like his brief pages for piano, among the most notable being those which bear the title Microcosmos [1935], plays a role similar to the works of small dimensions in Stravinsky's production, where the procedure appears as limited and clean-cut as in a chemical formula, even though such formulas are as numerous as they are witty.) Contrasts they are: in their sound value (as one speaks of value in painting), and in their density, in the quantity of material enclosed in their timbre, aside from the contrasts of dynamic chiaroscuro. To each instrument there corresponds, as if it were specifically its own, a special thematic idea which is treated simultaneously but with complete independence, leading to harmonic combinations which do not depend on any harmonic center but which have an empirical origin proper to polyphony. The peculiar exoticism predominating in this work may proceed from Hungary (as Stravinsky's jazz derives from an inner popular complex which may be Russian or no matter what), but may also be related to North American music. The American idiom is present in the strong syncopation and in the very special and brilliant clarinet style of Benny Goodman, the virtuoso for whom the work was written. The contrapuntal writing affirms, with its canons of various kinds, the solidity of the structure.

Of the very brief pieces which make up the collection entitled Microcosmos it has been aptly said that they are a kind of *gradus ad Parnassum* of the twentieth century. That is to say, they may serve future generations as a kind of introduction in which perhaps they will see a method of study of each special case in harmony, in the treatment of dissonance, even in the keyboard technique. The procedure is familiar, from Schumann and Chopin to the Études of Debussy and to the Five Fingers pieces of Stravinsky. In contrast to Debussy, who begged his pianist friends not to add a digital hammer to those which the piano already has in its mechanical makeup, Bartók like Stravinsky understood the piano as a percussion instrument which is appropriate above all for nonharmonic but percussive dissonance.

Composers who start from folklore sometimes assert vehemently that their themes or motives have a popular flavor but that they are of their own invention and bear an inalienable copyright. However, it is really a matter of indifference whether the composer produces a melody from his own head or borrows it from a popular melody he hears in the neighborhood. The origin of the motive is without importance; what does matter is what the composer does with the motive. The four notes of the Fifth Symphony are within the reach of anyone: to construct upon them the entire movement of a symphony (perhaps the most powerful symphonic movement in existence) is quite another matter. A motive, popular or not, the invention of the author or a quotation, is no more than a point of departure, a signpost to point the way the composer has chosen to follow; it is a summary indication alluding to the general style in which he has conceived the page, to the predominating color on his palette.

The fact that some of Bartók's motives come from his Hungarian or Transylvanian collections; some of Stravinsky's, from the collection made by Rimsky; that one or another by Falla may or may not be heard at the fountain of Avellano in Granada or in the caves of Albaicín or are to be found in the old Castilian musical treatises like that of Salinas, or in the vihuela collections—all this is a matter of complete indifference so far as the composition itself is concerned. From certain points of view the fact may interest the critic, the analyst of an author's work, the student of a composer's mental processes. Those considerations, however, lie beyond the province of the listener.

The authenticity and origin of a popular motive or melody has intrinsic importance when we are dealing with compositions belonging to the elementary phase of musical nationalism, compositions which consist of little more than settings or arrangements of themes taken from folksong and harmonized according to the musician's taste. Such pieces are often composed without more art than that of stitching together motives to form suites which scarcely merit this classical name, since the true suite consisted of a series of closed forms each of a specific type and appropriately combined one with another. There are also the many rhapsodies from Liszt to Berlioz, some of which possess real merit. Again there are the potpourris, sometimes not without their charm and interest. Yet after the work of Stravinsky, Falla, and Bartók, such music can only be backward-looking.

Today, we see musical nationalism simply as one phase of the transition between the weakening and decline of tonality and of form at the height of the romantic period and their reaffirmation—on a very different plane—within our own time. Perhaps one may discern in this recent stage of musical art a new epoch in which the experiments of the first decades of the twentieth century are finding their realization. If this indeed be true, we are witnessing the birth of a new period which, for its achievement of a form suited to the material employed and for the equilibrium between the content and its vehicle, may be considered as the beginning of a new classicism. For classicism in any artistic age consists in that nicety of balance between the centrifugal forces of the search for expression and the unifying forces of the desire for form. The artistic plane of music based on literal adherence to popular tradition is restricted by its very sources; yet as this literalness is transcended, such music is raised to the lofty heights of individual creation. The process is, then, one in which music advances from the anonymous masses to the unique individuality of genius. The reader has been able to follow this progress throughout this book.

We shall bring this chapter to a close by citing the relevant example of the national music of Spain from Pedrell to Falla. As has already been stated, the meaning of national in Spanish music in our day may be said to date from the activities of the two most significant masters of the nineteenth century: Francisco Asenjo Barbieri and Felipe Pedrell. But strongly accented character and well-defined features have always been the constant qualities of Spanish music closely linked, as it is, to the popular spirit. Spanish musical inspiration has not proceeded, in the majority of cases, from highly cultivated intellects nor refined tastes but from the healthy temperaments of artists of the people. This popular basis and nonintellectual quality may be observed invariably in Spanish music, no matter what the degree of education nor how lofty the elements of style and technique in the individual artist. This explains the absurd phrase, which has become classic, concerning "the Moorish blood" in Victoria, the sixteenth-century Spanish composer. Victoria's contemporaries recognized that beneath his technique, as rich as that of Palestrina, pulsated a singular temperament whose rare capacities for expression were felt to result not from artistic but from racial qualities.

It is, to be sure, true that in the Europe of the Middle Ages and the Renaissance secular music and even much ecclesiastical music inseparably combined popular and artistic elements. Spanish secular polyphonic music is filled with an unmistakable popular flavor but so, too, is this same music in Germany or Italy. In Spain, however, the separation between the art of the court and that of the lower classes of society is more perceptible because the courts, of foreign origin, brought with them modes and manners which had few repercussions among the people. While the court festivals put on the fine airs of France or Italy, Spanish society satisfied its tastes in the smaller types of theater—with music such as the *entremeses, danzas, jácaras, mogigangas,* and *tonadillas*—which filled the seventeenth and eighteenth centuries. Some of these dances came from the salons of the court, others from the towns and the villages for the popular always has the two sources: the town and the country. The popular music of the town has its home on the modest stage of the popular theaters, the market place, the suburban inn, or the little cafés. Popular peasant music accompanies the worker at his tasks, serves youths for their serenades, and is heard in the village square on festival days.

While, as has been pointed out,[4] Pedrell failed to achieve in his historical operas that art based on national folklore to which he and many another postromantic nationalist composer aspired, he laid the foundations of a sound method of musicological and folkloristic research which has been developed and expanded by later Spanish scholars. Furthermore, he made available in various published collections a great number of popular melodies gathered not only from the fields and villages of his native Catalonia but from all Spain. His editions of the works of the great sixteenth-century Spanish polyphonists, as well as his collections of medieval monodic music, serve to reveal the unmistakable popular aroma which pervades all Spanish music from the earliest times.

Thus, while Pedrell's work as a composer had no direct influence on the following generations of Spanish musicians, his teachings and theories became rooted in the consciousness of young composers far more profoundly than their technical learning. It is therefore possible to say, for example, that Albéniz owes nothing to Pedrell in the sense that not a single bar of his music derives from any by the master. Only Manuel de Falla may be said to have been influenced directly, since he found his "road to Damascus" in the lectures given by Pedrell on the history of old Spanish music at the Athenaeum of Madrid, and perceived the significance of one or another page of *Los Pirineos*. Yet, essentially, all contemporary Spanish music, from Albéniz to Ernesto Halffter, is the spiritual consequence of the plane on which Pedrell had placed an art until then lacking in noble models and ideals.

Barbieri's talent as a composer of zarzuelas of real merit led to the development of a popular and authentic lyric theater in the nineteenth and early twentieth centuries. In addition, his investigations in the history of early music for the theater culminated in his edition of that happy discovery, the manuscript of the Cancionero de Palacio, a treasurehouse of Spanish secular polyphonic music of the fifteenth and sixteenth centuries. In his zarzuelas, Barbieri brought about that creation of the Madrilenian style developed so delightfully by Bretón, Chapí, Chueca, the Valverdes, and other lesser talents.

All this music for the lyric theater, although it followed a traditional vein, was strictly speaking a popularized musical idiom of individual creation. There has arisen a misconception regarding the folkloristic basis of much of this music, particularly as regards the development of the Andalusian style. Manuel García, to mention only the best known of these "confectioners" of Andalusian music, simply created musical types in a style which echoed that of his predecessors. The most inadequately studied section of Spanish popular music is the Andalusian; its formation is still not properly

[4] See Chapter VI.

understood. Nevertheless, it can be safely asserted that all of it since the nineteenth century or shortly before is of personal invention, although each individual proceeds along traditional lines. Types of popular Andalusian music are known by the names of their creators who, from the improvised stage in café or inn, continued to create this Andalusian style. Chapí, Jiménez, and others also contributed to its development which persisted even to the opening measures of *La Vida Breve.*

This same style, as we have indicated, was echoed in the Alhambran suites of Bretón and Chapí and in superficial, if agreeable, virtuoso pieces for string quartet or violin by such composers as Sarasate, Monasterio and Arbós. Piano music in the same vein formed the basis for the works of Isaac Albéniz (1860-1909) and Enrique Granados (1867-1916). Neither composer, unless by exception or as a quotation, utilized the popular document in its original form. As Albéniz advances in his career, his invention of a Spanish idiom which seeks to entwine itself in the great popular tradition forcibly dominates the original source melody, even though at times, as in Joaquín Turina and in Falla too, the original is perceptible.

As I have pointed out in the book entitled *La Música Contemporánea en España,* "The exploitation of character, of the typical feature, in an anecdotal sense, in Albéniz, becomes in Falla an effort to evoke the setting. It is no longer, then, the picturesque; it is the sonorous atmosphere which he seeks. An analogous attempt finds superb realization in the music of Claude Debussy. Falla meditated it at length, as his erasures testify. The commonplace of local color disappears to give way to the suggestion produced by greatly simplified means, by what might be called the seeds of style, by brief, allusive details of popular song subjected to a harmonic treatment which will adequately contribute to their suggestion. Such a procedure presents a triple advantage: [*a*] the indigenous element remains reduced to its vital nucleus which will have undergone development by passing through the composer's personality, instead of the old system in which the composer took it already made as a cook takes his vegetables; [*b*] in the second place, the poetic plane on which the composer places himself, more withdrawn from the direct impression, is more intense, possesses a greater evocative capacity while it requires a more intense concentration because it no longer works by means of presentations but by reflections; [*c*] in the third place, the composer, free of formulas, must create his own manner of expression every moment, something, naturally, highly desirable to the artist who lives exclusively for his creation, for what is authentically his." [5]

[5] In *La Música Contemporánea en España* the history of contemporary Spanish music is set forth in detail. Let me simply remark here that the most notable composers of the new generation are: Roberto Gerhard, 1896; Salvador Bacarisse, 1898; Rodolfo Halffter, 1900; Julián Bautista, F. Remacha, 1901; Joaquín Rodrigo, 1904; Ernesto Halffter, 1905; Gustavo Pittaluga, 1906.

Ernesto Halffter, who married the Portuguese pianist, Alicia de Cámara Santos, has resided

The three stages into which national music is divided, from its elementary exploitation of the folkloristic document until that of the untrammeled eloquence of a language with national elements yet inalienably the composer's, stand thus defined for the reader with sufficient clarity, I believe. But these three stages, which are to be found successively in those countries which discovered and formulated musical nationalism—Russia, Bohemia and the Scandinavian countries—*coexist* at the present moment in others which have founded their nationalist aesthetics somewhat forcedly and artificially, sometimes more from political feeiing than from a truly aesthetic one, more as a program than from inner necessity.

This happens especially in the youthful countries of America who think to find in this imitation an emancipation from their previous imitations. Yet an art may be just as academic and superficial when it copies a peasant man surrounded by his fruits as when it copies the Venus of Milo. The nationalism which believes it emancipates itself from the art of the conservatory because it substitutes folklore for the waltzes and redowas of the nineteenth century suffers from an ingenuous mistake. It is not the character of the model that creates a work of art but the artist's purpose and the adequate realization of that purpose. Those nationalist composers who have sought values of greater transcendence have created an art which, deeply rooted in their native tradition, is nonetheless universal.

---

for many years in Portugal. His most recent work is *Rapsodia Portuguesa* (1940-41) for orchestra and piano solo.

The most important Portuguese composer of the present generation is Luiz de Freitas Branco (1890), a composer who combines popular with classical elements; a notable pianist, he is director of the Conservatory of Lisbon. Rui Coelho (1891) has been one of the most ardent champions of modern music. Federico de Freitas (1902) seems to find inspiration, by preference, in French impressionism.

Chapter
TWENTY-NINE

IN THE young countries of America the music of our time reflects many of the trends we have traced in the course of this book. Chief among them, however, appears musical nationalism in its various forms. This is perhaps only natural in view of a certain self-consciousness always inseparable from youthfulness. Examples of the various stages of musical nationalism exist side by side in these countries; fortunately, however, among the considerable number of old-fashioned nationalist musicians appear exceptional figures who have transcended its more rudimentary phases and attained a true universality. The persistence of musical nationalism in its more obvious aspects results in part from the fact that nationalist doctrines in music were slow to reach this continent. This is especially true in Hispanic America where fundamental works such as those of Smetana or the *Boris* of Mussorgsky or the operas of Tchaikovsky were largely unknown. On the other hand, in the United States the influence of the German school, which remained aloof from the nationalist movement, predominated through a large part of the later nineteenth century and, in consequence, an interest in popular or musical folklore material has been of slow growth.

The culture of all the countries of the Americas varies so widely in origin, in character, and in degree of development that the critical discernment necessary to establish aesthetic values has often been slow of achievement. These values are, furthermore, blurred by the interpretation of nationalism or of native music. What is termed native refers in point of fact to importations from the Congo, Sudan, or Malabar. And in these countries, the fascination of the exotic has become confused with popular traditional roots. The "discovery" of jazz (kindred varieties of which existed in Europe long before Ernest Ansermet brought the first Negro orchestras to Europe from the United States) overshadowed for a moment the genuinely native music of the United States. The most serious composers, however, have long since left behind such vulgar sensationalism and have been able to bring the deepest and most truly American accents to their music; in so doing, they have passed beyond the first rudimentary stage of musical nationalism. I shall try to sketch, from this point of view and with especial emphasis on the essential figures, contemporary music in America and that of the United States in first place.

Yet the task is fraught with dangers. The author, who is not an American and who has resided in this country for only brief periods, moves dangerously between the Scylla and Charybdis of ignorance and pedantry. In so perilous an undertaking, it is obvious that the writer's only object is to present the picture already familiar to the reader from the point of view, not without its interest, perhaps, of the European looking at American music. Much of this music is known to him only through the reading of scores or through gramophone recordings. It is therefore not the writer's pretension to evaluate each one of the works discussed but rather to place the most significant composers and those who seem best to exemplify the main trends in the music of the new continent. This music is rich in names and works yet, on the other hand, how rich is it in definite achievement?

Historians of American music such as John Tasker Howard or W. S. B. Mathews,[1] begin their account with the early years of the seventeenth century, with the pilgrims and puritanism: the *Whole Booke of Psalms* and the hymns attributed to Conrad Beissel. Before the Pilgrims set foot on the soil of New England, however, there already existed a kind of culture in the territory destined to become the United States, and music was a part of it. In considering the various trends in the development of American music today, this fact must not be forgotten. During many decades, music in the United States was subject to a variety of influences from many sources.

Only in recent times, when the study of folklore came to be treated as a field of scientific research, did this aboriginal musical culture come to be appreciated in its own right. Then, some composers, preoccupied with the European notion of nationalism in art, came to see that this indigenous music might be utilized as a potent aid in the task of Americanizing their art. There appeared the desire to supplant the title Music in America with American Music. Yet, to ask what is American music is like asking what is American? One feels what is American better than one can describe it. And it is better so, for the stamp of an American formula would be intolerable. So it seemed to Daniel Gregory Mason who, some years ago, in the *Dilemma of American Music*,[2] cried out with excellent judgment against that standardization which the use of any type of nationalism as an aesthetic criterion may bring about. Nevertheless, his conclusion that "nationalism is excellent as an ingredient but disastrous as a dogma" may not appear definitive.

[1] John Tasker Howard, *Our American Music* (New York: 1939). W. S. B. Mathews, *A Hundred Years of Music in America* (Chicago: 1889).

[2] Daniel Gregory Mason, the *Dilemma of American Music* (New York: 1928).

It is not with ingredients that we are dealing but with more essential things. Those American composers who have passed beyond the initial stages of nationalism show that one can be American while composing in various European styles, utilizing Indian or Mexican themes, or writing courantes or passacaglias, and that, on the contrary, one may utilize jazz as an ingredient and compose music in a French idiom in imitation of Stravinsky.

It is all a question of feeling. But in order to bring one's feeling to realization a technique is necessary. To dominate one's technique, to use it as a means of translating directly an authentic feeling, has been the work of generations of American musicians, from the agreeable picturesqueness of MacDowell to the aggressive picturesqueness of Copland. As in all art, the successive phases of this stage of culture have come to coexist and mingle with each other. Thus it requires discernment and a critical judgment to discover in the present movement in America what are the main currents: the old, the new, the degenerate and the obsolete, and the seeds of future growth.

Contemporary American music divides itself into three principal phases. (*a*) The traditionalists: musicians who find that the aesthetics and the technique inherited from their predecessors suffice them. (*b*) The indigenists: those who seek local color in exotic music to be found within the confines of the country, whether the native Indian or the Negroid of more recent importation. (*c*) The independents: those whose first preoccupation it is to be a musician without ceasing, on that account, to be American. Thus, if it suits their purposes, they utilize native folklore or Negro jazz, baroque classicism or French impressionism, the sonata or the exotic dance, or else they make daring excursions into experimental fields.

Sometimes those are more American who do not consciously strive to be (that is, who do not adopt Americanism as their creed) than those who wish to be so at all costs. I believe Mason is right in saying: "When MacDowell meets and assimilates German romanticism and Loeffler meets and assimilates French impressionism, when Powell meets and assimilates Anglo-American folksong, let none cavil and define, let us rather rejoice and applaud. Were a single one of them to be forcibly Americanized, music in America would be the poorer." And he adds, perhaps not with the approval of all American musicians, "Music in America is the richer for each and all of them and music in America is a thing far more worth working for than American music." Yet the two things are not incompatible; musicians may work for the one without losing sight of the other. There is no dilemma such as Mason paints. Quite the contrary, the musician must make a single objective out of the two. If an authentically American feeling exists, unity will be achieved and the multitudinous variations in American music will only serve to reaffirm American unity. Have we already reached this moment?

The musical interests of Daniel Gregory Mason as composer, teacher, and critic were the natural result of the traditions of a distinguished musical family.[3] Within the lifetimes of his grandfather, Lowell Mason, and his uncle, William L. Mason, music in the United States passed through that first phase which led to the intense development we are witnessing today. Lowell Mason, who was born in the last decade of the eighteenth century and lived well on into the nineteenth, knew as a child only the sentimental ballads, the revolutionary marching songs or the ingenuous airs of a Hopkinson, flying sparks which foretold the awakening of national consciousness. In his youth a more serious art reached him from the Continent, redolent of an early romanticism, to amplify the efforts of those first native composers, those classics of music in the United States.

Toward the middle of the century, two dates of capital importance, one in Europe, the other in the United States, found Lowell Mason in his maturity. The first, 1848, was the year of the revolutions in Europe which poured into America a large number of individuals who brought with them seeds of artistic culture of many kinds. This was the time when the School of Leipzig, presided over by the influence of Mendelssohn and Schumann and the brilliance of Weimar, concentrated in the figure of Liszt, were illuminating all Europe from St. Petersburg to London. Across the Atlantic, America could not escape this influence.

Europe came to America, but America also went to Europe. William Lowell Mason went to Weimar. So did others of his own generation and of the following from John Knowles Paine, born in 1839 at the height of the romantic period, to MacDowell and H. W. Parker, born in the sixth decade of the century. MacDowell and William Mason both died in 1908. Parker died a decade later. These, with a few more, such as George W. Chadwick (1854), are the most distinguished personalities in a century of music which, at its close, saw the coming of age of American music. Let the reader recall what Mendelssohn and Brahms were to Victorian England. It has been said that MacDowell is the parallel of Grieg in this country; the comparison may be completed by saying that Parker stands in the role of Franck. The comparison, for what it is worth, serves to show that nineteenth-century German music fed musical roots in America, as elsewhere, but that the fruits of the new harvest were none the less native to American soil.

What 1848 was for Europe, the year 1864 was for the United States: the moment of crisis and maturity, of the blossoming of national consciousness. The earlier part of the century is filled with minor figures marked by unmistakably American characteristics. To this period belong the native, untutored melodic genius of Stephen C. Foster (1826-64) and the Creole ex-

[3] D. G. Mason was the pupil of Paine and Chadwick and later studied with Vincent d'Indy.

oticism of Louis Moreau Gottschalk (1829-69). The second half of the century finds the times and the men in their maturity. J. K. Paine, Chadwick, and Parker signify a substantial forward step. MacDowell is the culmination, firmly rounded as to style and refined in taste.[4] Many of these musicians were natives of, or made their home in, the New England of the Pilgrim Fathers. The Boston group served appropriately as a beacon light during the second half of the century; characteristically, they turned to Europe for their training and for the formation of their taste. Chadwick and Parker went to Leipzig and Munich as William Mason had gone to Weimar.

Arthur William Foote (1853-1937), one of the most outstanding of the group, did not leave the country, yet, together with Paine, he is one of the first to attune his muse to the inspiration of Brahms, the new prophet who had a most enthusiastic disciple in Arthur B. Whiting (1861-1936) of Cambridge. The music of Frederick S. Converse (born in Newton in 1871), who studied with Chadwick and completed his studies in Munich, is nevertheless touched with a French aroma. The only woman in the group, Mrs. H. H. A. Beach (1867-1944) who said that she wished first to be a composer and second to be an American composer, is among the first in America to echo in her music traditional themes out of the past; she has responded especially to Celtic melody.

In the somewhat aloof and solitary figure of Charles Martin Loeffler (born in Alsace, 1861, died in Medfield, Mass., 1935) appeared perhaps the most distinguished musical figure of his generation in the United States. His response to traditions and influences of a quite different kind from those of his contemporaries resulted from the varied and fruitful musical experiences of the first twenty years of his life when he lived in Russia and in France. Almost alone among musicians of his generation in this country he responded to the new subtleties of French postromanticism and impressionism, although evolving a definite personal style marked by extreme finish and brilliance in technique. These influences are reflected in his many songs and in his frequently heard Pagan Poem (1909) for piano and orchestra. The Music for Four String Instruments (1923) and *Canticum Fratris Solis* (1925) for solo voice and chamber orchestra are skillfully wrought outgrowths of his profound knowledge of Gregorian music and his feeling for the medieval. Again, his very active musical interests led him to use jazz rhythm in Clowns (1928) and in the third movement of his Partita (1930) for violin and piano.

Two somewhat younger composers who, after sound training in traditional technique at Harvard University, absorbed contemporary French manners of writing during study in Europe, are John Alden Carpenter (1876) of

[4] Lawrence Gilman said that in the piano music of the nineteenth century only the sonatas of MacDowell are to be compared with those of Beethoven for passion, dignity, and breadth of style.

Chicago and Edward B. Hill (1872) of Cambridge, Massachusetts. Carpenter has exploited most successfully his dramatic and pictorial sense in his compositions for ballet, *Birthday of the Infanta* (1919) and *Krazy Kat* (1921), and his frequently performed *Skyscrapers* (1926). On the other hand, E. B. Hill has confined himself almost entirely to composition for orchestra and chamber ensembles in the abstract forms. After his earlier tone poems, of which the best known is Lilacs (1927), he has continued to compose symphonic pieces and compositions for various combinations of chamber instruments, all notable for meticulous workmanship; although conservative in technique, he has a well-defined personal style.

The importance of influences from Europe, particularly Germany, began to find a counterweight in an interest in folklore material with the newfound sense of nationalism following the Civil War. The rich vein of Negro folk music came to be appreciated and exploited for the first time. The first musicians to cultivate Negro music seriously were not Negroes. Unfortunately, those to whom such folk material belongs by right of race have ordinarily lacked the requisite technique to raise their music to the category of serious art. Although an Indian or a Negro may use his own folklore with an authenticity unmatched by a European or a Euro-American composer, the simple use of Indian themes by an Indian or Negro themes by a Negro remains no more than a quotation of native folk materials unless artistic purpose and technique are present. At the present time, however, the Negro composer, William Grant Still (1895), has firmly established his reputation as a composer of genuine originality in the treatment of his material, culminating in his recent cantata, "And They Lynched Him on a Tree" (1940), and his piece for orchestra, Memorial to Colored Soldiers Who Died for Democracy (1944).

Henry F. Gilbert (1868-1928) was one of the first serious American composers who felt the fascination of Negro music and treated it with great originality in an effort to create American music. Two decades later John Powell, born in Virginia in 1882 and a firm and consistent advocate of the Anglo-Saxon tradition as fundamental to an American musical idiom, could affirm that Negro music is as national an element in the United States as the Anglo-Saxon. The difference between the composer who reproduces a certain species of folk music, such as that of the Negro, and the composer who creates a new music from such material may be easily appreciated, I believe, in comparing the compositions of Henry Thacker Burleigh (1866), a pioneer Negro composer, and those of David W. F. Guion (1895), a Texan who learned his technique in Europe but who realized that this music, like that of the cowboys in which he was also deeply interested, required a treatment that could not be learned at the Conservatory of Vienna.

Arthur Farwell (1872) of Minnesota, one of the early composers to emphasize the importance of the cultivation of native materials in American music, was among the first to interest himself in Indian music, together with Harvey Worthington Loomis (1865-1930) and Charles Sanford Skilton (1865). Somewhat younger composers who followed this same interest are Arthur Nevin (1871), who studied the music of the Blackfeet Indians, and Thurlow Lieurance (1878), who has devoted many years to the study and recording of Indian music.

Charles Wakefield Cadman, born in Pennsylvania in 1881, has made abundant use of Indian and other folk material. In his American Suite for string orchestra (published in 1938) he uses genuine themes of the Omaha Indians (in the first movement), Negro themes of South Carolina (in the second), and the charming old American fiddler tunes in Old Fiddler, with which the suite ends. Cadman restricts himself to "painting" anecdotic pictures or simply transcribes aboriginal songs and harmonizes them tastefully and discreetly, according to his understanding of them.

The music of the Indians has also attracted the versatile Frederick Jacobi (1891). In his youthful years, when he had acquired important musical experience, he gathered songs of the Pueblos of Arizona and New Mexico. These are reflected in such compositions as the String Quartet based on Indian themes (1924) and Indian Dances (1928). It would appear, up to the present at any rate, that the effort to use Indian material has not been very rewarding. For the most part it has been exploited by composers writing in the harmonic idiom of the nineteenth century and, so treated, has lost its true character. Despite the large collections of the original music made by folklorists in recent years, few of the younger composers with the exception of Jacobi and Henry Cowell in his Amerind Suite (1940) seem to have been attracted to its possibilities. There have been no works comparable to the fine handling of similar material by Carlos Chávez in Mexico.

It is to the development of new criteria as regards musical education that the United States owes in large measure the rich flowering of composers beginning with the generation born in the last decade of the nineteenth century. The predominance of German musical influences which shaped the taste and style of nineteenth-century American composers was supplanted by training of a quite different kind for the generation of 1890 to 1900 under such teachers as Vincent d'Indy, Nadia Boulanger, and Ernest Bloch. For this generation as well as for the succeeding one, opportunities to study under the leaders of the new Viennese school likewise proved very attractive. These new directions in training were matched by an eager interest in all the new trends in music characteristic of the early years of this century. The facile adoption of contemporary techniques and a tendency toward eclecticism in aesthetic attitudes which mark this generation of American composers explain the varied character of their inspiration and the wide range of stylistic treatment and technique of their work.

Jacobi belongs to this group stirred by the new influences at work in Europe; he is furthermore one of the American composers well known in European circles. This contact he never relinquished after his student days in Berlin. He has felt aesthetic preferences of various kinds. Sometimes it is the synagogue which inspires him or the vague Assyria of old in whose vast deserts he hears an inspired voice (the Assyrian Prayers, 1923; the "Poet in the Desert," 1925; "Three Excerpts from the Prophet Nehemiah," 1945). Much of his recent music has been in the conventional forms for orchestra (Concerto for Violoncello and Orchestra, 1936-37; Ave Rota, three pieces in multiple style for small orchestra, 1939; Ode for Orchestra, 1945) or chamber ensembles (Second Quartet, 1933 and Fantasy for Viola and Piano). It would be difficult to maintain that Jacobi's orchestral technique has kept pace with the distances traversed by his imagination.

The untimely death of Charles Tomlinson Griffes (1884-1920) brought to an end the work of an early and talented American explorer in impressionist harmonies. His symphonic poem, the Pleasure Dome of Kubla Khan (1919), and the Poem for flute and orchestra (1922) are the most important and fully developed examples of his effective harmonies and colorful orchestration. His piano pieces, notably the Roman Sketches, and his songs are still frequently performed.

Emerson Whithorne's (1884) romantic turn of mind found musical expression in the impressionist vein which his characteristic use of shifting and syncopated rhythmic patterns has impressed with a personal stamp. These qualities are notable in the Poem for piano and orchestra (1927), in the orchestral works, Fata Morgana (1928), Moon Trail (1933), and Sierra Morena (1938). His powers of musical description are given full play in the orchestral suite, New York Days and Nights, while his interest in Negro music has led to one of his best effects in the canticles of the Grim Troubadour (1927) for string quartet and baritone, and in settings of other texts of the Negro poet, Countee Cullen.

Marion Bauer (1887) likewise stems from French impressionism, but her concept of "writing" and her harmonic knowledge is as efficacious as it is thoughtful. These qualities, worked with a sure hand, are notably evident in her *Fantasia quasi una Sonata* for violin and piano (1928).

It is, however, in a highly original and keenly perceptive personality such as that of Virgil Thomson (1896) that the influence of Europe's ancient musical traditions and culture acquire new significance and bear new fruits in the American environment. Thomson's appreciation of French and Italian seventeenth- and eighteenth-century forms is transmuted into a personal style in such compositions as the *Sonata da Chiesa* (1926) scored for clarinet, trumpet, French horn, trombone, and viola, in his Passacaglia (1922) for organ and in various choral works, including the two *"Missa Brevis"* (1924 and 1934), the "Medea Choruses" (1934), and numerous songs. He learned to love the classic style in the Paris of Erik Satie and so his manner of focusing the neoclassic is strongly ironic in its desire to strip music of overemphasis and severity, to make it fresh, charming, and light, very much in the French postwar (World War I) spirit—the weightless spirit of *Les Six,* as in his Violin Sonata (1931), his two string quartets (1931 and 1932), and the many characteristic portraits (Five Portraits for quartet of clarinets, 1929; Seven Portraits for violin alone, 1928; Four Portraits for violin and piano, 1930, and Seventy-five Portraits for piano 1928-40); to these may be added, in more serious vein, another portrait for orchestra and tenor, the *Oraison Funèbre* (1930) on Bossuet's celebrated funeral oration for the Princess Marie-Henriette.

Yet in this cultivation of the neoclassic, Thomson has in no way relinquished his personality as a twentieth-century American as his Symphony on a Hymn Tune (written between 1926 and 1927 and revised in 1944) testifies. His collaboration with Gertrude Stein resulted in what may be described as the first original American opera, *Four Saints in Three Acts* (1928). Here his study of French classical methods of handling the matter of prosody led him to set Miss Stein's free rhythms with a fine musical adjustment to the richness and variety of the English language. The success which this opera immediately achieved through its perfect sense of theater and its spontaneity led to other compositions for the stage and films. There was incidental music for numerous plays, the ballet music, *Filling Station* (1937), and the music for the films: the Plough that Broke the Plains (1936), the River (1937), and Spanish Earth (1937), in collaboration with Marc Blitzstein. More recently Thomson has written music for Euripides' the *Trojan Women* (1940) for radio performance, and music for Sophocles' *Oedipus Tyrannus* (in Greek) for men's voices, wind instruments, and percussion (1941). His critical writing, sparkling with wit, in which great truths are often expressed in little phrases, makes Virgil Thomson, writer and critic, the equal of Virgil Thomson, composer.

The extension of the great musical tradition of Europe in the more general and universal sense and its development in the hands of composers of strong individuality and surely developed technical equipment may be observed in the works of Roger Sessions (1896) and Walter Piston (1894). The work of both is highly intellectual and excludes any admixture of extramusical qualities. Composers with this serious approach to their art understand the profound need for a technique which will correspond to the exigencies of thought and style; they do not try to dissimulate their conviction nor to adopt Americanizing titles which sometimes have a certain air of camouflage.

Sessions' compositions show the development of a greatly broadened tonal system. Structurally they often display a complexity which is nonetheless surely controlled and fundamentally clear. All of his work is in the abstract forms with the exception of incidental music for the *Black Maskers* of Andreyev (1933). He has among other works three symphonies, a very interesting Quintet for Violin and Strings (1935), and a String Quartet in E Minor (1936) which effectively demonstrates his extension of tonality and his ingenious contrapuntal treatment never obscuring the musical flow.[5] More recently have been heard two characteristic pieces for piano, Pages from a Musical Diary (1940). His relatively small output suggests the great thought and care expended on his compositions.

Walter Piston has likewise restricted his compositions almost exclusively to the abstract forms. He has written a considerable amount of chamber music: two string quartets (1933 and 1935), a Trio for Violin, Violoncello, and Piano (1935), as well as suites and sonatas for other combinations of instruments. His fine Sonata for Violin and Piano (1939) is a recent summation of his aesthetic and technical criteria in its directness and intensity of expression presented with the ease and grace of flawless technique. Here, in addition to the characteristic contrapuntal weaving, is a harmonic breadth which adds a new dramatic quality to his style.

This broadening of technical resources to intensify the expression finds its true scope in his orchestral writing, as in the Second Symphony (1945). This is the most recent of numerous works for orchestra which include a Concertino for Piano and Chamber Orchestra (1937), a Suite (1929), and Concerto for Orchestra (1933). All his writing shows an elegance and wit which is highly personal but the gaiety, the rhythmic and melodic charm of his single excursion into ballet music, the *Incredible Flutist* (1939), comes as a pleasant surprise in the work of this serious composer. Piston's recent treatise *Harmony* demonstrates the soundness of his artistic criteria and of his purpose both as composer and teacher.

Another composer who belongs to the group of Americans interested in music for its own sake and but little concerned with literary or nationalistic preoccupations is Quincy Porter (1897). He has devoted himself largely to the composition of chamber music, of which the six string quartets (1923-36) form the most important part. He has gradually left behind earlier French influences to develop a pleasant and consistent personal style. He has also written shorter pieces for orchestra and incidental music to "Sweeney Agonistes" (1933) of T. S. Eliot and music for Shakespeare's *Anthony and Cleopatra* (1935).

[5] See the interesting article on this quartet by Edward T. Cone in *Modern Music* (March-April, 1941), XVIII, no. 3, 159.

Bernard Rogers (1893) studied with Percy Goetschius, Ernest Bloch, and Nadia Boulanger; he reflects the influence of French impressionism and the exoticism of the Debussy-Ravel-Schmitt-Roussel stage in his early works such as *Fuji in the Sunset Glow* (1927). New aspects in the use of sonorities may be seen in "Two American Frescoes" (1931) and the "Three Eastern Dances" (1928), and a new subtlety in his "Characters from Hans Andersen" (1944). His orchestral works show an interest in rhythmic experiments and a consequent emphasis on the balance in the percussion section. This interest in rhythmic complexities is linked with an unusual ability as an orchestrator (Third Symphony, 1936; The Dance of Salome, 1939; The Plains: Three Landscapes, 1940). Some of Rogers' most important writing, however, has been in the field of choral composition. His works in this medium have recently culminated in the powerful cantata, "The Passion" (1941-42), which is dramatic yet deeply felt religious music.

Experiments in rhythms and sonorities quite naturally go hand in hand. The experiments in the latter direction, particularly, made by the Frenchman, Edgar Varèse (1885), who came to the United States in 1919, have influenced some of the younger American experimentalists. In his youth, Varèse carried on his musical studies under Roussel and d'Indy simultaneously with the study of mathematics and sciences in the École Polytechnique and, since he came to America, has dedicated himself to glorifying in music the modern triumphs of pure science.

After having new musical instruments constructed capable of expressing the new spirit of the age, he astonished the layman by singing of such abstract entities as Integrals, Hyperprism, Ionization (1931), and Density 21.5 (1936) which are somewhat abstruse to those of us who have not studied in polytechnical schools. Indeed, Varèse himself entitles one of his compositions Arcana (Mysteries). Before this he had written *Amériques* and Equatorial for organ, percussion, trumpets, trombones, Thereminvox, bass-baritone voice (1937). It is curious that the orchestral poem entitled Metal (1932) is written only for orchestra and soprano voice and that, while Density 21.5 is expressed by a solo flute, Ionization required no less than thirteen percussion instruments to the exclusion of any other kind. This falls within the arcana of the spirit of a new age and we have no reason to question it. The most recent works of Varèse, among them his First Symphony with solos and chorus romantically entitled *Espace,* are dated 1937.

The study of jazz in its sonorous aspects (its aesthetic aspects, too) undoubtedly awakens stimuli in the composer, for example for its combinations of time values and its superpositions of rhythms on a constant monorhythmic base with its one beat which permits, obviously, of every variety of superimposed polyrhythms. Nonetheless such combinations do not necessarily mean richness of rhythm, for musical rhythm has an organic character and is not simply mechanical. It is not obtained by dislocations of the components of the measure nor is it the arithmetical sum of groups of ten sixteenth notes against those of seventeen, or of twelve eighth notes against eight eighth notes or five quarter notes or triplets of quarters and eighths as in one example in Charles E. Ives.[6] Such combinations, like the dislocations of a normal measure in irregular groupings, produce simply an effect of rubato, not really a polyrhythm; yet these attempts, very characteristic of American composers, have an interest in themselves and in their practical application. European composers have made such experiments both with rhythms, often of an exotic character, and with microtonic intervals.

Charles Ives (1874) is justly considered a pioneer in similar investigations in America. He was born in Connecticut, the son of local musicians who had made experiments in the acoustical aspects of music. Ives, from his childhood, was attracted by the off-rhythms and the off-key character of the music of popular bands and of church hymns played on a harmonium not very well tuned. Later he thought of the possibility of utilizing artistically these peculiarities of popular music and, indeed, they provided the motive for various compositions which came into being during the second decade of the century. In them Ives showed a desire for original innovations which give him, to my mind, a certain air of an experimentalist not always successful.

Nevertheless, Ives has in Henry Cowell an enthusiastic commentator who does him full justice. On a foundation of the traditional music of New England, Ives early began his tonal experiments, not by way of purely intellectual speculation but with the object of accentuating the expressive quality of his art and of his own ideas as a composer. The dynamics of the piece may change according to the feeling of the interpreter while its agogic accents may suggest to him different modes of expression as it undergoes temperamental variations. This possibility of interpretation at every moment is typical of jazz. But in point of fact it is a principle which has always existed in the music of all countries at all times, and orchestral directors and performers are very familiar with it. The freedom in performance leads to the rubato; this, in turn, to time combinations which European composers prefer not to write or which they suggest with some brief indications of shading and accent. Others follow the path of microtonic intonations.

Ives was one of the first Americans to feel the attraction for quarter tones and smaller intervals, which (as in the case of complex rhythms) are often *superimposed* on clear tonal bases. Freedom in the use of dissonance derives from experiments in the field of texture as dissonant counterpoint. Cowell says that, while Schönberg began to write in his dissonant style in 1909, the first complete works of Ives were heard publicly beginning in 1910 at a period when there was no knowledge in America of Schönberg's experiments.

[6] See Ch. xx in Henry Cowell, *American Composers on American Music* (1933).

Ives's first essays on high chordal agglomerations, atonal passages, harmonic and rhythmic combinations, melodic motives with wide leaps, jazz rhythms and other, at that time, heterodox formulas, date from the period between 1895 and 1907 after which there followed a space of nearly ten years in which his technical ideas were maturing. The general musical significance of Ives's music, however, has less interest or novelty than his experiments with musical material. His works (which include four symphonies, four sonatas for violin and piano, various choral, vocal, chamber, and orchestral compositions) are, for this reason, little played. Except for the Fourth Symphony (1910-20), Three Places in New England, and Concord, Mass. (1911-15), his works remain unpublished. Ives has been called "the oldest of the ultramoderns" and the founder of truly American music. He is therefore often considered the pioneer composer who has indicated the road toward the development of the American musical idiom. He has made great use of American folk and popular songs for the thematic material of his symphonies and other works. The first performance in its entirety of his Second Sonata (1909-11) for piano, the Concord, in 1939, first brought his music to the attention of the general public.

Henry Cowell stands out, at least speculatively, above the rest of those composers most strongly stimulated by the vision of progress. The realm in which Cowell carries out his new concepts in the materials of harmony is, simply, ruled paper and the keyboard of his piano. If Ives thought it necessary to strike a whole group of keys by means of a foot rule, Cowell is content to use the forearm for this purpose, a procedure which, like that of Ives, harmony teachers resolved readily by saying that it was a question of a chord of the dominant with appoggiaturas. The curious thing is that Cowell, who needs to fill out his chordal sensation with all these sounds, scorns the suggestion of ninths and elevenths and proceeds by mass duplications in works like his Shipshape Overture. He also scorns the possibility of developing short phrases or motives, in which he wishes to preserve always a perfectly clear tonal atmosphere. The overture, which appeared in 1941, may perhaps indicate a return to safe waters.

Cowell, in spite of all, does not require inner complications in his music and those which he uses, despite his *New Musical Resources,* are rather complications by accumulation than the consequence of profound aesthetic problems. A work in which this agglomerated criterion may be clearly appreciated in a very amusing way is his Amerind Suite, published in 1939. It consists of three small fragments for piano, each of which appears written in various ways. That is to say, manner (1) presents the melody in simple notes (A, E, D, etc.). Manner (2) adds for each note two more notes in such a way that instead of A we have D-E-A, instead of E we have A-D-E. In manner (3) the original A is composed of a little cluster D-E-G-A, the original E will be A-C-D-E, etc. In some versions the melody appears unadorned; in others it is doubled in fourths, in another in fifths and sixths above discreet arpeggios; finally the melody appears in closed chords with a fifth or an octave and the accompaniment is made fuller.

The advantage that Cowell offers his performers is that these may include first-year piano students, second-year students, those more advanced, the exceptionally trained and the virtuosos; all may play the five versions at the same time, either simultaneously or successively or in all kinds of combinations: the first with the third, the fifth with the second, etc., etc. The pity is that, unlike some eighteenth-century contrapuntal essays, the pentatonic melodies of the Amerind Suite are not capable of being superimposed one on the other and that the Power of the Big Worm may not be played simultaneously with the Lover Plays his Lute, and with the Deer Dance.

Henry Dixon Cowell (1897) was born in Menlo Park, California. At one time he toured Europe with the idea of making a career as a concert pianist. His love of investigation carried him far; his books today are worth more than a mere reputation for manual agility. In the field of instrumental investigations Cowell has collaborated with Theremin in the construction of an instrument called a rhythmicon which, according to definition, is "designed to produce all kinds of rhythms and cross rhythms" and which was made known, without further consequences, in New York in 1932. A work by Cowell for this instrument is entitled Rhythmicana and might have been included in the mechanistic works such as Steel and Stone (1931).

Some of Cowell's works bear the general designation of Symphonietta (1928), Concerto (1929), Quartet (1927), and Concerto (piano, 1929). But he prefers more abstract titles in which the aesthetic intention is kept secret: Communication, Vestiges (1924), Synchrony (1930), Two Appositions (1931), Four Continuations, Polyphonica (1930), Six Casual Developments. Some are more explicit: Exultation, Heroic Dance. A few belong to the good old times of popular evocations like his Irish Suite (1933) and Shoon Three, while the composition entitled Chrysanthemums (1937) seems to allude to a sort of *pince sans rire* in the style of Erik Satie. Cowell's more recent works include compositions for orchestra and chamber ensembles and songs; in all of them, he continues his original experiments in sonorities as well as rhythms. Among them are a Symphonic Set; the Chorale and Ostinato, No. 1 and No. 2, for oboe and piano; and Festive Occasion. The Toccata for flute, violoncello, piano, and soprano vocalise was given its first performance in the spring of 1945.

These experiments in rhythms and sonorities have been noted and continued by some of the younger independents. Four young composers on the Pacific coast—Ray Green, Gerald Strang, John Cage, and Lou Harrison—have recently experimented with orchestras made up solely of a wide variety of percussion instruments. Cage has already become known as an explorer in new sonorous effects with his book of music for two pianos and his Three Dances (1945) for two pianos provided with mutes in different places.

Ray Green's (1908) interests have led him to compose on themes from classical antiquity as a means to experiment in new ways of writing. He has written an orchestral work (1934) based on the *Birds* of Aristophanes (which lends itself to an entirely up-to-date manner and style of writing) and also an Overture, March and Finale for *Iphigenia in Tauris* (1935). He has also written choral and vocal works and the music for Martha Graham's "American Document."

Gerald Strang (1908), assistant to Schönberg at the University of California, has been attracted to the beauties of dissonant counterpoint as his Mirrorism and Sonatina for Clarinet Alone (1932) indicate. Adolph Weiss (1891), an older pupil of Schönberg's and one of the original cultivators of atonality, has written chamber music and a *Kammersymphonie* (1928) for ten instruments. A Theme and Variations (1931) leads in this field to his Three Pieces for Orchestra (1937) and to a String Quartet.

There is no doubt but that the rapid development and widespread interest in the modern dance in the United States has greatly stimulated composers to experiments in these directions. The functional character and free rhythmic development of the modern dance as contrasted with the ballet has offered a new field to musicians who have undertaken to compose accompaniments for this new form of the art.

One of the most successful composers in this field is Wallingford Riegger (1885). After his early works in romantic vein, *La Belle Dame sans Merci* (1924) for chamber orchestra and four solo voices and the Trio in B minor (1921), he became interested in experiments in atonality and has become one of the most skilled exponents of the twelve-tone system. His accomplished handling of this technique may be observed in such pieces of abstract music as Study in Sonority for ten violins (1927), Dichotomy for thirteen instruments (1932), and the recent String Quartet (1940). He has, however, given much interest to composing for modern dance groups such as those of Martha Graham, Doris Humphrey, Charles Weidman, Hanya Holm, and others (New Dance, 1935; With My Red Fires, 1936; Chronicle, 1936 and Trend, 1937). Riegger has also made curious experiments in music to accompany films as, for example, Frenetic Rhythms for piano, voice, and three wind instruments (1932) which was preceded by a Bacchanale for piano, four hands (1931).

Before proceeding to a consideration of the developments and ramifications of that special kind of rhythm, jazz, generally thought of as typically American, let us consider some composers who wish to represent other, and no less characteristic, aspects of American music. Randall Thompson (1899), without concerning himself overmuch with the extremes in contemporary musical idioms, has written simply and directly as a composer reflecting more especially the traditional aspects of the American scene.

He has composed two symphonies (1929-31); the slow movement of the Second stands out as a fine piece of poetic writing. Jazz Poem for orchestra with piano (1928) and some chamber music figure among his instrumental works. His choral works, however, represent perhaps his most successful and personal writing, for Thompson is an example of that special talent for vocal writing so eminently characteristic of Anglo-Saxon musicians in all periods. His vein is often satiric, as in Americana (1932) to inane texts chosen as the butt of Mencken's irony in the *American Mercury*. "The Peaceable Kingdom," for mixed voices *a cappella* (1936), with the subtitle "A sequence of sacred choruses—text from Isaiah," was suggested by an eighteenth-century American painting. It is an outstanding contribution to the literature of choral music of modern times. His most recent choral work, "The Testament of Freedom" (1944), is arranged for orchestra and men's voices to texts from the political writings of Thomas Jefferson. The choice of texts does not seem apt for musical setting and the composition suffers from a certain stiff and unbending quality, even approaching pompousness, that makes it less attractive than earlier works in spite of his mastery of choral writing.

A special gift for vocal lyricism with an attendant sensitivity to the rhythms of English poetry has distinguished the work of Douglas Moore (1893). With a keen perception of the poetry and the drama of the American scene, his music, whether vocal or purely instrumental, draws on the store of American folklore and literature. The well-known Pageant of P. T. Barnum (1924) was followed by other orchestral works in similar vein, Moby Dick (1928), Overture on an American Tune (1931) and, more recently, Village Music (1942). His choral works and songs, largely to texts of American poets, include: "The Ballad of William Sycamore" to the poem of Stephen Vincent Benét for baritone, flute, trombone, and piano (1926); "Simon Legree" to the text of Vachel Lindsay, for men's chorus and piano (1937); "Dedication" to a poem of Archibald MacLeish, for mixed voices, *a cappella* (1938).

Moore's active interest in the theater has given full play to his ability as a composer of dramatic music. After various pieces of incidental music for the theater, he wrote a three-act opera, *White Wings* (1935); an operetta, the *Headless Horseman,* to a libretto by S. V. Benét (1936); and, in 1938, the one-act opera, the *Devil and Daniel Webster,* which is a distinguished contribution to the little-exploited field of opera on American themes, remarkable for its skillful setting of the text and its dramatic intensity. Moore has composed some of his finest songs to poems of John Donne: "Three Divine Sonnets" and "The Token" (1942). After his early studies with Parker, d'Indy, Bloch, and Boulanger, Moore has set himself to develop a personal style which utilizes whatever technical means the special problem in hand seems to demand. In the field of the abstract forms he has written a Symphony of Autumn (1930), a String Quartet (1933), and a Quintet for woodwinds and horn (1942).

Howard Hanson (1896), as director of the Eastman School of Music for many years, where he inaugurated the American Composers' Concerts, has devoted himself wholeheartedly to encouraging young composers and to furthering the cause of American music. He has also composed many orchestral and choral works as well as an opera, *Merry Mount* (1932), on an episode laid in the New England of the Pilgrims. His orchestral works include several symphonic poems in romantic vein, Exaltation (1920), *Lux Aeterna* (1923), and Pan and the Priest (1926), among others, and four symphonies: Nordic, no. 1 (1922); Romantic, no. 2 (1930); the Third Symphony (1937) written for radio performance on commission of the Columbia Broadcasting System; and the recent Fourth in memory of his father. Of his Third Symphony the composer has said, "Like my second or Romantic Symphony the third one, too, stands as an avowal against a certain coldly abstract would-be nonsentimental music professed by certain composers of high gifts." This symphony, he feels, approaches more nearly than any of his other works the ends he has striven for in music. Hanson's first important choral work was the "Lament for Beowulf" (1925) for mixed chorus and full orchestra. More recently he has set "Three Poems from Walt Whitman," songs from "Drum Taps" (1935).

One of the young composers actively intent on writing American music is William Schuman (1910). He has composed works for orchestra: two symphonies (1935 and 1937), Concerto for piano and small orchestra (1938), and American Festival Overture (1939). He also demonstrates the Anglo-Saxon bent for choral music in his numerous choral compositions: "Four Chorale Canons" (1933); "Prelude" (1936); "Pioneers!" (1937); "Chorale Étude" (1937) for mixed voices *a cappella,* and, more recently, the cantata "This is Our Time" (1940); "A Free Song" (ca. 1943) for chorus and orchestra and a *"Te Deum"* for chorus together with a song, "Orpheus with His Lute" (1945) designed as incidental music to Shakespeare's *Henry VIII.*

Among the younger group who show a special interest in the composition of choral music, songs, and chamber works in a manner which shows their chief preoccupation to be with purely musical considerations may be mentioned Paul Creston (1906) and David Diamond (1915). Whatever may have been his apprentice training, Creston has transformed it into independent material. He is considered to be self-taught in the elements which go to make up his compositions. His Prelude and Dance (1932, edited ten years later as a piano piece) displays the sure hand of the composer in its modern writing. The Prelude is interesting for its great dissonant masses. The short dance has a finely personal beginning which is later diluted although as a whole it forms a clever contrast to the introductory piece. Creston has written a Partita (1937) for flute, violin, and strings; a symphony; a sonata for piano; a Suite for Viola and Piano; and a piece for small orchestra, Out of the Cradle Endlessly Rocking (1934), to which the principle of the old *moto perpetuo* of the spinner may be applied.

As a pupil of Rogers, Sessions, and Boulanger, David Diamond's compositions show a severe criterion of workmanship and an almost exclusive preoccupation with abstract forms. His works for orchestra include a Sinfonietta (1934), Symphony in D Major (1935), a Concerto for Violin (1936), and a Concerto for Harpsichord and Chamber Orchestra (1937). He has written for chamber performance compositions for various instruments and ensembles including a Partita for Oboe, Bassoon and Piano (1935), sonatas and sonatinas, a Trio in G Major (1937), and a Quintet in B Minor for flute, string trio, and piano (1937). In the field of vocal music are his "A Night Litany" (1935) to text by Ezra Pound, for tenor, mixed chorus, and orchestra, "Two A Cappella Choruses" (1935), and a number of songs, notably sensitive settings to Shelley's "Music When Soft Voices Die" and to verses in Shakespeare's *Tempest* (1945).

An interest in the contributions of exotic music for the enrichment of contemporary idioms distinguishes two other musicians of the young group: Colin McPhee (1901) and Paul Frederic Bowles (1911). After an early interest in the most modern experiments as a pupil of Paul Le Flem in Paris and the mechanistic Varèse in New York to whose influence may be attributed McPhee's music for cinema, Mechanical Principles and H_2O, both of 1931, as well as a Concerto for Piano and Orchestra (1923), a Symphony in One Movement (1930), and a Concerto for Piano and Wind Octet (1928), McPhee went to Bali. There he remained for six years, returning with a symphonic work, Bali (1936), and transcriptions of Balinese ceremonial music for two pianos. He has also written a choral work, "From the Revelation of St. John the Divine" (1935) for men's chorus, two pianos, three trumpets and tympani, and incidental music for Paul Robeson's performance of Eugene O'Neill's *Emperor Jones* (1940).

Paul Bowles sought the exotic in southern Spain and northern Africa as well as Central and South America, gathering relatively virgin song material on which he later worked with Copland and Thomson. He has written Two Huapangos, Melodia (1937), and Pastorale Suite which reflect these experiences with popular and folk music in a singularly personal way. He has written numerous pieces for the theater, among them: *Colloque Sentimentale* and *Yankee Clipper* (1936), both ballets; *Denmark Vesey,* an opera (1937), and more recently a musical setting, entitled the Wind Remains, for the masque in the last act of Garcia Lorca's *Así que pasen cinco años.*

Aside from its obviously fundamental rhythmic interest, jazz has connotations of an aesthetic and social character which have made it the mainspring for much of the music written in the United States. It was George Antheil (1900) who early carried to Europe this outstanding feature of Americanism when he presented his symphonic composition Zingareska (1921) in Berlin to the protests of the more circumspect musicians who figured in the audience. Another work based on jazz is the Jazz Symphony for twenty-two instruments (1925). Antheil has also written three sonatas for violin and piano (1923-24), two quartets (1924-28), and two chamber concertos (1932 and 1933). His contribution to mechanistic music is a *Ballet Mécanique* (1925); to Americanism, his American Symphony (1937); his share in Parisian irony appears in his Femme 100 têtes, a piano composition; while his Plainsman is film music. An opera, *Transatlantic* (1929), a ballet, *Fighting the Waves* (1929), and incidental music for *Oedipus* (1928) made Antheil's name known in Europe where he was one of the first Americans to be applauded.

Yet of course it is the name of George Gershwin (1898-1937) which has become classic in the realm of jazz. Indeed, at the present time a certain popular nationalistic feeling centers about his music. The Rhapsody in Blue (1924), the Second Rhapsody, the Concerto in F for piano (1925), An American in Paris (1928) retain their popularity, as recent new recordings of several of these works show. Perhaps his truest claim to distinction in the history of American music will rest on his Negro folk opera, *Porgy and Bess* (1935).

Louis Gruenberg (1884), a Russian who arrived in America at the age of two, may have Russian blood in his veins but externally his music seeks American accents, if indeed jazz is their best exponent. Jazz Suite (1925), "Daniel Jazz" (1923), Jazzettes, Jazzberries, and Jazz Epigrams suggest that Gruenberg sought in jazz a type of music which, as in classical times, might serve equally for the grand symphonic forms and for simple pages of piano music. Besides these he has written music in the more or less traditional forms like his symphony and chamber music; others inspired in romantic vein such as Vagabondia (1920) and the Enchanted Isle, which received the prize of the Juilliard Foundation in 1927; and considerable music for the stage, including a nonvisual opera for the radio entitled *Green Mansions* (1937).

In 1930, Gruenberg produced an opera which was presented by the Juilliard School of Music in 1931. This work entitled *Jack and the Beanstalk* to John Erskine's libretto, which the authors subtitled A Fairy Opera for the Child-like, is a gay satire with an exceptionally apt and rollicking melodious score. Gruenberg's serious attempt in opera, *Emperor Jones* (1932), is certainly the most satisfactory grand opera produced by an American up to the present time. It is characterized by a primitive intensity that is conveyed by rhythmic and melodic effects organically worked out from Negro musical sources. In his most recent work, Concerto for Violin and Orchestra (1945), Gruenberg again displays his ability to develop folk material and jazz rhythms in an organic and satisfying manner in the composition of a work in traditional form.

Another European by birth, Nicolas Slonimsky (born in Russia, 1894), who came to this country at an already mature age (in 1923), has experimented in his own way with atonalism and jazz. His originality consists less in the material of his harmonic elements than in his manner of combining them and of superposing atonal groups previously utilized. Works like his Studies in Black and White, for piano (1929), make use of a consonant counterpoint in each line of chords which are then combined in polytonal superpositions. Such ways of conceiving melody and harmony are expounded by Slonimsky, a perspicacious critic, in his essay on "The Plurality of Melodic and Harmonic Systems" (1938).

Marc Blitzstein (1905) passed in his student days from the classes of Nadia Boulanger to the experimental theaters of Vienna where Schönberg was the principal figure. His facile absorption of the atonal experiments of the young Viennese school is evident in his various orchestral and chamber works and his reaction to the new theater is to be seen in the one act opera-ballet, *Parabola and Circula* (1929), which may be understood as a *blague à froid* in the sense of his *Triple Sec* (1928), the opera farce where the dryness may be found in the chords of the chamber orchestra.

But these and other ingenious pieces lack the serious sense of direction which he was to describe allegorically in his radio song-play, *I've Got the Tune* (1937), and to demonstrate in his opera, the *Cradle Will Rock* (1936). In this highly successful music drama, Blitzstein puts his study of the music drama of Schönberg and his group at the service of social and political problems. The result, thanks to Blitzstein's sure sense of the theater, combines music, dialogue, and action with a sincere presentation of the problem of the underprivileged masses, in one of the most important contributions to the music theater in the United States. He has since continued to use his musical talents in the cause of political and social justice in *No for an Answer* (1937), another music drama, and in Spanish Earth, incidental music for a film, written in collaboration with Virgil Thomson in 1937.

One of the younger group, Robert Guyn McBride (1911), has drawn upon the experiences of his youthful years when he played in jazz bands and local theater orchestras in his native Arizona on a variety of instruments, from saxophone to piano. He has written the Go Choruses (1936), the Workout (1936), Swing Music (1937), and a Fugato on a Well-Known Theme (1935). Works reflecting a more serious reaction to the contemporary scene are Prelude to a Tragedy (1935) and Depression (1934), a sonata for violin and piano. He has likewise responded to the folk music of Mexico in Mexican Rhapsody for orchestra (1934). His more recent works are a ballet, *Show Piece* (1937), the characteristically entitled Hot-Shot Divertimento (1939), and a quintet, Wise-Apple Five (1940).

But those who today can be considered as classical masters in the artistic use of jazz, as an element of construction in compositions, are Gershwin and Copland. Copland, furthermore, has written an essay which can be extremely useful to the foreign reader as well as to the American and which in a way is like a declaration of principles for this aesthetics. This is his "Jazz Structure and Influence," published in *Modern Music* (January, 1927). To this study should be added that of Newman Levy, "The Jazz Formula," published in the same review in June, 1924. And if one wishes to hear the voice of one of the authentic practitioners of jazz itself, there is an essay by Paul Whiteman together with Mary Margaret McBride, also entitled "Jazz" and printed in New York in 1926. The essay of Copland has been followed by much writing on this interesting aspect of American music, among others two recent books, *Jazz; Hot and Hybrid* (New York, 1938) by Winthrop Sargeant, and *American Jazz Music* (New York, 1939) by Hobson Wilder.

With Aaron Copland and some of his contemporaries, we reach a high point in American music of today. I have made the preceding résumé simply to show the richness of the varied aspects presented by the American musical scene. Now we must pause in our narrative and consider two musicians who, among so many, have a particular attraction for the foreign observer. Copland is a man, born with the century, who started his studies in the year in which World War I terminated and a period of clarity, animation, and happy independence of ideas and invention arose in France. One of its consequences was the school which Nadia Boulanger founded in Fontainebleau and to which Copland repaired at the age of twenty-one. Whatever may have been the influence of French technique on Copland, it seems clear that this composer derived from it his manner of investigating searchingly the material which he chooses as expressive means.

"Technical imagination," it may be termed, which makes of him not a poet nor a painter nor a confectioner of exquisite enamels but, fundamentally, an artist who works with certain materials which fall within the category of what we understand as music. Copland is above all a musical artificer, a worker who, with certain rhythmic, harmonic, melodic, and especially sonorous materials fashions musical goods. If the reader remembers what was said before about the dry, mechanistic quality which the genius of Ravel assumed in certain of its aspects or what Stravinsky meant when he called himself a "musical engineer," he will understand better to what class of musician Aaron Copland belongs and why his music is not the best qualified to appeal to the man-in-the-street and the office girl. The music of Copland is the product of a musician for other musicians.

Notwithstanding this, it is the kind of music that usefully serves the purpose for which it is written; that is to say, it serves the client who has come to solicit in Copland's factory a certain amount of music for the theater or for the ballet or for the radio or for a group of chamber musicians. This quality of music "to order" appears in a great deal of Stravinsky's best music; Ravel himself did not disdain it—for example in his last concertos for piano. Once someone asked Paul Valéry why he had been silent for many years as a poet and he replied that "no one had ordered any poems of him." The romantic idea of the poet who writes his verses on the shores of a lake or on the top of a mountain is an old-fashioned one which hampers the present day listener because he continues to believe in a certain type of romantic inspiration, poetic, pictorial, or amatory.

But Copland proceeds from the diametrically opposed point of view, as do many modern composers. Like the architect or mason who is asked to build a certain edifice, Copland seeks, as did all musicians prior to the Beethovenian era, the materials which will be the most appropriate to fulfill his order, materials, furthermore, which are at hand in the country where he is to build his edifice. Once collected, he examines them coldly, as a professional technician, and uses them to construct an architecture with a functional meaning, although not a decorative one.

Various works will serve to demonstrate this, from the Symphony for Organ and Orchestra, which is one of his early works (1924), to his Concerto for Piano and Orchestra (1926) in which Copland, still very young, seems to have found his idiom. A work like that entitled, Music for the Theater, of 1925, is surprising for the maturity of workmanship and technique in a composer of twenty-five. The orchestration is sober, not going beyond the classical plan except for the use of a military drum and a xylophone, in addition to a piano. The title Burlesque of one of the pieces might, in point of fact, have served as title for the entire work; throughout, Copland deals with rather insignificant materials, contriving music that is designed to be performed and not to explain itself.

Thus, for example, his concept of the tonality is indifferent in itself, depending somewhat on haphazard combinations and superpositions of the different orchestral strata. Certain short motives, incisive in their rhythm and profile, lend spice while the whole is based on pedal figures and consonant basses in octaves or fifths or fourths. The binding material, a bit crude, can be concealed with some simple or double appoggiaturas.

That the aim is to give to the whole a sonorous bass and not a harmonic one is proved by the fact that the bass in the piano part does not always coincide harmonically with that of the orchestra; the piano is conceived as a means of color rather than as the harmonic nucleus of the whole. The harmony itself is conceived as color; a chord is like a tube of blue, green, or ocher paint and is used when it is desired that the passage have a blue, green, or ocher color; tonalities which are too crude are dressed with chromatics like cellophane wrappings. Dissonance is not a harmonic value but, as it appeared in Wagnerian times, is used to prick the ear on occasion. The instruments always preserve their personal and characteristic color and are almost always presented above clear, percussive rhythms.

Copland's treatment of his materials depends on the general idea which he has of the work as a whole: its use, its sonorous volume, the combination of instruments chosen, and its duration. This calculation is fundamental in the art of composition. One does not write a quartet like a piano sonata, or a prelude like a symphony. Yet this obvious truth, always foremost in the mind of the composers of the classic era, is forgotten by many composers; it may be, I believe, one of the truths that Nadia Boulanger teaches her pupils from the beginning. With this factor in mind, it is easier to achieve a work which possesses equilibrium; Copland's products always have this virtue, whether he writes a Symphony for Organ and Orchestra, or whether he designs a study on a melody (Vitebsk, trio for violin, violoncello, and piano).

The appropriateness of the work to its setting, that is to say, to the taste or requirements of the client who commissions it, is equally important for Copland. The Dance Symphony of 1930, commissioned by the RCA Victor Company, is a notable example of perfect calculation of climaxes and of sureness in the seeking of contrasts which permit the movement to continue without waste of the rhythmic potentialities. The Outdoor Overture, 1938, written for the Music Department of a New York high school, might be thought of as a school exercise composed by a master. Clear in ideas, classical in harmony, and with the normal orchestration *a due,* it has, indeed, a certain outdoor air and a certain quality of an overture for a play, perhaps a play by students. The motives, brief but well drawn, never undergo a complicated development; its variations are simple, scarcely more than a multiplication of the values. Copland's melodic ideas do not constitute his richest vein and the writing of an andante of symphonic proportions is a problem in itself; but Copland resolves the problem very wittily by giving the long singing phrase to the trumpet and, in so doing, underlines its meager melodic value, acknowledging its weakness by accenting it.

The idea of the music's application stands out particularly in Copland's compositions for the theater, in his ballets especially. Among his more recent works there are two: *Billy the Kid* and *Rodeo,* which utilize a minimum of local melodic color. Nevertheless, the result is plastically perfect and one is inclined to believe that more insistent and sharply characterized music would have hampered the realization of both ballets from the point of view of the dance. From that point of view, instead, they figure among the most successfully realized in the present repertory.

Copland has recently added to his list of works the short *a cappella* chorus, "Las Agachados" (the "Shake-Down Song," 1941) for a Schola Cantorum concert to commemorate Kurt Schindler, the Schola's first director. The chorus is based on one of the melodies in Schindler's collection, *Folk Music and Poetry of Spain and Portugal,* and demonstrates Copland's happy gift of utilizing folk material. He has composed a new ballet, *Appalachian Spring* (1945) for Martha Graham. His latest orchestral compositions are Quiet City, for trumpet, English horn and strings (1940); and A Lincoln Portrait (1943), for orchestra accompanied by a speaker.

Whether Copland utilizes the songs of the cowboys, those of Mexican cabarets (as in *El Salón México,* 1936), or those of American cabarets (Three Cabaret Dances, 1937), the effect is always one in which the thematic material does not predominate nor obtrude even though it may constitute the program of the composition, the heart of the anecdote. With Mexican material or with American material, Copland is always an independent composer, quite beyond any consideration of national music. His nationalism has been largely surmounted; if he is American, he is so by nature, not for the character of his melodies or his rhythms.

This is, in other musical fields, what has happened with Roy Harris. He is another of the composers of the present moment who is clearly and unmistakably American but whose inspiration and materials proceed from the free areas of thought without any restricting ties to political or aesthetic programs.

There are composers of whom it may be said, to paraphrase Chesterton, that they have learned their trade like the blacksmith by hammering or, like a certain violinist, by playing the violin. So there are composers who learn to compose by composing; this, in a sense, seems very natural, since a child learns to walk by walking, first on all fours on the ground, but not by studying the mechanics of the human body nor its equilibrium on a plane.

Roy Harris might be cited as an example of this class of composers who follow relatively late the conventional curriculum in which others, younger than they, have the advantage but in whose apprenticeship there is nothing which does not come from within. In his development, nothing is literal, everything is vital. For this reason, his technique may develop slowly; his first works may be inferior in the "writing" to those of a pupil with more technique but in this difficult and voluntary struggle to achieve genuine expression, his works—even those which seem to turn out badly—have the advantage over others in that the technical means of which the composer avails himself have been "found" after a struggle with the material in order to express something personal. Roy Harris, who has found new kinds of music and so it seems to me types which are wholly American, has avoided from the beginning the use of the formulas of the modernist school or recipes in the latest fashion. For this reason, and with the need to tread firm ground, Harris began writing traditional works in which the sonorous material derived from the European scales.

Harris, who was born two years before the end of the last century, only began to produce in 1925 (Symphonic Poem for chorus and trio, Andante for orchestra, 1926), after which there followed chamber works and works of large dimensions which indicate a serious meditation of the great classics—Beethoven especially—so far as the symphonic concept is concerned. Harris' symphonic concept accentuates its character in the course of a not inconsiderable number of works up to these last years when, in his Third Symphony, he seems to have brought his ideas in this form to maturity. This symphony is lengthily discursive yet its accent is concentrated and it gives the impression of a long meditative recitation in a type of discourse which sometimes approaches Brahms or Franck; the first, in the opaque and morose character of the melodic phrases; the second, in the construction of its phrases, for example in the themes of the first movement.

The sonorous mass is thick due to the lack of rhythmic vivacity, the slow harmonic development, and the form of the melody. Harris manipulates the normal accents of the measure in such a way that irregular successions of time values are produced, such as $\frac{7}{8}$, $\frac{8}{8}$, $\frac{5}{8}$, something which is considered very American. This may give exactitude to the melodic declamation but no rhythmic pulsation for it converts the melody into a kind of recitative; furthermore, it prevents the harmony from being constructed rhythmically, which would have been avoided by a normal articulation of the melody and by accenting it instead with dynamic and expressive shadings.

Sometimes the long and diffuse melody glides upon a base of interwoven arpeggios which, proceeding from a harmony of the seventh (A-C♯-E-G♯) is distributed in two forms of perfect arpeggiated chords (C♯-E-G♯ and E-A-C♯) with bitonal effects. The result, although subtle and ethereal, is nevertheless insistent, and the melody for the English horn seems diffuse and undecided. What matters, however, is that the expressive quality is always personal, and there is in the depths of this melody something which compels one to listen to it not simply with patience but with respectful pleasure. Harris' music frequently inspires such pleasure as, for an example of the briefest kind, in the melody entitled Four Minutes and Twenty Seconds (1943) for string quartet and flute in which the flute, above a background of tranquil harmonies, sings a lyrical melody of modal character.

Harris' meditative nature which determines his career as composer becomes clearly evident in a comparison of some of his works, for example, his Folksong Symphony (published in 1940) and a sort of concert overture which he calls Johnny Comes Marching Home, commissioned by the Victor Company. In the overture, a kind of slow meditation or orchestral amplification of a simple melody, the tune is spread over a succession of periods, each becoming more complicated in texture with rests for the purpose of finding the necessary contrasts which are underlined by dynamic shadings (*p-ff*). The clear harmony seeks novel effects in the modulatory leading. The melodic fragments form well-defined periods while the rhythms are a simple basis for harmonies arpeggiated by the brasses for sonorous fullness. An orthodox treatment of the orchestra and the composition leads naturally to tremolos which introduce the finale.

In his Symphony, similar characteristics appear and the very simple treatment of the voices—almost always in unison or in octaves, rarely in complicated contrapuntal variations—has a popular aroma. The thematic material derives from the folk song, "Welcome Party," a cowboy song, "Western Cowboy," the "Mountaineer Love Song," and a Negro melody, "Oh, Lawd! De trumpet sounds it in my soul." The first exclamatory words, "Oh, Lawd!" repeated insistently with the obsession of an anguished supplication, provide Harris with one of his most happy devices. It consists in the regular manner in which he causes the succession A♮-A♭ to be sung in the middle register of the singer's voice, making it susceptible to all the shadings of vocal expression from a cry to a scarcely whispered murmur.

Harris carries this formula to another of his compositions which, in my opinion, holds first place at the moment in American music: it is the second fragment, entitled "Tears," in his "Symphony for Voices" (1935), for a chorus of mixed voices *a cappella*. The formula is sung on the word "tears," followed by two trochees in a descending succession with diminuendo which is very effective; a sliding of the voice like tears themselves; sobs which burst from the depths of the manly breast as from the mother's heart. The "Symphony for Voices" is written to passages from poems by Walt Whitman and has the robust vitality of that admirable poet. The initial phrase in the first movement, found by Harris for the words with which the "Song for all seas, all ships" begins, is based on the C-major chord and has a grandeur in its simplicity, comparable in a sense to that in which Beethoven comments on the verses of Gellert. In the simplicity and economy of the sonorous medium chosen, in the austerity of his phrase, in the natural harmonies to which it is so difficult to return without becoming banal, in the succinct form, free as well as precise, Roy Harris achieves something, in the opinion of a critic who is *not* an American, which conveys the most exact idea of what *is* American; certainly something which is not European and is as far from English choral music as from the Central European concept of the symphony. The work was meditated by Harris over a long period. A suite to texts from Whitman for chorus and two pianos (1927), "Song for Occupations" (mixed chorus in eight parts, *a cappella,* 1934), and the "Story of Noah" (for the same combination, 1934) preceded the "Symphony for Voices" and gave Harris his security in the handling of his material and in the simplicity of his expression.

Harris has recently composed numerous pieces of chamber music, including a Sonata for Violin and Piano, Third String Quartet (1938), and a Viola Quintet (1940), and, for orchestra, a Folksong Symphony (1940); and Fifth and Sixth symphonies. The Fifth Symphony (1943) is dedicated to the U.S.S.R. Other compositions which seem to reflect the stress of the times are the Ode to Truth (1941) and the American Creed (1940). For the first time Harris has recently essayed music for the dance in What So Proudly We Hail, and Namesake, for Hanya Holm.

In Brazil, Negroid acquisitions have mingled their novelty (for exportation) with the European heritage and its consequent Creole tradition: that is to say, with "colonial" music. But even when a composer of as much fiber and talent as Heitor Villa-Lobos (1881) [7] takes account from the beginning of the relative values of the picturesque elements in Brazilian music (which has had its classical composer in the Italian manner in Antonio Carlos Gomes) and proposes to "raise" them to the heights of European music by means of a strong dose of technical sophistication, he has not succeeded, even in an enormous flood of compositions, in creating with the *modinha* or the *carioca* what Ravel did in *La Valse*. For that matter, neither Amadeo Roldán nor Alejandro Caturla, the young Cubans prematurely lost to music, were able to achieve it with the Afro-Cuban rumba.

The nationalism of Villa-Lobos has its ups and downs in his enormous production but in its general lines it belongs to what we have called the second phase of musical nationalism: to that which converts the commonplaces of local color into elements of style with which the composer works to create compositions in independent form more or less distant from the popular forms of its origin. It is, as has been said, the nationalism of Albéniz and of

[7] Heitor Villa-Lobos had as his predecessors in the study of folklore, Mario de Andrade and Luiz Heitor Correa de Azevedo. Alberto Nepomuceno (1864-1920) was the precursor of the present generation of nationalists followed by Brazilio Itiberé (1846-1913) and Francisco Braga (1868). Beside Villa-Lobos may be mentioned Oscar Lorenzo Fernández (1897), Francisco Mignone (1897), Barrozo-Netto (1881-1941), Fructuoso Viana, Luiz Cosme, Radamés Gnattali, Camargo Guarneri.

Falla's early production. It corresponds to the stage of Rimsky-Korsakov and to the earliest Stravinsky, who had already emancipated himself from it by the time of *Petrouchka;* while that same picturesque quality is the great attraction in the works of Villa-Lobos. Because of it the audacities in his "writing" hold a secondary place, unnoticed by the average listener whose attention is otherwise absorbed.

Now if one does not hear or does not listen to what is written, why write it? There is an important reason, namely, that these harmonic and tonal combinations, their use of dissonance, of rhythm, etc. are capable of producing a sonorous material of supreme interest, rich in color and in its suggestion of atmosphere. This interest exists in some of the works of Villa-Lobos and not in others, at least not always to the same extent. This is far from being a reproach but it happens that when the native-picturesque element drops, the ultramodern texture in Villa-Lobos also loses interest, as in some of his chamber works and pieces for piano. Apparently, then, the modern qualities in his writing must be integrally united to the folkloristic elements. Such also seems to be the case with his colleagues, less rich than he in technique and power, so that in them the national picturesque quality falls back to the initial stage of nationalism in all its crudity.

This case is the most prevalent in Mexico, where composers of a rudimentary nationalism are abundant. But it must be said in their defense that those who utilize elements of a little-known folklore (which they have found in the impenetrable forests and mountains here and there in the vast republic) or, indeed, those who utilize elements which are considered as relics of the ancient native cultures have few models to inspire them. In doubt, they cling to the popular or archaeological document and treat it simply, without seriously disfiguring it with technical artifices. It is obvious that the result must be extremely primitive.

What, in Villa-Lobos, is an agglomeration of technical means, an art to arouse *stupore* as the first Italian futurists said, a way to shock the observer, dazzled by the brilliant orchestral coloring and the wealth of motives and rhythms, is matched by the Mexicans with a praiseworthy technical simplicity. Anything else would be artificial redundance. This simplicity includes an obsessive reiteration of the short, incisive motives, accompanied by native percussion instruments (as also in Villa-Lobos, Caturla, etc.) and this crudeness, progressively accented, is its greatest merit. This very simple and elemental stage of Mexican musical nationalism is about comparable to what nationalist architecture produces in its field; as art, it does not go much beyond what Mexican artisans in metal do in their reproductions of models found in archaeological excavations nor, in some cases, does it surpass what the industrial arts achieve. Their ancestral techniques were brilliant, attractive, and rich with a strong originality. But when their primitive qualities are weakened and succumb to the complacencies of cheap adaptations, they run the grave risk of being converted into bric-a-brac for exportation, into Mexican curios destined for the country which has presented this phrase as a gift to the Castilian tongue.

This danger is, of course, common everywhere in America. The cabaret, the grand hotel waylay the rumba, the *carioca,* or the *corrido*. Those Cuban or Mexican composers who restrict themselves to putting on paper Negro, Creole, mestizo music have no place in this book. Strictly speaking, their labors, however praiseworthy, belong rather to an exploitation of folklore; when it is commercial (as in the case of the Mexican curios), it is simply an industrial art—a business.

Besides this elementary nationalism, there are in the Hispano-American countries composers of far higher rank. In general, there are nationalists in the romantic style but there are also composers who, having passed through the different stages of nationalism, have reached the final stage of a creative transformation of the source material.[8]

A clear example of poematic nationalism is the landscape of delicate romantic tints, the Isle of the Ceibos, by the Uruguayan, Fabini, while Julián Aguirre clings closer to the "document" of the pampas in his famous *"Huella y Gato."* A part of the production of the Mexican, Manuel M. Ponce, such as Chapultepec and Ferial, belong to this stage of descriptive and colorist nationalism; the motives, instead of being drawn from popular "documents," are the composer's own creations on a plane comparable to that typified by Albéniz in Spanish music (without suggesting a comparison between the two temperaments and talents). This is also true, it seems to me, of Enrique Soro in Chile and that of his fellow countryman, Humberto Allende, in his *Tonadas* while the Voice of the Streets (*La voz de las calles* by the poet, Pedro Prado) and even his Country Scenes (*Escenas Campesinas*) might be considered on a plane with Vaughan Williams (disregarding again, the individuality of both composers). An outstanding personality for his invention of popular motives is seen in Alberto Ginastera, in Argentina, with whom impressionism—more notable in South America than in North America—is to be felt in the sensuous effects of some of his harmonies. They are to be found, too, in another Hispano-American composer, the Colombian, Guillermo Uribe-Holguín.

In general terms, American composers have considered it an unavoidable obligation to cultivate nationalism in their music for the same reason that writers frequently cultivate local idioms. The personality of the artist and the originality of his art, it is currently thought, must be based on these

[8] These conclusions are necessarily provisional. A knowledge of Hispano-American music is difficult unless it is acquired on the spot on account of the scarcity of performances and especially of publications.

premises; but the example of their great universal poets like Rubén Dario, Lugones, and Nervo (not to mention many others of our contemporaries) shows that that point of view can only be provisional and that the relationship of an artist to the culture of the world is a much more profound ambition than the cultivation of the "typical accent," however attractive, subtle, or interesting the latter may be. The quality of immortality is naked and unadorned; it does not lie in picturesque trappings and the artist (of any age) who does not deeply aspire to this transcendental category will have to be content finally as the director of some conservatory.

The feeling that leads Hispano-American composers to consider the cultivation of the popular song of their countries as an unavoidable obligation seems, nevertheless, easy to understand. In the majority of cases, it is the only way in which these artists, like their colleagues in painting and literature, can distinguish themselves from one another since their respective countries are nations in the full process of formation and with a common cultural heritage.

Yet today there are a considerable number of Hispano-American composers who, having settled their account with patriotic nationalism, aspire to serve their country's cause in music in a more fundamental way, basing their values not on the trite picturesqueness of the local scene but on the universality of the spirit. Thus we find that the work of the most notable may be divided into progressive stages which, as with Manuel de Falla, display the gradual transformation of their criteria as artists in proportion as universal values supersede those of purely circumstantial importance.

In the production of Manuel Ponce (1886), pieces of picturesque-national character (I do not speak of his innumerable popular songs which, like those of so many by his compatriots, belong in another category) coexist with those of an absolute or abstract character. The latter include his concertos and sonatas which seem to reflect Ponce's notable sympathy for the Parisian aesthetics of the Schola Cantorum. His youthful Concerto for piano and orchestra (1910) is a good example of this Europeanized tendency at a time when picturesque nationalism was everywhere rampant. Another concerto, this time for violin and orchestra, completed in 1942, reaffirms that direction in the newest sense.

This, it seems to me, is the case likewise with José Rolón (1883-1945) in his Concerto for piano and orchestra, also dated 1942, and in which the abstractness of the idiom is occasionally enlivened by passages of popular origin which are absorbed into the predominating current, austere in color and severe in its expression. Rolón shares with Ponce the distinction of dean of the musical profession in Mexico. Both have taught the better part of the young composers of the country, such as Candelario Huizar (1899). The last of Huizar's symphonies (1942) makes use, not without some forcing, of melodico-rhythmic materials of the Coras, Huicholes, and other Indian tribes of the Pacific coast; Huizar has encased these materials in a form and a harmonic language much nearer to the classic than to the archaeological.

The magnetic force of German atonalism seems to attract the Argentinian, Juan Carlos Paz (1899). The twelve-tone technique has found in him a careful, patient, and sincere collaborator. In another Argentinian, Juan José Castro, is to be found in full development that transcendence of nationalism which has freed itself from the restrictions of folkloristic contacts in order to imbue with a noble substance the material necessary for the composition of extended forms, as in his Argentine Symphony and his Symphony of the Fields.

One means of emancipation from an elementary nationalism may be found by way of a great technique. On the other hand, a certain ultramodern technique lends itself, as we have already seen, with perhaps too great facility to an exaggerated picturesque nationalism. Paz seems to represent a good example of the first case, as do also Domingo Santa Cruz Wilson of Chile and Juan Lecuna of Venezuela. In Lecuna's piano pieces the aroma of Venezuelan popular song becomes transformed into permanent values. Picturesque overemphasis in the manner of the fresco painting so much enjoyed by Mexicans (of which Diego Rivera and Clemente Orozco are masters) makes use of the technique in which percussive harmony predominates with its consequent polyrhythm and polytonalism (or simply heterophony), its use and abuse of the pedal, of incessantly repeated figures, of dissonances *a fortiori,* and of the insistence on instrumental timbres. The latter derive directly from Stravinsky and Milhaud. Villa-Lobos, with his enthusiastic and robust personality and the spontaneity of his craftsmanship and agile mind, has carried these techniques and this picturesque color to the point where the mediocre spiritual value of his inspirations has become transfigured. But this has not been repeated with those who saw in Villa-Lobos a model to be followed and who followed it too facilely.

This occurred in the case of Caturla (1906-40) in Cuba, whose technique was too uncertain, and of Silvestre Revueltas (1899-1940) in Mexico. Revueltas was a musician of real temperament, of keen intuition, extremely sensitive to instrumental color, and with a fine ear for the color of dissonance. Yet one can hardly discover in his works a really harmonic procedure; there are only planes in juxtaposition or, better, sections in which a sensation of a tonic dominates, well concealed by dissonant adhesions, to be followed directly by another section similarly constructed. This is what happens in the composition called *Planos* which is, in my opinion, the most successfully realized and possesses the most authentic value of all the compositions by this composer. This piece (1934) displays a complete mastery of a modern technique consisting of chordal agglomerations, pedals, sharply percussive dissonances, elisions, and substitutions of congruous materials in which the folkloristic origin is scarcely discernible, in contrast to other works of Revueltas in which the popular material appears disfigured and caricatured yet easily recognizable. *Planos* presents the final result with greater logic and coherence, maintained by a vivid rhythmic feeling. Revueltas' songs to texts by Federico Garcia Lorca, accompanied by several instruments, display subtle brush strokes of original and interesting color. Along with the work just mentioned it is perhaps these little compositions which will longest endure.

The rest of Revueltas' production belongs to that nationalism *al fresco* characterized by violent coloring typical of the attractive and varied popular arts of Mexico. Curiously enough, countries in which living Indian music has an especially delightful quality as in Bolivia, Ecuador, or Peru, can show little beyond some brief pages for voice and piano, scarcely more than transcriptions of the original folklore material. Those harmonized by Beclard d'Harcourt constitute a most pleasing example but native composers have not gone much further. It would appear that along this line Moíses Vivanco in Peru has achieved reproductions of the original which, it is said, have as true a quality and authenticity as those of Gilberto Valdés for Cuban Negro music. Their works are far, however, from the art of true musical creation.[9]

It should be remarked, on the other hand, that Cuban composers have failed to make the most of their exquisite colonial music of French and Spanish origin with its highly original accents. The influence of this music is, however, very much alive in the lesser Antilles.

The young Mexican composers, Eduardo Hernández Moncada, Luis Sandi, Pablo Moncayo, Blas Galindo, and others, have assiduously practiced this kind of reproduction of folkloristic material. Nevertheless, they now give indubitable evidence of wishing to go beyond this rudimentary stage and have recently shown signs of doing so. Moncada in his Symphony in C (1942) gives concise and logical handling of certain short motives whose chromaticism does not endanger the feeling for tonality and which, without sentimentality, are expressed in warm and concentrated tones suggestive of native embroideries. Galindo approaches this sense of opaque, dense coloring in his Concerto for piano and orchestra, also dated 1942, in which the popular source seems very remote from the composer's consciousness even though it may beat deeply and soundlessly within him. Galindo's case is interesting because he is of pure aboriginal descent, of the Huichole race, if I am not mistaken.

The progressive stages in the transformation of this type of nationalism (sometimes popular, again archaeological) can be seen with great clarity in the work of Carlos Chávez, the musician of greatest distinction and of highest achievement in Mexico. Only a composer who has reached the final phase

[9] Composers' names and titles of their works, but not an evaluation of the works themselves, may be found in Nicolas Slonimsky, *Music of Latin America* (New York: 1945).

of his development and who has successfully resolved considerations of national sentiment and fully mastered technical problems would be capable of utilizing thematic elements of such crudeness and simplicity in a manner so completely satisfying artistically. If I am not seriously mistaken, such a composer is Carlos Chávez (1899); not, of course, from the first moment, but certainly at the present time. His earliest compositions, such as the *New Fire* (1921) and his ballet the *Four Suns,* resulted from that pre-Cortesian primitivism inspired by the example of the *Sacre du Printemps* in the same way that his Three Hexagons seems to derive from Stravinsky's little pieces. I am speaking here of this type of composition not as a direct influence yet, if one were to mention a contemporary composer as a point of reference for the art of Chávez, it would be Stravinsky.

An example of the most literal use of material derived from what is considered to be indigenous Mexican music appears in the music for pre-Cortesian instruments entitled Xochipili-Macuixochitl. Following it, the symphony H. P. (1932) based on the music of the ballet is pure folklore, rich in elements of colonial music, as is also Chávez's arrangement of the waltz, the Blue Dove (*La Paloma Azul*). Both have the picturesqueness of a Mexican mural, the first highly colored, the second with the delicate tones of eighteenth-century salon music given an ironic orchestration. The Sinfonía India, written in New York between 1935 and 1936, is a kind of summing up of these archaeological elements, sometimes imaginary, sometimes the pale reflection of ancient sources. After a painstaking study of their peculiarities, Chávez treats them simply but logically; the total result possesses a coherence which permits the ready acceptance of the generic title symphony for the composition even if in an allegorical sense.

Chávez had already confronted this problem some years before, when he wrote the incidental music for the *Antigone* of Sophocles arranged by Jean Cocteau. From it he made, in 1933, a kind of dramatic overture, very simple in its line. Its clear orchestration corresponds quite closely to the concept held by Italian composers of opera in the seventeenth century of the pieces with which they opened their operatic spectacles, under the usual title of sinfonia, and it therefore suggests the idea of the symphony in its more general meaning. If the Symphony of Antigone only roughly follows the thematic alternation appropriate to the early symphony, its material has nothing to do with that appropriate to European art and still less to that of the classical period.

When one listens to this work, so sure in its lines and in its construction, immediately after the Sinfonía India (both works are recorded), it is clearly evident that its thematic material (as well as certain instrumental combinations of a raucous, vivid coloring) derives very remotely yet indubitably from the same sources as the much more extended Sinfonía. It provides, then, a very remarkable example of the transformation of the primitive material into original substance; in this case it is national material elevated to the highest plane. Its substance is American to the depths of its spirit and makes of the Greek heroine not a character reconstructed according to present day literary taste but, it can be said without a trace of irony, an Aztec Antigone.

The Sinfonía India is probably Chávez's farewell to indigenous primitivism. The Symphony of Antigone seems, then, to open before him a new path in the objective treatment of nonfolkloristic material, however much it may be impregnated with an all-pervading feeling of an ancient inheritance. A Sonata for Four Horns followed in 1937 as the first stage in this new phase of the Mexican composer's career. This composition, amplified as to its sonorous medium shortly after, was first performed in 1939 as a Concerto for Four Horns. Finally there is, in my opinion, Chávez's most significant work: his Concerto for Piano and Orchestra first performed in New York in 1942. I believe that, at the present time, this work, so concise, well knit and finely balanced, reaches a culminating point in Chávez's music and perhaps in the music of Latin America today.

On bringing this book to a conclusion, the author believes it necessary to add a word of caution as regards the music of Latin American composers. The author has been accused by critics and propagandists of the various Latin American republics of a meager knowledge of the music of their countries and of not including in the Spanish edition of this work names and works of second or third rank. These critics appear not to have read the subtitle of that edition which clearly states that it—like the present English version—is concerned only with "the main currents of the music of our day." They also seem to have overlooked the fact that throughout the book the names of musicians in all countries, Spain included, who are not closely related to these "main currents" have been omitted as a matter of course. It has therefore been impossible to proceed differently in the case of Latin American composers who have not made contributions to these fundamental trends whatever may be their individual merit or the importance which they may possess in their own countries. All the young composers mentioned appear, not for the sake of providing information concerning their works, but because they are the most recent exponents of the important trends with which the book deals.

It must be added that unfortunately the author has frequently been disillusioned in cases where he has had the opportunity to examine the music of composers frequently mentioned in essays, bulletins, or entire books devoted to the music of Latin America. Much purely literary information exists concerning this music, frequently on the part of musicians and critics who have only passing acquaintance with those countries. But very little of this music has appeared in print, still less in recordings; performances, moreover, are so rare that the major part of this music is inaccessible to the critic. It is scarcely admissible in a serious work to rely on second-hand information which may be tinged with national or political bias. Discreet silence only is possible. The reader should maintain an attitude of reserve regarding all such literature and should urge that he be given opportunity to hear actual performances. If the reader will reflect on the expressed aim and plan of this book, I think he will agree that the author has endeavored to follow a consistent course not without erring on the side of generosity. Even at the risk of wounding national sensibilities, further deviations from its avowed intention would be inappropriate in a book which is not addressed to any nation but, so far as it is possible, to the universal reader.

Bibliography

Abraham, Gerald, *A Hundred Years of Music.* London: 1938.

———, *Chopin's Musical Style.* Oxford: 1939.

———, *Eight Soviet Composers* (Dmitri Shostakovitch, Sergey Prokofiev, Aram Khachaturyan, Lev Knnipper, Vissarion Shebalin, Dmitri Kabalevsky, Ivan Dzerzhinsky, Yary Shaporin). London: Oxford University Press, 1943. The author had the opportunity to consult the scores of some young Soviet composers not yet accessible to American critics.

———, *On Russian Music; Critical and Historical Studies.* New York: 1939.

———, *Studies in Russian Music.* London: 1935.

Adler, Guido, ed., *Handbuch der Musikgeschichte,* 2nd edition. Berlin: 1930.

Armitage, Merle, ed., *Igor Stravinsky.* New York: 1936.

———, *Schönberg.* New York: 1937.

Bartók, Béla, "Hungarian Peasant Music," *Musical Quarterly* (July, 1933).

Baudelaire, Charles, "Richard Wagner et Tannhäuser à Paris," *L'Art romantique,* E. Raynaud, ed. Paris: 1931.

Bauer, Marion, "Darius Milhaud," *Musical Quarterly* (New York: April, 1942).

———, *Twentieth Century Music.* New York: 1933.

Bekker, Paul, *Briefe an zeitgenössische musiker.* Berlin: 1932.

———, *Das Musikdrama der Gegenwart.* Stuttgart: 1909.

———, *Die Sinfonie von Beethoven bis Mahler.* 1918.

———, *Gustav Mahlers Sinfonien.* 1921.

———, *Klang und Eros.* Stuttgart: 1922.

———, *Kritische Zeitbilder.* Berlin: 1921.

Bekker, Paul, *The Changing Opera.* New York: 1935.

———, *The Story of Music. An historical sketch of the changes in musical form.* New York: 1927.

Belaief, V., *Les Noces.* London: 1928.

Benningsen, Olga, "A Bizarre Friendship," *Musical Quarterly* (October, 1936).

———, "More Tschaikowsky—von Meck Correspondence," *Musical Quarterly* (April, 1938).

Berlioz, Hector, *A Critical Study of Beethoven's Nine Symphonies,* translated by Edwin Evans. London: 1913.

———, *À travers chants.* Paris: 1862.

———, *Evenings in the Orchestra,* English translation by Ch. E. Roche. New York: 1929.

———, *Les Grotesques de la Musique.* 1859.

———, *Life and Letters of Berlioz,* translated by H. Mainwaring Dunstan. London: 1882.

———, *Memoirs,* English translation by E. Newman. New York: 1932.

———, *Voyage musical en Allemagne et en Italie.* (Studies of Beethoven, Gluck and Weber). Paris: 1843.

Bie, Oscar, *Das deutsche Lied.* Berlin: 1926.

———, *Die moderne Musik und Richard Strauss.* Berlin: 1906.

Billy, André, *La Littérature française contemporaine.* Paris: 1939.

Blitzstein, M., "The Phenomenon of Stravinsky," *Musical Quarterly* (July, 1935).

Bloch, Ernest, "Man and Music," *Musical Quarterly* (October, 1933).

Blom, E., *Tchaikowsky's Orchestral Works.* London: 1927.

Borgex, L., *Vincent d'Indy, sa vie et son œuvre.* Paris: 1913.
Bowen, C. Drinker, and Meck, Barbara von, *Beloved Friend.* New York: 1940.
Brian, Havergal, "Arnold Schönberg," *Musical Opinion,* LX (London: 1937), 1035-1036.
Bruneau, A., *La vie et les œuvres de Gabriel Fauré.* Paris: 1925.
Brunet, Georges, *Victor Hugo.* Paris: 1935.
Brunner, F., *Bruckner.* Linz: 1895.
Buck, P. C., *Acoustics for Musicians.* London: 1918.
Bücken, Ernst, *Musik des 19. Jahrhunderts bis zur Moderne.* Potsdam: 1929.
Bulletin d'Information, published by the U.S.S.R. Embassy in Washington (July 18 and August 20, 1942).
Busoni, Ferruccio, *Sketch of a New Aesthetic of Music,* English translation by Theodore Baker. New York: 1911.
Calvocoressi, M. D., *Mussorgsky.* Paris: 1913.
Calvocoressi, M. D., and Abraham, G., *Masters of Russian Music.* New York: 1943.
Casella, A., *Igor Stravinsky.* Rome: 1926.
Chantavoine, Jean, *De Couperin à Debussy.* Paris: 1921.
———, *Liszt.* Paris: 1910.
Chase, G., "Falla's Music for Piano Solo," *Chesterian* (1940).
———, *The Music of Spain.* New York: 1941.
Chávez, Carlos, *Toward a New Music.* New York: 1937.
Closson, E., *Edvard Grieg et la musique scandinave.* Paris: 1892.
Cobbett's Cyclopedic Survey of Chamber Music. London: 1929.
Coeuroy, André, "Concerning Arnold Schönberg," *Chesterian,* IX (1928).
———, *Debussy.* 1930.
———, *La musique française moderne.* Paris: 1922.
———, *Panorama de la musique contemporaine.* Paris: 1928.
Collaer, Paul, "Le cas Schönberg," *La Revue internationale de la musique,* I (Brussels: 1938).
Collaer, Paul, *Stravinsky.* Berlin: 1930.
Collet, Henri, *Albéniz et Granados.* Paris: 1925.
Copland, A., "Darius Milhaud," *Modern Music* (New York: 1929).
———, *Our New Music.* London, New York: 1941.
Cortot, A., *La Musique française de piano.* Paris: 1930.
———, *L'Œuvre pianistique de E. Chabrier.* Paris: 1926.
———, *The Piano Music of Claude Debussy.* 1922.
Cowell, Henry, ed., *American Composers on American Music.* Stanford University Press, 1938.
———, *New Musical Resources.* New York: 1931.
Craven, Thomas, *Men of Art.* New York: 1934.
Debussy, Claude, *Monsieur Croche, the dilettante hater,* from the French of Claude Debussy with a foreword by Lawrence Gilman. New York: 1928.
Decsey, Ernest, *Debussy.* 1933.
———, *Hugo Wolf.* Berlin: 1919.
Dent, Edward J., *Busoni.* London: 1936.
d'Indy, Vincent, *César Franck.* Paris: 1906.
———, *Cours de Composition Musicale.* Paris: 1912.
———, *Richard Wagner et son influence sur l'art musical français.* Paris: 1930.
Dujet, A., *Gabriel Fauré, biographie critique.* Paris: 1921.
Dunhill, Thomas, *Sir Edward Elgar.* London: 1938.
Dunk, John L., *The Structure of the Musical Scale.* London: 1940.
Dyson, George, *The New Music.* Oxford: 1924.
Elliot, John Harold, *Berlioz.* New York: 1938.
Emmanuel, M., *Pelléas et Mélisande.* Paris: 1926.
Erlanger, Baron R. de, "La Musique Arabe," *Revue Musicale* (Paris: August, 1932).

Evans, Edwin, "Arnold Bax," *Musical Quarterly* (April, 1923).

———, *Tchaikovsky*. London: 1935.

———, *The Fire Bird and Petruchka*. Oxford, London: 1933.

Fardel, Max Durand, *Stravinsky et les ballets-russes*. Nice: 1941.

Ferguson, Donald N., *A History of Musical Thought*. New York: 1935.

Finck, H. T., *Grieg and His Music*. New York: 1929.

———, *Richard Strauss: The Man and His Works*. Boston: 1917.

Fuller Maitland, J. A., *English Music in the 19th Century*. London: 1902.

———, *The Music of Parry and Stanford*. London: 1934.

Gatscher, E., *Die Fugentechnik Regers in ihrer Entwicklung*. Stuttgart: 1925.

Gatti, G. M., "Ernest Bloch," *Musical Quarterly* (1921).

———, *Musicisti moderni d'Italia e di fuori*. Turin: 1927.

———, *The Stage Works of Ferruccio Busoni*. 1934.

George, A., *Arthur Honegger*. Paris: 1926.

Gilman, L., *Aspects of Modern Opera*. New York: 1908.

———, *Debussy's Pelléas et Mélisande*. New York: 1907.

Giraud, Jean, *L'École romantique française*. Paris: 1938.

Goldberg, Isaac, *George Gershwin, a Study in American Music*. New York: 1931.

Gourmont, Rémy de, *Promenades littéraires*. Paris: 1905-9.

Grace, H., "The Late Max Reger as Organ Composer," *The Musical Times* (London: 1916).

Graves, G. L., *Hubert Parry, His Life and Work*. London: 1926.

Gray, Cecil, *A Survey of Contemporary Music*, 2nd edition. London: 1927.

———, *Sibelius*, 2nd edition. London: 1934.

Green, Dunton L., "Arnold Schönberg," *Chesterian*, VI (July-August, 1925).

Greene, H. Plunket, *Charles Villiers Stanford*. London: 1935.

Gwynn, Stephen, *Claude Monet and His Garden*. New York: 1934-35.

Hába, Alois, *Neue Harmonielehre*. Leipzig: 1927.

———, *Von der Psychologie der Musikalischen Gestaltung*. Vienna: 1925.

———, *Von neuer Musik* (Die Theorie der Vierteltone; Grundlagen der Tondifferenzierung und der neuer Stilmoglichkeiten in der Musik). Cologne: 1925.

Hadow, W. H., "Antonin Dvořák," *Studies in Modern Music*, 2nd series (London: 1895, 2nd edition, 1904).

Halm, A., *Die Symphonie Anton Bruckners*. 1914.

Harászti, E. *Béla Bartók*. London: 1938.

———, "La Musique de Chambre de Béla Bartók," *Revue Musicale* (Paris: 1930).

Hauer, Josef Mathias, *Vom Melos zur Pauke*. Vienna: 1925.

———, *Vom Wesen des Musikalischen*. Leipzig: 1920.

———, *Zwölftontechnik*. Vienna: 1926.

Heiden, Bernhard, "Hindemith's System: a New Approach," *Modern Music* (New York: 1942).

Hill, E. B., *Modern French Composers*. New York: 1924.

Hill, Richard S., "Schönberg's Tone-Rows and the Tonal System of the Future," *Musical Quarterly* (New York: January, 1936).

Hindemith, Paul, *The Craft of Musical Composition*. New York: 1941-43.

Holde, Arthur, "Is There a Future in Quarter-Tone Music?" *Musical Quarterly* (October, 1938).

Hollaender, Hans, "Alban Berg," *Musical Quarterly* (New York: October, 1936).

Hostinsky, O., *Erinnerungen an Fibich*. 1909.

Howard, John Tasker, *Our American Music, Three Hundred Years of It*. New York: 1939.

———, *Our Contemporary Composers*. New York: 1941.

Huch, Ricarda, *Les Romantiques Allemands*. Paris: 1930.

Hueffer, Francis, *Half-a-Century of Music in England*. London: 1889.

Hull, A. Eaglefield, "A Survey of the Pianoforte Works of Scriabin," *Musical Quarterly* (1916).
———, *Modern Harmony*. London: 1914.
———, *Music: Classical, Romantic, and Modern*. London: 1927.
———, "Scriabin's Scientific Derivation of Harmony versus Empirical Methods," in *Proceedings of the Musical Association*. London: 1917.
Hull, R. H., *A Handbook on Arnold Bax's Symphonies*. London: 1932.
Huneker, J., *Essays*. New York: 1932.
Hunt, Violet, *The Wife of Rossetti*. London: 1934.
Istel, E., "Albéniz," *Musical Quarterly* (1929).
———, "Manuel de Falla," *Musical Quarterly* (October, 1926).
Jean-Aubry, G., "Isaac Albeniz," *Musical Times* (December, 1917).
———, *La Musique française d'aujourd'hui*. Paris: 1916.
———, "Manuel de Falla," *Musical Times* (April, 1917).
———, "Some Recollections of Debussy," *Musical Times* (May, 1918).
Jemnitz, Alexander, "Béla Bartók," *Musical Quarterly* (July, 1933).
———, *Béla Bartók: His Life and Music*. Hungarian Reference Library. New York: 1940.
Kall, A., "Stravinsky in the Chair of Poetry," *Musical Quarterly* (July, 1940).
Kapp, Julius, *Das Dreigestirn: Berlioz-Liszt-Wagner*. 1920.
———, *R. Wagner und F. Liszt*. 1908.
Karatygin, V., "To the Memory of Sergei Ivanovitch Taneiev," *Musical Quarterly* (October, 1927).
Klein, H., "Albéniz's Opera, Pepita Jiménez," *Musical Times* (March, 1918).
Koechlin, Charles, *Debussy*. Paris: 1927.
———, *Gabriel Fauré*. Paris: 1927.
———, "Les tendances de la musique moderne française," *Encyclopédie de la Musique du Conservatoire de Paris*, Second Part, I (Paris: 1925).
———, "Souvenirs sur Debussy, la Schola et la S. M. I.," *Revue Musicale* (November, 1934).
Koechlin, Charles, *Traité de l'Harmonie*. Paris: 1925-30.
Křenek, Ernst, *Music Here and Now*. New York: 1939.
———, *Studies in Counterpoint*. New York: 1940.
Kurth, Ernst, *Anton Bruckner*. Berlin: 1925.
———, *Romantische Harmonik und ihre Krise in Wagners Tristan*. Berlin: 1920.
Lachmann, Robert, *Musik des Orients*. Breslau: 1929.
Laloy, L., *Claude Debussy*. Paris: 1909.
———, *La Musique Chinoise*. Paris: 1910.
———, *Notes sur la musique cambodgienne*. Basle: 1907.
La Méri, *The Gesture of the Hindu Dance*. New York: Columbia University Press, 1941.
Landormy, Paul, *Vincent d'Indy*. Paris: 1932.
Lanson, Gustave, *Histoire de la Littérature française*. Paris: 1912.
Leichtentritt, H., "F. Busoni as a Composer," *Musical Quarterly* (January, 1917).
Lenormand, René, *Étude sur l'Harmonie Moderne*. Paris: 1912.
Liebich, L. S., "An Englishwoman's Memories of Claude Debussy," *Musical Times* (June, 1918).
———, *Claude-Achille Debussy*. London: 1908.
Lloyd, L. S., *Decibels and Phons*. Oxford: 1940.
———, *Music and Sound*. Oxford: 1937.
———, *The Musical Ear*. Oxford: 1940.
Lockspeiser, E., *Debussy*. London: 1936.
———, "Debussy, Tchaikovsky and Mme. von Meck," *Musical Quarterly* (January, 1936).
———, "Mussorgsky and Debussy," *Musical Quarterly* (1937).
Lyle, Watson, *Rachmaninoff*. London: 1938.
MacColl, D. S., *What Is Art?* London: 1931.
Maecklenburg, A., "Hugo Wolf and An-

ton Bruckner," *Musical Quarterly* (New York: 1938).

Maine, Basil, *Elgar, His Life and Work*. London: 1933.

Manuel, Roland, *Arthur Honegger*. Paris: 1925.

———, *Manuel de Falla*. Paris: 1930.

———, *Maurice Ravel et son œuvre dramatique*. Paris: 1928.

Marliave, Joseph de, *Études Musicales*. Paris: 1917.

Martineau, René, *Emmanuel Chabrier*. Paris: 1911.

Martino, P., *Le Naturalisme français*. Paris: 1938.

———, *Parnasse et Symbolisme*. Paris: 1938.

Mason, Daniel Gregory, *The Dilemma of American Music*. New York: 1928.

Mathews, W. S. B., *A Hundred Years of Music in America*. Chicago: G. L. Howe, 1889.

Mauclair, Camille, *Histoire de l'impressionisme*. Paris: 1904.

Mersmann, H., *Kammermusik*. 1930-33.

———, *Moderne Musik*. Potsdam: 1929.

Milhaud, Darius, "Polytonalité et Atonalité," *Revue Musicale* (Paris: 1923).

Modern Music, articles on composers and current musical activities. New York: League of Composers.

Montagu-Nathan, M., *Contemporary Russian Composers*. London: 1917.

———, *Glinka*. London: 1916.

———, *Mussorgsky*. London: 1916.

———, "Prokofiev's First Pianoforte Concerto," *Musical Times* (January, 1917).

———, *Rimsky-Korsakov*. London: 1916.

———, "Sergei Prokofiev," *Musical Times* (October, 1916).

Morillo, R. Garcia, "Karol Szymanowsky," *Nosotros*, LXXXIII (Buenos Aires: 1943).

Nejedly, Zdenék, *Frederick Smetana*. London: 1924.

Newman, E., *Hugo Wolf*. London: 1907.

———, *Richard Strauss*. London: 1908.

———, "The Development of Debussy," *Musical Times* (May-August, 1918).

Newmarch, Rosa, *Antonin Dvořák*. London: 1928.

———, *Jean Sibelius*. Boston: 1939.

———, "Leoš Janáček and Moravian Music Drama," *Slavonic Review* (University of London, December, 1922).

———, *Tchaikovsky, His Life and Works*. London, New York: 1900.

———, *The Russian Opera*. London: 1914.

———, "Vitězslav Novák," *Chesterian* (July, 1931).

Niecks, Friederick, *Frédéric Chopin*. 1888-1902.

Niemann, Walter, *Brahms*. New York: 1929.

Pannain, Guido, *Modern Composers*. London: 1932.

———, "Paul Hindemith," *Modern Composers*. London: 1932. (*Musicisti dei Tempi Novi*. Turin: 1932.)

Paoli, D. de, *Igor Stravinsky*. Turin: 1934.

Parry, C. H. H., *Style in Musical Art*. London: 1911.

Pellissier, G., *Le mouvement littéraire contemporain*. Paris: 1901.

Picht, Hermann, *J. M. Hauer, ein Vorkaempfer geistiger musikauffassung*. Stuttgart: 1934.

Pike, D. E., "Arnold Schönberg as Song Writer," *Chesterian*, IX (1928).

Piston, Walter, *Harmony*. New York: 1941.

Prout, E., *Harmony*. London: 1889.

Prunières, Henry, "G. Francesco Malipiero," *Musical Quarterly* (July, 1920).

Rameau, Jean Philippe, *Démonstration du principe de l'harmonie*. Paris: 1750.

———, *Nouveau système de musique théorique*. Paris: 1726.

———, *Traité de l'harmonie reduite à ses principes naturels*. Paris: 1722.

Ramuz, G. F., *Souvenirs sur Igor Stravinsky*. Paris: 1929.

Reich, Willi, "Alban Berg's Lulu," *Musical Quarterly* (1936).

———, "Anton von Webern," *Die Musik*. Berlin: 1930.

———, "Paul Hindemith," *Musical Quarterly* (New York: 1931).

Reich, Willi, *Wozzeck* (a guide to the words and music). New York: The League of Composers, 1931.

Reis, Claire, *American Composers*. New York: 1932.

———, *Composers in America*. New York: 1937.

Revue Musicale (May-June, 1939). Special Stravinsky issue.

Richard, P. J., *La Gamme*. Paris: 1930.

Riesemann, O. von, *Sergei Rachmaninoff: Recollections*. New York: 1934.

Rimsky-Korsakov, N., *My Musical Life*, translated by J. A. Joffe. New York: 1923.

Ritter, William, "Smetana," *Maîtres de la musique*. Paris: 1907.

Rolland, Romain, *A Musical Tour through the Land of the Past*, translated by Bernard Miall. London: 1922.

———, *Beethoven: Les grandes époques creatrices*. Paris: 1928.

———, *Histoire de l'Opéra en Europe avant Lully et Scarlatti*. Paris: 1895.

———, *Musiciens d'Aujourd'hui*. Paris: 1908.

———, *Musiciens d'Autrefois*. Paris: 1908.

Rosenfeld, Paul, *An Hour with American Music*. Philadelphia, London: 1929.

———, *Discoveries of a Music Critic*. New York: 1936.

———, *Musical Portraits*. 1920.

Rossi-Doria, G., "Le théâtre et l'oratorio de G. F. Malipiero," *Musique* (December, 1929-January, 1930).

———, "Mario Castelnuovo-Tedesco," *Chesterian* (January-February, 1926).

Rottger, H., *Das Formproblem bei R. Strauss*. Berlin: 1937.

Sabaneiev, L., *Modern Russian Composers*. New York: 1927.

Saint-Saëns, C., *Germanophilie*. Paris: 1916.

Salazar, Adolfo, *El Siglo Romantico*. Madrid: 1935.

———, *La música actual en Europa y sus problemas*. Madrid: 1935.

———, *La música contemporánea en España*. Madrid: 1930.

Salazar, Adolfo, *La Rosa de los Vientos en la Música Europa*. Mexico: 1940.

———, *Música y Músicos de Hoy*. Madrid: 1928.

———, "Prerafaelismo," *Hazlitt el Egoísta y otros papeles* (Madrid: 1935).

———, *Sinfonía y Ballet*. Madrid: 1929.

Samazeuilh, G., *Paul Dukas*. Paris: 1913-36.

Schaeffner, A., *Igor Stravinsky*. Paris: 1931.

Schauffler, Robert Haven, *The Unknown Brahms*. New York: 1940.

Schloezer, B. de, *Igor Stravinsky*. Paris: 1926.

Schönberg, Arnold, *Harmonielehre*, 3rd revised and enlarged edition. 1922.

———, "Problems of Harmony," *Modern Music* (New York: 1934).

Seligman, H., *Karl Nielsen*. Copenhagen: 1931.

Séré, O., *Musiciens français d'aujourd'hui*, 2nd edition. Paris: 1911.

Servières, G., *E. Chabrier*. Paris: 1912.

Sessions, Roger, "Ernest Bloch," *Modern Music* (1927).

Sharp, Cecil J., and Karpeles, Maud, *Folksongs from the Southern Appalachians*. London: 1932.

Shirlaw, Mathew, *The Theory of Harmony*. An inquiry into the natural principles of harmony, with an examination of the chief systems of harmony from Rameau to the present day. London: 1917.

Slonimsky, Nicolas, "Dmitri Dmitrovitch Shostakovitch," *Musical Quarterly* (October, 1942).

———, *Music of Latin America*. New York: 1945.

———, *Music since 1900*. New York: 1937.

———, "The Man of Eighteen Symphonies," *The American Quarterly on the Soviet Union* (April, 1938).

Specht, Richard, *Gustav Mahler*. Berlin: 1916.

Stackpole, R., "Ernest Bloch," *Modern Music* (1927).

Stanford, Ch. V., *Studies and Memories.* London: 1910.
Stefan, Paul, *Anton Dvořák.* New York: 1941.
———, *Gustav Mahler, a Study of His Personality and Work,* English translation by T. E. Clark. New York: 1912.
———, *Neue Musik und Wien.* Leipzig, Vienna, Zurich: 1921.
———, "Schönberg's Operas," *Modern Music* (New York: 1929-30).
Stein, E., "Anton von Webern," *Chesterian* (October, 1923).
Stoecklin, P. de, *E. Grieg.* Paris: 1926.
Stravinsky, Igor, *Chronicle of My Life.* New York: 1936.
Streatfield, R. A., *The Opera,* 5th edition. London: 1925.
Swan, Alfred J., *Scriabin.* London: 1922.
———, "The Znamenny Chant of the Russian Church," *Musical Quarterly* (New York: 1940).
Symonds, Arthur, *Essays on Seven Arts.* London: 1908.
Tchaikovsky, Modeste, *The Life of Peter Ilitch Tchaikovsky.* London: 1905.
Thompson, O., *The International Cyclopedia of Music and Musicians.* New York: 1938.
Tiersot, Julien, *Smetana.* Paris: 1926.
———, *Un demi-siècle de musique française entre les deux guerres, 1870-1917.* Paris: 1918.
Tóth, A. von, "Zoltán Kodály," *Revue Musicale* (1929).
Trend, J. B., *Manuel de Falla and Spanish Music.* New York: 1929; new edition, 1935.
Vallas, L., *Claude Debussy et son temps.* Paris: 1932. English translation, London: 1933.
———, *Les Idées de Claude Debussy.* Paris: 1926.
Various authors, "Satie," *Revue Musicale* (Paris: March, 1924).
Villar, Rogelio, *Falla y su "Concerto de Cámara."* Madrid: 1931.
Vojan, J. E. S., *Antonin Dvořák.* Chicago: 1941.
Wagner-Liszt, *Briefwechsel zwischen Wagner und Liszt.* Leipzig: 1887.
Walter, Bruno, *Gustav Mahler.* Leipzig: 1936. English translation by James Galston with biographical essay by Ernst Křenek. New York: 1941.
Webern, Anton von, *Arnold Schönberg.* Munich: 1912.
Weissmann, A., "Ernst Křenek," *Modern Music* (1928).
———, *The Problems of Modern Music.* London: 1925.
Wellesz, Egon, "Anton Bruckner and the Process of Musical Creation," *Musical Quarterly* (July, 1938).
———, *Arnold Schönberg.* Vienna: 1925.
Westphal, K., *Paul Hindemith,* 3rd edition. Berlin: 1937.
Wiesengrund-Adorno, Theodor, "Berg and Webern—Schönberg's Heirs," *Modern Music* (New York: January-February, 1931).
Willems, Franz, "Paul Hindemith," *Von neuer Musik.* Cologne: 1925.
Yasser, Joseph, *A Theory of Evolving Tonality.* New York: 1932.
Zachimecki, Z., "Karol Szymanowski," *Musical Quarterly* (January, 1922).

Acknowledgments

The author wishes to express his thanks to the following publishers for their kindness in permitting him to use extended excerpts from works owned by them.

Reprinted by permission of the copyright owner, Associated Music Publishers, Inc., New York:

Page 239—Alban Berg, *Lulu*

Page 257—Manuel de Falla, Concerto for Harpsichord and Small Orchestra

Page 263—Darius Milhaud, Serenade

Page 241-2—Anton von Webern, Six Bagatelles for String Quartet, Op. 9

Permission granted by Durand & Cie, Paris, and Elkan-Vogel Co., Inc., Philadelphia, Pa., Copyright Owners:

Page 190-1—Maurice Ravel, *"Le Grillon"*

Index of Composers and Compositions

TALLAHASSEE COMMUNITY COLLEGE
LIBRARY